MW01286434

The Beauty's Brother

Leon Hart

Copyright © 2016 Leon Hart

All rights reserved.

ISBN: 1532906544
ISBN-13: 978-1532906541

DEDICATION

To all who have had the fortune of finding true
love and to those who one day will.

CONTENTS

CHAPTER 1 - PERDU

Trespassers were to be discouraged and scared away if they posed a hazard, but the old merchant was no threat. He was prey. Positioned at the top of a pine tree, Crow could tell the man was healthy, sane, and more likely than not, here to loot on a whim.

As soon as he set foot on the remote Castle Cadrer's grounds, Crow gave the warning call: a series of scratchy caws.

The man paused when from within the woods a wolf howled. His hairs prickled up, but he ignored his instincts, pulling his thick furs closer against the late autumn chill. He approached the main entrance. Rubbing his graying beard, he inspected the double doors that showed no signs of use for many years, perhaps over a decade. The handles refused to budge. He even put his sack down and pulled with both hands.

Crow impatiently clacked his beak. He flew down, over the man's head, startling him. Landing in a dead apple tree next to the servant door, he let loose one caw and flew off again.

Take the hint, old man.

The merchant smiled, thinking the idea his, and proceeded to the side door. Crow leaned down, bobbing his head slightly, willing the man to hurry. The man pulled the door open with enough ease, took one quick look around, and walked in.

Stupid looter, thought Crow smugly. *You shouldn't have entered.*

He let off three caws and flew down to the ground. A squirrel responded with a series of chatter. Using his sleek body, beak, and head, Crow carefully closed the door, slipping inside before it clicked shut.

The man had already left the servant hall. Crow listened carefully, hearing the increasingly hesitant steps enter the impressive grand hall.

Crow flew up a stairwell to the second level, having memorized these passages by heart. As quietly as he could, he landed on the rail of a balcony overlooking the hall. A mouse, seated at the rail's edge, acknowledge him with a glance, not with the usual eyes of fearful prey but comradery.

"Hello?" called out the man.

The curtains were drawn over the stained windows, the furniture covered in sheets, and even the chandeliers had some form of drapery over them. The gothic ceilings were dark and hellish. The floor, unpolished for years, threw up dust, fur, and feathers every time the man stepped upon it. Through the dark, the human eye would not be able to see the massive form positioning itself at the top of the grand stairs.

Unaware, the man made his way towards a display case. He wiped the dust off the top, trying to see if what it contained was worth breaking the glass.

"Why are you here?" demanded a deep, coarse voice. The master.

The man jumped back from the case, but held his ground.

"Who's there? Show yourself!"

"Answer me, trespasser."

"I am a humble, lost merchant-"

The master's pitiless chuckles reverberated in the hall. The merchant wavered. His hands trembled. He held them up, backing away slowly. His eyes widened as he desperately sought any movement.

"If you speak the truth, you have ill luck," said the master. "If you are lying, you are even more a fool to infringe here. I do not take guests."

The master took a couple steps down, revealing his lower form in the dim light. He was half naked, with fur, scales and feathers instead of human skin.

"Monster! No… I mean…Have mercy! I didn't mean to trespass."

"Yet you did. And unless you can offer me something in compensation-"

"My wares!"

The master growled while descending the stairs step by step.

"What wares could you possess that I don't have? I want equal compensation. People. Do you have female children? Grandchildren?"

"My… My daughter... Hélène," the man managed to whisper. He reached the locked doors, his back hitting against them. The sound echoed.

"You have until midnight. Send your daughter here and you will be spared. If you don't, or tell anyone about this, my servants will kill you and your family."

"Ss…servants?"

"They are always watching. They will be watching you. Does your thievish mind understand?"

A dog growled from the corridor leading to the ballroom. A couple mice squeaked and a cat hissed.

"Yes! Yes, please don't hurt me!"

"What is your name?"

"Monsieur Duval," cried the man. "Please, I won't speak a word of this place for as long as I live! I swear I'll honor the bargain."

Duval wept madly, face down on the floor, as the master let off a roar. He repeated his promises between sobs until he realized the master was gone. He scurried away in retreat.

Crow jumped off the balcony, pursuing Duval. He'd be punished if he lost him. He landed on his favorite pine tree when he spotted the man dashing across the grounds. The merchant's legs kept giving out every few steps, accompanied by whimpers. His panic only worsened at the ominous, iron gates, opened just wide enough for him. On each side stood a wolf and a bear. Neither moved as he scuffled by, but their presence was enough.

Duval ran down the overgrown road to his weathered nag. He lingered only to dump his wares and then rode away at full speed, Crow in aerial pursuit.

#

They returned half an hour before midnight. With only a sliver of the moon shining, the surroundings were barely lit.

A couple yards from the gate, Duval helped a heavily cloaked girl off the horse. Duval's eyes darted knowingly for predators, but they'd long since returned to hiding. He ushered the girl along the path and stumbled on a misplaced stone.

"Father," whispered the girl, clasping her hands around her father's arm. "There are no lights on."

"Please, Hélène. It is for the best. You need to stay here for a while."

"But what about you? You've shunned Roi, Anna is married, and Giselle is engaged! Who will look after the home?"

"You should have been more concerned about finding yourself a suitor than caring for me," muttered her father. Duval's anger was towards his own cowardice, but Hélène went silent at her father's irate tone. "There, the door beside the main entrance. You are expected. Tell them I sent you."

"You aren't coming with me?"

Father and daughter jumped at the sudden approach of a black and white, mid-sized herding dog. Crow was surprised White, one of the three head servants, had come outside. White looked at Hélène and wagged her old tail welcomingly. The girl gently reached out to pet her.

"See, the family dog," said Duval. "Now, I must go. I have a busy day tomorrow."

"But when will you fetch me?"

"I don't have time for your questions," said Duval, backing towards the gate. "Hélène..." His voice wavered. Crow tilted his head. Finally some fatherly love? Self-preservation and greed perhaps would not pull through? "You'll be fine," he answered after far too long a silence.

Crow landed on the gate. He pecked at the man's hat, startling him and sending him running back to his horse. Crow's satisfaction diminished as he saw the daughter's forlorn face. She didn't yell or run after him. Alone, just like the castle. Unloved. Given up. And eventually to be forgotten.

We have no choice. We are just as trapped here as you.

White licked the scared girl's hand, then slowly edged towards the servant door. Hélène wiped her nose with her cloak, forcing a grimace of a smile.

As Hélène entered with White, he flew to the roof. He entered through a small window in the turret attic. He considered this his room, so he could always count on the window being open.

He landed on the small pile of blankets stashed in a corner as his nest of sorts. A trunk stood next to it with various, old collectables on top. If he cared to open the trunk, several of his favorite books and a couple letters would be found. He considered these his belongings, though most of it had been pilfered over the years. He had no memories of the past; the time spent cursed had eroded them.

He dived through a hole in the floor, spreading his wings last minute, enjoying the exhilaration. These small levels of challenge and excursions kept his mind busy, a necessary exercise if he wanted to keep his sanity longer.

Arriving at the main hall, he saw a few candles had been lit in their stands, better revealing the unkempt room. He had missed the start of the encounter. The master was hiding behind a column. Hélène stood alone in the room's center.

"My father said you were his friend."

"Your father lied," said the master. "You are my prisoner. He traded your life for his."

Hélène brought her hands to her mouth, horrified at the thought, but clearly disbelieving.

"You will stay in a room prepared for you," continued the master. "You will do as I say."

"Why?"

"Don't question me," he growled.

"If you won't show yourself, then I'll leave."

Hélène folded her arms and turned towards the servant passage. She let out a startled cry. A bear blocked the exit.

Her cloak caught under her foot, tripping her. She grabbed a near armchair without realizing it was home to rodents, who scurried away.

The master stomped across the room, knocking aside a table. All remaining color drained from Hélène's face as she caught sight of the master's beastly form. He reached out his massive hand, as if to help her, then, seeing her mouth open and eyes widen in dread, grabbed her arm. She would bruise.

"If you can't be obedient, then I'll lock you in your room," he snarled, half dragging the girl towards the stairs. "You are mine. You will never leave this castle."

Her free hand uselessly beat against the master's arm. Her body twisted left and right, trying to escape the steel grip. She stumbled and nearly stepped on a snake.

Snake turned and hissed. He drew back to strike. From where she hid, White released a bark.

Perdu!

Crow swooped down and caught hold of Snake's neck just below the head. Snake's body was one long writhing muscle. Crow's talons fought to keep hold.

The bugger is heavier than I'd guessed.

He flew through the halls, making his way to the heavily locked door at the back of the servant quarters. The guard, Toad, transformed into a plump, mole covered woman with ogling eyes. A former scullery maid, she was of the decreasing percent of staff who could still hold their human form.

Take your time, thought Crow sarcastically.

Apathetically, Toad opened the door but did not go in. A lone candle lit the space. The dungeon occupants' nightmarish calls echoed up to them; desperate, angry, perdu, and scared. Furthest in, a puma yowled, temporarily silencing the room. Two servants had died before her capture. The place was a reminder to the still sane of what awaited them.

Flying into the hellish space, Crow ignored the regular cells. If they could use the cells they would, but various holding containers had been collected and assembled along the wall for smaller sizes. He dropped Snake into a high box and roosted on a wooden chair. Snake frantically slithered up the corner of the box, but was unable to reach the top.

Crow shifted uncomfortably, looking with disdain at Snake as he waited to make certain the reptile couldn't escape.

You must have ignored your daze warnings. You know entering dazes are a pre-form to perdu. What a fool. As a predator, you will be a lot less forgiven by the triumvirate when you snap out of this and are reassessed. If you snap out of it.

Crow shivered. Every time perdu happened, it grew more difficult to resist. Some simply gave up.

Unable to linger in the room any longer, Crow flew back to the now empty grand hall and landed on the banister at the top of the stairwell. From here he could see the second level hallway and guest room doors.

A female white tailed deer approached the door, pushing a silver cart with several plates. Delicately, she picked up the nearest plate with her mouth and brought it down to the floor. The plate was flat, with a few thin slices of cheese, to fit under the skinny slot that had been ruggedly carved at the bottom of the door.

"Some food, Miss," said the doe softly.

"I'm not hungry," replied a defiant voice from the other side.

Crow tilted his head curiously.

I wonder if Hélène would respond so if she knew she was talking to a deer. It's become so normal for me. I can't remember a time when the staff were not animals.

"As you say, Miss," said the doe. She returned to the trolley and headed back down the hall.

An exasperated sigh caused Crow to start. Boar sat below, also watching the scene. Usually managing staff behind the scenes, Crow guessed he'd volunteered first shift to watch the hall.

"Don't leave," called Hélène. "Who are you? Why are you helping that… that beast? Let me out, please let me out!"

Hélène banged against the thick oak door.

Her words aren't always clear, but I can hear her desperation and fear, thought Crow sadly.

White approached the stairs as a dog and transformed into human at the top. Crow avoided watching the actual transformation. Everyone did such as common courtesy.

An elderly lady, White had gray hair held back in a tight bun and wore a dark, outdated dress. She was in charge of the female staff with the exception of the cooks who fell under Boar's harsh control, though it was not uncommon for staffing roles to cross over.

Crow had very little to do with her. His job was external patrol and news, which didn't really fall under any of the triumvirate. But more often than not, Crow tended to report his findings to Fierté, the third head servant. Fierté had a better hold of his temper than Boar. When Boar got angry, you cleared the room immediately.

White's mouth stretched tight in concern as she bustled past them towards the door.

"Wait," said Boar, transforming to reveal a husky man with graying auburn hair and large sideburns. "The master doesn't want any of us tending to her."

Crow perked up.

You and I just watched one of the maids deliver some food… You must have intended to look the other way only once. It is actually surprising you did that at all.

White took a polite objective stance.

"The poor dear is terrified," said White. "If I could just comfort her-"

"We aren't even supposed to speak to her. The master's word is final."

"Then perhaps it's time we spoke with the master," said White. "This way will never win her love. And if he forces things, goodness knows, it is damnation for us all."

Boar brought his hands up to his temple and squeezed, "I trust you more on the arrangements of wooing and love, but we can't exactly change his ways overnight."

"All three of us should speak to him," said White. "We'll address him as one. If only there was another way to beak the curse, I'd take it. Well, we should quickly figure out some possibilities that the master may find reasonable for her. Restricted to the East Wing should be well enough. A servant to be with her at all times, who in turn will report to us. Only have her see us in human form, to avoid further fear. Where is Fierté? He should be at the center of this."

Boar did a swift intake of the hall, wincing at a particularly loud bang on the door.

"Crow," snapped Boar. Crow fluttered his feathers. He hadn't been sure they'd noticed him. "You're acting too curious of our guest. Be useful and fetch Fierté."

Crow gave a curt nod, glad his crow form hid his contempt for Boar.

He left the conspiring servants, flying to Fierté's office on the third level. He landed outside the door. A patch of rug next to the entryway was well worn and had a pile of bear hair building against the wall.

Steven was a former gardener turned guard thanks to his bear form. He usually chose to sit here, taking turns outside each of the triumvirate's rooms. The triumvirate had never really asked him to, but it was his method of keeping safe and sane.

Crow tapped his beak against the door, but received no response. Doubting Fierté would ignore a knock, Crow made his way along the hall, spotting the stag looking out a window at the end.

Fierté was normally extroverted, proud, and aware. The still, melancholic pose he held had Crow feeling disconcerted.

"Sir?"

Fierté looked at him with a particular expression Crow was not familiar with, but felt faintly wrong. Crow fought the urge to step back. It made his skin crawl. He looked down at his feet and when he looked up, Fierté was in human form, adjusting his white cravat. Fierté was the best dressed of the staff with a rich blue, tailored overcoat, gold buttons and a clean white blouse. Even his slightly heeled boots added a sense of confidence to his rank. His dark blond hair was held back with a stylistic ribbon.

"What is it?" asked Fierté, slightly groggy.

"White and Boar wish to speak with you about the guest."

It didn't take White and Boar any convincing to get Fierté on board. Crow resumed his position on the railing, staring at his reflection off of a brass vase while listening.

"If you start nitpicking every detail, like you did with the search for that runaway subordinate of yours, then you and White can manage this alone," Boar warned Fierté.

"A successful strategy covers everything," replied Fierté. "Now, who should remain human to emphasize our point to the master?"

Boar grumbled.

When the triumvirate had a plan, they entered the west wing. The master had not gone to his bedroom, his common tromping grounds, but to the library that was filled with a vast number of books.

Boar politely knocked on the door before opening it.

"Master East?"

"Go away."

Boar signaled the other two to enter with him, reluctantly ignoring the order. He transformed to a boar, but the other two remained human.

Fierté, while closing the door, mouthed, "Wait here," at Crow.

Crow pressed his head against the door. Further conversation was impossible to hear through the thick wood. The servants remained in the room for no longer than fifteen minutes and when they exited, they were silent with their heads bowed. Fierté closed the door and looked at his colleagues with a smirk forming.

Crow, presumed forgotten, trailed after the triumvirate as they started down the hall.

"White, I assume you'll find a suitable candidate from your staff?" Fierté whispered, in case their voices carried.

"I've it narrowed down to two," said White. "I'll see to it now. I'll also alert the seamstress. We can't expect the poor girl to stay in the same clothes the whole time."

Boar nodded, "I'll have the cooks come up with some appetizing meals for the week. Maybe we can win her over with food. And I can have Wolf and Steven clean the courtyard between the two wings."

"Don't forget to have your staff clean the ballroom," said Fierté, "We want her dining in the best this castle can offer when she's let out tomorrow. I'll have the halls and other rooms she might take looked after."

White let out a joyful chuckle, "Oh, this should be wonderful, just what is needed to get the staff up and running with hope again."

I wish I could hope, like many of the servants will, thought Crow. *But far stronger is my fear this girl is just another lamb for the slaughter. At least she will be safe and as comfortable as she can be for the week.*

Whether Hélène was confined in her room or free, the master would stay brooding in his room for several days. And even when he gained the initiative and courage to meet with the girl again, it would be brief. Crow could only hope, before then, the servants would have won the girl's trust. It was a pity though, that if any of them directly told Hélène about what she must do to break the curse, the curse would make her void. They had discovered that in their desperation with the first girl, and now she was buried in the cemetery, near forgotten by all.

Fierté stopped as the other two continued and looked down at Crow, losing his enigmatic facade. "I want you double patrolling for the next few days. If Hélène goes out to the garden, watch from afar. I want nothing interfering. And keep an eye on Wolf. We don't need his overenthusiasm resulting in another innocent death."

Crow nodded.

I never liked helping out with the duller servant tasks anyways.

#

A distant vertical line of smoke rose in the dim evening sky. Crow tilted his head, waiting to see if it would disappear. It had been three days since Hélène's arrival; the usual last day for when pursuers, if any, would show.

As the smoke persisted higher, Crow took off from the weathervane to inspect.

Arriving at a makeshift, human camp, he landed on a near branch, half expecting to see Hélène's father. Instead, a young man in his twenties, wearing a dark, wool cloak, sat by the fire. He rested on his pack, working at getting twigs from his short blond hair. A mediocre collection of sticks held a pot over the fire, warming a meager, half-eaten supper. The good-natured face highlighted by the flames didn't fit the usual travelers who passed through this part of the woods; thieves and lost souls.

Crow flew to a closer branch to get a better look, only to give a crowish grunt when he realized the man had spotted him.

"Hello, ill omen. If I had but found you an hour ago, I would have added you to my stew."

Stew! No hunter can catch me. Crow laughed inside. To show his confidence, Crow flapped down onto a rock across from the fire. He preened, enjoying the warmth the fire threw. *His voice is nice to listen to. It has a local dialect. Maybe he'll talk some more.*

The young man grinned.

"A fearless fellow, eh?"

He reached into his pouch and pulled out some stale bread, tossing it beside him for Crow. Crow carefully hopped around the fire, eyeing the bread.

A true crow wouldn't be picky, but… Thank goodness, mold free!

"You must beg from every traveler that passes through here. I don't suppose you saw my sister?"

Crow stopped attacking the bread and studied the man's eyes. The brown color matched Hélène's. Crow internally swore.

Hélène's brother is searching for her! I remember Hélène mentioned his name. Roi. Crow tilted his head to the side. *Roi Duval, then? He has the same nose, but otherwise his face is not as thin as Hélène's, nor are his cheekbones as prominent, though still defined. I actually like his looks better than Hélène's.*

Roi broke into a dejected laugh. He ran his fingers over his weary eyes.

"I'm asking a crow for information and it almost looks like it knows. I should have gone home and restarted afresh tomorrow. No. I can't. Days have already passed, and each one lessens my chances. Curse you, old man. Where did you send her?"

Roi tossed another piece of bread over at Crow, even though Crow had stopped eating.

Crow hunched, guilt nibbling at him.

The father, in fear of the master, has refused to tell his son anything. Good to know our performance worked so well. But I doubt Roi will give up until he finds his sister, which means he will come across the castle at some point. I wouldn't say this is my retribution for being involved with Hélène's holding, but I could bring Roi to the castle grounds and find something to assure him that Hélène is alright. Then, Roi could stay the night in the woods. That will be difficult, but a problem for when the time comes. And then-

Crow stopped himself. He was thinking too far ahead. First, he needed to confirm. It was times like these that he was grateful for the versatility of a crow's voice box.

"Hélène," he croaked out, using his crow voice.

Roi's head turned towards him fast.

"What?"

"Hélène."

"Hélène. You've seen her? Are you imitating her name?"

Crow bobbed his head several times, then flew on top of the horse's saddle.

Roi leapt to his feet, swinging his pack over his back. His eyes were alight with hope; a desperate kind that was willing to believe anything.

Crow got Roi to reluctantly leave his horse behind, after several pecks to the fingers. He then guided Roi along the more inconspicuous trails to the castle. When the tops of the castle's spires showed through the trees, Crow listened for any of the castle's closer patrollers; namely Wolf. The front was always watched from the windows and the back was Wolf's favorite grounds. Barely visible in the night, Crow took Roi to the western wall on the side of the castle; stacked blocks of sandstone with blackened spires poking out of the wall's top.

Roi struggled loudly over the wall, swearing as a spike poked him, but he made it over unscathed and said nothing through the overgrown garden until they reached a small side door to the castle. Crow knew it was locked.

"Wait," said Crow.

"Where is this place?" whispered Roi, causing Crow to pause. "I can see some lights on the second level... but this feels abandoned. I don't want to be trespassing on- ah, what am I doing? I just followed a crow."

"Wait."

Crow took off. Entering through the attic, he flew to the guestrooms. Hélène's door was locked for the night, causing Crow to pace outside it. Hélène would not have her window open in this cold weather and Nanny, her assigned servant girl, would be supervising inside. There was a secret servant passage to the room, but White, all these years, had kept its location to herself.

He flicked his tail when an alternative came to mind. He flew to the basement's laundry room. The iron was heating on the stove, but no one was around. Crow hopped on the counter, spotting a thick ribbon Hélène had worn to the castle. He bunched it in his beak. His heart beating rapidly, he swiftly returned to the side door, this time from the inside.

Memory allowed him to find and unlock the bolt in the unlit darkness. He put down the ribbon, shivering from the intruding cold air as Roi opened the door. Confident that Roi would stay in place, being unable to see, Crow flew off to find light. Shortly before the main hall, he found a lit candelabras. With five candles burning at once, one wouldn't be missed. He tilted his head and grabbed the candle, wiggling it back and forth until it was free. A candle acquired, he walked back, resisting the temptation to simply turn human.

Turning a corner, he squawked.

"There you are," whispered Roi, picking up the candle. Crow spotted the ribbon tied around Roi's wrist. "You brought me light! What a clever one you are. But I'm assuming I won't be welcomed here, so we must sneak about to find Hélène."

Roi peered through a keyhole, seemed satisfied, and opened the door to a servant stairwell. Crow flew past him, stopping in front.

He's only supposed to find the ribbon and be satisfied. I need to say something to get him out of here.

"Tomorrow," he croaked, wincing at his crow vocals.

"I can't wait another day," said Roi, moving around Crow.

Crow pecked undeterred at Roi's boot, "Tomorrow."

Roi firmly pushed him aside with his boot. Crow glowered, his feathers fluffed.

"Curse," warned Crow.

"My, what a vocabulary you have," muttered Roi dubiously.

As Roi's light footsteps retreated around the stairwell, Crow's mind rapidly spun.

This is too out of hand. I need to inform someone of the intrusion. I even have an excuse ready: I was unknowingly followed to the castle and the intruder slipped in before I could call out. Easy. Simple.

Crow closed his eyes, unable to condemn Roi like that.

The devoted brother deserves better. I need a new plan, something that will work without either side severely compromising. But I can't see many outcomes that don't end in Roi's death.

Crow caught his breath.

What Hélène wouldn't do to keep her brother unharmed! Roi can be kept as a hostage to keep Hélène obedient. She's already tried two unsuccessful escape attempts. But first, Roi needs to be caught alive.

Crow pursued Roi's direction to the quiet second level, but there was no sign of him. Frustrated, Crow flew towards the main hall, remembering someone had been patrolling there. If it was-

Boar was immediately alert as Crow landed in front of him.

"You don't usually approach me so brazenly," said Boar. "What the devils the matter?

Crow took in a deep breath, "There's a young man roaming the castle. I lost him in the west wing."

Boar's eyes bulged.

"A thief! Alert Fierté and warn anyone else. I'll go inform the master."

"Boar," snapped Crow. He flinched and tried to look apologetic under Boar's glare. "There's no time. What if he runs into Wolf or a perdu before we can question him? Wolf's your subordinate. You know he's more uncontrollable and aggressive than most of us."

"West wing you said?"

Boar charged towards the wing, Crow in flight behind him.

"You start at the far end," ordered Boar. "We'll move inwards. Transform. It'll be easier opening doors."

Crow flew to the ground as Boar opened the first door with his gruff hands. He took a couple steps before he transformed, wobbled to the side, and caught his balance by grabbing the frame of a painting. It was of Master East, back when he'd been human. Dust had built up on it, but a bright faced man in his twenties stared out, an eerie ghost of a past long gone.

Crow brushed aside his curly strands of hair that hung in his sight, the same black as his wings, but without the iridescent effect. Everything human went to a void when they were animals, including the clothes they wore at their last transformation. His clothes were a composition of grey, blue and brown; basic riding boots, shirt, vest, pants and belt. He did not wear a suit, like most of the male staff, and couldn't remember what his original uniform had been. His clothing collection came from a pile he'd found in a box in the attic. Most had presumed his old role to be a messenger or a scribe, since he could write.

Crow youthfully ran down the hall, his boots making light thuds against the red, floral carpet. Every few feet, the wood under the carpet creaked. At the first door closest to the window, he winced as his fingers formed clumsily around the handle. It was locked.

A crash sounded from a room further up the hall, nearer Boar. Crow jumped, tripping back on the rug and landing inelegantly on the floor.

Boar raced out from inspecting his first room as an ear-splitting roar sounded. His eyes narrowed at the set of library doors. He flung the left side door open and rushed in.

The door was left partly open, so after he'd struggled to his feet, Crow peered in, rather than enter. Boar stood partially in his view, but Crow's dark, gray eyes widened as he spotted Roi. His form was clearly lit by the library's ever burning fireplace. The young man was facing away from Crow and Boar, frozen in fear. Opposite of him was the master, who had been resting at the back of the library.

The master stormed towards Roi.

"Trespasser!"

Roi turned to run, but the master's massive paw-like hands caught his cloak in a swipe. The master snarled as he tried to free his hand, ripping the struggling Roi closer to him. Unbalanced, Roi hit his head on the side of a table. Instantly unconscious, he fell face down onto the floor. His cloak sprawled across his body as the master freed himself. Crow felt his stomach sink further.

"Master!" shouted Boar, running forward. "Are you hurt?"

"How did this rat get in the castle?"

The master glared at Roi, ready for the slightest provocation. He kicked a small, sheathed dagger across the floor. Likely Roi's. If it had been unsheathed, the master would have immediately killed him. Boar collected the dagger.

"Is he alone?" asked the master.

"If my information is correct, I believe so," answered Boar. "I've only just found out."

The master was silent for a good minute.

"With Hélène here, I can't risk anything. Kill him."

"Wait, wait!" shouted Crow, stumbling into the room and over the unconscious Roi. "I led him here."

Boar's eyes bulged and Crow shrank under the master's piercing stare.

"So he could kill me?" the master asked in a cold, unwavering voice. There was an eerie sense of stillness in how he was holding himself.

"No, sir. This is Hélène's brother. He was searching for her in the woods and would have eventually come across the castle. I thought we might use him as a bribe."

The master effortlessly flipped Roi over with his foot. Roi's head limply rolled to the side.

"Hm," grunted Boar. "They do appear similar. The dungeon then, sir?"

"If we treat him well, perhaps he will help keep Hélène compliant," persisted Crow. "We can house him in the guest room next to Hélène's."

"Do you think you're allowed a say in this?" demanded Boar. "Two-"

"We'll try his suggestion," growled the master.

"Master! This is not-"

"Are you saying, Boar, you are unable to manage two guests? I hadn't thought you were that incompetent. Confirm he is Hélène's kin and lock him in the room. When he wakes, tell him the rules. If he attempts anything... Make this clear to him."

"Yes sir," said Boar, bowing under the penetrative stare. "And what should we do about Crow?"

The master's eyes fell on Crow and Crow bowed low, unsure what else to do.

"If you ever pull such a stunt again, I will not be forgiving."

Boar grew bright red, restraining his objections.

Crow bowed deeper. The master, though usually having nothing to do with Crow, had always been easier on him.

But I'm as clueless as Boar. Either my past-self did something really good for him or he thinks I know something. I've never really bothered to question it. Whatever it may be, it's a godsend.

The master lumbered from the room, leaving the new guest to Crow and Boar.

Subtle, curious whispers came from the hall. Many servants had gathered outside the door. Boar briskly slammed it shut. Then he grabbed Crow's collar, easily drawing him close with his muscular arms. Crow, slightly taller than Boar, had to look down. He kept very still.

"If any trouble comes from this man the next few days, anything at all, I will hold you responsible," hissed Boar. "You're crafty and I don't like it. The amount of freedom the master gives you is disgusting. Behave properly, or you won't be able to fly when I'm done with you. Am I clear?"

Crow managed a grunt. Boar released him, then straightened Crow's outfit out of habit. Crow curled his hands to hide his trembling.

Boar's voice became unpleasantly sweet, "You brought him here, so you can carry him to his new room. Make sure to have him there before he wakes up. No slip ups." Boar opened the door and began hollering at the staff, "Make sure Hélène stays in her room. I don't want her knowing about this. You three, quit your staring and prepare the gentlemen's guest room. Clean what you can within the hour. You! Find White and…"

Crow nearly fell bending down, placing his hand under Roi's nose to detect steady breathing. He gave a sigh of relief. He then settled with dragging Roi as fast as he could towards the grand hall. He would have preferred carrying, but his human muscles were cramping as it was.

The gentleman's guestroom was unlocked. Roi's cloak became further destroyed as Crow stepped on it, trying to awkwardly lift the unconscious man onto the dust-covered bed. As soon as he was successful, he gave the body a few good shoves to make it centered.

Panting, Crow sat on the edge, waiting to cool off in his human form. His eyes scanned the room. Like the rest of the castle, the room was dark with its burgundy wallpaper, thick curtains, and ornate furniture. There was a fireplace, but it had been empty for years. The stack of wood beside it looked half decomposed.

A small cup coaster sat askew on the side table, from the use of a guest long ago. Crow absently straightened it. Underneath a guest had graffiti the counter. Initials were indented into the wood.

CC.

"You should leave," interrupted a cleaning servant curtly.

Acting indifferent to their scorn, Crow transformed and hid in the shadows outside the door.

I was expecting derision. I endangered everyone with this risk, so it makes sense they want me out of the way. Normally I'd oblige and go to my attic, but I found him. This is my plan. I want to be around when he wakes up. I want to hear what he says.

Crow was starting prepare for a light nap, when Boar stormed by. Boar opened the door and slammed it shut behind him. Crow pressed his ear against it in time to hear Roi woken by a rough shaking. He could only hear muffled hostility as Boar jumped right into an intimidating speech.

The sound of clipped footsteps caused Crow to draw back.

Fierté approached. His mouth slightly twitched when he spotted Crow. He signaled with a flick of his hand for Crow to stand further back. Silently, Fierté opened the door a crack to eavesdrop. An entertained smile crept along the butler's face as the heated words between Boar and Roi became clear.

Adjusting the smile to appear more endearing, Fierté strolled into the room. Crow scurried back to the door's entrance.

"Monsieur, I had thought you would be a model guest, seeing as you have a chance to see your sister."

"Hélène?" said Roi frantically. "All this bloats been shouting at me is rules and threats."

"If the boy had shut up, I would have gotten to it," snapped Boar.

"Ah," said Fierté, unsurprised. His gaze shifted to look down at Crow peering in. Fierté's eyes glinted. His foot lightly tapped the door, sending it on a slow journey to closure.

Fierté continued, "Perhaps I might present the expectations and benefits in a better composed manner. Firstly, in order to see your sister, neither you nor she may ever enter the west wing or ask after the master. When out of your room, you must be in Hélène's or an assigned staff's presence. Any form of aggressive-"

The door clicked shut. Crow clacked his beak irritated. He strutted back to his earlier hiding spot and settled down, his feather's fluffed. Reluctantly he fell asleep, waiting for the door to open again.

#

At first light, Crow carefully avoided all servants as he snuck into the ball room. A few curtains were open, highlighting the floor's rich mosaic of gold and purple marbles and making the regal room feel warmer. The cherry wood table was at the center, with eight chairs distributed around it. The two chairs at opposite ends were the only ones with plates and utensils set.

Crow flew up to a high ledge at the top of the columns that ran between the windows. He brushed his wings against the surface, cleaning the layers of dust that had built on it so that he could have a suitable perch.

Fierté arrived first. Escorting Hélène into the room, his long steps echoed. There was an energetic bounce in his stride, nothing to hint a late night. He gracefully moved ahead at the table, to theatrically pull Hélène's chair out for her.

"Mademoiselle," he said, giving his eloquent smile.

"Thank you, Fierté."

Fierté bowed, then picked up a silver pitcher from the table's center. He began to fill her glass with water, carefully making sure the glass and pitcher did not touch.

"Breakfast will be temporarily postponed for-"

"Oh, is the master finally joining today?" asked Hélène. There was a hint of scorn in her voice, but she did her best to maintain pleasantries.

Fierté's smile twitched.

Crow quietly chuckled.

A servant would have been slapped for interrupting him.

"Not quite, though I admit you will be having lunch with him tomorrow… Just a short snack to give you a better impression."

Hélène quickly hid her doubt by smiling as she leaned forward. "So then, what is this morning's surprise?"

"One that should please you greatly. And shall be here, so long as we continue to get along."

Fierté raised his hand dramatically and snapped his fingers.

"Hélène?" whispered Roi, taking a few steps into the room. His brow furrowed.

Hélène ran to him, and he hugged her tightly while she burst into tears. She lifted her hands and touched his face, "I can't believe you're here!"

Crow leaned to the edge of his perch, searching for signs of last night's run in with the master.

His bruising must all be covered by his clothing and hair.

"I can't believe I found you," said Roi, kissing the top of her head. "And I swear, until this is all sorted out, I won't leave you."

"Your rooms are next to each other," said Fierté, politely signaling them to the table. "You will have all day to catch up. But as the food is ready…"

"Of course," said Hélène, the palm of her hands drew across her eyes to wipe away tears. "Roi, all things considered, their food is excellent."

Roi lifted an eyebrow. His gaze shifted to Fierté. The butler's head lightly tilted towards the far end of the table. Roi started to scowl, but he quickly covered it with false ease when Hélène looked at him again. He complied with Fierté's subtle hint and separated from his sister's side to sit at the table's opposite end.

Fierté signaled to the kitchen door and two waiters in human form entered with the start of the meal. The aroma of bacon and eggs wafted up to Crow. Crow swallowed, trying to imagine his meal of dried berries and jerky would be just as appealing. Fierté took his leave with a bow, but remained by the entrance to the room, his sharp eyes never leaving the siblings. He reluctantly left only when one of the waiter's rushed over to him. Crow read his lips. "Boar has received word that the master wishes to speak with you. Boar will watch the guests."

"So the animals here talk," said Roi, sitting back with a full stomach as the waiter returned from speaking to Fierté and began to remove the plates. He scrutinized the human-form waiter, waiting to see if he'd transform.

"All the residents are cursed," said Hélène. "They frustratingly won't tell me much. From what I've heard and seen, they can still turn into humans for certain amounts of time. Nanny, my servant, she'll appear sometimes human, sometimes a bichon dog. And then there's the master. I've only seen him in his animal form… if he has any other form… and he is-"

"-A beast," finished Roi. "I had the pleasure of meeting him last night."

Hélène waited for the waiter to disappear through the serving doors before declaring, "They think I can somehow break this curse, but they won't tell me anything more."

"You? How does kidnapping a girl break any curse? Does it necessarily have to be you?"

Hélène shrugged.

Roi looked towards the servant door and spotted Boar watching through the small circular window. Roi glared.

"Then if no one is going to explain anything, I don't see why we should cooperate."

Boar opened the door. His jaw was clenched.

"Mr. Duval, you are dangerously close to breaking our agreement," said Boar, lacking the elegant flair Fierté had to calm situations.

Roi narrowed his eyes, standing up, "Trust me, old man, this is behaving for me."

"Roi," said Hélène sharply. "Don't make it worse."

"I'm afraid, Mademoiselle, that you will have to wait for tomorrow to see your brother again," said Boar. "He's earned a day of isolation, reviewing his manners and our arrangement."

"If you want me to attend lunch with your master, you'll-"

"Mademoiselle, this is the more hospitable solution."

Hélène paled and Roi stood still, studying Hélène and Boar carefully. He internally concluded something, for he bowed.

"My apologies for my brash mouth. I'll accept your judgment and will be careful in the future."

Boar gave Roi the same look he gave Crow when he thought him up to something. Allowing a brief farewell, Boar stiffly led Roi away.

Crow also took leave for patrol. At the end of the day, he cut his third flight short to eat and forage. He wrapped his humble finds in scrap parchment from his attic.

Returning outside with the package in beak, he located the windows belonging to the guests. The guestrooms looked into the courtyard: an assortment of stone, garden, and leafless bushes, with taller pine trees towards the back. Crow landed on Roi's windowsill and placed the package down. He craned his neck against the glass, attempting to see if Roi was even in the room.

Crow jumped and had to regain his footing when the curtain was pulled back. Roi stood there, studying him. With no clouds blocking the moon, they could see each other clearly.

Roi frowned and set about finding the window's lock, which was wedged tightly from lack of use. He managed to open the window on the side that Crow was not standing on.

"We meet again," said Roi, in pleased bitterness.

Crow tapped the package to draw Roi's attention, wary that Roi might grab at him. Roi picked up the small package, chuckling at the humble selection of food Crow had scavenged.

"For me, I assume," said Roi. He squeezed onto the window ledge to sit. "Thank you, my stomach was getting hungry."

Roi poked through the selections and settled with taking the dried berries out one at a time. He looked around carefully as he ate. He didn't seem bothered by the chilly air.

Crow allowed himself to feel the short sighted satisfaction that his gift had been accepted.

"Well, I think I can lower and then jump down without hurting myself too badly," muttered Roi.

Crow jerked out of his contentment and made a disagreeing sound.

"I'm not sure whether you're friend or foe," Roi responded to Crow. "...Or even a crow... whether you lead me here in pity or as a trap...?"

Crow didn't respond. Boar had ordered everyone not to speak in animal form to the guests, but something else held him back from speaking-shame and fear.

"Phf," snapped Roi as he angled himself further out the window.

Crow desperately let out a couple loud caws, usually used as a role call for outside. Wolf, loyally, answered with a howl from his current patrol in the woods. Crow looked back at Roi, his head tilting in an, "understand?" expression.

A rustle came from some bushes further in the garden and a fox calmly walked out. The moonlight reflected eerily on her eyes. Fox was normally even shyer than Nanny. But she would go out to hunt rabbit or quall when food was needed. Crow realized her hunter role had been changed to guard for the evening.

"Got it," sighed Roi, turning away from the window and throwing a pillow at the wall. "But what-"

As he looked back, Crow was no longer there.

Crow listened as Roi warily closed and locked the window. He hid on the ledge above, ready to watch all night to make sure Roi did not attempt to escape. Every creak and groan had Crow look wildly around. He knew tomorrow he'd be exhausted, but Boar's threat kept him vigilant.

Crow also kept watch of Hélène. Her curtain was drawn back. She stayed up late, reading a book from a collection she'd found in her room. She'd laid a couple already read books to the side, Crow suspected, to give to Roi tomorrow. Crow wished he could show them the library, but it was in the west wing, and only the master was allowed to use it.

CHAPTER 2 – THE WEST WING

A week after Roi's arrival, Boar untethered Crow's fate from being so closely linked to Roi's.

Crow hadn't rested so well; this being his first sleep back in the castle and not chilled above Roi's window sill. He found a cozy spot on the second floor, next to a hidden vent in the west wing that was leaking out warmth. He closed his eyes, enjoying the luxury. Since Boar had started the furnace up again, only certain rooms were given heat. The attic was not one of them.

As he hunkered down to enjoy an hour of snoozing, he contemplated an evening trip to the nearest town to find food. The servant's food selections had gone down quite a bit since the guests had shown up, though these days most ate what their animal form sought.

"Crow!" whispered Squirrel, alarmed.

Crow opened an eye. Squirrel flicked his tail, anxiously looking up at Crow from the floor. The common servants were on speaking terms with him again, not that they spoke often in the first place. Crow couldn't decide whether this was good or bad. With his shunning, no one had asked him to do anything extra. Even Boar and Fierté, when he quickly met to give his patrol reports, didn't talk with him much.

"It's an emergency," chattered Squirrel, failing to keep his voice down.

"What is?" inquired Crow calmly. He assumed Squirrel would request he fly a message. He lazily stretched his wings.

"Hélène and her brother! They've entered the west wing!"

"What! How?"

"I don't know!" said Squirrel. "Porcupine and I arrived to give the library a dusting. We'd left it unlocked earlier to fetch the supplies, and we're not used to locking rooms in the first place, and when we returned, they were there!"

"Nanny?"

"Not there!" confirmed Squirrel. "The master is in his room meeting with Fierté and White. I think Boar is outside, but all our heads will be had if he finds out!"

If Crow had been in human form, he would have bitten his lip. Squirrel was right about all their heads. Boar was still angry enough that Crow would get some of the wrath, even if he wasn't directly involved. If any of the triumvirate found out-

"We need to get them out and be quiet about it," said Crow.

He hopped off his roost, landing alongside Squirrel. They rushed down the hall as fast as their conditions allowed them. Porcupine scurried out from the shadows to join them.

"We are not allowed to speak to Hélène in animal form," said Squirrel. "We need a human."

"Ugh," groaned Crow, lowering his voice as they approached the closed library doors. "And I suppose neither of you can take form anymore."

"We haven't for years. And not by choice, laddie. Please, we need to hurry!"

Crow swiftly transformed, wobbling for a few seconds as he readjusted. Having not aged for a decade, he felt like an imposter in his body. He knew he appeared near the same physical age as Hélène, around eighteen.

"I'm not really even dressed correctly," he muttered under his breath. He wiped a stray strand of hair aside and fidgeted with his vest.

Squirrel waved a dismissive paw. Porcupine silently nodded his encouragement while gesturing desperately towards the door.

Crow took in a deep breath. He grimaced as he quietly opened the door just wide enough to fit.

The library had numerous shelves that rose all the way to the ceiling. The tall, bay windows at the back allowed in natural light, which would have obsoleted the lit fireplace, were it not providing sufficient warmth. Closest to the door was a hutch table with several books laid out on it. The siblings sat opposite of each other, studiously going over pages and whispering.

Crow knocked lightly on the side of the door. The siblings were startled. Roi got to his feet, crossing his arms as he inspected the interrupter of their reading. A frown graced his shapely lips. His eyes locked angrily onto Crow's and, under direct scrutiny, Crow momentarily forgot all about the curse, all about the library, and all about the reason he was there.

No one here comes close to his good looks. He's a little taller than me and definitely more athletic. Shit, his eyes are studying scraggily me. I wonder what he's thinking?

Crow shifted uneasily.

"Sorry to interrupt," Crow said softly to cover the roughness of his voice, "But the library is part of the west wing, and so, is off limits to guests."

Roi's eyes grew wider as Crow spoke.

"Who are you?" demanded Roi.

Crow felt the brief pangs of sorrow of not knowing his original identity. But a reassuring murmur from Squirrel behind him had Crow maintain his formal composure.

Though no more than a middle class man, Roi could compete with the master for having a sense of entitlement. At least his unpolished mannerisms help offset these ridiculous thoughts I'm having towards his appearance. It must be my crow-self's attraction to pretty things getting in the way. Okay Crow, focus on the situation.

"I'm a messenger for the master."

"You look young," commented Hélène.

"The master is hardly picky about age, so long as we accomplish our jobs. If you really care much for this conversation, I will gladly answer your questions outside, but for now, I request you exit this room. There are plenty of other rooms to read in."

Hélène and Roi exchanged looks.

"There are no other libraries," said Hélène.

Crow shrugged. When met with uncooperative silence he sighed.

"Not that you would care, but my neck is on the line with this."

"May we take a few books with us?"

As one of the few servants who could read, Crow eyed their collection of books on history and maps. *Escape? Simple curiosity?* Crow didn't care. He just needed them out of the wing.

"Fine, but hide them in your rooms," he whispered. "Three days, then I'll collect them to put them back."

"You think we'll be here that long?" said Roi, tucking several thick books under one arm.

"I don't know about you," said Crow. "You were foolish to follow her here, but Hélène, unless the curse breaks, will be here until she dies."

Hélène shivered.

As soon as they stepped outside the library, Roi shoved Crow against the wall with his free arm. Hélène gave a slight exclamation, then looked hesitant, noticing the two animal servants by the door.

Caught off guard, Crow didn't struggle. Roi's sharp gaze captivated him. Strands of curled hair slipped in front of his eyes, but he stayed very still.

"Everyone has mentioned this curse, but they won't explain it properly or how to break it," said Roi angrily. "Fact is, you're the only one who has given a straight enough answer. I'm tired of this dance. What is going on?"

"Roi," said Hélène softly.

"If I told you to your satisfaction, then it would obsolete the solution," Crow answered carefully. "And we are in dire need of the solution as our time runs out. We're all too scared to talk about it, in fear of revealing more than we safely should."

"Too bad," hissed Roi dangerously. He pushed his arm up from Crow's chest to against his neck. Crow resisted the desire to physically retaliate. Roi looked like he could and would take him on. He'd always had a preference for speech over actions anyways.

"You just said I'd told you more than anyone else. Please leave it at that and threaten another servant at a later time. Or would you prefer that I inform Boar of the missing books?"

Roi glared as he released him.

"You tell him and you'll regret it."

"I would," muttered Crow under his breath. He'd be an idiot to tell the triumvirate that he'd even contemplated allowing the siblings the books. He glared at Squirrel and Porcupine, warning them to stay quiet. He was more predator than them; he had some confidence they'd hold their tongues.

Masking his face servantly once again, Crow politely motioned the siblings the way out from the wing. He followed quietly, gently rubbing his throat. With them carrying so many books, his eyes carefully scanned for servants.

When they entered Hélène's room, he remained vigilant at the door.

"Make sure to hide them carefully. If a single one is discovered-"

"Yeah, we got it," said Roi, plucking a couple from Hélène's collection. "I'll keep most of them in my room. There's more clothes and crannies I can hide them in. So why did a messenger, of all your castle residents, come to check on us?"

"I had the misfortune of being in the vicinity," replied Crow duly.

"Psh," said Roi, leaving to his room. "A little blatant, aren't you?"

Crow debated which sibling to oversee and decided Roi, since he continued talking to Crow.

Even though they dislike me, it's thrilling walking beside genuine humans; to converse with them! It is addictive.

"I'm not saying the honesty isn't appreciated though," continued Roi.

"Not everyone here are all masked smiles and threats," said Crow. "Those happen to be Fierté and Boar's specialties."

Roi absently opened the door with books still in hand. Crow unconsciously made an impressed noise, which Roi heard and grinned. He spoke as he set the books down on the bed, "I run a book shop and archive back in our hometown, Beauclair. I've lots of practice getting around with books."

"Will you be missed?" asked Crow curiously. He was sure the triumvirate had sorted this all out earlier, but none of the other servants had been privy.

Roi shrugged, "By some," and left it at that. "Would you close the door? I don't want prying eyes."

Crow stepped inside, closing the door softly. He remained by the door, feeling somewhat like an intruder. His farsightedness allowed him to read the few titles he'd missed before.

"That's a lot of books," commented Crow. "Will you be able to read them all in three days?"

"I'm proficient," said Roi, opening drawers and wrapping the books in various clothes. "I'll finish them by then."

"Why those specific books?"

A look similar to the one Roi gave when he restrained himself in front of the triumvirate passed his face. This solemnly reminded Crow to remain wary.

"The local history, maps, records on nobility, enchantment history," pursued Crow. "You aren't reading for pleasure."

Roi's expression shifted to a calculating one.

"You do want me to keep my mouth shut?" said Crow. "While I'm obliging this one time, you must keep in mind that if I am not aware of your intentions, then I can't help."

"You want to help us?" said Roi, his expression becoming puzzled. His eyes turned from the bed and looked at Crow, as if looking at him fully for the first time.

This wasn't what Crow had intended. He'd simply used the wrong wording to express that as long as he was aware of what they intended to use the books for, then he could keep his mouth shut to the triumvirate, because any hint of related delinquency from them, he'd be able to be on top of it, albeit secretly.

However, he remained quiet as Roi studied him. The ticking of the grandfather clock in the corner became penetrative.

"Why would you want to help us?" asked Roi quietly.

"Some sympathy towards your situation," said Crow. He figured it wouldn't hurt to be on the siblings' good side. "Guilt. But understand, between my master and you, I would take the master's side. I'm not to be counted as an ally for whatever you and Mademoiselle Hélène do."

"Not to worry," said Roi, after giving a snort. "I'll trust you the day we grow wings and fly."

Roi went back to hiding the remaining two books.

"Now then, would you care to explain why you need the books?" asked Crow.

"Research," said Roi. "Because none of you will tell us anything useful, we're trying to figure these things out ourselves!"

"Hélène is here to help break the curse," said Crow. "You're here to help Hélène in that matter."

"Please," said Roi angry again. He tossed the remaining book on the ground and stormed towards Crow. This time he didn't attack him. He stopped short. Crow restrained his desire to retreat. "Keeping us prisoner isn't exactly encouraging us to help."

"Opposed to previous options, this is the best. Especially for you."

Roi laughed harshly, which irritated Crow.

"Many favored you be killed," said Crow, referring to Roi's first night. Roi looked like he was ready to punch Crow, so Crow quickly back peddled. "None-the-less, I personally would like everyone to come out alive… For what it's worth, don't waste time reading these books if you are solely seeking information on the curse. They're all written prior."

Crow quickly took his leave of the room, shutting the door before Roi could respond. The hall was still empty, so he went back to Hélène's room, whose door was still open. At first glance, he noticed Hélène had already hidden the books, something he did not like. Then he spotted a small dog laying limply on a loveseat at the back of the room. He rushed over to her and knelt down on his knees, wincing at his muscle's protest. He placed a hand over her nose and felt her lightly breathing.

"Nanny!" he hissed worriedly.

"You can't just run into a lady's room like that!" protested Hélène, alarmed and in the middle of changing shoes. The clever girl had been wearing slippers for sneaking to the library. Now she'd placed on her usual skinny, leather boots.

"What happened to her?" asked Crow, carefully inspecting Nanny for any injuries. He'd really wanted to say, 'what did *you* do to her?' He and Nanny weren't friends, but they still got along well enough.

"She was very tired, so she fell asleep," said Hélène. "Really, she's alright."

"Please don't lie."

"Why would I lie?" said Hélène, trying to sound innocent. She was not a natural liar like Roi.

"I know Nanny isn't sleeping naturally," snapped Crow. "I thought you two got along well enough that you'd never hurt her. She'd never hurt you. She admires you."

Hélène flushed as her brows furrowed and she refused to meet his accusing stare.

"She drank some sleeping herbs," said Hélène softly. "The last few days, I told White I couldn't sleep and she gave me some herbs to put in my water at night. I saved them and placed them in a tea I gave to Nanny."

Crow carefully picked Nanny up in a cradle. "I have to report this. You gave her several portions meant for a full grown human. Nanny, in dog form, could have died. White will need to check her."

Hélène went pale and brought her hands to her face. As she looked at Crow, her watering eyes revealed she had not intended to be malicious. She'd just been ignorant. Roi, who had likely influenced this plan, probably knew the possible side effects of overdosing.

"Please don't get us in trouble!" said Hélène.

"This is about Nanny," said Crow. "She might get in trouble too."

Worried his tongue would get too sharp, Crow walked briskly to the door, nearly walking into Roi. Roi guiltily stepped aside, his eyes moving from Crow to Nanny.

Crow stopped, alert and intent, and softly he rasped, "I will keep quiet of the library, but I must report this. If anyone inquires, I stopped you two from heading into the west wing."

"Isn't she alright?" asked Roi.

"Stay in your rooms, Monsieur Duval," Crow stated coolly. "I suspect it will help with whatever is to come."

Crow passed Nanny off to the female staff in the basement. White was still meeting with the master.

Having gotten his share of human exercise, Crow changed back to a crow. He felt drained. He wasn't sure how the triumvirate did it so often and concluded practice had something to do with it. He'd once tried to stay human for as long as he could a few years back. He'd successfully reached eight straight hours, but afterwards had slept double the time and had a slight perdu moment.

While Crow preferred reporting to Fierté, he knew he was still with the master and White. Reporting sooner was better than later. This left Boar as the only option.

He found Boar at the stables, sitting awkwardly in his animal form next to an old horse named Vincent, a groomsman who had fully gone perdu long ago. Based on the supplies set around, Boar had just finished taking care of the horse and was tired. He ignored Crow's approach.

"We've had a slight incident with the guests," said Crow, landing on a post.

Boar agitatedly looked over at him.

Crow continued, "The siblings managed to become unsupervised and were entering the west wing. I transformed and redirected them to their rooms."

"Are they supervised now?" demanded Boar, starting a trot towards the castle.

Crow fluttered from perch to perch.

"No."

"Idiot," snapped Boar. "You left them unattended! Where the hell is Nanny?"

"Hélène and Nanny took to preparing tea on their own in Hélène's room. Sleeping herbs were accidently used, causing Nanny to fall asleep."

Crow flinched, feeling the unease in his stomach of having manipulated the situation.

"Are you sure it was an accident?" asked Boar.

"I didn't witness it. I found Nanny asleep in Hélène's room after escorting them away from the west wing. Others are tending to Nanny now."

"Should've gone back to keep watch and sent someone else to find me," snapped Boar, ever unhappy. Crow shrugged it off. "Get yourself back to the main hall and keep watch until otherwise."

Crow first confirmed the siblings were both still in Hélène's room by listening at their doors. Hélène was crying. Settling on the nearby rail, Crow didn't need to wait long before a couple of Boar's underservants came to replace him. More reliable individuals, in Boar's view.

Unable to handle the complications arising, Crow restlessly took off for a long patrol. He regretted letting the siblings take the books, and Nanny's limp figure kept cropping up in his mind, reminding him of what the siblings wouldn't hesitate to do.

And yet, I still feel for them.

He let off a frustrated caw.

When he returned well past noon, he decided he'd rather not encounter Boar, and so sought out Fierté to give his report. Fierté was in the study. The door was open and Fierté, in human form, sat at a well-lit desk, sorting through papers. He appeared quite at ease, indicating Crow's worries of his book smuggling involvement had not been found out. Crow released a breath he hadn't realized he'd been holding.

"Good afternoon, sir," said Crow, his usual greeting when he brought the reports.

"Ah, Crow," said Fierté, placing his papers aside. He signaled Crow to take a seat, twiddling a quill in the other hand. Crow landed on the padded armchair across from Fierté. "Anything of interest today?"

"Aside from chilling winds, nothing much. I suspect snowfall within the week. Food is scarcer as well. Fox and Wolf will have a difficult time acquiring any game."

"A rather uneventful time, compared to this morning, no?" said Fierté. He always had a way of speaking that sounded like an innocent inquiry, but

Crow's wariness always rose at the tone. Fierté noticed this. "I'm not overly concerned about the morning event. It seems it was all just a misunderstanding by the guests. Sometimes you can get turned around in these hall if you're not so directionally inclined. Squirrel and Porcupine both claimed you did an outstanding job in redirecting them. In fact, our guests have become even more passive from it. Hélène has agreed to several further arrangements to dine and chat with the master."

"That's excellent news, sir," said Crow, wondering why Fierté was telling him. Normally he'd hear this sort of news second hand.

"Yes," said Fierté, smiling happily. "So allow me to thank you for keeping on your toes and stopping them from entering the west wing."

"Of course, sir. I wouldn't have normally interfered, but I was the only one who could transform nearby."

Crow hopped onto the chair's handle to take his leave.

"One more thing," said Fierté. He waved his hand for Crow return to the chair's center. "Mr. Duval visited me personally and apologized for the incident. An appreciated improvement in his behavior. And while here, we had a deep discussion on what we could do so such accidents wouldn't occur again. He also expressed a deep desire to not be restricted to his room so often." Fierté gave a smile that crinkled his eyes as he picked up a particular sheet and read, while giving a classier imitation of Roi's voice, "Hélène has Nanny as a watcher and servant, so I want one as well. I want the boy who I talked with earlier today."

Crow was glad he was in crow form, as he paled significantly.

"I was under the impression you had escorted them back to their rooms and left it at that," said Fierté. "But Mr. Duval appears to remember that you in fact had a good chat."

"I... talked a bit," said Crow. "But mostly it was just warning them away from the hall and the incident with Nanny."

"I'm not angry. I know you wouldn't betray us in any way. As such, I am granting Mr. Duval's request."

"What?"

"You will be with him for at least half a day, every day, to watch and assist," said Fierté while adding an extra note to the paper. "The remaining daylight hours are for patrol and recon. Night, as per usual, is for yourself. Questions?"

Crow's beak hung open.

Fierté laughed while asking, "Transform please."

Crow obeyed. He leaned against the back of the seat, his hands gripping the arms.

"During your serving hours, I require you to be human," said Fierté, still jovial but very serious in his statement. "I don't want either guest to know your animal form. It is to our advantage."

"Right," said Crow, still in shock.

"I know you'll be able to manage the hours," continued Fierté. "Though it will be a tough first week as you warm up. Make sure to appear clean. They're already familiar with your clothing, so I won't have you change into something more suitable."

"So… you just… want me to watch them?"

"Roi Duval," said Fierté. "Your priority is Roi. Watch and assist. If anything is in the least suspicious of him, report immediately. In fact, I want reports every one to two days."

Crow nodded, aware that Fierté could see his poorly hidden lack of enthusiasm.

"This isn't a choice," said Fierté.

"I know sir. I just don't understand why he'd trust me. I thought he hated us."

"Oh, he doesn't hate you. Actually, he sounded rather fond of you, though that won't last if he learns you led him here. Your human-self left a good impression, maybe because you appear around their age. It's your job to figure that out and maintain it. The staff is in the process of being informed."

"When did you want me to start?"

"Dinner," said Fierté. "It will make a pleasant surprise for them. And I know I don't need to remind you, but I'll do so just for an ease of mind; don't speak about the curse." Slight guilt crossed Crow's face, but Fierté misread it. "Relax. You'll do fine. I know you've never served before, but you've seen us manage many times and you can always ask me any questions."

Crow nodded and made his way, weak-kneed, from the room.

Just before dinner, he headed to the laundry room, where the servant baths were also kept. He found a fresh washbasin and quickly gave his face a good cleaning. He rubbed it dry with a brittle towel. He then dipped his fingers in the water and ran them through his hair, hoping that in its unruliness, it would somewhat stay back.

His procession to the dining room alternated in speed as conflicting thoughts battled in his head. When he finally got to there, Fierté was just leaving. Fierté's presentation smile remained on his face as he winked at Crow. Crow only tightened his clenched hands.

As he approached the table, he could sense servants watching him. He thought he saw Boar peer in through the waiter door's porthole. Roi's back was to him, focused on pouring himself another glass of wine, while the waiter looked on flustered at not being able to do his job. Hélène looked up, noticed Crow, and gave a smile. The smile was a disguised warning to Roi, rather than a greeting to him. Roi turned his head to see Crow and a grin made its way along his face.

Crow stopped at the edge of the table, bringing his feet together sharply, causing his boots to click.

"Good evening Monsieur and Mademoiselle. As you may or may not have been informed, I am to be Mr. Duval's *assistant*."

"How nice to see you again," said Hélène warmly.

"Call me Roi," said Roi.

"Roi," said Crow quietly, and then gave Hélène a bow, "It is a pleasure to see you again as well."

"Oho," said Roi. "Being more mannerly now, are we? I liked it better when you were blunt."

That was when I wasn't your nanny and I thought I wouldn't have to deal with you face to face again, thought Crow grimly.

"I'm afraid I was caught off guard with everything that occurred. I apologize for any rudeness I displayed. Please expect better behavior henceforth."

Roi made a noise at the back of his throat.

"Please have a seat and dine with us," said Hélène.

"Thank you for the offer, but I shall wait by the door," said Crow.

Nanny usually stood over there, but she was still not present. Crow stood sternly, wishing he could sit by the end. He took turns placing weight on each foot.

When finished with his meal, Roi walked over to Crow and placed his arm over Crow's shoulder. Roi didn't hesitate placing his full weight down. Crow could smell the wine from his breath and his cheeks appeared a bit flushed.

"Alright," said Roi. "Let's go get acquainted! Hélène! Are you coming?"

Hélène walked alongside them as they moved into the main hall. Crow spotted a few animals watching from the shadows.

"Can you walk on your own?" asked Crow as politely as he could through clenched teeth.

Roi put down even more weight causing them to swerve.

"Ahhhhhh, I'm a little tipsy. 'm sorry."

Assisting drunks had not been in Crow's plans.

Not even the good looking ones.

Crow struggled to get Roi up the stairs, internally venting over what he considered his new, particularly degrading role. He further fumed when Hélène passed and reached the top well before they were half way. At the top, he saw Hélène and White had crossed paths.

"I'll bring it right away," said White, before giving a courteous curtsy and heading off.

"I requested some tea be brought to my room," said Hélène to Crow. "Please, would you sit with us there?"

Her large eyes looked like a doe's as she gazed at him. Crow was fed up with standing and he was going to have to watch them until curfew anyways. He forced a small smile.

"Perhaps for a short while, so long as I'm not intruding."

"Of course not!"

At her room, Roi forced more weight on Crow as they walked through the door, causing Crow to hit the frame. He held back a curse and pretended not to hurt.

A small table had been set up in the room's center, with four chairs. Crow got Roi seated and then had to stand behind him, holding his shoulders until Roi stopped swaying.

"Stable, sir?"

"Yep," replied Roi cheerfully.

Crow pulled a seat out for Hélène, then rushed to help White as she entered the room pushing a trolley. The cups and saucers were placed on the table. White poured the first round of tea before placing the teapot in the center.

"Tonight is a simple chamomile tea to help with everyone's resting."

Roi already looked half asleep.

"Thank you so much," said Hélène.

White gave a motherly smile before turning the trolley around to leave.

"Curfew is in an hour. Nanny will be back tomorrow. Will the young miss be alright the night alone? There will be a safe guard posted outside your door."

"I shall be fine," said Hélène. "I'm glad Nanny will be alright. I feel positively awful about her."

Crow held his breath, doubting White was as fine as indicated by the smile on her face.

"Don't fret dear," said White at the door. "Accidents, no matter how we strive, are bound to happen. Sweet dreams."

White left the door open, as was expected when opposite sexes were in the room. Crow took a seat, and they were all quiet for a good ten minutes. Crow let his eyes shift to a painting where a peephole was said to be; part of the secret passage White knew about.

"Tomorrow I'd like some fresh air," said Hélène, breaking the silence. "Care to join me in the courtyard? Roi? Err… I'm sorry, I don't believe I know your name?"

Crow stared at her blankly. His name? His original was unknown. His current name would give him away as the crow. His mind racked for something to say.

"Don't you have a name?" asked Roi, suddenly quite sober and focused.

"I…," struggled Crow.

"Are you not allowed to tell us?" pressed Hélène.

"Something like that," said Crow reluctantly.

"Then what would you like us to call you?"

"Anon," decided Roi. "Short for anonymous."

"You can't just decide for him," said Hélène, glaring at her brother. "And it was horrible that you made him work so hard to get you here."

"I had to make it look convincing," said Roi.

Crow resisted narrowing his eyes. He touched where his shoulder was still smarting from the run in with the doorframe.

"Anon is fine," he said. "Though I don't understand why you were acting drunk."

"So they wouldn't think we were up to anything," said Roi. He leaned on the table, blowing on the tea. His eyes shrewdly watched Crow.

"We aren't up to anything," said Crow calmly.

"Of course we aren't," said Roi sardonically.

Crow stiffened.

"Gentlemen," said Hélène, "Let's not get upset over specifics." She turned to Crow and grabbed his hand that he had rested loosely on his tea cup handle. Crow tried to politely pull away. "Thank you so much for not giving us away. We don't intend to pull you into anything unfair, really. We just wanted someone trustworthy to be watching over Roi so he can read in peace without worry of interruption."

Crow began to feel relieved. A slight smile started on his lips.

"And tell me anything I can't snoop out for myself," added Roi.

And the relief was gone. Crow looked across the table, vexed, and met Roi's gaze. Roi smirked.

"There we go. There's the spirit you had."

"Let's not abuse this relationship," said Crow decidedly. He picked up his tea cup and took a quick sip.

Roi snorted and muttered to Hélène, "Heh, two fingers. He drinks like a rich man."

Crow flushed and set the cup down, now aware of his drinking habit.

"Roi!" said Hélène angrily. "Don't be rude."

Crow forced a smile much like Fierté's.

"All of us at the castle strive to uphold top class civility and manners, and thus I avoid methods of drinking performed by lower class men."

"I'm middle class," said Roi.

"Of course," said Crow, blinking innocently. "I didn't state otherwise."

Hélène quickly changed the topic.

"Well, Anon, I know this is pressing our friendship forward quite quickly, but is there anything you could tell us about the castle or the curse? With no one here to listen in…"

"I'm sorry," said Crow. "But I've told you all I-"

"How old are you?" interrupted Roi.

"Roi!" said Hélène exasperated.

"This isn't rude. I want to know how old my servant is."

"Assistant," corrected Crow. "And I'm older than you."

"I doubt that," said Roi, sitting back and crossing his arms. "You look younger. I bet you lied that you were older in order to get a castle position."

Oh, you're sneaky. If you were an animal, I bet you'd be a fox. Crow let a little smile show through. "Subtle and clever, but I won't fill in the blanks."

Roi just shrugged and the room went awkwardly silent again.

"Before curfew is in effect, there are a few things I'd like to discuss with Roi privately," Hélène hesitantly broke the silence.

Crow got up and bowed. Needing to keep them in sight for the remainder of the hour, he stood by the door. He kept eyeing his tea cup, wishing he'd drunk more.

The siblings kept their voices low, but he picked up parts of their conversation. A lot of it was safe topics, such as worrying about their town and family, which contributed to Crow's level of guilt. That was, until Roi's, "I'll work my charm. He'll loosen up. And don't worry, I changed the hiding spots."

Cow felt his hairs bristle, but he pretended not to hear.

CHAPTER 3 – DON'T TRUST RODENTS

"What's that noise?" asked Roi, cupping his hand to his ear as they finished touring the servant quarters.

Crow's eyes lingered on the closed dungeon door. The occupants were quiet, but a steady scratching could be heard.

"Chickens for tonight's dinner."

"Speaking of which, I'm getting hungry."

Crow watched Roi canter down another hall. For the twelfth time that day, he peered curiously through an open door.

"We can go to the dining room," said Crow. "I'll inform the cooks."

"This will finally give you something useful to do! You're like a jealous lover. All you've been doing is watching me all day. "

"And cleaning up after you," muttered Crow. He flexed his fingers.

All the silly chores Roi had him do, Crow suspected, were tests, some strange method of seeing Crow's flexibility and capabilities. That morning, clothes had intentionally been left sprawled across Roi's room. Three times, Roi accidently knocked ornaments off the counter when Crow was nearby to catch. Twice, he'd gone to the garderobes and not returned until Crow went to fetch him. It had been a relief, the hours when Roi sat down and read.

In the dining room, Crow pulled out a seat and Roi sat down, placing on a mocking air of spoiled aristocracy.

"Food!"

"One minute," said Crow, sighing and heading for the servant doors.

Walking down the waiter hall, Crow smelled a roast waft up from the kitchens further down. His saliva started to build.

"Lunch for the brother?" inquired a mouse waiter, sitting on a cart.

"Are you able to serve him anything this soon?"

The mouse nodded, and then added, "Boar wants an update on him."

"I informed Fierté yesterday."

"Fierté is not Boar."

The mouse scurried down a strand of yarn that had been tied to the cart handle, heading to inform the kitchens. Crow backtracked to the dining room. Peeking in, he spotted Roi attempting to make conversation with a sparrow resting on one of the chandeliers. The sparrow had only hunched down in response, but this didn't deter Roi.

With Roi occupied, Crow skipped steps down the servant stairs to the basement, walking in big strides to get to Boar's office quickly. It was going to be a pain if both Fierté and Boar wanted him to update every day. He hoped White wouldn't feel left out and become demanding too.

At the corner before Boar's office, Porcupine stood talking quietly with Spencer. Hearing footsteps, Porcupine looked Crow's way. The small animal tensed, and then hustled away at a pace unexpected of the creature. Spencer hurried in front of Boar's door. He appeared more docile than normal and his burly bear shoulders twitched with apprehension.

"He's a little preoccupied right now," said Spencer quickly. "Let me inform him you're here."

"I'm just giving a quick report," said Crow, crossing his arms.

Spencer swiftly knocked a couple times, then opened the door to poke his head in, "Sir, Crow is here to report." Spencer looked back at Crow apologetically. "Just letting him transform."

When Spencer opened the door for Crow, Boar stood in the middle of the room. As soon as Crow was inside, Boar snapped his fingers and Spencer slammed the door shut. Crow looked back. Boar grabbed hold of his shoulders and roughly turned him to face him.

"You're not assigned to be their abettor, boy."

Crow's eyes widened at the accusation.

"I understand," said Crow shakily, though he had very little notion.

Boar released him and turned away laughing, "It amuses me because I agree. I think you understand exactly. I also think you are deceitful and a liar. How far did the siblings get when you stopped them in the forbidden wing?"

"Not too far. Just outside the library."

"Outside the library or in the library?"

Crow internally swore, but maintained his neutral demeanor.

"The library door was open."

"Oh," said Boar. "Well, I've just learned the siblings in fact got inside the library. Is that all that happened?"

"They did step foot in the library by the time I managed to transform," said Crow. "But I got them out quickly. I felt there was no reason to mention it."

"That's all?"

"Yes."

Bang!

A book was pulled from under Boar's desk and slammed on top. Crow recognized the cover as one of the books supposed to be hidden in Roi's room. It contained local maps, albeit, outdated by two decades. His whole body went still and a cold crept through his arms.

Boar took hold of Crow's shirt collar, dragging him right up to the table. He looked like he was considering shoving Crow's face into the book. But instead, Boar released him, circling the room agitatedly.

"Just caught them in the library," said Boar, his volume raising, but not yet reaching a yell. "And you just swore to my face that nothing else occurred. That's funny, since it was also reported both siblings took several books from the room! And, after a search of their rooms, we found five."

Crow determinedly stared down at the book. His throat felt tight. He didn't dare look away. The fact that Boar wasn't at full throttle in yelling yet was unnerving. The room was ominous, building up to explode.

"Strange how you hadn't noticed big books in their hands," seethed Boar vehemently. "Is there anything you'd like to add to this? Any further knowledge… before judgment?"

"No."

"Are you certain? Because I know more than you might think."

Crow's mind scrambled. Porcupine must have squealed. The only thing he could think of was that the siblings had taken more than five books. Porcupine had not likely counted. He'd been down pretty low to see the full stacks. Was it something further back?

His breathing increased as he sought to think of anything else. Unsuccessful, he settled with slowly shaking his head. He restrained his hands from shaking by curling his fingers.

Boar cuffed the back of Crow's head. From Boar, a cuff was as bad as a punch. Crow stumbled, grabbing a shelf to keep his balance as his eyes pooled with tears. Then came an actual punch to the side of his stomach. Crow fell to his knees, curling up as his arms clenched around his stomach and he sought to breathe properly.

"I won't have traitors in the master's castle," snarled Boar.

"I'm not a traitor!"

"Then you're an idiot! Allowing the siblings to use you or whatever the cause may be. Let's hope there's nothing else."

"There isn't."

Boar angrily struck out with a kick, catching Crow's left arm. The momentum sprawled Crow back against the shelf as his arm surged with pain. The pulsing foretold more than a simple bruising.

"Why. Are. You. So. Fucking. Defiant?" snarled Boar, kicking Crow with each word. The exertion caused Boar's face to purple, spit to fly, and sweat to form along his hairline.

Crow fought not to yell, finding the best refuge by curling up against the shelf. He hated his powerlessness. He'd been at the edge of Boar's wrath before, though not to this extent or so cornered. It was a matter of waiting it out. Boar's beatings were infamous, but he'd never killed anyone.

Cringing as he waited for the next strike, Crow glanced up to see Boar had settled on looking down at him with contempt.

"What have you learned from this?"

Crow swallowed, striving to get enough air between ragged breaths, "That I shouldn't have overstepped my boundaries-" He flinched as his body protested at his attempts to get in enough air to speak. "I'm just a servant. I'm only to follow orders. The castle comes before anything else."

Boar looked at him, disgusted, but he nodded.

Tasting blood in his mouth, Crow narrowed his eyes as he couldn't resist but to add, "and don't trust rodents to keep their mouth shut."

Boar struck Crow on the side of the face, causing Crow's vision to suddenly cease. He groaned as he slid down all the way to lying on the floor, pain blending with nausea and dizziness. The approaching sense of sleep was welcomed.

As he drifted off, Boar got near his ear, close enough that Boar's sideburns scratched against his cheek. Amidst his ear's ringing, he heard Boar snarl, "If you weren't so damn useful, I'd break your wings."

#

Crow woke up to the humming of a couple servants a room over.

Blinking slowly, he realized he'd been placed in the small infirmary; a mediocre room intended only for servant use. The master and guests were always tended directly in their rooms.

A clock hung on the far wall, indicating dinnertime. The medicine cabinets and hanging herbs took up the remaining wall space. The plants were common found, like garlic and oregano. Fierté had the rarer dried plants in his office, a collector back during the curse-free days.

Crow flinched. Someone had kindly bound his left arm and placed it in a sling. Testing it, he concluded it was sprained and thankfully not broken. He lifted his good arm up slowly and felt around the tender skin under his eye. The bruising didn't hesitate in making tears form at his touch. He felt grateful he hadn't transformed during Boar's rage filled outburst. His crow form was fragile.

He attempted sitting and bit back a cry as sharp pain shot through his chest. Slowly he got to his feet, his legs heavy and cumbersome. He used the furniture to regain balance.

After successfully sneaking a drink and painkiller from the kitchen without being noticed, Crow made his way back to the main level. His foot hit against something solid, causing him to stumble and barely catch his balance. He winced as his body protested.

"You really should watch where you step in these halls," said a young voice.

Crow looked down at Gustav, who was tilting his rabbit head up at Crow. Gustav was younger than him and hadn't been able to transform to human for years. Fuzzily remembering his human appearance, Crow placed him around fourteen. He wasn't particularly nice looking and his arrogant personality around the lower servants made him isolated. However, he was good at his job and very loyal to Fierté.

"What happened to you?"

"An angry pig," said Crow uncaringly, but he'd already checked to make sure no Boar loyalists were around.

"What did you do this time?" asked Gustav, wrinkling his nose. Crow couldn't tell if Gustav was amused or exasperated.

"None of your business," said Crow stiffly. "Don't you have Fierté's errands to run?"

Gustav twitched an ear, and then headed off without a word.

Crow entered the dining room through the main hall, avoiding the waiter hall where Boar loyalists would judge him. The dining room door was closed to preserve heat; the main hall was still chilly. Crow took in a deep breath, and then opened the door, strutting into the ball room like nothing was the matter.

Approaching from behind, Roi and Hélène both appeared unharmed by the book raid, though Hélène was glaring at her food as she ate. Roi chatted continuously, unbothered. Crow bitterly bet Roi had finished the books they'd found already. He wondered if he'd be able to retrieve and return the remaining books without suspicion. Right now it seemed better to simply leave them.

Crow quietly joined Nanny at the side. Nanny was watching in dog form. Her eyes shifted from the siblings to Crow. Thankfully, she said nothing.

A servant brought forth a dessert.

"Pudding!" declared Roi. "Excellent! Back home in Beauclair I'd heard that the East cooks' specialties are their puddings."

The waiter froze. Crow heard someone gasp. With a satisfied smirk, Roi took the ladle from the waiter's hand and presumed to serve himself.

"Of course, it was a hunch," continued Roi. "This was either an East or Pierre-mont estate. No one reacted like this to my Pierre-mont references earlier. Interesting. Thank you sir, for confirming which family this castle belongs to."

The waiter blinked, quickly retrieved the ladle Roi left in the pudding pot and gave Hélène a couple distracted scoops before rushing off. Hélène stared after the waiter, her mood slightly improved.

"Anon, I heard you enter," said Roi, not bothering to turn in his seat as he proudly started on his pudding. "Since this doesn't concern the curse, I'm sure you can confirm for me; does everyone here serve Lord East? Is your master a relative, regent, or keeper of this castle?"

Crow stepped forward, irritated by Roi's good mood. Roi appeared ignorant of the repercussions his words could cause. Crow reached across Roi's field of vision to straighten a spoon, drawing Roi's smug attention from the pudding to the utensil. Roi's eyes flickered from Crow's hand, to his sling, to his face. Crow felt the satisfaction of seeing Roi sober up.

"One of your rules is to not ask after the master," answered Crow. "But as Francis did react so strongly; yes, we are an East household."

"You-" Roi started, completely surprised.

"All actions and words have repercussions," said Crow sharply, retrieving a napkin that had fallen off the table. He kept his voice even, even though it hurt to bend. "And while you are an honored guest, I request you remember the rules that are keeping you in this position. I was expecting repentant behavior after your stash's discovery."

Roi's eyes widened and Crow internally swore.

Roi and Hélène don't know the books have been found yet. Bastard Boar. He must have simply taken the books and left the rooms spotless- No, that's too clean for him. It must have been White and she'd told Boar. This means Hélène is upset about something else...

Hélène looked like she was about to say something but White approached, "Mademoiselle Hélène, your bath is ready. Please accompany me right away, so the water won't cool."

Hélène bit her lip as she exchanged concerned looks with Roi. She turned and wordlessly followed White. Roi stood up from his seat, watching Hélène leave. He then turned to Crow, his eyes still wide and troubled. He ventured closer, to get a better look at Crow's bruised face. His hand rose, mesmerized, but stopped short of touching.

"What happened to you?"

Spoken more curiously than concerned, Crow bitterly remembered Roi perceived him as a captor before anything else. Any compassion, even seeming friendship, was falsified. Crow suddenly felt too tired and sore to deal with Roi any longer.

"Just a sprain and bruising due to my own follies," said Crow, unaware of his observable bitterness. "You needn't concern yourself about it. Will you need me for anything this evening? I'm afraid I have some other duties to attend to."

Two waiters entered the room to clean the table. They watched Roi and Crow closely.

"No, I'll see myself to my room," said Roi, suddenly distracted. "I'll see you tomorrow."

Crow bowed aside as Roi left the room. To play it safe, he listened at the stairwell until he heard Roi close his door, to search his room uninterrupted.

Gustav popped up beside Crow. Feeling unsociable, Crow looked down at Gustav apathetically and pushed the rabbit away lightly with his foot. Gustav glared at him. Using his small paws, he rubbed where Crow's boot had touched, as if wiping off Crow's taint.

"If you're done for the evening, Fierté would like to talk with you."

Crow leaned, frustrated, against a rail, staring up at the ceiling. The day wouldn't end! He'd never been a great servant, but even he recognized he'd become more unruly than normal. Whether from the siblings or his own stir-craziness, he needed to watch himself. Another beating from Boar or even Fierté, who rarely resorted to what he considered below his taste, would have him crawling on his knees.

"Where?" asked Crow.

"No wonder Boar gave you a lesson, with such an attitude."

Crow snorted.

"Where is Fierté?" repeated Crow.

Gustav took him to the third floor, so Crow knew Fierté was in his office. He went just fast enough that it was uncomfortable for Crow to keep up. Crow privately plotted payback.

At the door, Gustav gave Crow another glare before hopping off on another errand. Fierté's door was open, so Crow knocked on the panel first. He poked his head inside.

"Sir, did you ask for me?"

He immediately stepped back. Boar stood only a few paces inside.

"Come in, please," said Fierté.

Crow reluctantly stepped inside. Biting his lip, Crow did a little bow. Any agitation and bravery had disappeared instantly in the presence of the two power houses.

"Well, speak of the devil," said Boar. "I'll take my leave."

Crow released a quiet breath of relief as Boar turned in his usual gruff manner. He shrunk back as Boar passed. Boar ignored him.

Fierté gave a weary look after Boar, and then focused on Crow. His mustache twitched as he quirked the corner of his mouth.

"What did Roi say when he saw you like this?"

"He just inquired casually. You can ask the dining staff."

Fierté sat down at the desk, his finger thrumming a pattern on an ink bottle lid. He studied Crow thoughtfully. Crow fiddled under the stare.

"I don't agree with such visible beatings, but Boar was right to get angry and you know punishment was due. You have handled yourself well otherwise, though. Roi trusts you, so make sure to keep him in line."

Crow nodded.

"How is your human form handling?" asked Fierté.

"I can still last several hours each day."

"Good," said Fierté. His face firmed as he settled on a resolution. He got out of his seat to stand in front of Crow. His hand reached out and confidently grasped Crow's good forearm. "From now on, report to only me, not Boar. Understand?"

This close, Crow could see the stag in Fierté's eyes. Fierté was smiling, standing in a straight, calm posture. Even his hand gave a kindly squeeze before releasing Crow. But this wasn't a good will gesture to protect him from Boar. He was claiming an asset.

Crow silently nodded. Between brutal Boar and egocentric Fierté, Crow preferred kissing the feet of the latter.

"Good. And let's make sure to maintain professionalism and loyalty through all this... because I would hate to have to discipline you. With Elliot not around, my temper isn't as good."

Crow immediately stiffened. Elliot was a young servant Fierté had been particularly close to. That summer he'd permanently caved to perdu. Furthermore, he had escaped to the woods and had not been seen since. Because of this, there were dark rumors that Fierté's love was one sided and forced.

Fierté reached out and held Crow's chin. He lowered his head so they were face to face. Crow could feel the top of Fierté's fingers brush lightly against his bruised cheek.

"Will I need to discipline you?"

"I won't let you down, sir," Crow forced out.

A rueful smirk crossed Fierté's face. He released Crow and turned towards his desk.

"Now get out."

CHAPTER 4 – A RELUCTANT CONSPIRATOR

The following days, Crow kept his distance and carefully played the role of the silent servant shadow. This left Roi rather confused. He initially displayed some intent to dispel Crow's cold behavior, but by the third day appeared defeated. Or to better say, caught interest in a different subject, which Crow had the misfortune to stumble upon, literally.

His arm no longer in a sling, he brought candles into Hélène's room where the two siblings were occupied in their own activities. His foot hit against some knee-high solid which sent him stumbling. Regaining his balance, he noticed the number of inanimate objects lying about the room; mostly hunting trophies brought over from Roi's room. A male pheasant stood in the center, two rabbits near the foot of the bed, a skunk by the window, and a small fox by the door, the instigator of his fall.

This would have appeared random, but having flown the surrounding area many of times, Crow immediately recognized the layout modelled after the region's landscape. The animals represented the major towns. Even the towels strewn in a line across the floor represented the river.

Roi stared at Crow sheepishly with a stuffed weasel under one arm.

"Want to join the game? I'm playing house. This weasel here is Uncle Pierre. He's visiting the rabbits in order to convince them not to elope. Mrs. Fox, who you've met, is…"

"No thank you," said Crow, finding he just didn't care enough to call Roi out. Other than recreating the landscape, there didn't appear to be much else going on.

Roi shrugged and positioned the weasel near the wardrobe.

Crow placed the candles on the counter-side, scanning the remaining room carefully. Hélène was looking melancholic by the window. Nanny was lying comfortably on the end of Hélène's bed.

Curious towards the pensive expression Hélène wore, Crow carefully made his way around Roi's landscape to the window.

"Is there something I might help you with, Mademoiselle?"

Hélène gave a passive grimace. Crow was ready for her usual 'let me go home' or 'tell me why I can't leave'.

"Has your master always been such a self-centered brute?"

Crow's mouth hung open. A chuckle escaped before he quickly controlled himself. His poorly hidden amusement caused Hélène to smile. Crow cleared his throat.

"As long as I remember, he's been this way. Think of him as a forlorn brute. He's spent so many years warped in his beastly form that his manners went dormant. If anyone can reawaken them, I believe it'd be you."

Hélène moved to sit next to Nanny, absently stroking her head.

"It's hard, when I'm with limited freedom and knowledge," said Hélène. "He requests to see me every day now. I know you all think this is necessary for some curse, but his character is just so-." Her eyes narrowed as she straightened up while looking around the room. "For goodness sakes Roi, clean this mess."

Roi saluted.

After a sigh, Hélène continued, "I'm starting to think your master knows the most out of everyone here. I don't mean to insult you, Anon, but I suspect you don't tell us much because you simply don't know."

Were he in crow form, he would have fluffed up. As a human, he merely kept his face neutral.

I know as much as any other servant! But then, Fierté and the master have their journals…

"If you befriend him, he may reveal more," offered Crow, wincing as Roi tripped and beheaded a rabbit on a chair. "He's… especially keen to follow chivalry."

"Well, I'm afraid I don't know how I can befriend him to-"

"Maybe you could seduce him to be nicer," suggested Roi, tromping back over to them. The stuffed animals were all tucked away in the far corner. "A lusting man will reveal many things."

Hélène rolled her eyes and gave Roi a disgusted look. Crow also doubted Roi was fully serious. However-

"The master has a weak spot for affection."

"You want me to flirt so that we can get more freedom and find out more?"

"You don't have to get intimate," said Crow.

"Oh, but a kiss would wipe him off his feet," said Roi. "It doesn't have to be on the lips, for example-"

Roi caught Crow's shoulders, pulling him in quickly, he pressed his lips between Crow's eyebrows. Roi's lips were tender and soft. Crow had always imagined lips to feel harsh. This close, he could study Roi's face in-depth; impulsive, passionate eyes, the light freckles and pores, a few missed hairs from shaving…

What am I doing, studying Roi like this? These thoughts are absurd. I've never focused on these things before and I certainly won't start now. Especially not with him! The ass just kissed me without a hint of decency. This is all just a joke; a performance put on by a jester.

Coming to his senses, Crow jabbed his elbow into Roi's rib cage, causing a swift release. Roi managed a mischievous grin while he clutched his chest.

"Of course, it only works if the other party wants you or is deprived," said Roi weakly. "I'd imagine Master East is both. And we can count on his noble upbringing to make sure he doesn't take it any further."

Everyone blanched at the thought.

"Your brother is very physical though," said Crow, roughly rubbing the spot Roi had touched. It still tingled. "A kiss isn't necessary. Simpler affections will do. Something simple, like…"

He looked at Nanny. He kneeled onto the floor at the bed's edge, facing her at eye level. Lifting his hand, he lightly caressed Nanny's face, staring into her eyes. Nanny looked enduring, but Crow sensed she was very embarrassed. He placed on a conserved smile, "You're so beautiful. Your large, intoxicating eyes, this close…"

Crow chuckled, unable to take it seriously any longer.

"I've seen better technique," said Roi. "Hélène, you know I've flirted a lot, I'll give you several options. Come here Anon."

"I'm not going to be your pretend partner. Take Nanny. She closest resembles the master right now."

Hélène burst into laughter and patted Nanny's head, "Oh Nanny, you are much nicer looking."

"I don't want to use a dog," said Roi, but his expression hinted something slightly different; something Crow couldn't quite grasp. "Besides, you're my height."

"Just talk to the air," said Crow.

Roi stared at Crow, puckering his lips in a pleading pout. Crow stared unwaveringly back. Roi tilted his head and Crow remained unmoved. Roi then raised an eyebrow. From the corner of his eye, Crow saw Hélène shake in withheld laughter, and when Roi brought his hands together in an exaggerated plead, Crow released an amused snort at the antics.

Crow's attempt to remain proper diminished as Roi took to chasing him. He initially retreated in reaction to Roi's sudden movement, but quickly grasped the playful intention. They raced around the room, Crow agilely keeping a few steps ahead of Roi.

Hélène's giggling? Good. I can fool around if this is going to benefit her.

Roi doubled his efforts when Crow gave a frisky grin. Laughing from the exhilaration, Crow and Roi came to a tie at opposite sides of the table.

"Come back to me, my love," said Roi.

"I'm dumping you, sir, you're too arrogant."

"I'll have you know that's confidence! All my lovers have admired it. They also admire my flirtatious techniques. So stay put and let me show my sister…"

Crow feinted one way, and then took off in the other. He raced around the table with the intentions of reaching Hélène as a safe haven. Roi caught his hand. Crow staggered as sharp pains shot up through his healing arm.

Calling out victoriously, Roi used his momentum to push Crow onto the bed. Crow's back flumped onto the sheets, his legs hanging over the edge. Roi's hands pressed down on Crow's shoulders. His one leg pushed against the ground to weigh Crow down, while his other snaked between Crow's legs, Crow presumed for balance. He was pinned.

"Oh yes," laughed Hélène, "I definitely will try that move on Master East. Such a catcher."

Roi looked up at his sister, happy to see her laugh. Crow took the opportunity.

"Oh, your moves have won my heart," said Crow. He grabbed the unsuspecting Roi's shirt collar, pulling him down and drawing his attention. Their chests lightly met, the fabric ruffling. He stared directly into Roi's eyes as he whispered, "Now I'll tell you all my secrets."

Roi's mouth opened agape. Crow sniggered and shoved the suddenly weak Roi aside. Crow stretched as he stood back up, and then massaged his tender arm.

Hélène gave Roi an amused 'seriously?' look, before stating, "Well boys, as much as you are trying to help, this is proving just to be a comedy for my amusement. Why don't you two run off and continue playing honeymoon while I talk with Nanny?"

"Hélène, I know-"

"Its fine, Roi. Eating silently in the beast's company is not getting us anywhere. We can only acquire so much from the servants, and the servants who are our friends get beaten if they tell us anything more. White starved Nanny for two days simply because Nanny accidently let slip at the start that not everyone could transform into humans. Anon too, for looking the other way at the library."

Nanny whined, telling Hélène it was no one's fault. Hélène gave a pained smile.

"I'll start with some minor things… but I need Nanny to help me decide what to say," continued Hélène. "To mentally prepare myself. While you two are hilarious distractions, I need woman time."

"I understand," said Roi, looking downtrodden. "But don't do anything you feel forced to. There are always other plans. If this curse's cure is reliant on you not knowing, then maybe something can come of it by me knowing."

Roi returned to his room, Crow on his trail. Roi closed the door swiftly after them.

"Nice of you to break your cold treatment to comfort Hélène," said Roi.

Crow debated whether there was genuine warmth in Roi's voice or if it was a snide statement. Regardless, Roi was looking at him differently again, waiting for Crow to respond, clearly expecting Crow's burst of social speech to continue.

"I'm afraid I can't be of much more use," said Crow.

"And there you're wrong. I don't intend to ask for any more information from you, lest you go tight-lipped again… or punished." Disgust flitted Roi's face. "I'd rather avoid any drama."

"Like the game of house you were playing?" asked Crow, unable to resist. "I think you beheaded Cherteaux… oh, wait, it was the eloping rabbit. My apologies, I always mix up dramas with maps."

Roi brought the point of his index finger down on the table, causing a distinct thud.

"That's why I like you, Anon. You and Nanny are good people, and you're particularly vigilant. Hélène is resolved to trying to solve this under castle rules. I'm not. I'll be damned if Hélène shoulders all this. I want to find out what the townspeople know. I want to know the extent of this curse. Anon, can you help me find a way to sneak out?"

Crow coughed and double checked the door was closed as he regained his composure.

"Are you mad?" hissed Crow. "Not a minute ago you are blabbing about love and now you want to run away?"

"Not run away… an excursion. I studied the maps before the book was taken back. Beauclair is too far, but there are three nearer towns. Granted most of their archived documents are kept in Beauclair for safe keeping, but I could talk around. I know people in most of the towns."

Crow shook his head.

"You can't talk about this."

"I can. No one's listening."

"I am."

"No one will know if you don't say anything."

"They'll notice you're gone," said Crow. "They'll know it was my job to watch you. Roi, I'm supposed to report to Fierté everything that you say and do."

"But you won't," said Roi, looking at him from the corner of his eye.

"You hold too much faith in me."

"So you'll report to him that I kissed you?" asked Roi slyly. "I've been thinking carefully about this for a couple days now. I can head out straight that direction, slightly left for two hours and at a good pace I can get to the nearest town, Cherteaux. They have a monastery there."

"It is also a popular stop for soldiers," said Crow darkly, remembering his patrols to the town. "A place for you to get some potential raiders."

Roi quieted.

Finally, he continued, "I would have done that a week ago. But I know now there are some good people here... and Hélène remains hostage. I doubt I'd win with that strategy. I just want to acquire any additional information I can about this place. Any knowledge of local curses or rumors."

"Even if you sneak past the perimeter guards, they'll find your trail," said Crow reluctantly. He winced at even considering the plan pliable. "The perimeter guards here will kill you."

"They can only get at me during the few minutes I'm passing through the gardens."

"Some of us can go a fair ways," said Crow reluctantly, and then bit his lip.

"Oh, come off it," said Roi, snickering. "I already figured something like that. A crow led me here all the way from Creek Crossroads. Hey, maybe they could help us."

"No, they can't."

"No, no, hear me out! Is the crow a perimeter guard? I think they're like you, they can compromise and be negotiated with."

"I assure you, this is far out of the question. If you told Hélène this plan, even she-"

"Don't tell Hélène," threatened Roi.

Shit. Hélène always comes first for him. I was speaking too familiarly. Even the goofing around we did in the other room was purposed for Hélène.

Crow distanced himself. They lingered in their thoughts.

"We'll pull a Nanny," suggested Roi, quick to recuperate. "I'll set up a lovely tea party in here and sneak out. You get to relax while watching the room. If anyone notices, you can pretend I drugged your tea and you fell asleep. That way, your hind is covered. Let the crow and I do the work."

"Why would the crow help you and what makes you think I could find him?"

"Is it a he? I thought so, but I didn't want to be quick to judge. I think he led me here out of pity and I didn't listen when he tried to warn me. If I'd waited... But I had no clue what trouble Hélène was in. Even though this is far from ideal, I was imagining worse."

Crow fidgeted with his sleeves, his gaze avoiding Roi and looking outside.

"The crow is a loner. Even if I persuaded him to help, what did you want him to do?"

"As the eyes in the sky, he can help me get across the grounds undetected and keep an eye on me for the rest of the time, for your satisfaction of course."

Crow closed his eyes. The plan was far more complicated when he was expected to play two roles he didn't want to do in the first place. Crow only needed to peek at Roi to see the man had a flare to his eye. He was going to try, with or without him.

What do the towns know? The castle must have been popular before the curse made it forgotten. If there was documentation of the castle at the monastery, which should be protected from curse magic, perhaps it would give clues. Why were we cursed? Are there other ways to break it? The rules had always seemed so black and white, but stupid Roi's mixing everything gray.

"I'll talk to him," said Crow.

Roi grabbed his hand.

"Thank you! If it's too much trouble, you could just send him to my room."

"No, I'll talk to him," said Crow. "Wait here."

"You'll do it now?"

"You'll need to do this before tomorrow night's storm," said Crow. "And you'd better take the time to pray that it works out as smoothly as you hope."

CHAPTER 5 – THE EXCURSION

"Go to the middle of the garden," whispered Crow. "Wait there for five minutes. The crow will caw when the coast is clear. Stick along the hedge and run right up and over the wall. Don't stop running until the castle is out of sight. Even then, keep moving quickly and silently. If a perimeter guard catches wind of you, they'll be on your trail quickly. There is an old hunting trail you will eventually come across, by then you might think you're safe, but-"

"Keep moving quickly," said Roi, brushing off Crow. "I got it."

"And five hours," snapped Crow, shoving a small pack at Roi. "You passing up breakfast won't make much of a worry, but missing two meals will cause suspicion."

Roi adjusted the pack to fit neatly under his coat. They'd dressed to look like they were going for a garden stroll.

"Understood," said Roi. "You don't need to keep going over this."

"You're treating this far too laid back," muttered Crow, opening the side door to the back garden.

Roi sauntered past, taking in a deep breath of crisp morning air. As he exhaled, he released a giant mist.

"No running yet!" added Crow adamantly, pointing his finger as if at a dog. "Wait for the crow."

He closed the door and raced back along the halls they'd painstakingly snuck along to get here unnoticed. He slowed his pace at Hélène's door. He lightly knocked.

Nanny opened it in human form, holding some ribbons in her hand, preparing Hélène's outfit for the day.

"Roi had a reaction to the tea I gave him this morning," said Crow pretending to badly hide amusement with solemnness, when really he just felt guilt and nervousness. "His face is rather swollen. He's passing on

55

breakfast, but the reaction should be down by lunch. Please inform Hélène he is rather embarrassed of his current appearance and asks she not seek him until his recovery."

Nanny silently nodded, closing the door.

Crow then slipped over to Roi's room, locking the room from the inside. Quickly he stuffed the pillows under the bed covers, giving a false shape for someone to see, in case anyone decided to briefly check on Roi. He paused, sitting on the edge of the bed. His fingers felt along the CC engraved deeply into the side table.

"Nothing has come of following the rules so far," Crow whispered to the silence, a desperate speech to justify his waywardness. "No clues, no cure. It's long overdue to take a leap of faith with others."

With that, he briskly stood up. He strode across to the window, opening it and climbing onto the edge. He closed the curtains the best he could. Within seconds he transformed, and with great effort, he drew the window as close to closed as he could.

He took off, flying to the top of the castle and landing on the highest point of the slated roof. He fumbled to get a good balance against the wind, his near-healed wing still stiff. With the high bird's eye view, he carefully scanned the land and angled his head to listen. Fox was out hunting, but to the north. Not a threat. The only one on perimeter duty at this hour was Wolf. Crow knew the unnerving member of the household's schedule only because duty required they sometimes work together; Crow was the eyes in the sky while Wolf was the nose and ears on the ground.

He did a swift flight checking the castle windows, trying to look past the reflections to see if anyone was looking out. Satisfied, he landed on a tall pine, just outside the wall.

Here we go.

He released a caw.

The top of Roi's head began to bob up and down above the garden hedges within Crow's sight from where he stood.

Crow scanned along the wall, making sure Wolf was still not near. When he looked back, his stomach knotted. Roi had disappeared. Crow's eyes whisked back and forth, looking at each path Roi might have pursued.

The idiot was supposed to follow the hedges directly! Right to the wall and over!

A light whistle sounded below. Crow looked down and released an exasperated grunt. Roi was crouched at the bottom of the tree, looking up at him. Roi gave a little acknowledged salute, and then continued along into the woods.

He's quicker and quieter than I remember. I'll give credit where due, this is good for getting by the guards, but I don't like that he's able to slip out of my sight so easily. I'd rather be the invisible one.

Crow took off, moving ahead higher.

They reached the skinny hunting trail within the hour, at which point Crow felt satisfied enough that they'd successfully left with no one trailing them. Now it was a matter of trust that Roi would do as he said.

The town of Cherteaux eventually came into Crow's view, the small chimneys sending smoky tendrils into the air from the fires keeping the homes warm. The monastery was positioned at the highest point of the town, at the top of a rocky hill. Stone steps led up to it, zigzagging steeply.

Crow landed on top of the monastery, studying the different buildings. Most were small dwellings where farmers, hunters, and herdsmen slept. Their fields were visible eastward, intermixed with a few dairy pastures. The local inn was the most successful businesses there, next to a bakery and stable. Fortunately, only two horses were stabled, so if there were any soldiers in town, it would be stragglers. Only a couple people were out in the chilly morning.

But all it takes is one messenger.

Roi took to the road as he arrived at the outskirts. He walked slowly. Passing the inn, he paused. The way his body stood, it was clear he wanted to go in.

Crow shifted his stance to lean apprehensively over the edge of the roof, shuffling his wings. If he had been in Roi's position, he would have sought a way out, lying with just as much ease. He just didn't like the realization that someone could lie so easily to him, to give him all the right reassurances and to gain his trust, something Crow gave little of.

He's going to go in. He's going to betray us. I'm such a fool to have trusted him.

Roi took a couple steps towards the door, stopping as someone left through it.

The man was a husky looking gentleman, bundled in furs for the day. The two of them approached each other, after Roi had clearly addressed him. For a moment they talked, Roi throwing his hands expressively around and the man laughing and pointing towards the hill.

This doesn't look like duplicity.

Crow shivered with relief as Roi continued along the road and then up the path. Breathless at the top, Roi entered the building unhindered and was welcomed with open arms by a monk.

Unable to enter the monastery, Crow circled the building, peering into windows, but was unsuccessful in spotting Roi. He settled on the top of a statue by the entrance, giving him easy watch for Roi's exit.

The sky grayed despite the sun being up, though not forbiddingly dark. The storm was still hours away. Though able to handle it with relative ease, Crow could feel the strain and summon of the castle's curse starting inside him. It would still be hours before it would overtake him, but the mild feeling was not pleasant; something like having the notion that you'd eaten bad food and repercussions would inevitably come. When he had been overcome in the past, ignoring the warning signs, he would perdu and his animal instincts would bring him back to the castle's range, where he recovered quickly enough.

When Roi exited, his expression was unreadable, giving no indication of what had happened or been found. His pack was hidden under his cloak. He carried a piece of bread in hand. Roi broke off a piece and held it out towards Crow. Crow tried to look dignified on the statue's head.

"Hello, wary friend."

Crow responded with a suspicious study of the bread. Roi gave the bread a little wave, giving Crow a last chance. Crow swooped and grabbed the piece, landing along the stone wall to eat it. The bread was fresh, made right at the monastery.

He released a grumble, to which Roi grinned and replied, "You're welcome."

Roi started down the path. Crow was ready for him to dash away, but the bread had been an offering of peace, an attempt to reassure Crow. They took the same route back through the woods. This time Crow stayed near, savoring each other's silent company in the lonely, cold forest. The closer they got the castle, the less the curse strained him. He felt himself relax.

As they drew near the back of grounds, Crow took off above the trees. They were close enough that at this point he had faith Roi would stick to the plan. If Roi were to turn tail and run, he wouldn't get far.

Crow glided to Roi's window. He peered inside, confirming the room had been undisturbed. Then he released a caw towards the grounds, used for roll call. He waited for Wolf to respond but heard nothing. With lunch upon them, most of the residents would be slipping to the basement kitchens for a bite to eat, while those more nocturnal would be catching some rest. They were in luck for approaching the castle undetected.

Crow flew towards the part of the wall Roi would attempt re-entry through. Roi was still not in sight, but he would reach it soon. An alarming snarl sounded from Roi's direction and Crow flapped crazily to regain his composure before landing on the nearest branch. Muffled words responded, spoken by Roi, but the snarling didn't stop.

Wolf.

Should I abandon Roi and play dumb, perhaps facing some time in the dungeon for falling asleep on the job, or-.

Roi's scream rang through the forest.

"Damn it all," swore Crow.

He took off, flying through the thicker trees while following the sounds, emerging in time to see Roi and Wolf in a struggle. Roi was pinned to the ground, Wolf's jaws locked on the right side of his body. Crow cringed. A gash made by claws had been raggedly slashed across Roi's cheek, from nose to ear. Wolf himself was unharmed, clearly unmatched.

Roi kicked out, giving something of a cry from the effort. Wolf released him and backed up, aiming for the next strike.

Crow swooped down, transforming midair a few steps from Wolf. He stepped between them. His hair stood on end before the large canine. He prayed his human body had the size his crow formed lacked to give Wolf a moment's pause.

"Cease!" ordered Crow. "I've got this."

"Out of the way," growled Wolf, his words barely discernable. "This is my catch."

"Dammit, Wolf! This is my charge. I have this under control."

Wolf snarled. He hadn't been in human form for years, though Crow suspected he could if he wanted to; he was one of the few inhabitants who truly enjoyed his form.

"Your ward stepped over the wall. Unexpected intruders or escapees are to be killed."

"He's not worth killing yet."

Crow angled himself more directly in front of Roi, facing Wolf with his hands out like wings to hinder Wolf's view. He could hear Roi painfully moving backwards on his back and elbows.

Wolf took a step forward, his face inches from Crow. He turned his head to keep an eye on Roi. His cold nose brushed Crow's hand. Crow's fingers twitched. One snap and Crow would be joining Roi. Crow used all his willpower not to retreat and take flight.

"Your watch failed," said Wolf. "Let me do my job."

"You kill him and you ruin all chances for Master East."

Keep him talking...

Wolf sneered.

"The master wants the female. You idiot, you're going to-"

"Hélène would never forgive anyone, and anyone associated, if her brother is killed! I already can't guarantee anything with his current condition. Only a real idiot would attack first."

Wolf snapped in warning at Crow's fingers. Crow swiftly raised his hand in time, but kept his stance. His heart hammered in his chest. Wolf sniffed the air, leering as he scented Crow's fear.

"Do you want to be eaten, Crow?"

"Go inform Boar," said Crow evenly. "I'll escort our guest back to his room. Tell Boar I'll lock him in, so he will not have freedom of the castle anymore. Let our betters decide his fate."

Wolf cocked his head skeptically to the side. He began to turn, walking horizontal of Crow and Roi. Crow lowered his arms, releasing a relieved breath. Wolf's ear twitched. He then turned and leapt towards Roi. Crow found his voice stuck as Roi cried out for the both of them. Wolf stopped short, giving Roi an angry snort and a snap towards Crow, then turned around, saying nothing more as he trailed away.

Crow remained in his stance until he was certain Wolf was truly gone. His knees became shaky, but he willed himself to remain standing. He turned to see Roi and winced at the sight.

Blood seeped through the bite on the side of his chest, his arms were scratched and the face injury was deeper than first observed. Somehow, the pack had been missed in the maiming, peeking out loosely under his coat.

Roi struggled backwards as Crow started towards him. Crow stomped a foot down on the end of Roi's coat, stopping his retreat. Roi's eyes were wide with fear. Crow gritted his teeth, forcing himself to keep calm.

"We need to get you back now."

"You…" said Roi, confused amidst his shock and pain. "You were the crow."

"We can talk later. If I can get you to your room before Boar or Fierté take action, they may overlook some of this."

Crow held out a hand. Roi stared at it as if it had become a foreign object. Roi's hand raised slowly as Crow shifted from foot to foot impatiently, repeatedly looking where Wolf had disappeared off to.

As their hands clasped, Roi grunted as Crow helped him up. Thankfully, Roi's legs worked fine, though the rest of his body profusely bled from each movement. Roi leaned desperately on Crow for support, releasing hisses and grunts. Neither said anything. Crow was too worried and Roi was in too much pain. Adrenaline seemed to be the only thing keeping them moving.

Crow took him the quickest route, aware of more than a couple eyes spotting them. He struggled to open the door at Roi's room and then helped Roi across to his bed, laying him down while pulling out the pillows from under the covers. He undid Roi's blood soaked jacket and did his best to remove it with his trembling hands. Roi released a few curses between clenched teeth. Then Crow removed the notably bulkier pack, accidently dropping it on the floor due to his shaking. He kicked it under the wardrobe.

"Who was that?" mumbled Roi, as Crow prepared the washbasin and washcloth.

Crow assumed he was referring to, "Wolf, the castle's constant perimeter guard. He's killed before, so we can consider you lucky. Give me your left arm."

Crow ignored the blood that had gotten on his own clothing and hands. He did a quick wipe down of the blood on Roi's arms and face. He had no faith to try working on the main body. Roi flinched from every touch.

"I'll find someone who can help with your injuries," said Crow, turning to leave. "If you can, take your shirt off so they can get a clear look at the bite."

Roi grabbed his arm suddenly.

"Wait."

Crow clenched his jaw and easily pulled out of his hold.

"Anon…" said Roi weakly.

"Don't move, you've lost a lot of blood."

"You will be back?"

Crow looked at him, the concern and pain in Roi's eyes caused him to cave. He couldn't hide the pity in his facial expression.

"I honestly don't know. They'll probably drug you for a while. And if you're locked in here, there's no need for me."

"Promise me you'll come back. At least watch Hélène."

Crow winced a smile. "I'll try."

Roi wanted to say more but Crow fled the room and locked the door. Wolf would have informed Boar by now. He needed to inform Fierté.

Hélène called curiously from her room as Crow passed. He ignored her. He raced up the steps to the third level, stumbling at the top. He noticed through a window that the skies had started to snow. Mercifully, Roi's trail would be masked.

He knocked quickly at Fierté's door.

What if Fierté has already been informed?

There was a slight noise, which Crow knew was a transformation, and then Fierté opened the door. Seeing Crow, his smile faltered. His eyes studied Crow up and down, his forehead scrunching as his eyes widened.

"Sir, a situation has occurred," said Crow, hearing the underlying hysterics in his voice.

Fierté checked the hall to see only Gustav hoping around the far end, and then he opened the door wider for Crow to enter.

"Why is there blood on your sleeves and hands?" asked Fierté. He grabbed the nearest container, a silver pitcher, and dipped a napkin in the water before passing it to Crow's trembling fingers.

"Roi got stir crazy and stepped over the castle ground's boundary," said Crow.

Fierté looked at Crow, astounded.

"You killed him!"

"No!" said Crow, stumbling and grabbing the nearest chair. "As… As soon as I realized it, I pursued him and caught him near the wall. But Wolf got to him first. Roi was attacked. I managed to stop Wolf from killing him. He's… badly injured."

Crow began to hyperventilate, bringing his hands to his face.

"Slow down. Breathe," said Fierté. He bent down in front of Crow, resting his steady hands caringly on Crow's knees. "You're not harmed, are you? Good. Is he unattended?"

"I locked him in his room," said Crow, managing to clumsily produce the key and place it in Fierté's raised hand.

Grasping Fierté's calmness, Crow gulped and pulled himself back together. He wiped his face on his shoulder and ran his fingers through his hair. At least he'd gotten to Fierté first. But the worry for Roi's condition and what Fierté was thinking kept him on edge.

"White will tend to him," said Fierté, after a moment of silence. "She's grown rather experienced with the accidents we've had in the past. You were right to stop Wolf. Hélène would have shut us out."

Boar's enraged voice shouted from down the hall, "Fierté! Fierté, that crow has endangered us again!"

Crow shuddered and Fierté adopted an exasperated expression as he barely managed to straighten up before Boar stormed into the room.

"Boar," Fierté casually greeted his equal. "I see you've heard the news as well."

"Oh, Wolf informed me thoroughly," said Boar. "Thanks to this," he glared at Crow, "little bird here not doing his job, the man was unwatched for who knows how long."

Crow glowered.

Fierté looked at him nonchalantly, "Actually, Crow, you had skipped that part. What were you doing that allowed Roi the unsupervised time?"

Crow hadn't thought this part through yet. His heart was still racing from the attack.

"I…" he stuttered, looking away.

"You. Were. What?" demanded Boar, stomping across the room and grabbing Crow by his hair, yanking his head back sharply. Crow let out a pained whine. He felt like throwing up when he saw Fierté make no effort to stop Boar's abuse, watching intently with a slight smile curled on his lips.

Sadist, thought Crow angrily. *Getting off on feeling powerful. You could stop this.*

Boar's grip tightened and the pain tripled.

"I was in perdu!" shouted Crow desperately. His right hand reached up but was roughly slapped aside. "He seemed content reading in the courtyard, so I changed and watched from the roof. I got lost in the crow for a minute and when I came to he was near the wall. I swear, I didn't mean to neglect him."

"What an inconvenient time to perdu," said Fierté, finally placing a hand on Boar's arm.

Boar released Crow after one final tug. Crow clutched his head. But this was short lived, as Fierté grabbed Crow's chin, forcing direct eye contact. Fierté brought their faces close, so close they could feel each other's exhales Despite Fierté's nonchalant facade, Crow could read the threat in his eyes.

"Crow, is this really what happened? You wouldn't be trying to cover for anything?"

"I wouldn't joke about perdu," said Crow. He flinched at Boar's snort.

"You know that being in perdu for a minute is a vast step in your progression," said Fierté. "We all know that you're rather good at fighting the curse. If you've gotten worse without us knowing, right at the castle… Crow, how often has it happened?"

Crow got the bitter sense he was digging a different grave for himself.

"This was the first time… other than when I'm far out from the castle for too long," said Crow. "It had to be a fluke…"

Fierté looked thoughtful, and then released Crow.

"You believe him?" said Boar furiously.

"Why would he lie?" asked Fierté. "If he has entered a sudden progression, and it's not simple fluke, we'll need to test him."

Even Boar looked unsettled.

"The dungeon then?"

Fierté shook his head. "No, Crow keeps us updated on the world outside. In that way, he is important. I want to keep extra close watch of his condition. I'll keep him in my office for the next several days."

"If he has progressed and goes into perdu again, you'll have a wild bird flying around," said Boar.

"I'll have Pan bring one of the old bird cages."

Crow struggled out of the chair to his feet.

"Crow," said Fierté, patronizingly. "You know it's unavoidable and more than reasonable."

"Please don't," pleaded Crow. "I swear it was fluke. At least put me in a dungeon cell; there are some things to do there. But a bird cage… a cage! I'll barely be able to move."

Fierté grimaced in false sympathy, "It's the only way I can adequately observe you."

"It'll speed my progression with nothing to occupy my mind! Send me into a daze!"

"It will hardly impact you permanently, to be in it for a few days," said Boar.

Crow took a dreading step away from Fierté and Boar. Superiors or not, there was a limit to his obedience.

Boar recognized Crow's defiant expression and instantly grabbed for him. Crow nimbly jumped to the side, but only served in instigating Boar to charge forward, his large hands wrapping around Crow's thinner arms.

"Damn you, fat hog," snarled Crow as Boar struggled to keep hold.

Crow stamped down on Boar's boot, causing Boar to thunder in pain and momentarily let go. Crow took a step towards the door, but Boar and Fierté simultaneously reached and caught his clothes. Losing his footing, Crow fell to floor. Fierté held down his right arm while Boar moved to sit on his back, his foot pressing down on Crow's injured left arm.

"Steven, get in here," roared Boar.

"Pont, Gustav," shouted Fierté. Gustav was at the door instantly. "Find Pan and tell him to bring the largest bird cage immediately to my office."

Gustav nodded, eyes wide, and hopped from view. Pont, whose animal form was a cat, more cautiously entered in human form. His athletic figure was in its mid-thirties, his crewcut platinum hair, which had him stand out compared to the rest of the staff, indicated a militant history.

Steven, in bear form, lumbered in last and took over for Boar sitting on Crow. Crow gasped for air as the weight became thrice heavier. Fierté released Crow's arm.

"Don't care to change your story?" asked Boar.

Crow was unable to get enough breath to reply. He settled with a glare towards Boar.

Fierté strode over to his desk and moved aside half of the contents. Then he took to writing something down, while everyone else remained uneasy until Pan, something of a storage caretaker, arrived with the cage. Made of brass, it followed the traditional half oval shape of a birdcage. The interior only consisted of a stand, wooden and worn. At best, it was clean. The cage was placed on the cleared corner of Fierté's desk.

Fierté got down on his haunches before Crow. He used his quill to push aside some of Crow's disheveled hair from his face so they could see each other properly.

"Crow, Steven is going to get off of you and, for your own good, we would like you to transform cooperatively."

Steven slowly maneuvered off of Crow. Pont crouched next to him curiously, ready to grab him if he tried anything. Crow greedily took in the new air as he struggled up. He held his bruised arm.

"How long?" wheezed Crow.

"Three to five days," said Fierté, "Depending on my assessment. Now, transform."

Pont and Steven looked respectively away, though Pont kept track from the corner of his eye. Boar wanted to appear indifferent, but even he shuffled and appeared interested in Fierté's shelves. Fierté stared at Crow head-on.

Crow made it swift. He remained quiet, refusing to meet their eyes. He did step on Pont's hand, when offered, and Pont, kindly enough, brought him right to the stand in the cage so Crow didn't have to use his throbbing wing. Crow was feeling too upset to appreciate any gesture.

He faced the window, ignoring them. Pan showed Fierté how to lock the cage. The lock was too advanced for beak and talon.

"Fierté, we need to see what condition the brother is in and question him," said Boar.

As they followed Boar out, Fierté, appearing in the highest of moods, chuckled, "'Fat hog!' He described you spot on."

The door shut and Crow heard it lock from the outside. A candle remained burning, supplying some light and warmth. Crow suspected it wasn't out of consideration but forgetfulness.

He seethed with anger. The humiliation of being locked in a cage, useless and unable to escape. To be stared at and mocked. To feel his sanity ebbing away.

CHAPTER 6 - CAGED

The first full day of being caged, the snow constantly fell and the silence offered Crow considerable time to sleep and think. To entertain himself, he studied the different items in Fierté's office; piles of paper strewn on the desk, several cleaning articles, a few aging servant outfits, a glass cabinet filled with dried herbs, hung flowers, and bottled liquids that Fierté collected. Each was neatly labelled: tussilago farfara, papaver rhoeas, elderberry, etc. Another door in the far corner indicated his sleeping quarters. Crow never saw him go in.

Fierté remained in the office and in human form, scribbling away on papers. Sometimes he would mutter indecipherably and scratch something out viciously. From what Crow gathered, he was keeping a very detailed account of the household, perhaps to add to his memoir collection.

Crow refused to interact with him.

"Your confinement doesn't condemn you not to talk," said Fierté, the second day.

Crow continued to stare out the window at the darkening sky.

"Was it all hot air when you expressed concern of entering a daze?" persisted Fierté. "Talking helps annul dazing."

Keep wasting your words. I won't speak to you.

"Hm, I suppose you consider this punishing me for putting you in there?" concluded Fierté. He shook his head pityingly. "Foolish, youthful ignorance. Crow, your silence is only harming yourself."

The following silence was disturbed as Fierté released a resigned sigh and picked up his favorite writing quill. The feathered end slipped through the bars, tickling the tips of Crow's plumage. Crow resisted grabbing it and craned to the opposite end of his stand. Fierté persisted, slipping his fingers through the bars to allow the feather end to tickle Crow's chest. Crow let out something of a crow grumble, which got a smirk from Fierté as he pulled the quill back out.

Fierté had just lit the evening candles and was resuming his writing, when the door barged opened and Hélène walked in. He dropped his quill in surprise. Crow himself ruffled his feathers and barely managed to restrain a flap that would have hit the metal bars.

Hélène started strong and ended hesitant, "Fierté."

Nanny poked her head around the corner, looking guilty. Hélène proceeded to close the door with Nanny outside. She approached Fierté's desk, her eyes hungrily taking in his office. This was her first time in the room.

"It's unbecoming for a lady to be with a man behind closed doors," stated Fierté.

"I left a crack."

Fierté placed on his pleasant smile and gave a little bow, "Mademoiselle, you know, all you need to do is ring the bell in your room for service."

"I wanted to take a walk. And I wanted to talk specifically to you."

Fierté raised an eyebrow. He walked around the desk to offer her a seat.

"Nonetheless, please refrain from my office in the future," requested Fierté. Crow bet he was worried she'd walk in when he was a stag. "It's unbecoming for a guest to be in a servant's room, not to mention this counts as part of the forbidden wing. Now, what service may I provide?"

"I want my brother let out of his room," said Hélène determinedly. "He's been locked in for over a day and I haven't been allowed to see him once!"

"Your brother tried to leave the castle. I'm afraid he broke the agreement."

Hélène shook her head stubbornly, reminding Crow of Roi. He internally smiled.

"That's what I'm here to clear up," said Hélène. "I know my brother. He was just a bit stir crazy and merely went exploring. I'm certain he had no intention of running away. Besides, he'd never leave me here. At least let me visit him. I've heard he was injured."

"Nearly killed," said Fierté, his eyes twinkling as Hélène's hands covered her mouth, horrified. He gave her a few seconds to grapple with the information. "White has been healing him. You can ask her on his condition, though I've heard he's recovering speedily. I've also received reports that he's taken to entertaining himself by bouncing something against the wall, and hiding it whenever someone enters."

Crow bet the real entertainment for Roi was having the servants come in to try finding the object, rather than the actual bouncing. He imagined

Roi as bored as he was. It occurred to Crow that he might be able to convince Fierté to give Roi some freedom again, but his pride remained too strong to break his silence.

Hélène placed her fingers through Crow's bars and absently started stroking his feathers. Crow suspected she thought him stuffed. He remained still, not wanting to scare her.

"What happened?" asked Hélène softly.

"Our perimeter guards are not as… tame and civil as us," answered Fierté, giving a look of sorrow. "Fortunately, one of my men was there to save him."

"Please thank him for me."

"He will be informed."

"But I still want to at least visit my brother. If you want me to have a meal with your master every morning, I must request this."

Fierté paused, a finger rubbing his chin, thinking of how he could make this situation beneficial. "I understand your feelings towards family." He helped Hélène up from the chair and escorted her towards the door, "I will speak with Boar and White and see what we can do. Please understand, our castle occupants and safety come first. Your brother gave us a fright. If outer towns were to find out about us, I doubt they would be kind."

"Thank you!"

Fierté gave another bow and a well-wishing before closing the door with her outside. He absently stared out the window, standing still by the door.

Plotting, thought Crow.

Fierté's eyes rested upon him.

"Don't mind a beauty's hand caressing you, hmm?"

Crow maintained silence.

Fierté bolted the door, and then walked over to the cabinet. He took out some cheese, bread, and candied nuts, setting them meticulously by height on an empty corner of his desk. The cheese's aroma wafted over to Crow and he felt his stomach growl. He got scraps of bread in the mornings, along with a small cup of water which his beak could only manage to drink half of, but it was nowhere close to a proper meal.

"Boar would have you caged until the end of the assessment," he continued, "but if you promise good behavior I'll allow you out for a stretch. I have food, wine, and at least some walking space in this room. Do we have a deal?"

Trying to win me back? thought Crow grumpily. But the opportunity to stretch was too great. He gave a short nod of his head.

Fierté's grin irked Crow. He unlocked the cage and held his hand next to the stand. Crow refused to step on it.

"Now, now," said Fierté, arching his right eyebrow. He pulled his hand out of the way and held the cage door open.

Crow hopped onto the opening rail and then took a few flaps to the floor. He swiftly transformed and struggled to stand with his stiff joints and light-headedness. He stumbled to the side, unconsciously grabbing Fierté's arm for balance. Fierté grasped his elbow to support him. Flushing, Crow quickly let go and pulled from Fierté's light assistance.

Immediately he took Hélène's seat and began consuming the food. His throat felt parched and unused. He wasn't bothered using his fingers, since no utensils were provided and the food tasted heavenly.

Watching with amusement, Fierté took a seat in the armchair. His legs were alert, however, angled towards the door. Just in case, suspected Crow.

"Don't eat too fast," he chided.

As his stomach filled, Crow debated his silence. His curiosity again won and he rasped, "Will you actually consider Hélène's request?"

"I'll discuss it with Boar and White later. Good to know you can still speak."

Fierté got up and walked behind him. Crow moved onto the wine goblet Fierté had poured for himself earlier but hadn't drunk. Dehydrated, the wine went down quickly. He then reached for the water pitcher left on the side table.

Crow flinched from a muscle cramp as he attempted to pour the water into the goblet. He barely kept it from spilling as he quickly put it down. He released a frustrated breath. Fierté's hands came down on Crow's shoulders. Light, kindly enough, but with a testing, secondary purpose. Crow stiffened and flinched.

"I said to slow down," said Fierté, leaning down by Crow's ear. "Are you still sore?"

"Fine," muttered Crow. He shifted to the edge of the chair, out of Fierté's hold.

"Well, we'll need to get you some new clothing until the old ones can be cleaned," he commented, unaffected. "And your hair is a mess. Haven't you been… preening yourself?"

Fierté settled with adjusting Crow's hair and Crow let him have that, focused on attempting to pour the water again. When he was done drinking, Crow approached his cage and cleaned out the dirtied bottom. Fierté put on an innocent enough 'oh' expression as Crow placed in some paper, making a dramatic point of it.

Crow was allowed a short time more to stretch his muscles, and then it was back to crow form and in the cage. He readopted his earlier pose, staring towards the window and getting lost in thought while watching the snow and rolling clouds.

By the fourth day, Crow shifted in and out of a daze. Fierté had not let him out again, though it had to do with Fierté being busy. Nearing lunch, Pan showed up and unlocked the cage, wordless as usual.

Crow hopped out and onto the floor, transforming. The desire to be human had been building and it was an ecstatic relief to do so. He couldn't remember being this passionate over his human form before and blamed his assignment to the siblings in starting the obsession.

"Did Fierté give you permission?" asked Crow.

Pan gathered the cage while nodding.

"Am I free to go?" persisted Crow.

Pan nodded again and left the room.

Crow walked over to the window and opened the glass panes. He gave a wicked grin. The room would be freezing when Fierté returned. He transformed, hopped on the ledge, and then took off into the snow storm. The grounds would be deep in snow. He flew for some time, grateful for the feeling of his wings being free. He stayed out until the cold started to seep through him. He flew down to the grounds and entered through the kitchen servant door. The room's occupants ignored him as he walked through, focused on their duty to make the best desserts for the guests as possible. Crow wondered what Roi and Hélène would think if they learned the majority of their meals were made by animal forms. Only one cook could be human still, and even then, it was for no more than an hour. It made quite the sight; an Eurasian elk keeping the fire going, a goose sautéing with the side of its mouth, a weasel managing to grip a knife to cut to the vegetables, a dog plucking a chicken.

Crow walked along the skinny passage leading to the dining room. He paused, remembering Roi was locked away. So it would just be Hélène inside...

Hesitantly he approached the swinging door. He peered through the tiny porthole into the room. The dining table was beautifully lit with many candles in silver and golden holders. The food, as usual, was more than was necessary, but not as much as there had been the first week.

His heart did a flip when he saw there were two figures at the table. They'd let Roi out as well. Watching Roi work on some sort of salad took a weight off of Crow's mind. The siblings sat in their usual opposite ends. Hélène sat in the better lighted half, in obvious favor. But even in the less lit side of the table, the candle's made Roi's hair shimmer with a golden hue and he looked much healthier than the condition Crow had left him in.

Ow! What the-

Crow was grabbed by the ear and wordlessly dragged backwards. Around the corner he brought his hands up to defend but his attacker swiftly let him go, boxing his other ear. Crow stumbled, his ear ringing.

"You passed the test, hm?" said Boar. "How unsurprising."

Crow used the wall to steady himself and then met Boar's gaze. He opened his mouth to speak but Boar interrupted him.

"I don't want to hear it. You shouldn't be in these corridors anyways, you're not a waiter or a cook, so fly off to do patrol or something."

"But the siblings are in the dining room."

"Yes, how observant," said Boar sarcastically. "And you know who else, the waiters! Because they belong. You, on the other hand-"

"I'm supposed to be with them."

Boar snorted, "Used to. Even if you're not progressing, do you think we'd let you still be in charge of them?"

The despair that Crow felt bubble inside showed on his face and Boar made a disagreeable noise as he turned away, threatening, "Don't let me see you near them!"

Boar strode back around the corner.

"Honestly, boy, you're supposed to be a messenger anyways," squeaked a mouse who passed him along the hall. The mouse shifted into his waiter form. "Hélène has Nanny and the brother… well, he's only allowed out for breakfast and dinner, and Pont is his guard."

"Guard?" said Crow surprised.

The waiter shrugged and continued on to enter the ballroom to take away the course's dishes.

Crow felt drained as he headed through the back passages to the grand hall. He sat down on a love seat hidden in a corner, resting his feet on the coffee table and leaning his head back to look at the dark, gothic ceiling arches. He didn't much care if anyone saw him sitting. In fact, he partially hoped he was spotted, because then he could argue his frustration out. He hadn't felt this useless and empty for some time. He hoped it was the effects of the daze still upon him.

He took in a deep breath and closed his eyes. The room was cold and musty. The guests always only briefly passed through here to get to second floor or if summoned to the west wing.

Slowly, he got lost in thought.

Should I defy Boar, and assumedly Fierté, and find a way to speak to the siblings? I've never felt so close to anyone like I do with them… But they're outsiders. I've risked the castle occupants twice for them. Scheming was what held us together. There's no real connection. Ugh, right and wrong is such a muddle. Perhaps I deserve to be a crow forever. I need to do as I'm told, so I don't mess anything else up. But Roi… the happy look he gives me when-

A pinch to the cheek broke him from his daydream. Crow fell off his seat, flustered. His eyes focused open and he saw Roi standing beside him. Any bandaging for the bite was hidden under Roi's clothes, but the scratch along his face proudly stood out in red, angry scabs. A quiet curse escaped

Crow's lips as Roi gripped his arm and helped him back up. Roi remained standing as Crow retook his seat while crossing his arms.

Angry?

The tinkle of a bell sounded. Crow's eyes scanned for Pont, who wore a bell in cat form, but couldn't spot him. Crow figured Pont didn't think it worth stopping Roi and Crow from meeting. The cat could be dangerous, but he could also be lazy.

"Where the hell have you been?" demanded Roi, redrawing Crow's attention. "Here I am, worried sick about you, and I find you lounging!"

Crow winced and looked at the floor.

The irritation in Roi diminished as he let out a huge sigh. He sat down next to Crow, spreading his arms out along the seat's back.

"Seriously," said Roi, more calmly. "Hélène didn't even know where you went. You promised me to watch her."

He remembered that? I thought he'd forget, he was so anemic.

"Sorry," muttered Crow. "I-" He struggled with what to say and ended with saying nothing. He glanced at Roi and realized Roi had been studying his clothes.

"You're still wearing the outfit I got blood all over," said Roi, poking at a particularly bloody dried spot.

"I'll change later. You should head back to your room."

"You know my schedule?"

"Everyone does. You and Hélène are practically nobility here, remember?"

Roi let out a bitter laugh, "Oh, I'm infamous at least. Thank God our stories matched... no?"

"Well, that's the truth for you," said Crow, nodding to their surroundings and glad Roi grasped the hint.

"So, will you come with me to my room?" asked Roi. "Maybe play a few rounds of cards? I've had dry company for the last few days, and none except White when bedridden. Hell, why do wolf wounds take so long to heal?"

Crow's eyes followed the scratch lines. They would leave scars. His guilt built up. His heart started to palpitate like he was back standing between Roi and Wolf.

If I'm going to give up the siblings... This is better for everyone.

"Sorry, I've other duties."

"Duties," scoffed Roi. He started playing with a piece of Crow's hair by his ear; pulling it straight to watch it bounce back in a curl. "What, they don't want you in charge of me anymore? The cat taken over?"

Crow shrugged.

Roi swore and stood back up, "That shouldn't matter. We're friends."

Crow laughed bitterly before he could stop himself and Roi halted.

"Friends," said Crow scornfully, standing up. "Our ranks are far too different for that to even be fathomed. I'm a servant, Master Duval." He gave a mocking bow. "I took care of you, and anything beyond my duties was a mistake. If you want someone to play cards, Pont, the cat, knows how. Or you can request Boar or Fierté to find someone new for you to bully."

Roi looked absolutely taken aback. He took a couple steps away.

"Don't ever think anyone here is your friend," continued Crow, his voice becoming a low growl. "You're only being treated as a guest because you're useful."

"Where is this coming from?" demanded Roi.

Unable to stand the hurt expression building on Roi's face, Crow headed for the nearest passage.

"Someone wiser than you. You should never have come here."

"Who fucking led me here?" yelled Roi after him. "Whose fault is that?"

Roi's words bounced around in Crow's head as he retreated. He transformed only briefly to get up to his attic. Sitting in human form by the window, his finger ran over the blood spot Roi had touched. He hated himself for his conflicting desires. Frustrated, he struggled out of the tainted shirt and vest. He threw them into a corner. After sitting in the cold, cooling down for several minutes, he found some new clothes in his trunk and changed into them. They were similar, with only a few color tweaks.

Sparrow shortly found him and informed him that the head servants wanted to speak with him. As a crow, he silently followed Sparrow to Boar's office, where he could hear Boar, Fierté, and White talking. The small vent overhead was open, which the sparrow flew in ahead. Crow transformed into human, using his human hours while he could, and waited outside the door, listening in on the conversation that ensued.

"We all know if we are capable of it, Hélène's requests should be met," said White. "She has been obliging us, after all."

"I suspect even she is ignorant to her brother's true mischievous intents," commented Fierté dryly.

"This is beyond spoiling," declared Boar. "When we denied the boy's demands, the girl asks White. It's like the parent game we all played as children; father says no, so ask mother."

"Nonetheless," said Fierté, "her request is not unreasonable, nor Roi's. We'd denied him his to remind him his place, and though he worked around us through his sister, I believe our point has sunk in."

"Sir," piped Sparrow, but was hushed by White.

"Maybe so, but my main concern is the request," grumbled Boar. "You're too trusting of certain staff members."

"Crow?" said White, surprised. "I don't know him well, but because he has something of a head on his shoulders and used it to stop your wolf from mangling our guest is not a reason to distrust him. He knows our fates are tied together. Betrayal is death."

"Albeit impulsive and stubborn at times, he's loyal, Boar," added Fierté. "Don't tell me that this isn't jealousy that our black bird has finally sided under my command?"

Crow imagined Boar's flustered face. He shifted his feet uncomfortably. He knew he should announce his presence, yet listening in was giving an interesting perspective.

"I wish you had just used those journals of yours and established from the get go who he fell under," grunted Boar.

"His position had him under no one and it was best to let him drift the way he best fitted," said Fierté, uncharacteristically icy. "And I ask you leave my journals out of this. They are only for memoir."

"I'm going to see to Hélène for the evening," said White wearily. "If the two of you wish to continue debating, please wait until I'm gone. Just remember, we already ran this by the master and he approved."

The door opened and White exited in dog form, spotting Crow.

"And the lad is waiting outside, so please inform him."

Crow bit his lip and stepped in front of the doorway.

"Eavesdropping," muttered Boar. "Bloody messenger. Well Fierté, he's yours to punish. What shall it be?"

"You've been reassigned to Monsieur Roi, at Hélène's request," said Fierté, immediately adopting a business attitude. "Pont is still his official guard, but you are to keep him company, spy behind closed doors so to say. Service duties, such as fetching wood, will furthermore fall to you. Patrols also must continue."

Crow stared at the boar and stag as if it were a joke.

"I thought I was to refrain from all contact."

"Talking back, another demerit," muttered Boar.

"You're the one who told me."

Swiftly Crow transformed and was up on the cupboard as Boar stormed towards him.

"Fierté!" snapped Boar.

"You've become rather outspoken," said Fierté calmly. "Crow, remember to heed your tongue and respect your superiors. I don't think you'll be up for more discipline. Especially mine."

Crow nodded mutely. Boar punished brutally but swiftly; Fierté's was more strategic, dangerously psychological.

"Good. Remember to inform me each day, or Boar if I'm unavailable."

"I'm surprised they requested me," said Crow. "Roi and I briefly encountered in the hall and it wasn't a pleasant conversation."

"See," Fierté told Boar. "Albeit less detailed, it's just as Pont told us. I trust this puts aside your earlier issues."

"Get to your duties," Boar ordered Crow.

Crow took off, staying high. He made his way back to the familiar guest hall. Seeing no one was around, he transformed standing atop the banister, enjoying the slight euphoria at the risk and freedom. He jumped and landed softly on the richly carpeted floor. He spotted Pont lying diligently across from Roi's door, next to a vent from which heat was currently pouring.

Both guest doors were open, but the voices were all coming from Roi's room: Nanny, Hélène, Roi and White. Pont clearly had no interest in getting involved. A fancy saucer half filled with cream from the castle's best collection lay next to Pont, given kindly by White when she'd made her way to Hélène.

Though the avian and rodent population of the castle avoided Pont, Crow walked over to him, restraining the animal instinct to keep out of the feline's range. Gustav and Sparrow were terrified of him. But Pont, like Crow, had a good grasp of his humanity and resistance to the curse. Now that Fierté had fully claimed Crow as his subordinate, Crow wondered if Pont would associate with him more. At least they would through their current assignment, and that was why Crow forced himself to sit next to him.

The white haired cat looked at him, his eyes hooded. Pont was a selective talker, usually out of laziness, but Crow had heard him get quite talkative a few times, especially when there had been two other cats on staff. The other two had fallen victim to perdu too many times, dangerous to the less carnivorous staff, and were in the dungeon.

"I didn't get to thank you for assisting me four days back on the stand," said Crow. "My wing wasn't in the best condition."

"It will be a sad day when none of us can do a simple, helpful act for another," said Pont, his strong accent signaling a foreign past. "Though when that time comes, I intend to be one of the last and shall find myself some elderly woman to spoil me."

Pont closed his eyes, clearly envisioning his goal. He released a soft purr.

Crow didn't want to think about that time at all. It was also disconcerting that Pont, though unhappy about the civility that would be lost, seemed fine with the impending fate. Pont had no faith in Hélène breaking the curse and didn't seem to care.

"Have you been informed about me?" asked Crow.

"That Wolf wants to kill you the next time he sees you or that these children really want you serving them again?" asked Pont.

"I've been re-assigned to Roi."

"Yes, I've been informed."

"Excellent," said Crow, struggling to his feet. "Then we'll be seeing each other more often."

"Don't feel obligated to talk to me. I'm rather enjoying this position compared to all the other jumbles Fierté assigns me."

The cat was usually assigned to infestation control, of the non-staff sort. This meant Pont saw this assignment as something of a vacation- to be able to lie the hours away- though behind the lazy front, Crow got the sense Pont was quite alert. Pont always performed his duties and his mannerisms were deceptive. Their very conversation had probably been memorized and locked into Pont's secretive mind.

"Are you here all hours?" asked Crow, unsure how to respond.

"Yes. And in caveat, don't fuck up again. You're not the only one to report irregularities of anyone to Fierté."

Crow shivered and didn't respond. He knocked on Roi's doorframe before taking a step inside.

Roi's fireplace was roaring, making the room generously warm compared to the snowstorm outside. White had a tray in her hand as Nanny helped collect the remaining tea items from Roi's table.

Immediately, a confident smile drew across Roi's face. *Getting what he wanted again.* Crow did not reciprocate.

"Ah, please grab that cloth and wipe the table for us," requested White.

And back to servant work.

Crow took the cloth from Nanny, who went to fetch a spoon that had fallen under the bed. Immediately Crow thought of the pack under the wardrobe. He struggled to keep his eyes from straying that way. His chest lightened when Nanny returned without noticing. Not that it really mattered now. He had every intention to obediently live up to Fierté's orders, especially with Pont watching. What he wasn't sure of was the spy part. Was he to snoop through Roi's room? He already knew the pack existed, but that would bring proof that Crow's previous actions had been deceitful.

Crow restrained a sigh and placed the cloth folded on the tray.

"Did you need assistance with anything else, Madam White?"

"No, thank you," said White, offering him a smile, but he could see she was remembering he had eavesdropped earlier. "Mademoiselle Hélène, I'm afraid it's gotten quite late and is time for you retire for the evening."

"I am feeling rather faint," said Hélène, surprisingly willing from what Crow was used to. She lightly touched the back of Crow's hand as she passed. "I hope this isn't too inconvenient, it was more my request than Roi's. I have Nanny, and fearing my brother would become something of a lonely recluse, I requested you."

Crow stiffened at her touch, but forced a light smile.

"Fierté has informed me that I am assigned to accompany Roi during the waking hours."

White looked at Crow. "I've tended to him today. His bandaging and ointments are kept in the cupboard there. Will you be able to manage?"

"I will seek assistance if it proves too much," answered Crow.

Being nurse to Roi hadn't crossed his mind. He kept his eyes from straying towards Roi's face. Crow turned to follow the women out.

"I want you to stay with me."

Crow froze, knowing very well Roi was referring to him. He gritted his teeth and shifted around while asking, "Was there something else you needed before you retire for the evening?"

"Company for another hour of cards. My wound likes to really hurt at this hour, so sleep is out of the question, and I've had more than enough of my own company for the past evenings."

Bastard, thought Crow. *You're either keeping me behind to continue our argument or you're just going to test me again. Sorry to disappoint you, I'm going to maintain my composure.*

"Madam White," called Roi. "Is he not allowed to stay this late?"

White looked back, her intelligent eyes behind her humble smile assessed everything, "Please don't forget, Monsieur, that us servants require sleep as well. But I find no harm in a game of cards. Please keep it to an hour."

Roi gave White a sweet smile, before shifting it to a look of triumph at Crow. Crow glanced at White and for a moment they made eye contact. He gave her a little bow.

You want me to find out why Roi wants me and to tell Fierté if it is anything important. Fine.

"I'm going to lock the door," said White. "Just knock on the door and Pont will unlock it when you need out."

Or I could not rely on Pont and just fly out the window.

The door clicked closed, followed by the scrapings of it being locked. Crow could feel a faint headache starting up. It was going to be a long hour.

Crow stood hesitantly by the fireplace. His head tilted curiously as Roi energetically pulled an arm chair over from the chess table to the main table, rather than bring out the cards. He then grabbed the spare wine and glasses kept on the counter, placing them inelegantly on the table's center. Crow pondered on what could be making Roi so excited, when suddenly there was a clicking sound and from behind the giant tapestry that covered the wall next to the fireplace, a human body took shape.

Crow's mouth dropped open as Hélène made her way out from behind the tapestry. He was silenced as Hélène giggled and put a finger to her mouth. She tiptoed to the door, listened, and then looked satisfied. The siblings greeted each other happily, embracing, and Roi affectionately kissed the top of her head, completely ignoring Crow. They spoke hushed, so their voices wouldn't carry out of the room, but it wasn't too soft. The walls were thick. It was like they hadn't seen each other mere minutes ago.

Hesitantly, Crow approached the tapestry. His fingers curled around the fraying ends and lifted the heavy fabric away from the wall. Tall and narrow, the discreet door had been left opened inward. No one on the staff had mentioned this passage, meaning it was forgotten. It was both ingenious and dangerous of the siblings to find it. Worse, they had just shown it in front of him.

"You've been visiting each other all along," murmured Crow, with his head still behind the curtain.

When he pulled back, he saw Hélène grin and Roi look at him cockily.

"How long?" he asked, taking another peek behind the tapestry.

"Oh, shortly after the library incident," answered Hélène. "We were trying to find good hiding places and we both noticed the wall sounded hollow, so we played around until we discovered the latches."

Crow turned back to face them. "So then, when I saw you demand to Fierté to let you see Roi, it was all an act, you'd been seeing him anyways. Impressive, even I believed the desperation on your face."

The siblings brimmed.

"Fierté and Boar aren't the only ones playing games," said Hélène. She giggled. This reminded Crow of how young she was. Crow only looked young like them, but he had a decade on his appearance. He was at least five years older than Roi. Crow pulled a chair out at the table for Hélène to sit in. "But how did you know about my request to Fierté?"

Crow backtracked quickly as he pulled the other chair out for Roi, who politely declined with a wave of his hand and chose to sit on the bed's edge.

"Ah, Fierté discussed it with a number of servants to find a solution."

"But you said you saw her," said Roi. "Were you following her in crow form?"

Hélène indicated no surprise when Roi gave away Crow's animal form. Crow assumed Roi must have informed her. However, her hands started to fiddle.

"He couldn't have because I met with Fierté alone in his office…," said Hélène, puzzled. "Oh my God! Was that you in the cage?"

Crow took a step back, trying to think how he could lie. Then he shook his head.

To hell with it.

As Fierté's spy, he could decide which side to betray after their honest conversation here. He pushed aside his servant demeanor and flopped into the armchair in 'devil may care' style, gazing towards the window.

"I brought it on myself. I didn't prepare my lies properly."

"They know the truth!" exclaimed Roi. "Impossible! Wait, you were in a cage?"

Crow chuckled at Roi's alarm before answering. "The excuse I gave them made it sound like I was progressing in the curse. Fierté and Boar may not have totally believed me, but they accepted it nonetheless and locked me up as part test, part 'don't mess with us.'"

Hélène jumped up from her seat and pounced on Crow, giving him a hug. He remained uneasily still. His face started to pink and he awkwardly tapped her shoulder gently when held for longer than a second. His shoulders relaxed as she released.

"You poor thing! You couldn't even stretch in there! Why didn't you talk to me? I could have helped!"

Hélène returned to her seat, genuinely upset. Her pity for him was touching. But Crow felt she deserved more pity than him.

"How long did they have you locked up?" asked Roi, his voice unusually coarse. His hand gripped the bed post like the bed might come alive and shake him off any second.

"Not too long," answered Crow light-heartedly.

Roi slammed his hand against the bed post, shaking the entire support. "How long?"

Crow jumped. He wasn't used to Roi's physical aggression showing up on any topic other than towards Hélène's situation. It worried him. But an inkling of satisfaction also rose up inside him.

Crow reluctantly answered, "I was released today."

Roi restrained himself after Hélène gave him a hard look.

"Can you tell us your name now?" asked Hélène, shifting the topic. "Unless you prefer to go with Anon still."

"I go by Crow. Anyone who has an animal name has long since forgotten any trace of their original name."

"Crow," tested Roi, looking pleased when Crow looked at him. Crow was pleased as well, though he hid it. He liked hearing his name from non-servant lips.

"Didn't you ever try to track down your real name or family outside of this castle?" asked Hélène.

For the first time, it was Hélène who'd asked something unexpected. Roi shook his head, but didn't chastise, likely as curious.

Crow crossed his arms and bit the corner of his lip. He was silent for several seconds, listening to the crackling of the flames as his mind fought to remember. It was like fighting through a blizzard where distant silhouettes of memory would mockingly appear, impossible to reach or discern.

"I probably did," said Crow finally, quietly. "Most things that either of you think you'd try if cursed like us, I probably tried. The first year is rather... blurry, for all of us. Hélène, I'm truly sorry you were drawn into this."

"Let's put regrets to the side," said Hélène. "However, Roi, in regards to the whole wolf tragedy- don't roll your eyes! I will repeat this as many times until it sinks in. I understand that you don't tell me everything so that I can have the amnesty of denial. But your escapade leaving the perimeter grounds for clues was reckless."

"You're the vanguard keeping the beast busy in this operation," replied Roi. "You don't need these things weighing on you."

Crow's eyes trailed over to the wardrobe again. Roi shifted on the bed, following Crow's line of sight. When Crow looked back at Roi, their eyes met, Crow's dark against Roi's honey brown.

"What does Hélène know?" demanded Crow, disliking the building tension. "What does Nanny know? What have you found out? And what are your plans?"

"Nanny knows enough," said Hélène. "She's kind enough to look the other way, like she knows to sleep when I sneak in here, but she doesn't know that Roi and I do more than visit."

"You're plotting."

"Nanny has a sweet, naive mind," said Hélène smiling.

"Not so," said Crow. "Anything direct and she will report you."

The fact that there was no mention of the passage in prior days, despite Nanny clearly being aware of it, meant Nanny was playing her own game with the siblings. Crow was envious that Nanny's involvement was simpler- probably won over by Hélène's kindness. Crow was stuck with the arrogant Roi, which did not allow for feigned servant ignorance.

"That's why only you are in here," said Hélène.

Crow frowned.

"You've placed your fate with us," said Roi. "You let me loose, you kept my secrets, and you've more than proven yourself."

"You're really viewing me... as an ally," said Crow, his heart sinking. Asset perhaps, but not full on ally.

"Ally and friend," said Hélène, grabbing Crow's hands and forcing him to uncross his arms. "You saved my brother from death! Crow, we will be forever in your debt!"

"So you don't consider my questions at all pert or demanding?"

"No, though I am still pissed about your jerk treatment in the grand hall," said Roi. "But I know your personality by now, and I know you wouldn't speak like that if not for a reason. Now I know it was because you'd been locked in a cage like an animal but didn't say a word that might have gotten you out of it sooner. You were distancing yourself to protect us."

No. You misinterpreted that.

Crow opened his mouth, but Roi shook his head, silencing him.

"We are all on the same page," said Roi firmly. "The curse needs to be broken. We are all bound one way or another. So it is my priority to solve this as much as Hélène's, as yours, or even as Master East's. We will find an alternate way. I wanted to meet tonight to make it official. Hélène is frontline, so she's on need to know basis, aware we are working on it in the background. Crow, you're the runner, undercover. And I am the researcher."

Roi reached under his covers and pulled out some tightly bound scrolls.

"The monastery," said Crow.

"Which I am still irked you recklessly did," said Hélène. "But since it's been done, I'm going to let this pass… once. If you sneak out this castle again, Roi, frontline or not, you need to tell me. And you too, Crow." She pointed a determined finger at him. "If my brother oversteps, tell me immediately."

Crow grimaced.

Roi unraveled two scrolls, passing one to Hélène and the other to Crow.

"I've had a lot of time to read through these while healing and locked in here," said Roi. "I know them by heart. They are loaned, so I'd like to return them eventually."

As Hélène unraveled hers, she glanced at Crow, "So he really can read?"

Crow raised his head.

"Did you assume I just looked at pictures and placed my best guess? I'm one of the best readers on staff. I even have a few books and letters in my room."

"But that means you're well educated," said Hélène.

"Have I sounded uneducated?" inquired Crow, genuinely curious.

While all servants knew how to speak appropriately, there were distinct differences amongst certain ranks, especially in vocabulary. The least educated ones were mostly perdu nowadays, but Crow had always considered himself at least par with Pont. Definitely better than Nanny, who could barely spell her name.

"Don't seek flattery," said Roi, walking behind Crow and hitting him lightly with a scroll on the head. Then to Hélène, "He's a messenger. He probably knows how to write too."

I can print and write.

"I wasn't seeking flattery," muttered Crow, rubbing his head.

"Oh, no?" said Roi. Resting his arms on Crow's shoulders from behind, he plopped his chin down on Crow's head. Crow had developed a sort of tolerant endurance to the very touchy Roi. "Sounded to me like you were bragging, followed by praise seeking."

"Says the king of arrogance," said Crow dryly.

Hélène let off a wispy laugh before looking at her scroll.

"Cadrer Castle … this is a monk's recording from two decades ago of his observations when invited to a large party hosted by Lord East and his sons. At the party, Lord East gave this castle to his third son, Goodwin, as his upcoming tenth birthday gift. So the master here is the third son of Lord East."

Roi nodded. Then he tapped Crow's scroll.

Crow, skimming like Hélène, observed out loud, "This is a letter from Cadrer Castle to the monks about buying two years' worth of mead. It's dated half a year before the curse, which means the castle was involved with the surrounding towns right up to the curse… And it's signed."

Crow stopped and bit the corner of his lip again.

"Do you know this person?" asked Roi. "You might have even delivered the message. The monks kept it because the receipt of the transaction is on the back."

"I… I don't remember delivering it."

"Who signed it?" asked Hélène.

Still on Crow's head, Roi read out loud, "Written on behalf of Master Goodwin East, son of Lord East, Head Cook, Cornelius Schwine." Crow could feel Roi's words vibrate.

"If the staffing hasn't changed too much, that would be Boar," said Crow. "How fitting."

But it's disappointing that there's no memories coming forth that it is indeed Boar. Maybe I can try to find something he's written later and compare writing styles.

Roi chuckled, "We should start calling him Swine."

"Only if you have a death wish." Crow bumped Roi off of him and placed the paper onto the table. "Speaking of whom, Boar does not trust me at all. He will be watching us closely. We'll have to be careful with our interactions. Perhaps even feign some distance."

Roi scratched his jaw while pacing around the table.

"Us being too friendly right now would raise suspicion. How about in public I give you a hard time and you pretend to be bitter about me? It should be a convincing start. They won't suspect that we really are friends."

Friends. Even after my spiel in the grand hall about this, he still claims we're friends? Shit. He really believes we are. I thought-

Crow felt his throat tighten and he quickly changed the subject, "Hélène, how are your breakfasts with the master?"

"Awkward as usual," said Hélène, not bothering to flower her response as she would to anyone else. "Sitting at a table and staring at my meal. Frustratingly waiting for him to say something, but he is either too shy or scared. Absolutely nothing is coming of this."

"Time to up the offensive, little sister," said Roi.

"I'm not using your charming tactics, dear brother," said Hélène. "If you recall, Crow got the up on you during that demonstration."

"I meant on the befriending front," said Roi, grinning at the memory. "You already have the head servants adoring you. Test the waters again. Ask for something that only he can give you that wouldn't be deemed unreasonable. It will make him feel manly. If it helps us, that would be all the better, but don't put yourself in danger."

"Actually, I do have something in mind." Her lips pursed secretively. "But it's only for the vanguards to know at the moment."

"Come on! The researcher and spymaster need to be kept in all loops."

"Nope."

"Not even for family? Well, I suppose Crow isn't-"

"He's closest to a supportive little brother I could ever get," said Hélène, sticking her tongue out at Roi. "Crow, are you okay?"

Crow had grown taut as the siblings had bickered.

All this planning and genuine trust, can I throw it to the wind while reporting this evening to Fierté?

"I'm just… not… used to this," said Crow, clearing his throat from the tightness. He stood up, as if the action alleviated some of the guilt.

Roi's brows furrowed, "All the conspiring?"

"What? No. Hah, no, that's more familiar than I'd like."

"Friendship," said Hélène softly, but her voice echoed to Crow.

Bulls eye. Can I really throw this to the wind when I report to Fierté?

When Crow said nothing, Hélène nodded. She reached out and caught Crow's hand to sympathetically hold. Crow stood uneasily in his stance. He appreciated her gesture, but he gently removed her from him. He turned towards the fireplace. He didn't want them to read his emotions.

"I've never really connected and gotten close to anyone here that I could confidently say was a friend. Hah, and now the prisoners are calling me one."

"What about Nanny?" asked Roi. "She's your age."

"Associates. We get along but…" Crow shrugged. He thought of the master, who had even less contact with people. "I was reassigned with the priority to spy on you. Not to just be around like Nanny, but to truly warm up to you two and find out anything."

The siblings were quiet. Crow turned to face them, his eyes glistening. The flames reflected in his eyes the fierceness he felt.

"You don't need to worry about that," said Crow. "Forget the rules. I'm going to be bird brained in the coming years anyhow. I might as well go down fighting and conspiring until the end. I'll lie right to Boar, Fierté, hell, even the master's face for us to succeed. I've gotten away with small ones before. There's got to be more than one damn way to break the curse. Roi, Hélène, I'm yours."

He saw Roi shiver.

Crow crossed back to the table and sat back down in the arm chair. His body was flooding with adrenaline and a weightlessness that made him high. He crossed his legs, resting his elbows on the table's edge, looking at the siblings who had moved closer to each other during his monologue. He let a smirk cross his face.

"So, let's conspire a proper game plan."

CHAPTER 7 – FOREWARNING LETTERS

Several days had passed since his oath. Despite their planning, little was done. For Roi and Crow, it was more about fooling the staff and regaining trust.

Crow told Roi about the internal, female voice the cursed residents had all experienced when they first fell prey to it, informing them of how the curse could be broken. Over time, the exact words faded from their memories, so they relied on what had been recorded: specifically; an unmagicked girl needed to fall in love with the master and the master with her, and the girl could not know this was the key to breaking the spell. With this, Roi knew as much as anyone about how to break the curse. He promised not to tell Hélène this until they found an alternative way. He knew if Hélène voided her usefulness for the castle, there would be no happy ending for them.

Sitting in the attic, Crow looked at his humble book collection. He hadn't read them for a couple years, so leisurely breaking open the spines again might have been a good pleasure were he not distracted with thinking about Roi.

I know I placed them in one of the books...

He picked up the thickest book, a collection of memoirs to some old war. It wasn't from the library. Crow couldn't remember where he'd scavenged it from, but the original owner was likely very into history. He opened the yellowed pages, the book cracking and threatening to fall apart. He could imagine Roi cringing at its treatment and preservation.

A couple envelopes fell from the pages they'd been precariously tucked into. Crow picked the envelopes up, feeling the letters inside. They'd come with the book – or at least he thought they did. They were worn and frail from times earlier he'd opened and closed them to read. They were thought-provoking letters.

Crow placed the book aside and flipped the nearest envelope open, the paper scraping against itself and the edge rewarding Crow with a cut. Crow placed his finger in his mouth, continuing to pull the letters out with his other hand.

The first letter was the shortest, dated a little over a decade ago; a week or so before the curse. It mostly lectured the receiver to look after themselves, be polite to Master East, and to gain favor. The second letter was two pages. The first page of the second letter had been washed out by spilled peppermint tea, the scent still lingered, but the second page was clear.

Crow remembered studying the washed letters back in his days of boredom, before he'd dived obsessively into his patrol role. He hadn't looked at them for some time. But perhaps they would help Roi with figuring out more about the curse. These letters… He couldn't deny he felt protective of them. He was pretty certain, despite lack of evidence, that these might have been his last delivery, perhaps the very thing that had brought him to Cadrer Castle right at the time of the curse.

The second page was ominous. Crow had curiously read it many times, but had never felt compelled to act further on it. Crow skimmed the contents, surprising himself by coming to a few conclusions he hadn't thought of before.

Because I hadn't been thinking with a conspiring mind.

No names were mentioned through the letter, except for the signature. The writer's penmanship was well practiced and several lines seemed to give multiple messages. Past the first full paragraph, the wording changed and sentences were arranged strangely. Crow had since figured out the code and could just stare at the coded words and know their proper order.

"-of which I'm certain you may hold your own against.

My own schedule has taken a rather steep incline of my time, which increases the prosperity of not just my own but my clients' finances, and my nerves. Perhaps it is this that causes stakes and daggers to be seen much more than normal, but I must say this particular one persists. I would have thought myself finally passing into the eccentricities of neuroticism, had careful conversations with others not confirmed my suspicions, though they themselves are too dull to even see the puzzle and its pieces. Which is why I am putting great faith in you by telling you this. However, I am informing you not to set you to action, but to hear warning and retreat.

The brother, the very one you labelled as "unhealthily hungry," has tightened his circles closer and these circles have become dark. I am certain that a particular elderly woman visiting court has magic blood, and studying her eyes from afar with this knowledge, of no easy task, has confirmed a being even older than I've ever witnessed. I've recoiled from pursuing her for the time being, in favor of safety. Some things so old are not meant to be confronted… at least not when allies are spread thin hunting other worries.

I know not what is to happen, but please keep close eyes on this brother until your leave. It could be towards one of the others, for the amount of snake and claws that goes on between them, but I fear the favored one will be dark magic's target. Our Lord seems unable to notice how his sons sour towards each other, how so blandly favoring leads to such jealousy to turn to the dark arts.

Be wary of any magic, even a magician for entertainment. Keep close your wit. I know you've yet to achieve your errands, but I urge you to finish up in the next few days and return to Remais. I do not think collateral is cared for in the minds of the jealous.

Keep this to yourself. Leave hints of warning for your host to heed if you will, as long as you are not associated, but do not linger. I will be awaiting your return eagerly and I admittedly regret the ill timing of all this.

Remain sharp.

-Corvus"

"Corvus," said Crow out loud. "You knew about this curse. Or at least, you suspected something was coming."

Should I tell or show Roi the letters?

Crow grabbed the bucket he'd filled with snow yesterday and had left in his attic to melt. He broke the thin layer of ice and began scrubbing his face and surrounding hair with the chilling water. The cold seeped through his skin, eliciting clarity in his internal debate. Despite the deep-seated instinct to keep his possessions away from anyone, he would show the letters to Roi.

He grabbed a clean shirt and used it to dry the rivulets of water off his face. Transforming, he adroitly grabbed the papers in his beak and flew over his barricade, down into the castle hall. He immediately returned to his human form and tucked the letters carefully in his pocket. As a human he could keep them safer. Excitement overcame caution as he raced along the halls.

"Careful!"

Crow did a dance to avoid running into Fierté, who'd just walked out from one of the master's rooms. Slight amusement gleamed in Fierté's weary eyes as he watched Crow regain composure and give a minor bow of the head.

"Sorry sir!"

"Back from morning patrol?"

"Nothing to report, aside from cold winds," nodded Crow. His hand absently went to his pocket. Fierté's eyes followed, but didn't register. "Are you tired sir?"

Fierté sighed. "It shows, does it?" He stood straighter, stretching his back. "When the master wants to chat, my goodness he goes on."

As the head butler, he had a bond closer to the master than any of the servants, but it was nothing past professionalism.

Fierté started down the hall towards a draped window, his index finger beckoned Crow. Crow looked in the direction of the grand hall, but reluctantly obeyed Fierté.

"Do you think it will snow or just remain windy?" asked Fierté, drawing the drapery back with enough force that it stayed open.

Crow stopped beside him, staring out. Frost lined the window's edges. The view of the snow covered grounds and woods was enchanting as the sun peeked over the tree line.

"There's some eastern clouds approaching, but I doubt any snow will come," said Crow. It was a guess. He'd been lost in the thought of the letters during most of his flight.

Fierté nodded absently.

When weary and nostalgic, he would enter a daze, but Crow had never heard of him going full on perdu. Crow could empathize. This was something that Roi could not fully understand; what was always haunting the back of servants' minds day and night. Cursed, watching their friends and subordinates slip away, wondering when they too would inevitably change... Crow felt his comradeship rise. Through the silence, he built up courage.

"Do you know of anyone named Corvus?" asked Crow.

Fierté's gaze stirred from the window to Crow, the daze leaving his eyes.

"Who?" asked Fierté, genuinely interested. But if Fierté held no knowledge, Crow didn't want to draw the butler in further.

"Corvus," he repeated dismissively. "I heard a traveler on the road mention the name and it stood out. I think I might have heard it back... back when-"

"We were human," finished Fierté.

Crow nodded.

Fierté looked thoughtful, "I'm afraid I can't help you with that. My mind is holding, but any prior names by memory were lost as much as yours." Then he looked amused. "Did you know, I once had a similar feeling towards the name "Adalost." Later, in the cellar with Boar, I discovered it was a cheese. Perhaps it's something like that? I know Boar found it absolutely amusing."

Crow tried to imitate Fierté's amusement.

"Is there something more?" asked Fierté, sensing Crow building distance between them again. Fierté's gaze searched for what his messenger was not saying. Crow regretted saying anything at all. He should have researched further first. He'd just been sucked into Fierté's aura of amity and had taken a chance.

Crow gazed back out the window, using it as an excuse to avoid Fierté's inquiring look.

"No, it was probably nothing. I'll likely forget about it by tomorrow."

"Crow," said Fierté next to his ear, enforcing his name. A compassionate hand rested on his shoulder, though it shifted further in towards Crow's neck, hinting dominance. "There's been a lot of pressure on you, especially with having to serve our special rebel. If-"

"It's fine."

He wanted to move, but Fierté's grip tightened.

"Are you really fine? Roi isn't making you do anything? There's nothing you're holding back from telling me?"

"Other than being an arrogant, immature man, he's been well-behaved, sir."

"Heh," chuckled Fierté. He patted Crow on the shoulder while releasing him.

As Crow turned, he saw Fierté was staring at him; an inquiring, dangerous, pursuant look was on his face. The stag would protect its herd fiercely, even to the point of possessiveness. Crow felt his crow-self tighten his talons.

"Fierté!" called the master, causing them both to jump.

Fierté elegantly twirled around, loyally returning to the master's room. Just before entering, he glanced back at Crow. "Remember Crow, no secrets, no matter how above suspicion."

Crow briskly made his way to Roi's room. He encountered Doe, pushing her trolley of freshly cleaned towels towards the guest rooms. Usually these were left on side tables outside the doors, to be brought in by other servants when the siblings were absent. Crow grabbed a couple, giving Doe a grin.

At his approach, Pont was human and on his feet, unlocking the door before changing back to a cat, his bell jingling slightly as he resumed his sleepy sprawl.

Crow opened the door without warning, striding into the room, shouting out, "Rise and shine, Master Roi! It's another cold, chilly day, but the sun is shining."

He heard Pont chuckle in the hall as the door closed in on its own. Crow felt satisfied in his performance to make the servants think he was doing his utmost to make Roi miserable while still maintaining his duties. Roi would undoubtedly do something in turn that day.

For now, Roi only groaned, dragging the covers over his head to block out Crow's voice.

Crow dumped the towels, going over to the window to draw back the curtains. He then trudged back to the fireplace and set about starting a fire.

"Must you barge in?" complained Roi, as Crow made no effort to stifle his noisy preparations.

"You stayed up too late on your own. Dawn has passed, breakfast will be soon."

"I could still sleep half an hour more," grumbled Roi.

Crow strode over and grabbed the covers. Dragging them downwards, he revealed Roi's head and night shirt.

"Ugh, cold room."

"The fire is going," said Crow unsympathetically. "Besides, I want you to see something good before the day gets started."

"I promise to admire you in half an hour."

"Not me, you dolt," said Crow, having a seat on Roi's bed and pulling out the letters.

The crinkling of paper had Roi alert and shifting to sit next to Crow. He winced slightly from his healing injury. His night shirt and pants were wrinkled from a restless night.

"Letters?"

"Two. I've had these in the attic and almost forgot them for years now. I think I was to deliver them back before the curse. That, or I simply collected them when I went through a book scavenging phase. But I'm pretty certain they were meant for someone here. They're dated just before the curse."

Roi took them with even more gentleness than Crow had treated the letters, making Crow feel assured in sharing. Roi's respect for written items was unmatched. The unnamed envelopes were carefully inspected before even opened. Then with nimble care, Roi unfolded the letters.

The only time Crow interrupted the silence was to help Roi with the coded part of the second letter, which he caught on to with natural ease. Then he reread them, quiet and enthralled.

"This makes me think of two questions," said Roi at last. "We knew the place was cursed and I'd gathered that it was an enchantress of sorts, based on the curses rules you all dreamed. And it confirms an East relative intended this. Unfortunately, it does not specify the curse or any way to break it."

"Likely why I never showed the letters to others and forgot their contents," said Crow.

"But it establishes that someone at Cadrer Castle knew something was going to happen. Whether they're still here or not is the question. You probably were to deliver this to them, and as you still have it, they didn't get it in time. You also have one dated a week earlier, which means some delay might have occurred for the letters, making you too late and ill-timely cursed."

"Do you think this person is still here?"

"A good chance," said Roi. "On the other hand, they might have noticed signs without Corvus' warning and booked it safely before cursed. Another reason for why you might still have the letters. But...."

"The male guest room has always been oddly stocked," said Crow thoughtfully.

"You noticed. Hélène's room is distinctly personalized; arranged and brought about by White. If there was also a female guest, her stuff has long since been cleared for the beast's captives. This room, which I doubt has ever been touched this decade," Crow nodded confirmation, "has unique supplies in it, untampered. The tailored clothing in the wardrobe that has always weirded me out, for example. I bet they belong to the letter's receiver."

"So they're here," said Crow, trying to think who. Pont stuck out as foreign, but his background had always been heavily supported as former security and he had a fitting bodyguard uniform kept in his quarters.

"I think something happened to them, beyond simply the curse, to have the room abandoned," said Roi, "Or this room belonged to someone else entirely and the real receiver of the letter was working here under guise. The letter is shifty."

"Either way, no one has memories."

"No, they don't," agreed Roi. "So we'll pursue that part as backup, albeit, if they were a guest, I suspect a clue lies in the graffiti."

Crow looked at Roi, bewildered, and Roi tapped the bed stand. CC still stuck out in the engraved wood.

"You think the intended receiver left that?"

"No sure," said Roi. "But I think it was made after the curse. The servants would have replaced anything damaged like this prior. But let's focus on the name we know."

"Corvus."

"Yes, Corvus," said Roi thoughtfully. "We know he wrote from the province capital, Remais, and is associated with the court and the East family. It sounds like he isn't nobility, or not high at least, but he has high influence and association. And the brothers... Lord East has four sons... No, five, because Goodwin here seems to be erased from all history except for the faith-protected monastery and Cadrer Castle's personal records. So one of the brothers, "the hungry one," which I assume means power hungry, took out Goodwin through a connection. Which means we need to find more about the curse's source."

"The old lady enchantress," said Crow. An odd expression slid across Roi's face. "You figured something out?"

"I need to dwell on it. For now, I think we should tell Hélène the name so she can also keep an eye out."

Crow reached for the letters.

Roi held them away and gave Crow a rueful smile, "I'd like to keep them to analyze closer."

Crow struggled to keep his possessiveness at bay.

"You need to make sure they're very well hidden," he finally snapped, pointing a commanding finger at Roi.

"In the tapestry passage."

"Wrapped in something to protect them."

"Absolutely."

Roi stated it dryly, indicating Roi felt this was already obvious.

Embarrassed, Crow quickly changed the subject, "Take your shirt off, I'll change your dressings."

Roi had finally given up trying to wear his own clothes all the time. The guest room clothing gave Roi a more aristocratic look, though his manners were definitely still middle class. Now that they had their suspicions from the letter, Crow wondered about the original owner of the clothing.

Crow grabbed the roll of fresh bindings from the shelf and watched Roi remove his shirt. The fact that Roi had managed to keep himself fit, despite being locked in a room all this time impressed Crow. He wasn't bulging with muscles, but he clearly did some heavy work back in his normal life. Boxes of books, Crow supposed.

Crow unwrapped the cloth on Roi's wound. It didn't bleed anymore, but still looked painful.

"You took a bath this morning," commented Roi as Crow got close. "You look and smell good today."

Crow brushed his hand over his damp hair, "I only bathe when the water is fresh. It's disgusting, the thought of sharing the same water with everyone else. I just washed my face and hair in a bucket. Preening as a crow seems to help."

"If the curse is ever broken, would you stay here?"

Crow's eyes darted up to study Roi's face. He didn't get Roi's thought process half of the time.

Roi started to laugh, ruining the start of the new binding, "When you looked up it looked like you were seducing me."

Crow sighed as he gathered and restarted the binding. He grabbed Roi's firm shoulders and made them still.

"Move again and I'll wrap some salt in," he threatened.

"But seriously, would you stay at the castle?" asked Roi stopping Crow's hands in his own.

Crow's cold hands drew in the warmth from Roi's. It felt good being warmed, though it wasn't Roi's intention. Then he felt guilty about his cold hands touching Roi's body during bandaging.

Crow sat back on the stool, removing his hands, "No, I wouldn't."

"Where would you go?"

Crow thought for a few seconds, and then shrugged, "If our memories return, home? But then, it's been a decade, so if there is anyone…."

"Wait, you're not from here?"

"I don't really know. A messenger could be from anywhere, really."

"You have the same accent, so you're at least from this province. Would you come with me to my town? Even if just while you're getting back on your feet."

"To Beauclair? Maybe."

"Really!" said Roi pleased. "Well, now there's a second incentive to end this curse."

"It's a very minor maybe," grumbled Crow, getting back to work.

Roi watched him work closely. His eyes followed every movement Crow's fingers made. Crow suspected to make sure everything was done right. He only winced a few times, leaning a little closer to Crow each time.

A light knock came at the door.

"I can't finish a simple redressing without interruption," grumbled Crow.

He impatiently leaned up against Roi's shoulder, the angle allowing for quicker work. His jaw gently brushed against Roi's hair as he looked down to keep track of the binding. Roi smelled of smoke and old pages. Swiftly looping the remaining bandaging around the body and tying a practical knot, he pulled back and strode over to open the door.

Nanny stood clutching the skirt of her dress shyly, her round eyes staring at Crow.

"Hélène is having a simple breakfast in her room today and wishes for her brother to join her."

Nanny's eyes shifted to Roi, still half undressed on the bed. Crow angled the door, worried of the letters that sat visibly on the counter beside Roi.

"I'm sure he'd be delighted," said Crow. "He'll be over shortly."

He shut the door.

"I didn't overstep saying you'd like to attend?" asked Crow.

"It's perfect actually," said Roi. "And your effort to hide me from her was amusing. Jealous of my body? Don't want to share it with anyone else? After that hug you gave me, I knew you were the possessive sort. Sometimes I forget my Adonis looks have men and ladies falling in love."

Hug? Why must he twist my actions?

"Your arrogance is your downfall. I'm pretty certain it's more eye candy for her than any love," said Crow, shaking his head. He leaned against the wall while watching Roi change himself; a perk of Roi growing up middle class made some chores easy. The pants were slightly too short, but worked with the boots Roi wore.

"Perhaps she gives similar peeks at you."

"Then it's just the way she looks at others. She's shy."

"You must be eye candy for her as well. Not the sweet, approachable kind like me... more a chilly, minty sort."

Roi placed the letters inside the pocket of one of the pants hanging in the closest. Crow winced, wanting to hide it properly in the passage, but realized it would take too long. Pont, who undoubtedly heard the conversation in the hall, would expect them to leave soon.

"The stuff that will come out of your mouth," said Crow, doing his best to place the letters at the back of his mind.

As they walked over to Hélène's room, they argued over what made a person handsome. Pont appeared to ignore them, lying with his eyes closed, though Crow knew well he was awake.

Hélène's door was open and she sat at her table.

"Today is a good day," said Hélène, seeing her brother enter.

Crow absently pulled a chair out for Roi. Roi gave an obnoxious smile at this, but then his focus was entirely on his sister.

"I've been granted access to the east wing's library, on the conditions that it is only an hour spent in there and in the company of the beast."

"That's both great and unfortunate news," said Roi, but focused on the positive. "A surprising luxury. So many books will be to your access. Are you allowed to take them out?"

"One at a time, after they have been approved by the beast."

"So he's finally spending more time with you," said Roi, looking thoughtful. "Maybe they will allow me to join?"

"Oh, I seriously wouldn't push your luck there," Crow stated.

Nanny shook her head, Crow uncertain whether to Roi's or his own impudence.

Her cheeks blushed as they always did when she talked to groups greater than one, "What shall you be having for today's breakfast?"

The siblings both ordered simple breakfasts compared to their usual feasts in the dining room. The meal was based on what they normally ate outside of the castle: scones, butter, and herbal tea for Hélène, French bread, boiled eggs, and earl gray for Roi.

Nanny curtsied and headed off with the order.

Roi leaned towards Hélène, his voice low. "We have a name of someone who suspected the castle was going to be cursed before it happened. Corvus. This person isn't a resident here, so we need to see if the library has any recording of them."

"Have you asked anyone?" asked Hélène.

Crow leaned down beside Roi.

"I did check with someone," said Crow. "If anyone knew a name associated with the castle, it'd be them. They were not familiar with it."

Roi looked at Crow, surprised. Crow shrugged it off. He'd forgotten to tell him earlier. He'd explain better later.

"I'll keep my eyes and ears open," promised Hélène.

"Only do so if it is discreet," said Roi. "I know that today's round is a test."

"And don't mention the name to anyone else," added Crow.

Nanny walked back into the room. Crow pretended he was scratching away some mess on the table. Roi leaned back in his chair.

"And that is why no one likes the taste of those herbs," said Roi.

Nanny's gaze met Crow's. She knew they'd been discussing something else, but she said nothing, a silent ally through ignorance.

Roi and Hélène filled the room with laughter and natural friendship. Their conversations were perfectly censored from anything that might draw worry from the servants. Crow was occasionally asked questions or to support a side. Nanny was not, but more due to her own shy preferences. She kept her eyes down, happy and satisfied; a proper servant. Crow momentarily felt envious before pushing it aside. He was good at his job. He just happened to be currently assigned a position not meant for him.

His eyes wandered the room, stopping at where the spy hole to Hélène's room was located. Some cloth had been very clearly wedged into the hole, which screamed more Roi's doing than Hélène's. Crow grinned. It had likely been there for a while and since no servant had removed it, the spy passage was either not being used or they gave up when realizing the siblings were aware of it and any attempt to remove the block would be obvious.

Three swift taps on the doorframe interrupted the room and all four occupants looked towards the door.

"Good morning," greeted Hélène.

"Good morning to you as well, Mademoiselle," said Fierté. "I'm afraid I must borrow your servants for a short time. White will be up with breakfast and tea, and Pont will be in hall, should you require anything."

Fierté had on his pleasant smile, the usual he showed to Hélène. The smile wasn't as false as it had been at the start of Hélène's captivity. Crow concluded Fierté really did like Hélène.

Nanny and Crow exchanged looks.

Nanny gave Hélène a brief curtsy with a whispered, "Excuse me, Mademoiselle," and pitter-pattered over to the hall.

Crow felt fortunate he had been looking somewhat servant-like, standing behind Roi's chair. He did a swift bow to the siblings, following Nanny more at a swagger, using the precious seconds to try and figure out why they were being called away. He didn't think, aside from his and Roi's secretive research, they had done anything out of step. In fact, they'd gotten their routine down to something near flawless.

Though Fierté was usually one to encourage them to be in human form, he requested they transform in the hall. It had been said with an added, "Let's not take from the human time you have to spend with our guests," but Crow suspected it was more to keep the master calm, as they arrived outside his room.

The door opened for them.

The large room was dark and dank, despite the clear signs of majestic wealth and comfort. The windows had thick curtains drawn about them. Crow could barely make them out on the far end. The fireplace, across from the bed and nearer the door's entrance, was the only light source and it was low to the master's preference.

Nanny slowly entered the room, stopping just inside the door. Her tail was low and Crow could tell she was resisting pulling it between her legs. Crow hobbled in after her, lightly brushing against her as comfort, not admitting it was to comfort for himself as well. He hopped up onto an iron stand that held the fire poker, not liking being so low.

A chair was beside the fire, facing them. Crow didn't initially see the master sitting in it, wrapped in a cloak and head down; motionless and quiet. In the flame-lit room, the shadows cast across his face contrasted the lines to further enhance the beastly side of him. Crow could not tell his mood and, in the dark atmosphere, he held his tongue.

Fierté closed the door, remaining in the room with them. As the master looked up from his hunched, brooding position, Crow regretted his self-entitled hop up on the stand. The stand was closer to the master than Nanny.

Crow felt like blessing her when she sidled closer to him.

"Sir, Nanny and Crow, as per requested," said Fierté. "They shall help enlighten the situation from *their* point of view."

The beast only nodded.

"Nanny," said Fierté. The small dog jumped. She usually only worked with White and never had been good with her nerves around Fierté and Boar. "Please inform the master of what Hélène's thoughts are of him and the castle."

Nanny released a whimper. She then looked at her paws as she said softly, "I have reported everything to Madam White, sir. She would better report than I."

"So White has," said Fierté. "But we'd like to hear your words and opinions directly. Particularly on Hélène's thoughts on being allowed more freedom."

"No sugar coating," said Crow under his breath, realizing the master wanted a rawer form of information. Lower servants were a swing and miss for this. Though they'd still remain polite, many didn't have the skill and flair of the experienced servants to bring up or ignore certain points.

Crow saw the beast's head tilt ever so slightly. Crow clamped his beak tightly shut.

Fierté gave Nanny an encouraging smile, though Nanny didn't remove her eyes from the floor.

"Sir," said Nanny, barely hearable, but no one asked her to speak up. Crow saw Fierté place his hands behind his back, as if restraining the desire to say something. He'd probably been requested not to by the master earlier. "She was overjoyed at the news to use the library. Books and stories appear to be strongly loved by her and her family."

Or a good way of escape, thought Crow, and restrained himself from chuckling bitterly.

The master shifted, and his gruff voice, restrained before the shy dog, demanded, "So she is happy?"

"Much happier," said Nanny.

"But is she happy," persisted the beast.

Nanny shivered.

"If I may-" started Fierté, but the beast's glare at him had him shutting up.

"What does she need to be happy?" demanded the beast.

"There are moments when she is happy and there are moments when she is sad," said Nanny. "She is sad… when she has time to think. She is happy, when there is something to do, speaking with others or reading."

"Are there any signs she will disobey me? What has she said about the library?"

"I've heard no talk of disobedience," said Nanny, stronger now. "And she was in a wonderful mood this morning, due to the library news. She will be more open with you."

"Good," said the beast sitting back with a sense of relief.

"As White and I had advised you, sir, the library was a grand move. These raw accounts are the same as our own," said Fierté.

"And for you?" asked the beast.

Crow realized the beast was addressing him. He could feel Fierté's gaze on him, a "careful how you speak."

"Nothing," lied Crow fluently. "Though Nanny knows Hélène better than I, I would heed her words more."

"And your charge?" asked the beast.

Crow went silent, thinking of the best phrasing. He could see all of them, even Nanny, had their eyes on him.

"No sugar coating," the beast whispered Crow's own words and Crow felt himself fluster.

"He acts out the more he is restrained," stated Crow. "While I would say his disobedience has been tamed by injury, he will still test and push boundary limits. He is close with Hélène, so I believe often he acts out believing it's on her behalf. But in Hélène's presence, he is of better manners."

The beast looked at Fierté, "We should be rid of him."

Crow caught his breath and did his best not to shiver. The beast wanted Roi dead, out of the way. He was being selfish. This was a life. Curse or no curse. And Crow wanted to shout at the beast that he was the same, if not worse than Roi on that level, but his fear held his tongue for the better.

"It is a possibility," said Fierté neutrally. "But I would request the master explain his reasoning."

"We are humoring him and he is not even a welcomed guest," said the beast. "He wastes the time of people who could be used elsewhere. He has caused more trouble than his worth."

We're trying to find an alternative method for everyone, thought Crow, disgruntled. He realized he'd let out a croak. The master was looking at him.

"He is a pain, but he is doing some good. Hélène feels less trapped because she has a family member here. His antics are almost always for her. His selfish moments are out of insecurity and feeling restrained, but he would do anything for his sister. And Hélène relies on this. Remove him by death, dungeon, or whatever it is you are thinking, and you will find yourself back at square one with Hélène, at best. I wouldn't be wasting my time with the man if I did not think there was a long run worthwhile goal towards the end."

"I know this has been going slow and you are feeling frustrated... sir... but you are further with Hélène than any of the other girls," said Fierté hesitantly. "Hélène has shown wisdom and a lovely heart. Keep the brother alive."

"I will keep the library test with Hélène as it is," said the beast. "Build my presence with her... and I would like to talk with her more. She has excellent stories. As for her brother..."

"Sir," piped up Crow, his wings twitching from his nervousness. All eyes went back on him. "This may sound demanding, so forgive me but I feel it's important. I would ask Roi is released from being locked in his room."

"Quiet, Crow," said Fierté, steely.

"Released from his room will allow him to spend more time with Hélène and soothe her," persisted Crow. "Tell Hélène you wish to make her comfortable, that you feel her brother has understood his lesson, and that even you can't stand the thought of someone being trapped and wish to provide as much freedom as you can. This will win her closer. She will respect you for your faith and trust in her brother."

"He doesn't deserve…" growled the beast.

"No, he doesn't," said Crow. "And this makes your deed all the more powerful to Hélène. She'll know you are doing it for her. She'll recognize the great gesture it is."

"I don't want him roaming my halls," said the beast darkly.

"I'll enforce he stays in the main and guest wing," said Crow. "It will be made clear, only Hélène has the luxury of accessing the library. This will show her your value of her. And when I am not around to watch Roi and Pont needs to sleep, have Roi locked in his room between midnight and seven. I think even Roi would appreciate what we are doing and it would reflect on Hélène."

The beast was quiet as he pondered this. Fierté had a funny expression on his face, which Crow couldn't read.

"Yes, Hélène would appreciate this gesture," the beast finally said.

His selfish desire for Hélène to look at him better had won, though Crow could sense a coil still bound tight and ready to spring any moment. Crow felt woozy with relief.

"Then you and I shall come up with a more detailed plan," said Fierté. "Is there anything else you wished to ask them?"

The master shook his head, signaling the door absentmindedly with his paw. "I'm done with them."

Fierté opened the doors. Nanny was out fast and Crow, not wanting to disturb the already tense mood, hopped off the stand and walked rather than flew from the room. Without a word, Fierté closed the door, leaving them alone in the hall.

The two servants wordlessly went back to their duties, both pondering the talk on their own. Crow dared to hope the master was actually changing. Hélène was working her magic.

#

Roi was confined to his room when Hélène left for the library, which meant Crow's suggestion had not been enforced yet. Bored, Roi threw a pillow at Crow, who'd been staring absently out the window. The pillow hit him in the face.

"Dead crow," said Roi. "You should be more aware of your surroundings. A hunter will take you someday."

"A desperate hunter," snorted Crow, grabbing the pillow and flinging it back.

Roi caught it. "You know, as strange as our situation is, we've become good friends. I don't have that many."

"I find that hard to believe."

"Well, no close friends," said Roi. "None that would take getting locked up to cover for me."

"I thought we'd agreed to drop that topic," said Crow. "My motives were self-protecting, I assure you."

"So you keep saying," chuckled Roi, flopping to lie back on the bed, his legs hanging over the edge, his hair strewn and highlighted against the covers. Crow liked staring at the rich golden color. He figured it was his crow side. He noticed it was a bit darker that day.

"Do you want me to arrange a tub to be brought so you can bath?" inquired Crow.

"Do I stink?"

"Not… particularly," said Crow. "You actually take decent care of yourself, but I know some people don't want to always use a washbasin to keep clean."

"Want to see me nude?" asked Roi, doing a sweep of his body as if he was already out of his clothes and on display. "We'll set it up at night, with candles along the counters lighting my body with a soft yet fiery light. And maybe I might even tempt you to enter the water with me."

"You've read too many romance novels," said Crow, smirking. "I see you half nude when I change your bandaging. That's already more Roi than I need."

Roi ignored him, going on with his mock fantasy.

"Slowly you'll strip out of your clothes to join me. Lulled by my seductive voice, you'd slide into the water and rest between my legs as my arms wrapped around you so we both fit. And then you'd say, 'Oh Roi, I loved you the moment I laid my dark, captivating crow eyes on you in the woods. You are the light to my dark.'"

Roi had gone high pitched, mocking Crow's voice, and Crow had retrieved the pillow. He pressed it down on Roi's face by the end, though Roi got his last line out sufficiently. He grinned ear to ear. Crow knew this was an intentional, playful jibe from Roi. Crow didn't get why he spoke these things, though at least the stories weren't spoken outside the room. His best guess attributed it to Roi's boredom and loneliness.

"If you keep this up I'll tell Hélène your stories and she'll give you the silent treatment," threatened Crow.

"Hélène is the only one in my family who still talks to me," said Roi suddenly solemn.

Crow didn't know what to say and so fell quiet.

"My sister is my closest friend- as kids, I always looked out for her," continued Roi. "When our family estranged me, our roles reversed. Then our father…" Roi bit back his anger. "I really care for her. And you. You've helped us a lot at your own risk, despite your futile claim to be cold-hearted."

"She'll be okay," said Crow. "We'll figure this all out. She dearly loves you as well. I can tell."

"Do you like me?"

"You can be a pain," joked Crow. "But I can live with it."

"Seriously," said Roi, slowly getting up.

"If I didn't, I wouldn't be helping you," said Crow, rolling his eyes. How Roi could be needy.

Roi smiled, suddenly shy, "Well, you should know… the main reason my family won't-"

The door opened abruptly, swinging to slam against the wall.

Crow and Roi jumped. Crow turned and saw Hélène alone.

Roi, who would normally sardonically comment at such an entrance, took one look at his sister before rushing to her side. He wrapped an arm around her as Hélène's beautiful face, flushed, tear-stained, and hair astray, shattered into uncontrollable weeping.

CHAPTER 8 – THE FLIGHT

Her words were mixed amongst heavy sobbing. Crow managed to discern 'brute,' 'insensitive,' and 'frightened.' Crow resisted going over to her, knowing he would not be a welcomed addition. If it was a servant's sympathies she'd wanted, she'd have sought Nanny.

Suspecting the cause of this disheveling behavior, Crow bit his lower lip. He watched Nanny's silent progress, in dog form, into the room. Looking out towards the hall he spotted Pont sitting alert, watching intently. Crow was tempted to close the door, but he remained still, worried any more movement might set off Roi or make Hélène even worse. He focused on Roi more than Hélène. He hated people crying and he preferred to steer clear of these emotions.

Roi clutched her close, his head next to hers while his hands rubbed her back soothingly. This was clearly not the first time the siblings had comforted each other so. Hélène's sobbing lowered, though tears continued to stream from her eyes. Briefly she noticed Crow, but he was swiftly ignored. Crow swallowed, feeling even more awkward.

Roi embraced his sister even closer against him. Crow closed his eyes, imagining the comfort those arms around him might bring if he were in such pain.

"I'm here," said Roi softly. "Cry your heart out. Tell me what happened when you're ready. I'm here."

He said more so softly that Crow couldn't hear it. Hélène reduced her sobbing to hiccups and the occasional shudder. She raised her sleeve and wiped her face.

"He truly is a beast."

Crow opened his eyes.

"I know," said Roi, shivering at his own memory. "What happened?"

"It started off so well," said Hélène. She took a shuddered breath. Crow thought she might sit down, but she remained standing, clutching Roi. Roi obliged her by standing still. "The library was amazing, the fireplace was running, so the room was so warm. He was tense with anticipation. A good kind. I suppose I was as well. We talked loosely at the start. He wanted to tell me something good I suspect, trying to figure out how to say it. The first half went well, but he couldn't seem to get the courage to tell me what was making him so... proud. Regardless, he was in an excited, good mood, so he hardly noticed my search for specific book topics on the shelves."

Her eyes strayed towards the open door and quieted on that particular topic. She had been seeking books for Roi.

"It was such a positive meeting, so I started asking questions about the castle, him, and the people here," continued Hélène. "He mostly answered them, but his mood started to change. He got more withdrawn, but I didn't want the opportunity to pass so I pressed on. And then I asked why I could not just simply access the library at any time and he freaked out. We yelled at each other... Oh Roi, he got so mad! He yelled I would never leave. He flung books from the shelves, while shouting my questions were none of my business. And of course, I replied it was my business as I am a prisoner here. And then he threw a chair, roaring! Roaring in terrible anger. I was so frightened! I ran. I ran here. If I stayed, I fear he would have hurt me."

Hélène trembled and lost strength as she sunk to sit on the floor, releasing Roi. There was more to be told, but Hélène would not tell it. Crow suddenly suspected the master had been a lot cruder, and he winced.

Forlorn and miserable, Hélène began to cry silently, keeping her mouth shut, lest she started sobbing again. Roi stood still staring at her, perhaps in some sort of shock. Then a tremble went through him.

"He's still in the library?" asked Roi. He'd not encountered the master since being caught. His mind had softened the encounter. "I'll-"

"Wait, don't," cried Hélène.

"No," snapped Crow.

Pont and anyone nearby would be hearing this. Their voices weren't exactly low. Roi ignored them, charging for the door, his hands in fists.

Crow wrapped an arm around Roi, intentionally pushing against the injury while his other hand grabbed Roi's shoulder. He pushed the pained brother away from the door, back against the wardrobe.

Roi looked past Crow, angrily, towards the door. Despite the pain, he raised a hand to shove Crow aside. Crow grabbed hold of the Roi's shirt collar and leaned in close. Their eyes were inches from each other.

"They will kill you."

Roi stared into Crow's eyes but he eventually released a breath sounding like a frustrated sob. Crow's own hands shook as they held Roi back. Slowly he released his hold, stepping away until he reached the door. Keeping his gaze steadily on Roi, his hand blindly felt the handle and he swung it shut. He released a sigh when the door clicked closed.

"We need to be clear minded before we react," he said so both siblings heard, but his voice wouldn't travel through the door.

Roi trembled with anger, but didn't move from against the wardrobe. Hélène buried her face into her hands. Nanny transformed and was next to her, placing a calming hand on Hélène's knee and braving to whisper words of comfort to her mistress.

Crow broke from watching Nanny when Roi moved. Crow tensed, but Roi was only reaching up squeeze his temple.

"You think they'd kill us?" he asked.

Hélène, no. You, yes. But Crow kept it to himself.

Between sniffling, Hélène held up a book in her hand that none of them had noticed she was holding, "Well, at least they didn't check the book I brought out in all this." She tried to force a smile, though it wobbled.

Crow's smile was more a grimace as he gently took the book from her and brought it over to Roi. He moved carefully, not wanting to set either of them off. Roi took the book but his concern was still towards his sister.

"Hélène, if he touched you-"

"He yelled and threw things, but didn't harm me."

"That's only the next step," hissed Roi.

Hélène shook her head, "I should have sensed he was off, despite the hope he was showing. I pressed the questions; I inquired and prodded too much. But still, you'd think, as a noble, he'd have the sense not to act with such a tantrum. His voice, I could feel it through my bones."

Crow bit his lip. The siblings talked to each other like he and Nanny weren't there. Crow felt his apprehension lessen when Hélène had Roi promise not to react.

"Remember the goal," she said, finally getting up with Nanny's help. "This is part of the vanguard." She laughed resignedly. "I can't have the researcher rushing into danger."

Roi looked like he'd like to object but held his tongue. Instead he said, "I won't do anything for now. But I promise, Hélène, I'm working hard to find another way."

Nanny's eyes grew wide, realizing that they were talking about what she kept herself ignorant of.

"Please, Mademoiselle," she whispered softly. "You need to lie down."

Hélène obeyed, following Nanny back to the door.

"I'll try to train him a bit," said Hélène, her hands shaking as she bit her lip, striving to appear in control. "I'll show him such behavior is not acceptable. If he wants conversation, he'll need to redeem himself."

The door closed after her and Roi whispered venomously to himself, "She shouldn't allow him to redeem himself." He looked at Crow, but Crow knew the anger wasn't at him. "Your master is a bastard."

"It is his inner beast. Always stuck between animal and man."

Roi crossed to Crow, speaking so quietly that Crow's hairs stood on end as heard, "If he killed himself, would the curse be broken for everyone?"

"He was the target, but we were all cursed," said Crow fearfully. "He is the key to unlocking the curse but not through death!"

"Are you certain?"

Crow shuddered.

But, like a flipped switch, Roi suddenly reached for a fray of Crow's hair and tugged it gently before going back to the bed, inspecting the book.

"We'll keep death as a last of all last resorts. But if he treats Hélène like that again-"

Crow said nothing and the silence drew for a long time as Roi fiddled through the book.

Finally, Crow asked, "What book did she bring?"

"A book on Remais," said Roi absently. Then, "I need to be alone, Crow."

Fierté wouldn't like that, though Roi did seem to have control again. Crow realized this was an excuse; he was personally worried for Roi.

"Are you sure?"

Roi looked at Crow, "I'm not mad at you."

"But usually you like to rant someone's ears off to feel better. I'm all ears."

"Thoughtful, but I need to get lost in a book. If she's not supposed to have this book, I need to read it and get it back to her before they notice. I imagine everyone else is in a tizzy right now."

Feeling like his throat was swollen, Crow nodded. Before he reached the door, he looked at Roi, who was watching him leave.

"I'm truly sorry," whispered Crow. He opened and closed the door softly behind him. Pont didn't bother to lock it.

Crow remained outside the door for hours. The time for dinner came and passed, but neither sibling left their room. White passed once, on her way to Hélène's room, and asked him how Roi was doing. Crow gave a shrug. Her grandmotherly face was on before she even knocked and entered Hélène's room. He heard Hélène burst into tears again when White entered.

When Doe came by with the trolley of tea for Hélène, Crow quickly filled a cup and saucer for Roi, wordlessly nodding thanks to Doe. He gently opened Roi's door, not bothering to knock.

Roi was sitting in the armchair, thickly engrossed in the book. His disheveled eyes and weary posture suggested some crying or the likes of it had occurred in Crow's absence. The fire was dying in the fireplace, but Crow didn't touch it. Roi could tend the fire later if he wanted to. A lit candle was on the table next to Roi's chair, supplying sparse reading light, now that darkness had fallen outside.

Crow set the saucer and cup next to the candle wordlessly.

As Crow turned to leave Roi whispered, "I might have a plan."

"Tell me during our evening cards when no interruptions are guaranteed," said Crow. "I need to first report in with Fierté."

Crow left the room. Roi's hunched, defeated position in the armchair pained him. He could only imagine how Hélène was. White had yet to leave her room.

When Crow arrived at Fierté's open door he waited outside for Fierté to finish giving Gustav instructions. Dismissing Gustav, Fierté signaled Crow to enter and when to stand behind his desk. Crow closed the door after himself.

"So, what is today's news?" inquired Fierté, as if nothing out of the ordinary had occurred.

"Hélène was quite upset about the master's behavior," said Crow bluntly.

Fierté, in the low candle light, said nothing. Crow couldn't quite make out his eyes.

"Roi comforted her as best he could and I believe got a bit riled, but he remains following the rules. He's almost taken a defeated position."

He didn't bother saying Hélène was back in her room with White. Fierté probably knew that already.

"I'm glad to hear he knows his limits," said Fierté.

Crow twitched.

"He has a right to actively oppose us this time."

"Does he really? I beg to differ."

"I admit I heard it second hand from Hélène, but it sounded like the master more than lost his temper. A chair thrown across the room? Books strewn from the shelves? Roaring? It's worse than when we perdu."

"It sounds to me that you are feeling affected by this yourself," said Fierté. "I assure you, it was no different from the master's usual breaks of temper. Hélène did not realize how much he has held back for her. And from this, it can be taken as a lesson to know her place. Words are as harsh a weapon as actions, and she was wielding hers."

"It is no excuse to lose one's temper. At least he should have some sense of chivalry or... I don't know... just a sense to leave if he's going to behave like that. No one should behave like that."

"Master East is an esteemed noble," said Fierté harshly and unflinching. "Nobility are on an entirely different level."

"Nobility or not, he can't act like that towards people!" snapped back Crow, his hands slamming down on Fierté's desk, trembling, remembering how upset Hélène was.

Fierté was suddenly leaning across the desk. His hands tightly clasped down on Crow's, keeping Crow from pulling back. Crow refused to flinch. It was Fierté's face, which was mere inches from his, that caused Crow to catch his tongue. Fierté's eyes flashed in warning as he said darkly, "Watch your tone."

Crow breathed deeply, restraining all he wanted to say. He reluctantly lowered his gaze to focus steadily down at the desk.

Fierté's grasp tightened further. "Do you understand Crow? The master may do as he pleases. He's done as he's pleased. Hélène has been treated the best of all the girls we've acquired. Or does your resurfaced insubordination beg to differ?"

Crow opened his mouth but said nothing. He exhaled with irritation and tried to pull his hands back, but Fierté held on. Startled, Crow looked up, temporarily meeting Fierté's gaze before glancing away again.

"Do you need a lesson?" demanded Fierté.

Crow had never received one from Fierté, but he knew and had seen Fierté always personalized them for servants when they'd reached a particularly bad point. It wouldn't be a harsh beating like Boar gave. It was catered, half psychological. One servant had refused several days in a row to go outside to fetch water during winter. They'd been made to sleep outdoors for a full week in the middle of a storm and given extra fetching duties. They'd nearly died, but never after that did they object any assignment. Another time, two servants had become rather public in showing their affections. Crow shivered remembering their punishment. One had long since gone perdu and the other never spoke to anyone about their love.

Crow shook his head.

"Answer me properly," said Fierté.

"No," Crow rasped out softly.

Fierté released one of his hands. He brought his own hand up to Crow's jaw line and grabbed it gently, but still with commanding authority. He forced him to look his way. Crow looked just below his eyes, but he could tell Fierté was staring right into his.

"I don't ever want to see this behavior again. It is never proper for a servant to act this way, even if their master is in the wrong."

Crow caught his breath. He nearly swore like Roi. Fierté released his hold of Crow's jaw.

"The master, White, Boar, and I had a long chat after the incident," said Fierté after several seconds. "Keeping this confidentially between us, he agrees he lost himself and will work towards his temper. However, Hélène was also in the wrong. I suspect your opinion will matter to her. To avoid future destruction, hint to her how she should behave."

The relief Crow had been feeling was replaced with contempt by the end of Fierté's words. It showed on his face. He barely held his tongue.

"You used to be so stoic before the siblings came," said Fierté after a sigh.

Fierté released him and walked around the table. Crow rubbed his hands, trying to get the feel of Fierté's grip off of them. He was stronger than he looked, though not as strong as Boar.

"I agree the master has been treating Hélène far better than the previous ones," said Crow. "But you made me connect with them, sir. You said connecting would be easier because of our nearer age. So I won't deny, I've grown sensitive to their treatment and I can't ignore it."

"Let's play a quick game. Let's pretend you are a servant, I am the head servant, and your master has just lost his temper with a guest."

Fierté twirled his finger around, signaling Crow to face the door. Reluctantly, Crow obeyed. He sensed a final warning.

Fierté walked around him, "Ignoring the fact that you do not wear the expected servant outfits, which is acceptable only because we are short, how should you be standing?"

Crow brought his legs closer together, imitating the way he'd seen the more submissive servants stand. He straightened his back, his arms falling to his side, eyes straight forward. The stance did not feel natural.

"Good," said Fierté. "And when I give an order, what do you do?"

"Follow it through."

"When the master gives an order?"

"Follow it."

"When the guests give an order?"

"Follow it, so long as it does not contradict yours and the master's orders."

"And does not place the rest of the residents in any sort of danger," nodded Fierté, still circling Crow. "What about your opinion?"

"It doesn't matter."

"Only when I ask for it. So when there's something you want to say, what should you do?"

"Make sure it follows all rules and regulations," answered Crow, spite in his words.

Fierté stopped behind him, adjusting Crow's outfit. His hands made their way around Crow, to manage the outfit's front.

"Are you a head servant, Crow?"

"No."

"Are you a guest?"

"No."

"Are you a noble?"

Crow hesitated as one of Fierté's hands got close to his neck.

"…No."

"Am I in my right to punish you for insubordination?" demanded Fierté, not liking Crow's hesitation.

"If I have done something wrong, yes," answered Crow.

"There are ways to punish and pleasure, that will make your lesson stand out in mind," said Fierté, his fingers pressing against the clothes, moving across Crow's stomach, downward, nearly reaching-.

Crow's eyes widened fearfully and he pulled from Fierté's hold, stumbling and turning to stare at the butler in disbelief.

"It is my job to keep everyone in line, Crow," said Fierté. There was a hunger in his eyes. "I know exactly what drives and hinders every servant under my command. Should I need to give a full lesson, I assure you, it will fully utilize your distastes; restraint and touch. When I give a full lesson, I never need to give it again. I'm placing faith in you to correct yourself with this reprimand. Is there a need for a lesson, Crow?"

Crow shook his head, backing towards the door.

"Same time tomorrow," said Fierté, waving a dismissive hand. "If you keep your tongue and behavior in line, the future meetings should be brief."

Turning, Crow shakily opened the door and slammed it behind him. He winced, then quickly started down the hall. When he got to a turret with an elegant, curtained window and dusty seating, Crow lost his strength and stumbled into the nearest chair. The area was dark; the moonlight barely made it through the curtain's crack. This hall was not cared for, as the guests didn't come this way and rarely did the master.

Crow leaned forward in his seat, releasing a frustrated curse. His knees supported his elbows as he held his head in his hands. He refused to cry, but he was close. He knew he needed to get back to Roi for their planned "card playing" evening, but he couldn't show himself in this condition.

Crow became absorbed in trying to reel in his frustration and build his stoic barrier, as Fierté had so called it. He had changed with the arrival of Roi and Hélène. He needed to back pedal. He still had every intention of helping the siblings, but this rebellious demeanor he had taken on almost naturally, *likely from stupid Roi's influence*, had to be restrained.

Damn Boar and his violence. Damn Fierté and his carefully carved threats. I'd curse the master, if it weren't already so.

A slight shuffle on the rug brought Crow out of his dark thoughts. He kept his hands still on his head, but glancing to the side, he saw a large cloaked form through the darkness. Master East. Through the dimness,

Crow saw the master's gaze note him. The master's sight in the dark was impeccable. Crow froze, aware his brooding frustration was more than apparent. But the master did not stop, though perhaps slowed, and continued down the hall.

Crow released his head and leaned back in the chair, staring up at the cobwebbed roof. Fierté would have been exasperated at Crow for not jumping to his feet, ready before the master. It hadn't even occurred to Crow until just now. But he doubted the master would tell Fierté. Crow wasn't important enough, and there had almost been... pity in his gaze? Yes, the master did feel some guilt about his servants suffering the curse, though he nearly never showed it. Crow had caught him off guard as much as the master had caught him.

A clock down the hall chimed ten. Crow took in a deep breath. He tried to reason with himself. There was nothing he could do about most of this, so it wasn't worth his focus. He needed to dwell on what he could do.

With this in mind, he returned to Roi's room. Pont, who didn't move to unlock the door, appeared to actually be sleeping. Crow tried the handle and was surprised it turned. The beast had listened to his suggestion. Roi's door would only be locked between midnight and seven, or if any discipline was again needed.

Crow cleared his throat as he walked in. Roi was several chapters through reading the book from the library. Crow read the spine, 'Provincial Capital, Remais.' Roi looked up to give his usual greeting, but his expression immediately hardened. The book was placed down and Roi moved over to him, wincing from the abrupt movement.

"What happened?"

"Just the usual evening report," said Crow, forcing a smile. "And servants getting on my nerves."

"You were gone for over an hour."

"Just servant stuff."

"Crow," said Roi forcefully. "We know each other well enough to see when the other is off."

"Fierté and I had an unpleasant conversation on how the master treated Hélène," Crow finally admitted. He didn't want to bad talk Fierté too much in front of Roi. Fierté was nerve-racking, but he was also excellent at keeping everything in order for all these years. Definitely better than Boar. Crow regretted having been so insolent to the better of the two head men.

"Surely Fierté knew it was wrong."

"He has a stance on both sides," said Crow, rubbing his temple and not wanting to think about it. "But his loyalty is always for the master. He told me to discreetly advise Hélène to tiptoe better when around the master."

Roi growled as he began to pace the room.

"Did you tell him how hard Hélène took it?"

"I attempted. I was reprimanded and reminded of my place."

"Attempted," spat Roi. "Reprimanded. Curse it all, Crow, she was trembling and in tears."

"I know," said Crow quietly.

Roi grabbed Crow's shoulders, shaking him, "But did he say he'd do anything? She's just a girl. She's-"

Roi stopped himself, seeing Crow's pained expression.

"You tried your best," softened Roi, releasing him. Then he embraced Crow much like Hélène did. "I'm sorry I torment you. You probably took a risk standing up for us."

The warmth of Roi's body seeped through the clothes into the surprised Crow and Crow wanted to draw it all in. Roi's fingers lightly curled against Crow's back. Crow could feel Roi's breathing against his neck. He leaned in. The empathy and kindness was a needed welcome. But then, he thought of Fierté, his arms wrapped around him earlier, hands moving down, the warning of a lesson.

Crow quickly tried to back out with attempted humor, but he was certain Roi had felt his sudden stiffness.

"The risk was for Hélène. You, on the other hand, bring what you deserve."

"Did I deserve to be attacked by Wolf?" asked Roi, refusing to turn to humor. He touched the forming scars on his face, and then placed his hands back on Crow's shoulder, studying Crow's face. Crow stared at Roi's hand.

"To a degree, but not like that," said Crow honestly. "You're trouble, but not bad. You certainly did not deserve the ravaging Wolf did to you. I shouldn't have left you."

Roi released Crow.

"You flew ahead because you trusted me. And I feel likewise."

Crow walked over to inspect the book so Roi wouldn't see his embarrassment. He quickly reverted the subject.

"It sounds like the beast did have another lesson on temper management from the triumvirate. He'll probably be sulking for the next few days, so Hélène should be safe. In fact, she might be in the library with just a servant tomorrow."

Roi's body relaxed as he closed his eyes, relieved. "That will make it easier on her." He moved next to Crow and flipped the book over, revealing a page that mapped the southern part of Remais. "How far can you fly?"

Crow frowned.

"You want to go to Remais?"

"I don't think I could make it there and back in time," said Roi. Then he looked bashful. "Plus I'm still wary of crossing Wolf again. At least, until I know the risk and plans are sounder."

"You want me to scout Remais?"

"I've been thinking it all day. Hélène's devastation only affirmed it. We can continue to encourage her, but there's no chance she'll fall in love with him." Deep silence followed. Crow knew Roi was thinking, 'And I don't want to encourage her.'

"I know."

"And while she's treated wonderfully by the servants, that and bribery won't work in matters of love," said Roi. "Love is needed by both sides. And even if Hélène was open to the idea, your master's heart must be too cruel to be open to love. Lust, perhaps. But love, I doubt he even loves himself."

Crow grimaced. They both stared absently at the map in silence.

"I can make it," said Crow into the emptiness. Roi jerked from his thoughts and looked at him. "If I fly fast I can get there in three hours, four at the most."

"Is it time or distance that affects you?" inquired Roi.

"Both. I flew to the outskirts of the city a few times long ago, when testing my boundaries. I've had little need these days, but I know I can still do it."

"How long can you spend there?" asked Roi.

"I doubt more than a couple hours," said Crow. He pointed a finger at the map, "That's the hill the noble residences are on. I'll search out the brothers and see if I can find anything about the curse, the enchantress, or Corvus."

"Especially Corvus," said Roi. "I bet they'd believe us if we needed to contact someone outside. If they are still alive and aware of all this. There's also the possibility, depending on the receiver of the letter, that Corvus isn't even their real name. But if we can find them, they may have at least kept track of the enchantress."

Crow nodded.

They looked at the grandfather clock.

"I should leave now, then."

"This is important, but Crow, if you can't manage it, come back. You're my only ally here."

Crow pulled back the curtains of the window, already formulating his flight plan, grateful for the distraction that had presented itself for him. He undid the latch and immediately the cold air was rushing in to the room.

"Turn," requested Crow, seeing Roi was watching him.

"Do you need to eat anything before you go?" asked Roi.

Crow shook his head, exasperatedly twirling his finger around. Roi exaggerated a turn. Crow transformed, feeling warmer in his feathered form, though he knew the cold would break through eventually.

"I'll return this way. So sleep with an ear open."

"I doubt I'll be able to sleep," said Roi. "I'll study the book, so we can be ready."

"And the letters."

"I did earlier today." Roi's face turned pink from the cold as he approached the window. He stuck a hand out and felt Crow's feathers. "I think we've gotten all we can from them, not to say they weren't a huge find. I'm grateful you brought them to my attention. Fly safely, my friend."

Crow did a quick, friendly nip at Roi's finger, and took off. Against the dark sky, no one would see him. The wind was harsh him, but didn't press him away from his destination. Crow flew higher and picked up speed. He wasn't patrolling the woods; he didn't need to keep an eye out for people. The clouds looked ready to spill their contents and Crow prayed they held until his trip was done.

The city lights eventually appeared as enlarging specks. Despite the length of the flight, Crow had enjoyed it. The call of the castle, willing him back, was rising steadily. He assured it soon, but not yet.

Entering the city, he landed on a townhouse, resting and getting better bearings. He matched up where he was based on his memory of the map. The map was outdated, but still the roads and most designs were the same. He startled away pigeons as he moved along the roof, craning his neck to see some of the buildings. The bell tower clock nearby showed it was nearing one. Nearly everyone was asleep, aside from the few soldiers that patrolled the street and those sauntering home from the red light district.

Crow gave a few hops, and then took flight again, flying towards the noble homes. This area proved less bird-friendly; spikes lay atop some buildings. He finally rested on a statue in the center of a plaza. A soldier spotted him and they stared at each other. Crow then pretended to preen himself, causing the soldier to mutter under his breath, questioning how much liquor he'd drunk, and continued on his way.

From this point, the night became more explorative. Crow's adrenaline spiked at the adventure as he approached each home. It wasn't too difficult to figure out the housings. Many had their names on the estate. The Lord's home was huge, a giant trail wound through a park before the giant, three story mansion even showed. Crow managed to get inside through an open servant window. The floors were covered with marble and the walls paneled with a rich burgundy wood Crow hadn't seen before. When he got out of the servant section, the ceilings became professionally decorated, ghostly painted faces peering down at him through the dark. The mansion was not as gothic as Castle Cadrer, but the building's wealth far exceeded it.

The Lord appeared out for the night, the staff all asleep. This allowed Crow to search the rooms unhindered. Each of the rooms meant for guests could fit Hélène and Roi's room together, but were all unoccupied. Aside from the furniture, they were kept so incredibly clean and void, that Crow picked up a small feather that had fallen from his wing and stuffed it behind a dresser to avoid feeling like he was contaminating the place. At the end of the third overly extravagant hall, Crow confirmed one of the sons still lived there, the youngest, by finding his possessions in his room. Unlike the other rooms, this one was disorganized, though it too held a sterile impression. An open bottle of red wine was on the bed stand. The bed was empty, but small wrinkles in the sheets indicated it had been sat upon. A letter was open next to the wine.

Crow flew onto the counter, using his talons to straighten the carelessly kept paper. It was from a lover, likely whose residence the brother was at now. He bent over the ledge and eased the drawer below open with his beak. He strove through the contents, finding further letters. Most were love letters from five other women, implicating the brother as quite carefree and not the sort of personality to curse another, let alone a relative. Two letters at the bottom proved more fruitful. The first was from the second oldest brother, away on military duty, lecturing his younger sibling to find a respectable occupation, instead of riding on their father's coattails. The second was from the third oldest, announcing the birth of his fourth daughter, from where he now lived two provinces away with his wife, whom he clearly adored. Neither implicated a hungry character, someone who would have distinctly benefitted from Goodwin's disappearance.

That left the oldest.

Crow left the East estate, flying by homes, holding his breath in hope of finding Corvus labelled on one, or another East. He even prayed for the remote chance to spot a suspicious woman on the streets who could be the enchantress.

He nearly flew by a marbled covered mansion, but abruptly stopped and landed on the stone paved ground before it. The East name was etched on a panel at the gate, though this was clearly not the Lord's. This was the heir's home, the oldest brother.

The front yard was large, though only a fraction of the size of the Lord's estate, and void of plant life. Crow stared at a life-sized stone statue of a man holding his head, his face distorted by the shadows to look like he was in pain. A shiver ran through Crow, as he realized his own pain building within him. His time was running out. If he'd been in human form, he'd be sweating.

Crow approached across the grounds. The lights were on. A small dinner party was going on in the main level of a large hall that even fit several grand marble statues and a fountain. There was live musicians for twelve guests who dined at the enormous table.

Crow hopped up onto the low window sill, peering through the glass. The men sat on one side, facing towards the window, and the women with their backs to Crow. They seemed to be enjoying themselves well enough.

A hand inside waved across his view, frightening Crow so badly he nearly went into purdu. Settling his ruffled feathers down, he saw it belonged to a frowning servant. They looked at him as they would a pest, trying to get rid of him without disturbing the diners. They closed the curtains.

Crow wished he'd had time to spot the brother. He flew up to the mansion's second level, getting inside through an opening in the attic and working his way through cracks until he was properly inside. He found his way to the heir's door, which was locked, but a fashionable window over the thick oak door was slightly open. Crow squeezed through. The office had many papers and locked cabinets. The heir's richly carved desk was strewn with papers. Crow clacked his beak. His time was running out. In a patrol, he would have long headed back when he first experienced these levels of light headedness and nauseous.

Are crow's able to throw up?

Crow set to work, skimming rather than reading properly. The curtains were open, allowing the dim moonlight shining through the clouds to light up some of the room.

Nothing in this estate report. Not anything helpful in this letter to either, though it's apparent he lusts for more power with the number of business scandals it lists him in. Next. No, just numbers. Shit, my head. Focus. Keep reading. No mention of an enchantress or Corvus. Just tons of records of unimportant names. Nothing convicts this brother! Keep reading, keep focusing… Ugh, I can't find anything!

Frustrated, Crow flew to the window, unlatched it, and took off into the night. His head felt like it separate of his body from the light-headedness and focus he'd forced. At least he could check the East homes off the list.

I can't explore anymore. I need to come back another night.

The thought left Crow feeling even more ragged. He wasn't supposed to be doing this. Not by servant rule, but by the curse's will.

Snow began to fall as Crow left the city's outskirt. His headache was slipping away, gratefully, but his daze was increasing. His thoughts felt like they were floating and there was the temptation to simply stop thinking at all.

The storm is picking up. Not good. Need to fly faster. So cold. Keep flying. Need warmth. Others. On branch. Warmer. Still ill. Why? Go… Need to go… to the castle!

Crow blinked himself back to focus. He was perched on a tree with several other birds. He'd entered a daze, possibly a perdu. Disturbed, he realized he couldn't push it like this again. Less than an hour in the city would have to be the limit, if at all, next time.

His stomach churned as he took flight from the branches cover. He made sure to keep thinking, to fight the daze. The clouds sent their full fury of snow down at him. He released a caw of relief when the barely visible grounds proved familiar thanks to a decade of flying over them in all seasons. He was little less than a half hour away from the castle.

It felt like hours, when the dark castle appeared through the whirling storm. Crow landed inelegantly on the window ledge, his legs giving out as he sat down and pecked lightly against the glass. He shivered as he waited, leaning against the glass, which felt warmer than the surrounding air. When no one appeared, he grimaced, summoning up his remaining energy.

Crow pecked against the window more viciously. A sleepy-looking Roi struggled through the curtains and, with the trouble of someone just woken up, opened the window only long enough for Crow to slip in. Crow transformed before Roi was finished locking the window.

"Y' find anything?" asked Roi tiredly. He rubbed his eyes with his palms, trying to wake up.

Crow shook the snow from his hair and body. It was chilly in the room. The fire had gone out some time ago. He crossed over to Roi's bed and sat on it, enjoying the heat that still emanated from the covers.

"Nothing," admitted Crow. "And I had to come back a bit early... I was starting to perdu. Flying that distance is quite a workout."

"Is it possible you missed anything?" asked Roi, becoming more awake and joining Crow on the bed.

"I never finished," said Crow. "Tomorrow I will. I searched the Lord and heir's houses, and explored the wealthy district, but haven't found anything. No sign that Goodwin East ever existed there, or of this Corvus."

"I had an idea when you were out. Corvus mentioned finances, or something like that, maybe check the banks. The rich and influential people would have their names with accounts there."

"I'll look there tomorrow... I guess today, since it's early morning," said Crow between yawns.

"You're exhausted."

Crow resisted rolling his eyes at Roi's pathetic observation. He swayed as he got to his feet. He headed for the door, tripped over the rug, and even more slowly got back up.

"My tired black bird, Pont's outside with the key," said Roi. "He might... wonder what we were up to in here at this hour."

Crow's cheeks flamed. He gave the window an unappealing look.

"Ugh, guess it's the cold again."

"Just stay the night here. At least for a few hours to warm up. I'm awake now. I'll do some reading, and in an hour I'll wake you."

The offer was tempting. Crow could barely stand straight, and he wouldn't put it past his crow form to perdu from the extreme weather and fatigue.

Roi grabbed his shoulders and directed Crow back to the bed, kindly enough pushing him onto it.

"Rest an hour," ordered Roi.

Crow worked his boots off with his feet and wriggled under the covers, taking delight in the warmth. He couldn't remember the last time he'd slept in a bed. Goosebumps rose along his skin.

"Half an hour," he muttered drowsily.

"Half an hour, then," confirmed Roi, picking up the boots to move them to the side.

Crow was asleep before Roi even set them down.

CHAPTER 9 – THE BANK

As Crow drowsily woke, he honed in on a ticking that shouldn't be sounding in his attic. Opening his eyes, his gaze rested on the grandfather clock across the room. *The guest room.* Sunlight streamed along the curtain edges. More than an hour had passed.

Crow abruptly sat up, the covers falling down from where they'd been tucked up to his neck. He scanned the room for Roi before realizing that the furnace the bed had become was largely due to Roi sleeping on the other side.

Crow fought to keep the swearing in as he squirmed out of the covers. He inched too close to the bed's edge and fell over with a sheet wrapped around his leg. He landed loudly on the floor, his entrapped leg sticking up over the bed like a flag of surrender. He groaned.

Roi leaned over the bed edge in a bright mood, looking like he hadn't lost any sleep.

"Good morning, sleeping beauty."

"Nothing is good about it," grumbled Crow, accepting Roi's help to free his leg. "What if Pont or White walked in! What were you thinking? Sharing a bed!"

As Crow got to his feet, he stepped on something soft. He jumped off the unexpected texture, looking down so fast that his stiff neck ached.

My shirt and vest?

Rubbing the back of his neck, he looked down at himself.

At least my pants are still on.

"Did you undress me?"

"Your clothes were damp from the snow," shrugged Roi. "And it gave me something nice to see."

"You should have woken me!" exclaimed Crow, flustered.

"I tried," said Roi, waving his hand exasperatedly. "You were waking for no man. Entirely conked out. And I was getting tired, too."

"I slept for hours in human form," grumbled Crow, collecting his clothes and scrambling to get them on. "I'm going to have to spend the day as a crow to accumulate some time again."

"Admit it was nice sharing a bed," said Roi. "We didn't have to rely only on our own heat."

Crow flushed as he tied his boots.

Grinning, Roi wriggled out of the covers and grabbed his own shirt. Crow noticed the bandages were becoming loose, but the dressings weren't as necessary anymore.

The scars will actually enhance Roi's allure.

Crow shook his head to rid his distracting thoughts. He headed over to the window. Roi joined him and undid the latch.

"I'll be back by evening," said Crow. "Pretend you're satisfied with reading and don't need me all day."

"I wouldn't mind your company as a crow. It's fascinating to see a talking ball of black feathers."

Crow raised his hand and flicked Roi's head, something he'd seen Hélène do when Roi was talking rubbish. Roi looked away. Crow transformed and took off.

Crow spent the remaining morning sleeping in the attic. After the nice bed it was difficult, but he needed to regain the energy. At noon, he did his patrol. Nothing as usual. The day was clear and the air was cold.

With a significant amount of hesitation, Crow reported to Fierté. He kept the report record short and fidgeting remained by the open doorway the entire time. Fierté acted indifferent. Everything appeared to be back to normal.

Crow returned to Roi's room for the evening game of cards. Hélène was with them for the first half, before catching on that her companions had something up their sleeves and retired early for the evening. With the door finally closed, they set about cleaning the table.

"If anyone comes checking for me, just tell them I flew out your window to do a patrol," said Crow, gathering the teacups onto a tray.

Roi helped wrangle the plates. Crow placed the tray on the back counter. He'd return it to the kitchens tomorrow. He now stood in front of the fireplace, enjoying the warmth the fire was still throwing. He stretched.

"I wish my room had a fireplace," said Crow enviously, closing his eyes.

"You could share this room with me."

Crow chuckled at the thought, and joked, "Don't tempt me."

He felt Roi's hands play with the back of his hair. Crow stopped stretching, opening his eyes. Roi was standing near enough that Crow could feel his warmth on his back.

"Your hair is just as black as a crow's. Lovely, really."

Crow pulled out of Roi's fingers as he bent towards the fireplace. He wasn't sure if the heat on his face was the fire's or his own, but he kept his back to Roi. He grabbed a log to add.

"Guess I'll head out earlier this time. The fire really has me warmed up."

Crow stood and followed the wall towards the window.

"Wait!" Roi's right arm went past Crow's head, his hand pressing against the wall. Crow froze. Roi's left reached up hesitantly, then began to follow the wrinkles and curves to Crow's outfit. At first it was light, but his finger pressed harder so that Crow could feel the drawing on his skin.

Crow's initial startle shifted to bewilderment. His mouth slightly parted open as his brows furrowed. He watched the tracing fingers, mesmerized. Then his gaze flickered up to Roi's and he took in a sharp breath. Roi was staring straight at him with a look in his eyes.

Wild? No. Predatory? No. Longing? Crow's mouth closed. His heart took on a quicker beat. *Being cooped up is obviously affecting Roi more than I had noticed these days. He's social. He likely met his sexual needs on a whim back at Beauclair.*

"I need to go," said Crow, feigning ignorance.

Roi's left hand stopped tracing and blocked Crow's retreat.

"You don't have anyone special, do you?" He stepped forward, causing Crow's back to meet the wall. It was cold compared to the rest of the room; compared to the heat coming from Roi.

"Romantic relationships amongst staff are rare," said Crow, trying to treat it as Roi's usual stupid comments.

"Have you ever loved? Women? Men? Both?"

"This… is not appropriate, even in jest."

"I- I find you quite attractive," murmured Roi. He leaned his head forward, stopping when their faces were inches apart. His lovely honey eyes reflected the fire's flames. He stared intently at Crow with no hint of jest.

Crow felt blood rush to his face. Even his ears had a burning sensation.

Say something, Crow thought angrily to himself. *Remember, he's not actually serious… not when he's in a normal mind state. You need to stop this.*

Roi leaned his head in a little further, so that their foreheads touched. He was pleasantly soft, but the sensation of skin to skin brought Crow from his frozen position. A desperate grin drew on Crow's face.

"You're horny because you've been locked up too long," said Crow, slipping fluidly under and out of Roi's arms. "The others can sometimes get like this with each other too." *Like Fierté.* "Especially during spring. There are handkerchiefs in the cupboard, just store them in a box when you're done. I don't want the room smelling. Have a fun night!"

He transformed by the window, hidden by the curtain, and then took off for his second outing without looking back at Roi. He thought he heard a sigh. In crow form, his confusion and worries cleared with the cold air. His thundering heart slowed to a rhythmic pace for flight. Repetitively, he assured his worrying mind, Roi would tend to himself and things would be back to normal. They had too. He just wished the slight pang, which he presumed was guilt, would also go away.

With some moonlight, it was easier finding the city. The streets were empty this late at night, and any watchmen were huddled around fire pits. He flew lower when he got to the middle class portion of the town. He scanned signs and posts. Approaching the richer districts, he spotted a sign with a bank emblem; the province's main bank.

He inspected the building's exterior, every nook and cranny, until he took to carefully going down the chimney. There was a grate at the bottom, but it did little for blocking him as he angled himself under the bars.

His feet clicked along the ground as he hobbled in the room. He carefully inspected it. No cats or dogs. Some snoring around the corner signaled a guard near the main entrance but otherwise the bank was empty for the night.

Crow continued to walk, rather than fly. He exited what he assumed was a manager's office and passed a series of desks in a marble built room. Everything was designed to display wealth. There were a couple stairwells going down to the safes. He only needed information. He figured it'd be on the main floor.

Eventually he came across a room with "records" written across it, indicating the employees were expected to know how to read. Crow clicked his beak unhappily. The door was shut with no way around to get in. Crow even checked for a way under the floor.

He let out a frustrated groan. But as a crow, and so far from the castle, it came out as a caw.

"Who's there?" called out the security guard, followed by a shout from the other side of the bank, "Did you hear someone?"

Two guards.

He shook his head at his carelessness. The footsteps approached the hall quickly and Crow pressed himself in the shadows between two chairs. He flinched as the guards' boots tromped by.

"Should we get the dog in?" asked a guard as they found their search unproductive.

As they checked the main room one more time, Crow quickly moved back to the cubicle room. Daring a few flaps, he hopped onto a desk. A neat stack of papers had been left on top, with numbers and diagrams.

Crow opened his beak as he moved along the desk's top, collecting most of the papers in his mouth. He carefully hoped onto a chair, and then to the floor, keeping his beak clamped shut tight.

"I think I heard some noise that way."

Crow hustled far under the desk with the papers. The guards strutted through the cubicle room.

"Think the rats are back again?"

"That's why I wanted to get the dog. The useless mutt just huddles at the door. He should be more useful than just an alarm."

Crow felt sorry for the dog.

When the guards got to the far end of the cubicles, with their lantern half-heartedly lighting up the shadows a human could hide in, Crow ran sideways around the corner as fast as his crow legs could handle. The papers sounded as they dragged against the floor.

"Over here!"

The two stumbled Crow's way.

Crow ruthlessly nudged the papers with his beak to get them as far under the closed 'records' door crack as he could. The pile was no longer straight. As the guards rounded the corner, he hopped back under the chairs, pressing himself against the wall and breathing heavily.

"Shit," whispered a guard. "Someone's in records."

His comrade pulled the keys from his belt. Then he attempted to unlock the room as quietly as he could, wanting to surprise the culprit. They flung the door open, giving a triumphant call, charging the opening.

The room was small, with shelves filled on three sides of record books, ink, and pens. A table was in the middle, high so one needed to stand to comfortably use it.

The guards spent several minutes in confusion. Crow took the time to pacify his nerves. They collected the papers and decided to put them in their lock box, since they weren't sure where they'd come from. One guard remained by the door as the other walked down the hall to wherever their lock box was. The guard remaining watched his companion go.

Crow moved so his talons wouldn't make a sound, but felt rather awkward and silly. He entered the room, staying in the guard's blind spot. When inside, he moved behind a basket on the lowest shelf.

The door was closed and locked, leaving Crow isolated. With little light other than what shone through a small porthole window, Crow got to work. He wished he could change into a human for this part.

He flew up on the table to study the shelves. One side was arranged numerically, the other side alphabetically. The alphabetical side was more promising. There were three C books. He aimed for the newest one, which itself looked like it had seen a couple decades.

There was no room for him to stand on the shelf ledge. Flapping frantically, he managed to attack the top of the book's spine, pulling it out and sending it to the floor. He landed next to the book and waited to see if the guards had heard the noise.

After a few minutes of silence, he dragged the book under the small light pocket shining on the floor from the window. Opening the book smoothly, for a crow, he began to skim the pages. The listed C name accounts were not alphabetical, but rather seemed to be entered in the order they'd been made.

He was unsure of the time he spent going through the pages, but he had to move the book twice to keep it in the moonlight. He also felt the perdu rising in the back of his mind.

Eventually he came across a name that had two pages reserved for it. Half of the page listed meaningless bank information, but at the top read "Corvus, Bertok." Crow released a sharp breath. Next to the name was a signature, a tight continuous flow that matched the letter's style. He skimmed to the end of the recordings to see the last recorded date was four months ago. Corvus was likely still alive.

Crow looked below the name and saw Corvus had a rank; Count. Below that, "Associates; Navan Corvus, son – serving at royal court. Lord East – Hirer, serves as Treasurer - Has special access to his lordship's accounts."

Crow noted the Lord's symbol; he'd seen it many times at the castle. Now Crow knew how Corvus was connected to the noble family. So surely Corvus would be able to identify the enchantress or perhaps even have records in a diary somewhere. He scanned the page but there was no listing of a residence, aside from the city name.

Crow carefully worked at ripping the Corvus page out. Then, with difficulty, he closed the book and shoved it to the back of the room. He rolled the page up tightly, keeping it in his talons. He flew to the top of a shelf nearest the door.

He took in a deep breath and managed to croak out, "Guards!" Speaking this far away from the castle, even with his crow voice, was difficult. He paused, then called several times more. He could hear them rushing down the hall.

"This room again," said one through the door. "That ain't no rodent."

"I knew this place was haunted. We locked this room and there was no one in it."

"Open," said Crow, flinching at voice's scratchiness. "Let my spirit out or be cursed."

"Lord protect me," muttered the first voice. Crow imagined him doing a symbol against evil.

"No, don't open it. It could be an evil spirit."

"I am the grandfather of Lord East," said Crow, his voice shaking from the effort, but it added a chilling effect. He flinched as he swallowed. "I wish to speak with his treasurer, Corvus, then go to rest peacefully."

"Count Corvus?"

Crow remained silent. So Corvus was known well enough.

"He's out of town," continued the guard. "He won't be back until to attend the Heir East's party two nights hence."

"Open the door, and be blessed," said Crow, shaking from the exertion. "Keep it closed and be cursed."

"Damn it all," muttered the more superstitious guard.

The jingling of keys sounded.

The guards sputtered of demons and ghosts when Crow flew out past their heads. He retraced his steps in flight, escaping without hindrance.

The flight back was swift. Being successful gave him extra energy. He landed on Roi's sill carefully, tweaking his wings and tail to maintain balance, and tapped the window with his beak.

This time, Roi had stayed up waiting. He was wearing a housecoat and an open book lay on the table next to the oil lamp. He opened the window immediately. Crow flew to the floor, leaving the page and transformed.

As Roi turned from adjusting the curtains, Crow picked up and passed the sheet to Roi with numb fingers.

"I found something," exclaimed Crow. "And heard something."

"There's some lukewarm tea over in the kettle by the fireplace," said Roi, sitting down in the armchair.

Crow let Roi read the page as he poured himself tea. He rested his hands on the pot. When he could close his fingers without feeling numb, he picked up the teacup and sat across the table from Roi. He had to make a mental note not to perch on his feet. He was glad his excitement had helped keep perdu at bay during the trip.

Roi took a long time reading the page. Crow finished his tea and refilled before Roi finally looked up. Crow watched a weary smile reveal on the otherwise emotionless face. "So, our elusive Corvus is alive and a Count. You know, I might have heard him mentioned before. But that's beside the point," said Roi. "Did you read it or only take it?"

"Just the top and bottom. I know there is no address or much helpful detail, aside from him being close with the East family. Their treasurer. But, I heard he'll be in the city two days from now, to attend a party hosted by Lord East's heir, apparently."

Roi stroked his chin, "Do you think you'd be able to manage a third flight so soon, remain aware, and in a crowd? I know there are limits."

Crow shrugged, finishing off the second cup. "I could, probably, with lots of rest leading up to the day."

"And then, you'll attend the party, maybe locate Corvus, and eavesdrop," said Roi. It sounded good to Crow, but Roi said it unenthusiastically. "Crow, this opportunity requires a human. I can talk to Corvus. I can ask around."

"Crows can mimic words to a degree."

"I'm sure Count Corvus would love to converse with a crow. I'm used to you, but I still find it creepy when Pont says something. I swear he waits for the perfect moment when he knows it will disturb me the most."

"And your plan works because Corvus is obviously attending the party here. You're a prisoner, remember?"

Roi went quiet.

Fine, don't say anything more, thought Crow grumpily. *I don't feel like thinking and talking anyways.*

Crow was nearly drifting off to sleep when Roi said, "I might have an idea, but I need to sleep on it. We'll talk in the morning. Want to sleep here?"

"I shouldn't risk a second night," mumbled Crow, getting to his feet. He looked unhappily at the window, where the cold could be felt radiating in through the glass.

"Just sleep in my bed," said Roi. "If it makes you self-conscious, I'll sleep on top of one sheet level and promise not to undress you. Okay?"

Crow looked at the bed longingly. He took a dazed step forward before he stopped himself. He crossed his arms, but his eyes lingered on the temptation.

So nice and soft, thought Crow. *And how wonderfully warm it got last time… right up until I remembered where I was and fell off. No, I need to resist. It's just a be-*

Roi wrapped an arm around Crow and brought him close. The warmth was like a siren song, causing Crow to lean closer to Roi.

"Just warming you up," said Roi. You did amazing tonight. You'll have to tell me the full story tomorrow when we aren't half asleep. Look, it's almost five. Stay here. I don't even notice you sleeping, you're so quiet. In the morning I'll have breakfast delivered and we can spend our time plotting until noon."

Crow gave in. He felt too groggy to function. He lay on top of the covers; the room felt warmer than him. He was asleep before Roi got to his side.

CHAPTER 10 – A TENTATIVE ALLY

Roi was already up, dressed, and studying the page at the table when Crow awoke. The door was closed and blocked by a side table Roi had put in front of it. It wouldn't stop any determined person, but it guaranteed a degree of privacy. On the main table was a silver tray with various small dishes of breakfast choices.

Roi grinned as he noticed Crow approach the food. "And good morning to you. Eat what you want. I'm not hungry. White delivered it. I told her I made you drink wine and stay up late at cards, so you passed out. She wasn't impressed, but I figured it was an acceptable excuse…"

"I can work with that," said Crow.

Fierté would not be impressed either, but he'd make Roi carry the weight and tell Fierté that Roi had been ornery. Plus, Fierté himself had told him to keep Roi happy and in line.

Crow pounced on a biscuit, unable to hide the pleasure of all this food available to him. He hadn't eaten such variety and so well in a long time. When he got to licking his fingers, comfortable enough with Roi to no longer be embarrassed of personal habits, Roi brought the sheet forward. Crow stopped halfway down his finger line.

"I think we need a third party," said Roi thoughtfully. "I was wondering who you think would be ideal. You know the staff better than me. They can't all be pompous, perdu, or stupid."

"Putting aside the stupidity of this idea, you want a castle member. Not Hélène?"

"Not yet," said Roi. "She'd jump at the chance, but she and I are limited and I don't want to strain her more than she's at as the distraction team. She's being obedient, making them think I'm doing my job, which makes them think you're doing your job."

"What sort of help did you want?" asked Crow, not many candidates coming to mind. He crossed his arms as he sat forward in his chair.

"Is there anyone who can leave the castle like you? Or can be trusted, at least? What about Pont?"

"Pont!" hissed Crow, and then shook his head. He kept forgetting that as much as Roi was a fast learner, he still didn't know much of the servants. "Pont is Fierté's man. He's possible to bribe, but he'd need a pretty big incentive. Curse breaking and goodwill isn't on that list. I wouldn't trust him."

"Then Fierté isn't an option either?" asked Roi. "Your servant bigwigs, they seem to be human a lot. So I'm guessing they're in better form, like you? They could head out?"

Crow finished cleaning his hands with his napkin, shaking his head. "Boar, Fierté, and White could probably all leave the castle, but certainly not in human form. I've personally never seen them step beyond the walls, so even if they could, I don't think they'd be able to make it as far as Remais. I'm used to pushing myself against the castle's pull. Plus, I don't think any of their animal forms would be welcomed at the party."

Roi gave a chuckle, "So they won't be having deer and pig at the celebration, then." Crow responded with a silent chuckle. "What animal is White?"

"She's a dog."

"Like Nanny?"

"More of a mid-sized herding dog. But at her age, she wouldn't make it far, physically. Plus, she'd never-"

Crow stopped mid-sentence.

"What?" asked Roi.

"Well, I'd never thought about it, but when Hélène first arrived, White had commented, 'if only there was another way, I'd take it'. She's always empathized for Hélène."

"Enough that we could trust her?"

"I'm not around her often to really know."

"Right, you work with Fierté and Boar," said Roi. "White is in charge of the female staffing."

Crow nodded. His head felt heavy. He let out a groan.

"What?" asked Roi.

"I slept as human again," grumbled Crow.

"So?"

"So, I won't be able to stay human much longer. Maybe another hour if I want to push it. I'll need to change to recuperate."

"Okay, but stay here," said Roi. "Don't go hide."

"I don't hide," said Crow indignantly. "I just go do other things. I sleep, scavenge, and patrol the forest!"

Roi snorted as he got up to throw a log on the fire.

"I don't mean to sound ungrateful of your company," added Crow. "Hanging around you and being human so often has me almost forgetting I'm cursed."

"Crow, I've seen you as a crow," said Roi. "And you pretty much just admitted you like my company. Stay with me as an animal."

Crow leaned back in his chair, stretching his arms.

"If you save me some sweets from your dinner, then you have a deal."

It will be interesting and less lonely. I'm not too sure why I feel the need to isolate myself from Roi when I change. Perhaps habit and shame. But Roi is being understanding. And there doesn't appear to be any of those strange looks from yesterday.

Roi looked surprised at Crow's sudden acceptance. Then very pleased.

"A deal, then!" he exclaimed, bouncing over to Crow and sticking his hand out. "With you as my wingman, nothing will stop us."

Crow released a laugh.

For the remainder of the morning they went over each staff member. White seemed increasingly the most viable, because of her high rank and sympathy. Aside from the triumvirate, the servants were either too incompetent, untrustworthy, or loyal to their hierarchy.

Around noon Hélène came to visit, catching the two huddled next to each other, debating over a list of supplies they believed they should gather. Crow had been in bird form up to a point, but had taken on his human form again as their debate had heightened and Roi had broken into laughter, "I can't take arguing with a bird seriously".

Crow immediately stepped back, pulling a chair out for Hélène. He read her bemused expression and felt relieved that nothing misfortunate had occurred during breakfast for her. Yesterday, he'd overheard Squirrel and Porcupine gossiping, "The master is tirelessly rereading all the books on etiquette to make up for all that he's lost".

"I was wondering what was keeping you so occupied," said Hélène. "Usually you'd have checked in on me by now. I see Crow is keeping you to himself these days."

"Hardly," said Crow, red creeping up his face. "Actually, it's good you're here. We need another person to overview with."

Hélène looked sweetly over to Nanny, "Nanny, I believe I've left my room rather a mess. It wouldn't look good if anyone were to enter and see its conditions. Would you mind fixing it up? I will keep company with my brother and Crow."

Nanny curtsied and left, closing the door after herself.

"She knows we're conspiring," muttered Crow.

"She knows a lot," said Hélène. "That's the problem when you get used to a quiet presence. They hear many things. But she won't say anything of us. She's a good friend."

Crow bit back the urge to criticize Hélène's use of "friend" towards a servant. He imagined the master and servant relations surely weren't this familiar under normal circumstances. He glanced momentarily at Roi before blinking the thought away.

Is our relationship normal?

Hélène reached over and lightly put her hands over top of Roi's, "I'm happy you and Crow get along so well." Then she pulled the supply list over. "Is this what you need help on?"

Roi gently took and placed the list aside.

"Actually, we'd planned to ask you about White," said Roi.

"Now I'm intrigued! White?"

"I was hoping for a more detailed version of your experiences with her? You're a good judge of character. Has she ever seemed selfish or upset by you? Are her actions genuine? How does she compare to the other-"

Hélène held up hands up, her left brow raised.

"Slow down! Her actions are always genuine and I suspect she cares deeply for me, almost like a grandmother-granddaughter relationship. If you're trying to find something bad on her, it will be tough... unless Crow knows something. Her worst fault that I can think of would be that she is inflexible to breaking any rules or expectations of the castle servants. I hope you don't plan on harming or exploiting the dear woman."

"She's a candidate for our cause," stated Roi. "I can't tell you fully for what, but there's an opportunity which she might be the best option to help us."

"Give her a series of tests, perhaps?" said Hélène.

"Discreetly, that might work. I can ask her questions about you, when you're with the beast, to judge her responses."

"And I can ask her questions to see how far she might go or do in certain situations," added Hélène. "Crow, might you ask her-"

Crow shook his head ruefully. "That would be too suspicious. We speak to each other rarely, never casually, and I'm still something of notoriety amongst staff."

"Then maybe you shouldn't be around at all, to avoid any affects your presence might have," said Roi, tapping his chin. "You could go do your flight around the castle routine."

"Patrol?" said Crow dryly. "How exciting."

"Right then, off you go."

"Now?"

"Yes, now!" said Roi, standing up and opening the window. "We've got limited time."

Crow restrained a smirk as Roi failed at attempting not to appear cold from the outside air gusting in. He transformed and took off, flying over Roi's head and causing him to duck.

Crow went on a brief patrol, but quickly snuck back into the castle and waited in the warmth of Roi's room. Taking on his human form, he paced Roi's room.

I doubt the siblings' questioning will produce anything new for me. White cares for Hélène, but to the point that she would conspire with us? I doubt it. The triumvirate will always place loyalty to the master before guests. But on the other hand, Roi is right. We need help.

"Done your patrol?" asked Roi, as he entered the room.

"You've been out in the castle for hours," complained Crow.

"I was snooping," said Roi proudly, "and then I went to have dinner. But besides that, Hélène feels certain that White could be convinced to not view our plan as any sort of betrayal."

"And you agree?"

"White is surprisingly hard to judge for me. However, I trust Hélène." Crow opened his mouth to object, but Roi continued, "Remember, we have a time limit. We have to make an abrupt decision of someone."

Crow ran his fingers through his hair, resuming his earlier pacing. He could feel Roi's eyes following him.

"Very well," said Crow, between his teeth.

Roi strode over and wove an arm around Crow's shoulder.

"Smile! This will all work out. Trust in Hélène. I filled her in on a few details, so she's going to help us convince White during tea. She's going to work her magic… figuratively speaking. Can I count on you for full support? White needs to see us united and certain."

Crow grinned, imagining White's expression at their revelation.

"I can do that."

"That's my black bird. I'll meet you in Hélène's room. I want to set up a couple things in here."

Crow reluctantly went on ahead.

Tea in Hélène's room after dinner was not outside their usual pattern. Crow nervously fiddled his fingers behind his back in anticipation as Roi arrived shortly ahead of White and Doe, who came with the trolley. White picked up the teapot, moving it to the table. Crow helped Nanny bring the cups and plates over. Hélène and White exchanged pleasant greetings as White placed a pot over the fire to heat up water, in case more tea was later wanted.

"Please, White, will you stay with me a while?" requested Hélène.

White blinked her elderly eyes a few times, "Is there something troubling you, my dear?"

"Not at all," said Hélène, smiling. "I just thought some wise insight would be a welcomed change for this evening, if you are not too busy."

"Never for you, dear." She signaled Doe to continue on without her.

Nanny pulled a chair out at the table for White as Crow walked quietly over to the door. He looked at Pont, who had his eyes closed. Crow believed he was sleeping this time, but still unsure, he shut the door quietly so Pont wouldn't hear.

As he turned back to the room, he heard White say, "Forgive me, but does this have anything to do with all the questions today?"

See Roi? You and Hélène underestimated her.

Roi smiled but held his tongue, leaning back in his chair.

"Indeed," said Hélène. "Nanny, please grab the paper I have over by the fireplace."

Nanny brought the paper delicately to Hélène. Hélène laid it down before White.

"What's this?" said White, picking up the paper. "I'm afraid my eyes aren't quite what they used to be."

"Allow me to summarize," said Roi, clearly attempting best behavior. "The fresher writing on the top is mine, listing the date that an important person is going to attend the heir of Lord East's party. This person themselves is on the account written below. Bertok Corvus."

White blinked a few more times, puzzled, and then put the paper down. "I'm afraid you have lost me."

"A man named Corvus knew the curse was going to happen before it did," said Crow as he headed back to the table.

White gave a slight jump at his voice, her head turning slightly to view him.

"And how might that be?" said White confused. "Wait now. Why is this even a subject? My dear, I'm afraid this seems a topic we should not be addressing."

"I disagree," said Roi, leaning forward. "Hélène still knows nothing of the words on how to break the spell."

White fought to maintain a neutral face, "And I suppose you do, young one."

Roi gave a grin that Crow now rather liked. But White did not find it comforting in the least. Watching her expressions intently, Crow could tell when all their questions earlier clicked into place for her.

"I'm incorrigible," said Roi. "When someone tells me I can't know something, I go find out."

"Nanny, Crow, I would hate to think you were involved in this," said White faintly.

Crow leaned on Roi's chair, "We all know which of us Roi acquired his knowledge from."

"And I pray Boar will not murder you on the spot."

"If he learns of it. But I don't think he'll know for a while."

"You can't expect-"

"Please listen to us," said Roi, his hands lightly covering hers in earnest, his eyes wide. White went extremely still. "We're trying to tell you that there might be another way. We, Crow and I, have found a possible alternative… and we can't go further without your help."

Roi said it quite convincingly, though Crow thought he overdid her importance.

"I'm sorry," said White, slipping her hands from his and standing up. "I'm afraid I must disagree with what is going on here. I must report-"

"Corvus wrote letters to a person in this castle, warning about the curse before it happened," said Crow, striding to stand between the door and White. "I've had them for a while, but never took action. We don't know who it was for, but we've tracked down the writer. This is the only time frame, the only chance we can find them. This person knows things. There's even a chance that they might be able to direct us to the enchantress and plead our case. A long shot, yes, but so is the main route if you think about it. We're just so used to this way that we're scared to break habit."

White thinned her lips.

"I will show you the proof," said Roi, standing. "If you trust us… if you trust Hélène, come to my room and I will better inform you."

"Please, White," said Hélène. "We've placed all our faith in you. You are the key, you can support or break us. Go with Roi and hear him out."

"And you?" whispered White.

"I'm the vanguard," said Hélène. "I continue the main route, whatever it is. Though I admit I've got a whiff of it. But as I have not been counted as void, it must not be quite right and I won't think about it. But Roi has been working hard. Please look at his work."

White looked more frightened than Crow had seen before. She clutched her pale hands in front of her and nodded. Roi pulled a wardrobe aside, revealing the passage that lead to Roi's room.

"You found it," said White surprised.

"You did know about it!" Crow whispered under his breath. He shut his mouth when he noticed White had heard him.

Roi sauntered over and offered White an arm, guiding her like a shocked grandmother through the passage. Crow stepped back to Hélène, whispering, "Two knocks means she's on board. Three, and we better be ready for Roi's and my execution."

"You can do it."

Crow followed after them. Roi had the letters laid out on the table. He seated White there and sat across, signaling Crow to hurry and sit as well. Crow sat on the edge of his seat, tense.

"I will hear you out," said White solemnly. She wasn't as grandmotherly without Hélène around.

Proving to be an excellent storyteller, Roi started from the beginning. Or rather, he began from when they stole from the library and disclosed right up to Crow's flights to Remais.

Crow scrutinized their wild card. White's face was not stoic. She even winced when Roi spoke of Wolf catching him. Crow had hoped to skip that, but Roi believed it would help get White's sympathies.

"This is quite the master plan, Monsieur Roi," said White when Roi finished. "Crow, I had no idea you were so double agent."

"I consider myself still loyal to the master," said Crow. "This is in his favor. I'm sure you can see that as well, after all of this."

"We knew we'd need the help of one of the triumvirate," said Roi. "Boar is… Boar doesn't like me or Crow, and seems too narrow-minded. Fierté is, well, loyal but insincere. I don't think he'd keep this secret like we're asking you, or might twist it somehow."

"And why was I chosen, then?" asked White. "Because you perceive me as weak."

"Hardly," said Roi. "You're the most human."

White straightened and smoothed her apron out while muttering flustered words. Her cheeks pinked and Crow had never seen her eyes shine so. Crow felt like kissing Roi in celebration, but he kept his face calmly on White.

"So, will you assist us?" asked Roi.

"With what you have shown me, and if nothing is being held back, I will for Hélène and the master," said White. "And Hélène is not informed of all this?"

"The beast can't punish her for what she doesn't know," said Roi.

White flinched at the word beast.

"I don't think we can inform the master," said Crow, to amend that. "Right now, his stubborn ways would condemn us for how we acquired the information, nor would he believe in us. I think he half believes he deserves this fate."

"Sadly, I agree," said White. "He is determined in his ways. Who else knows?"

"Just you," said Roi. "Nanny turns a blind eye, Hélène is on need to know, Crow is the runner, and I'm the researcher."

"And my role?" asked White curiously.

"I was thinking supplier or advisor," grinned Roi. "Because we need to figure a way to attend the party to meet Corvus."

"Finding this Corvus does sound like priority," said White, trying the name.

"Is it familiar?"

"No, but if I inquired to Fierté-"

"I tried already," said Crow. "He has no memory and he might get suspicious if you ask as well."

White nodded.

"So we need to figure out who should go," said Roi. "We've got only tomorrow left. Which is why we are being so forefront with you right away."

"You think you are the best candidate?" said White to Roi.

Crow snorted.

"And you think not?" observed White.

"He won't get away with sneaking out again," said Crow. "Pont keeps track of the door and tails him. There's the window, but Roi doesn't have wings and Wolf patrols the back especially carefully now."

"So you think a crow is a better choice for a party?"

"I just don't see how Roi could make it."

White went quiet, her lips pursed and her eyes distant. Crow almost feared she was entering a daze until she blinked and looked confidently at Roi.

"I think we can sneak you out," said White. "But what promise can you give that you won't betray us this time?"

"I can watch him," said Crow.

"Ah, but what's your guarantee your familiarity won't hinder your judgment?"

"Probably the same that you won't turn us over to the master," replied Crow. "And if I were to betray, I have no where I could go. The curse always pulls me back."

"I swear upon my life," said Roi. "You have my sister. Your staff has earned our respect. We will fix this."

White nodded, but wasn't fully convinced.

Nonetheless, she spoke, "Monsieur Roi will play ill tomorrow. Crow will tend to him, but will acquire the illness soon after, it being contagious. I will be the only one to tend the room after that, being the only one with clothes built against contagions. During this, Roi will head to the stables. Henry is on in his years, but he will manage a trip to the city."

"He's a horse," said Crow, noticing Roi's confusion.

"I thought only a few can leave the castle," said Roi.

"Henry's humanity is… fully gone," said White sadly. "He's only a horse now. We will have to procure some coin so that you can afford a horse back to the castle at the end of the outing. Henry, even in a horse frame of mind, will not be able to stay at the city. However, he will be able to find his way back home."

"I will fly along for as long as I can," offered Crow. "I'll also make a trip to Remais the following day, in case Roi need any help."

"Only if it doesn't harm you," said Roi, lightly touching Crow's shoulder. "I saw how hard those night flights were on you."

Crow bit his lip and looked away.

"When Monsieur Roi reaches Remais, he will need to find an inn and acquire an invitation and clothing; though the manner in how he gets these items will have to be worked out upon arrival," said White. "I will aim to place together a sizable purse this evening."

"That would be greatly appreciated," said Roi. "I think there's very little we can actually plan about the city portion. I was mostly worried about sneaking out of the castle."

"I've kept staff occupied to certain sections of the castle before," said White. Her eyes crinkled. "And, as you and Hélène have discovered, there are many passages. Tomorrow I'll suggest the best route."

"Thank you so much," said Roi, standing up and bowing. "I knew our faith was rightly placed."

"I think thanking me is a little too soon," said White, her mouth thinning again. "I will see what I can do, but I promise nothing."

"That's all I can ask."

"Well then, I best go collect the funds," said White.

Crow got up faster than White and raced over to the tapestry, holding it out of the way for White to exit back through Hélène's room. He knocked on the passage twice.

After a swift good night to Hélène, they exited into the empty hall. White stopped and turned to face Crow.

"Are you certain he won't take this as an opportunity to deceive us?"

He, as in Roi. White, I trust Roi ten times more than I trust you.

Crow shook his head, "He had a chance at the monastery."

"But that town doesn't have an adequate military. Taking this directly to court or the military in Remais might have a different effect. Magic is feared in these times, especially by the powerful. They associate the victims as needing to be rid of as well."

"I will be flying out to check on him."

"I want you to be with him the entire time, to keep an eye on him, and guide him. I get the sense that Roi will be hotheaded and indulgent to whim. That might not help with Corvus, who I assume to be the cool-headed sort. At least you're level-headed."

"I pushed myself staying out that far as I did. I'd like to, but I can't last."

"You are exceptional at resisting," nodded White. "Which means there's much going on in that head. Fierté noticed this. That is likely why he wanted you out of Boar's hands. Boar's managing is too rough for you."

Crow winced.

"I might have a solution," said White. "For now, keep Roi believing the main plan is his lone journey. I will let you know if my solution is possible tomorrow."

#

The next day, Crow reluctantly watched White slip something into Roi's drink during breakfast and three minutes later Roi was throwing up. Roi was sent to his room under Crow's care. On the bed lay a note.

Crow picked it up and read it out loud, "Henry will be ready an hour before sundown. I have arranged for all the servants to be occupied in locations away from the front of the estate."
He crumpled the note and threw it into the fire.

"Still have doubts about her?" asked Roi.

"This could all be too good to be true," said Crow. *But my respect of White has increased greatly.*

At noon, Crow faked illness in front of the staff when pretending to fetch food for Roi. White was around in seconds, ushering Crow to remain isolated with Roi in the guest room until they'd recovered. To lower their apprehension, Crow and Roi silently played cards until it was time for Roi to leave.

An hour before dusk, they took a secret passage White had revealed, following the winding paths until it led out to the yard. Crow took off in crow form, keeping an eye on the grounds, cawing to confirm it was clear for Roi to cross to the stables. Crow then flew back to Roi's room, entering through the open window. He changed into human form and nearly jumped back out when he saw White dressed in her contagion outfit: a white overcoat attached to a mask and hat.

"You're late," she said grimly.

"I wasn't aware you wanted to meet now."

"You accompanying Roi to the stables was not part of the plan."

"I played lookout."

"It was unnecessary. I told you I would occupy everyone."

"What if Wolf decided to take a stroll through the front? Can you really occupy Fierté or Boar? The master?"

White waved it aside, signaling him to sit. She removed the mask and sat across from him.

To Crow's bewilderment, she held out a spoon and had him hold it. She folded her hand firmly around his until Crow held it steady, then carefully dumped in it the contents from a small, embroidered pouch. Fine silver powder gathered in the spoon.

"Swallow this and then drink the water," said White, indicating a filled cup that sat in the middle of the table.

"That's, uh, that's metal," said Crow perturbed.

"Glass," White corrected him.

"Even better," said Crow sarcastically. "I always wanted small shards ravaging my stomach."

"Any of my girls would have taken it without question," muttered White.

"But I'm Fierté's, remember?"

"Are you still?" asked White. "Conspiracy aside."

Crow gave a "tch" sound and shook his head.

"It is enchanted glass- as powerful as the curse," stated White proudly. "While it cannot help against the curse, it will void it for a degree of time."

"How do you know this?" said Crow. "How did we get enchanted glass?"

"It was Master East's precious hand mirror that he gave into my care several years back when he couldn't stand watching the world anymore. It allows us to watch anyone like we are there, gazing through a muted window."

"Couldn't it have been used to find a way to alter the curse?" demanded Crow, and then he lowered his voice. "Track the enchantress or Corvus?"

"It is broken," said White regretfully. "He had thrown it at the wall and shattered it in frustration before placing it in my care. Most of the pieces have been rearranged, but you must know the person's true name and have met them in order for it to work. We don't know the enchantress' name. We have not met Corvus before. And we are forbidden from using it."

Crow looked distastefully at the glass.

"Won't it be noticed if a section is missing and ground into... this?" he lifted the spoon.

"Eventually. I've kept it locked up, so no one should notice for some time. Nonetheless, I don't want it mentioned."

"And how do you know this will work?" said Crow, wrestling with the thought of consuming the substance.

"Because Henry took some in his last days," said White. Her eyes grew wet, but her face remained stern. "We were desperate. We knew he would go soon anyway, so I took a sliver, ground it up, and fed it to him. We had an hour together when we were both human. And so we ground slivers every day for a month, just the two of us. Then he finally left for good. I wonder how much he knows he's helping us now by letting Roi ride him."

"How long will I have? What about my health?"

"The glass is magic, not actual glass," said White. "It will fade eventually, though you may feel a bit ill until it does. Remember, it only voids. This means your memories won't come back. I thought through everything carefully. This should give you two days. You leave together and return together."

Crow raised the spoon speculatively to his eyes, and then placed the spoon in his mouth, dumping the contents at the very back and swallowing. He began to cough from the dust fragments and grabbed the water. He drank the entire cup before stopping and attempting to clear his throat.

"You need to catch Roi before he leaves. Take the passage. You won't be able to transform and you'll soon feel the effects. They will lessen with time, but when you can't feel anything of it, its magic is about to end. Now go!"

Crow raced along the passage and onto the grounds. Half way across he stumbled, clutching his stomach. He grabbed onto a nearby statue, gritting his teeth together from the pain. White had assured it wasn't actual glass, but it certainly felt like there was glass in his stomach.

Time of the essence, Crow forced himself to stand up when the pain subsided to nausea. He made a few more steps before the need to throw up hit him fiercely. He leaned over a flowerbed, struggling to keep the contents down.

He remained in the pose until the nausea somewhat lowered. Then got to the stable before needing to stop again. Crow clenched his stomach. Taking in a breath to steady himself, he stepped inside, closing the door after him. A dozen empty stalls lined the stable with the largest at the very back opened. That was where Henry was kept. The old, hefty horse was in the aisle now, its thick brown coat shivering with the excitement of being ridden.

Roi was on the other side, tightening the saddle. He was humming a tune.

"The forest way should be clear for the next five minutes," said Crow, alerting Roi to his presence.

He removed his hand from his stomach when Roi stood on his tip toes to peer over Henry.

"Come to see me off?" he asked cheerfully.

"Actually, I've come to join you," said Crow, walking over to him like his stomach wasn't a bubbling miasma of magic glass.

"Excellent," said Roi, mounting Henry. "You can ride on my shoulder!"

He tapped his shoulder with his padded gloves.

Crow laughed and added, "In human form."

Roi looked puzzled. Crow grabbed the stable hand coat that hung unused. It smelt of mildew, but the woolen texture indicated it did a good job for warmth. He placed it on, leaving the front undone.

"White found a way to neutralize the curse on me for a few days. It freezes me as I am; I can't remember anything or transform, but I can travel with you as human with no side effects." Except feeling like he was sick at sea.

"She did magic?" said Roi surprised.

"She had… something in her possession of magical qualities that neutralizes the curse for anyone who consumes it. But best not to mention it."

"This proves she's on our side," said Roi with satisfaction. He eagerly lowered a hand to help Crow up behind him. Henry would easily be able to carry them.

"She's invested."

Crow adjusted himself behind Roi. Pressing against Roi's back as Roi moved Henry forward had the heat built up on his front and his uneasiness lowered.

Roi rode Henry hard. His pace to Remais was relentless, but still took twice the time it took Crow in flight. Roi talked a bit, but Crow mostly just listened or answered with one-liners, holding onto Roi with his eyes closed.

"You don't like riding horseback, do you?" Roi had commented to Crow's silence.

Crow grunted in response.

At the city gates, Roi let Henry free before entering the city. It was dark and nearing curfew, so they took to the nearest inn. Roi was asleep on the bed immediately. Crow, though weary, found he was too ill to sleep. He took one awkward position to the next, before finally passing out in the chair by the window.

CHAPTER 11 – SEEKING CORVUS

When morning came, Roi bought a loaf of bread from a local bakery. They sat silently on the bed, eating while dwelling in their own thoughts. Roi kept giving Crow sidelong glances. Crow found the food helped in keeping the illness down. He could now function without cramping, but he still felt sick.

"We'll split the tasks," said Crow, interrupting the pensive silence. "Your goal will be to acquire the invitations. I'll find appropriate outfits. If we can't acquire invitations, we'll have to try sneaking in as servants. Though arriving as guests is more productive."

"Agreed," said Roi. "And I'd make a lousy servant." He reached over and moved Crow's stray hairs aside. This time he smiled shyly, "It's strange to be with you outside the castle, but my freedom only confirms my feelings. I'm glad you came along. I mean, really glad."

A flicker of delight ran through Crow. He gave Roi a confident smile, which caused Roi to shiver. Crow quickly reached up and lightly felt Roi's forehead. Roi's eyes half-closed at his touch. His temperature felt normal, so Crow removed his hand, but Roi now had a dazed look in his eyes.

Crow frowned in concern, "Are you not feeling well?" *Because I should be the one shivering and wanting to vomit in a corner.*

"I've been restraining myself… but Crow- I really like you."

"Likewise," said Crow, running his hand through his dark hair and setting loose the stray ends. "It's hard finding good friends."

"No," said Roi, pinching his nose, then swinging his legs to the side of the bed to be nearer Crow. "I mean more than friendship. Crow, you need to know. My family, they estranged me because of my relationships. Only Hélène ever remained understanding. But for those who know me back home, they know I'm gay."

Crow was about to push it to the side, claiming he didn't care, but then he saw the worry in Roi's eyes. Roi took in a deep breath, releasing it nervously as his hands had become clenched. Crow reached out in concern, but froze when Roi caught his hand.

Roi chuckled warily. "At first it was just lust. You were someone nice to look at. Then I got to know you and it became a full on attraction. Crow, do you get it? You're driving me crazy because I don't know what you're thinking in turn. You avoid, ignore, or joke, but you never clearly confirm or reject. And sometimes, just the way you move or look at me... I feel like you're flirting in turn. I'm in love with you."

Crow dropped his remaining bread. It wasn't a surprise that Roi held some attraction, but the genuineness was not simply cabin fever or lust. He saw the tears of loving frustration in Roi's eyes and it left Crow feeling-

"I..." stuttered Crow. "I don't know."

Roi's posture lowered and a greater emotion of pain rose in his eyes.

Crow released a frustrated hiss and slid closer to Roi, forcing a smile.

He blushed fiercely as he stated, "But I won't deny, I've admired you when I thought you weren't looking. Clearly I wasn't as subtle as I'd thought." He felt some relief as the worried lines softened around Roi's eyes. But, the hope was back. Crow cursed himself. He didn't know how to manage these things.

"Roi... I'm not...," said Crow. "It's flattering, you can tell I'm all red, to know someone likes me in such a way, but I would not make for a good partner. Being cursed for the last ten years aside, I'm pretty much clueless on romance. I've never really found people attractive, I have trouble getting close to anyone in the first place, and I don't like to be touched."

"I touch you all the time."

"Yes, well, I was making an exception for you," said Crow. "I thought it was just in your unusual nature to touch people constantly."

Roi's grinning now! He was near tears a minute ago. What did I say?

"So you're new to all this," said Roi. "You're saying you at least think I'm good looking and that I just need to continue seducing you, albeit at a gentle pace, for you to eventually be mine."

"I am not saying that at all!"

Roi raised a hand, running it lightly along the top of Crow's hair, then down to Crow's eyes, pressing his fingers on Crow's lids to close them. Crow humored him.

"Keep them closed. I want you to try something," said Roi. "Consider this my incentive for today's task. If you don't want me to do this again, just let me know."

Crow held his breath. He heard the bed groan slightly as Roi leaned forward. He listened to the sound of Roi's breathing draw nearer. Then,

Roi's lips softly met his. It remained there for a second, then was gone. Crow opened his eyes.

"First true kiss?" asked Roi. "No objections?"

Crow glared. Roi laughed.

"Did you hate it?" asked Roi. "Or maybe you didn't experience it enough to have an opinion. Let's try again."

Roi leaned forward, catching Crow's lips and pressing more strongly. Crow tried to balance himself, but his hand slipped on the cover and he fell backwards. He grunted as his back landed on the hard mattress. Roi pursued, bringing his knees onto the bed and straddling Crow. He leaned down to kiss Crow for a third time.

Crow felt a warmth start up in his body. He felt a gentle suction as Roi's lips parted while still kissing, but Roi didn't go further. Releasing the kiss, Roi sat up. Realizing his eyes had closed mid-kiss, Crow opened them.

Roi tilted his head, "Well?"

"It… wasn't bad," muttered Crow. *Why do I sound like I've just taken a long flight?*

"From you, I'll take it as a compliment," said Roi, grinning as he got off the bed. "This should hold me over for now."

Acting like it was nothing, Roi pulled on his coat and pocketed the bribe money. He had an extra jump to his step and Crow couldn't help but feel amused amongst his mixed feelings. Roi was happy because of him. It left him feeling good. But as for all the rest, he still didn't understand what he should do, what he should feel, and what he should say.

Crow focused on remembering Remais' neighborhoods he'd flown over in crow form. He took to the streets. He had some money that Roi had passed to him, but it wasn't close to enough for getting the outfits they would need.

He found the tailoring road where a number of clothing shops were set up. They were finer wear, which made his own appearance stand out. His attire was not even that of a servant, but of a messenger. Most of the shops were labelled with words rather than symbols, to attract the educated and noble sides of population.

He passed a dress shop. A woman came out, proudly sporting a new winter coat. The gentleman waiting outside gave a whistle and the woman laughed happily. They proceeded to flirt and Crow realized he'd stopped and stared. Biting his lip, he focused back on the road.

He walked over to a hatter shop, considering it a good enough starting point. Entering through the door, he smoothed his hair back. While he couldn't pretend to be a gentleman, his carefully crafted composure gave him some level of trustworthiness.

"Can I help you?" asked the hatter.

"Yes, as a matter of fact. I've been sent to pick up a hat for Monsieur Goodwin of Beauclair. I've also got the coin for the fee. He'd been told it would be ready for today."

"Give me a moment to find the receipt," said the hatter, pulling out a box of hand written papers.

The hatter's fingers skimmed through the papers. Crow brought out the coin that would cover a couple hats. The hatter looked at the coin from the corner of his eyes. Unable to find any Goodwin for that day, he proceeded to look at the other dated receipts, in the case it was misplaced.

"Oh, he said he'd requested the receipt be kept in the hat's box," said Crow, as if he'd just remembered. "Sorry sir, I should have remembered that. Apparently he had a problem elsewhere last year with his hat being given to someone else, so he wanted to make sure it didn't happen again. I think that's why he went with your store this time. A good reputation."

"I don't normally keep receipts with the articles, but I'll take a look," said the hatter, turning and taking turns at opening the hat boxes on the shelf behind him.

Crow quickly grabbed several of the receipts in the box, hiding them in his pocket.

When the hatter was unable to find the fictional hat and receipt, Crow took his leave amongst the hatter's extreme apologies and promising that if Master Goodwin came in for a refitting, he would work on it immediately at a discount.

From this point, it became a matter of careful manipulation. He memorized the information on the sheets and started at the lower wealthy shops. He followed a routine; he'd been hired as scribe for a random name he'd memorized from the receipts, who wanted him to have fitting clothes and to put the cost on a tab. He took bits and pieces of the clothing and boots he acquired, choosing the pricier, matching portions, until he had a decent outfit. Something a young noble might have; not the richest noble, but one with some wealth. Best of all it fit him perfectly, since he got most of it tailored. He was dressed in the finery for the second round, going into new stores while claiming to buy some gentleman clothing for his cousin, and to put it under his Uncle's name. This time he used Corvus, half out of curiosity and half feeling the person could start helping right off the bat. He'd seen the man's wealthy accounts. Roi's clothes were not tailored, but Crow was quite pleased with the arrangement.

Upon returning to the room, it was still empty, so Crow took the opportunity to sleep. He hung the clothes on the chair and placed the boots under it. He lay down on the bed and was immediately asleep.

Crow woke up to Roi flicking him on the head.

"When I'm not around, do you just sleep?" asked Roi, then flashed an invitation in his hand.

"Just one?" said Crow with concern.

"For one plus guest," said Roi. "It's an invitation for a lower noble, so they weren't even bothered in being named on this thing, but the East seal is real, so this is an authentic invitation they should accept at the door."

"Did you have to use all the money?"

"Only to bribe a guard," said Roi. "I was talking with the servants at an estate whose masters were business associates with the Easts but were away on a pilgrimage. I didn't think nobles did that. Nonetheless, they had the invitation, but it was a waste. In trade for written work, they gave me the invitation."

"It couldn't be that simple."

"Pessimist. Well, I did have to go around talking up people to find out which families were acquainted with the Easts and then who might be away. My first try was an entire failure. And you know how long it took me to do their write-ups? I haven't had food since breakfast. Your castle has me used to three meals a day plus tea. My stomach is starving."

Crow fetched the remaining bread from the morning. He realized that despite Roi's lateness, it had not occurred to him to search for Roi; that Roi might have finally betrayed them. Looking at the man eat, slouched and relaxed at the edge of the bed, Crow felt a satisfaction that Roi was staying true to his word.

There's still room for deceit, but I trust him. Crow didn't know what to think of this building faith. *With the party drawing nearer, I have to rely on him. My stomach is twisted in knots, and not just from the glass. Corvus is our hope. We have to find him, or anyone who might be involved in the curse, or this is all for naught.*

A church bell nearby tolled nineteen times.

"The sun's starting to set," said Crow nervously. "We should go. The pre-party started already an hour ago. The main meal won't be for another hour, but we'll want to do most of the socializing away from the tables. And I'll be damned if we stick around for the dancing."

Crow gave Roi his outfit, and then changed in the far corner while keeping track of Roi from the corner of his eye. Roi's pants were slightly large, but the rest appeared to fit well. Crow felt pleased. He also felt confident, dressed in his own tailored outfit. There was a murky mirror hanging on the wall. He looked at his reflection, taking on a noble pose and placing on a confident smirk, making up the character that would be his disguise.

The lines around his eyes crinkled with mirth as he watched Roi, in the mirror's reflection, try to get a high styled boot on while hopping.

"Where's our servants to do this for us?" said Roi, finally stomping the boot on the bed to get it on. Crow burst into laughter. "Don't laugh. I have no experience with high society fashion."

Roi finished his getup by slipping the long coat over and Crow tried a whistle. Roi turned around, the coat billowing in a circle around him.

Like he has wings, thought Crow.

"You suit your clothes," said Roi.

Crow's tailed regency tailcoat was not as long, nor did it flutter with his movement. Roi walked over to Crow, tugging the floral designed vest and smoothing the dark crimson silk undershirt. Crow's heartrate started to increase.

"Likewise," said Crow, standing very still.

Roi ran his hands along the seams, like he was inspecting, but Crow suspected otherwise. A warmth started to grow in his belly. Roi was special and Roi liked him, more than as an ally, more than a friend... Roi had shown him his soul. Crow didn't want to taint it. He wasn't sure about it himself, but couldn't deny that his care for Roi was greater than simply his empathy for the two siblings.

Crow tilted his head sideways, frowning, "I still don't quite get you."

"You're going to give away your crow nature if you tilt your head like that at the party," said Roi, carefully placing his hand against Crow's cheek and righting his head up. Slowly his fingers drew across Crow's cheek, sensually, before leaving. "We need to look like important men."

Crow's legs weakened and his breathing quicken. His cheek tingled, like after the kiss. Any nausea from the magic glass was practically forgotten. *Is this what Roi was talking about? Is there more to love than just mentality? Is my body more certain than my mind?* Crow blinked out of his thoughts.

"Oh, you'll have the ladies heads turning at least," said Crow, adjusting Roi's button and standing back to nod proudly. "I have a ridiculously good fashion sense. Maybe I was a tailor."

"I could be butt naked and the men and women would be coming for a piece of me," said Roi, grinning arrogantly. Then, "But the clothes were a good choice."

Crow did a mock bow before turning towards the door. His hand reached for the handle and he paused, the importance of the evening weighing back down on him.

I can't step forward.

Roi's hand gently landed on Crow's shoulder.

"We'll find him," he whispered softly, his lips lightly touching Crow's ear.

Crow bit his lower lip.

Roi's other hand wound around Crow's chest and Crow felt Roi hold him close. He could feel Roi's heartbeat against his back. It was faster than normal. Roi was nervous, too.

"We can wait a half hour," suggested Roi softly.

"No. We have to use all the time we can get."

Then Crow felt a light kiss against his cheek, just passed his ear. It was light and quick, but he felt the warmth explode in his stomach, swelling right up into his chest. He relaxed slightly.

"You must have some magic," muttered Crow.

"No magic," whispered Roi. "Just me."

Crow leaned his head back onto Roi's shoulder, closing his eyes and enjoying the warmth. *If human contact like this has me feeling so wonderful, who knows what else the curse is keeping from me.* He took in a deep breath and then opened his eyes. Roi was looking at him encouragingly, trust and care in his gaze.

"We will find him."

Crow leaned off of Roi and blew out the candle by the door. They exited quietly from the inn and meandered through the dark streets. The soldiers near the estate area didn't give them a second look. Roi was ogling at the wealth they passed, but Crow was familiar with it all. He was thinking of all the work the servants did to keep these places looking so well.

Roi followed Crow, as Crow knew the way, though everything looked altered from a human perspective. The area at the heir's estate was full. Carriages were about, many with servants simply waiting or talking amongst themselves while their masters were inside. Some were going back to their masters' estates, obligated to return at a certain time.

Crow and Roi slipped through them effortlessly. At the gate, Crow held up the invitation envelope and the guard waved them through.

Crow picked up speed, his adrenaline increasing as they got closer. There were people hanging around the front talking and socializing, but the bigwigs would definitely be inside. At the doorway a footman asked for their invitations and Crow brought it out from the envelope, holding it loosely while gazing into the hall. He realized this made him look aloof, but this seemed normal to the servant, as he nodded at the invitation.

"Welcome to the party, sir."

Crow walked in as if it was something he did daily. But as they stepped through another double door at the end of the hall, Crow found himself standing straighter and his eyes widening. This was the vast hall, with a fountain in it, which Crow had seen through the windows. Stairwells rose on one side, leading to more of the mansion. There were several side doors, some for main use, others for servants. It was five times the size of Castle Cadrer. Everything was dripping in gold and the people were numerous, dressed in some of the most beautiful outfits Crow thought possible.

At the sight of the banquet table nearby, Crow was over and grabbing a cookie with a thick pile of icing on top. His intentions were to eat something filling to lessen the glass's nauseous effect, but as he bit down and closed his eyes, he found himself actually enjoying the devastating sweetness.

"We're on a mission you know," whispered Roi, having recovered from the initial awe.

Crow opened his eyes and saw that Roi was more amused than annoyed. He looked around at the gathering of people in the grand hall. The Lord Heir's home was huge. Finding Count Corvus would be difficult.

"I think splitting up might be best," said Crow.

"I disagree with that," said Roi strongly.

"Why? We'll cover more ground. We won't talk to him until we both get there."

"Why?" exclaimed Roi surprised. "Because, the Lord Heir might know you. The enchantress, if she's around, might know you. Anyone might know you. Count Corvus might even."

"If the Count does, that would be convenient. But you already confirmed that anyone at the castle is forgotten. No one will know me. And I especially doubt they'd remember servants."

"The curse makers might be exempt," said Roi darkly. "Just stick together."

Crow restrained a frustrated groan and gestured Roi to lead the way. They made their way around the room, mostly eavesdropping. When Crow finished his cookie, he took a cup of champagne from a passing waiter's tray with ease, holding the cup with few fingers. He knew he was enjoying the situation too much. Being out, free in human form, being served, too, it was all too good even for a day. Then he thought of White, the cost of this freedom, and he quickly sobered up. And it was in time, for Roi had taken to talking to a group of plump gentlemen, who seemed to be pressing too many questions of their own.

"Who exactly are you?" inquired the nearest gentleman.

"Roi Duval," said Roi. "I work for Count Corvus and I have a message for him."

"Why would a dressed up commoner be here?"

"Commoner?" said Roi, his voice taking on a tone.

"Please, we can see it in the unrefined way you speak and act," said the second gentleman. "You may work for Count Corvus, but I don't understand why or how you even got in."

"I brought him in with me," said Crow, stepping forward. He held himself with Master East's noble arrogance at the back of his mind. "He said he had a message for my uncle, had even borrowed some fancy clothes as an attempt not to disturb anyone, and now it appears he is being harassed."

He pushed in front of Roi, half shielding him from the oncoming slaughter he sensed.

"Count Corvus is your uncle?" said the first gentleman. Crow was ready for the laughter, but instead, the gentleman actually seemed to consider it. "I didn't know he had a nephew," said the gentleman after a few seconds of scrutinizing Crow.

Crow nodded his head, "I'm not normally in this province. But the message is of due importance and I can't supervise this messenger all night, so if any of you have seen my uncle, if you would kindly point us in the direction, my friend can drop off his message and I can be free to my entertainment."

"Last I saw, he was by the fountain," said the second gentleman, already growing bored of the situation.

"Thank you sirs," said Crow, giving a slight nod.

Roi took a humbled bow.

As they turned away, Roi drew close to Crow.

"As great of a reader as you are, your noble etiquette isn't up to par," grumbled Crow.

"But I have you here to make amends," said Roi, nudging Crow. "That was quick thinking."

"I had a few excuses lined up ahead of time," said Crow. He finished the champagne and left it on a ledge.

"You're lucky they didn't know too much about Count Corvus."

"I judged as much based on their expressions when you first asked," said Crow.

"And you were acting just like a spoiled nephew too," chuckled Roi. "Should I call you master?"

"Now who's not taking this seriously?" said Crow as they skirted around a large group of people and arrived at the fountain.

They leaned against the side as they studied the people around them.

"Over there," whispered Roi, leaning close to Crow's ear so no one could hear. Crow felt his breath tickle his hairs. He resisted the urge to lean in. "The man at the top of the stairs is the Lord Heir."

Crow looked and spotted a man in his late thirties, dressed with many fanciful ribbons and velvet, speaking with several bland men. Like the room, his outfit was fitted with many golden ornamentations. The man's face was similar to the portrait the beast kept. But this person looked older, sourer, and, even from this distance, Crow could read an unquenchable hunger in his eyes.

"I bet he is the brother," said Crow softly. "First born, felt threatened by Goodwin. Ambitious enough to turn to dark magic."

"Keep an open mind," said Roi. When the Lord Heir impatiently moved a woman out of his way to get down the stairs, Roi added, "But I think I agree with you."

Their eyes continued to sweep the room.

"Bertok!" exclaimed a female voice from the other side of the fountain. The higher than normal pitch made it stand out from the crowd. "How was your trip? Successful, I hope."

"Bertok Corvus," whispered Crow.

They couldn't see the woman or who she was talking to. He turned his head but the water and statues blocked his view. Crow started to make his way around the fountain. Roi took the other direction around.

"Monica," greeted Corvus, his voice deep and welcoming and with a slight rasp. "How is your husband?"

"Growing larger by the feast," laughed the woman. "It's hard to believe the two of you went to school together. He gets wider while you maintain your physique. I might have married the wrong man."

Corvus appeased her small talk with a laugh.

Crow released a breath as he got them in view.

Corvus and Monica, both handsome people, were facing each other like old friends. Corvus' black hair was pulled back tightly and hidden under a feathered hat. His height was on the taller side and his dark, almost black, eyes seemed to be calculating everything they rested on. Like most nobles, his skin was pale from the winter weather. He was dressed well, knowing the latest court fashions of blue, red, and purple, and at his side was a rapier. Though it wasn't uncommon, it still made Crow curious if Corvus wore it more than just a fashion statement. Both Corvus and the woman looked imposing enough to hold their own against the Lord Heir, or any other high end noble, with just words.

There was a business associate by Corvus' side, who seemed content to listen. Wearing a stylized blue hat over his mousey-brown hair, he had a slight scar on his lip and a trimmed mustache, appearing to Crow as middle class and an eager noble-wannabe.

Crow stopped several steps away in caution. Pretending to look through the crowds for someone, he carefully listened. They had to handle this carefully, but his eagerness had Crow's hands shaking.

"I hear you might be taking up the Lord Heir's treasury care," stated Monica.

"There has been some discussions, but nothing confirmed," answered the associate. "My apprenticeship under Bertok has been invaluable."

"Just take care not to bite off more than you can chew," warned Corvus lightly. "You've got quite the taste for property acquisition."

Their conversation switched fluently between small talk and a couple sentences of what Crow considered the actual passing of information they really wanted. The topics bored him, but he found the method of exchange fascinating.

Eventually Corvus excused himself from the company. Crow looked to see where he might be heading and felt his heart sink as Corvus deliberately stared straight at him. The man took direct steps towards Crow.

"Weren't you taught that eavesdropping is rude?" asked Corvus, stopping before Crow.

Crow felt his knees go weak and he leaned back against the fountain's edge, unable to bring forth the arrogant acting he'd managed with the plump gentlemen. Corvus waited patiently, but not at all impressed, his dark eyes taking in everything about Crow.

Crow opened his mouth but nothing came out. Panic bubbled within him. *He'll be able to deduce I'm a servant after one word!*

"He wasn't eavesdropping," said Roi, who came up from behind. He walked carefully around Corvus to stand beside Crow. "My friend is very shy and he wished to speak with you, but is scared of crowds."

Corvus raised an eyebrow and slightly turned his head, judging the excuse's plausibility.

"I don't know you," he said with certainty to Roi. Then to Crow, "Do I know you?"

"Possibly," said Roi. He nudged Crow and hissed, "Give him the letter."

Corvus' intensity was even getting to Roi, causing Roi to rush the encounter. Crow's hand scrambled into his pouch, retrieving the second letter, holding it out shakily to Corvus. With cat-like cautious curiosity, Corvus reached his gloved hand out and took the letter, his eyes still assessing them. Roi avoided the gaze.

"We want to know if you sent this," said Roi. "It's not recent. About a decade old."

"A decade," said Corvus, intrigued as he opened the letter swiftly. He hadn't needed to scan it more than for a few seconds before he folded it up and tucked it in his pocket.

Crow wanted to cry out and grab the letter back, but felt Roi grab his wrist.

"To whom did the letter belong?" asked Corvus, crossing his arms.

"I found it in my room," said Crow quietly. "But I don't know if it is mine."

"When did you find it and whose family do you belong?"

"I think, sir, that we would like your answer first," Roi dared to interrupt. "This should be more of an exchange than an interrogation, you see."

Corvus gave Roi a dangerous looking smile, before giving a slight twist of his head to signal it a tolerable agreement.

"It is in my writing and signature, but I don't recall ever writing such a letter. As for its contents, it invokes curiosity, but I shall be burning it."

"Could we get the letter back instead?" asked Roi, hiding his disappointment. "It was ours."

"It's more dangerous than a sword," said Corvus. "The accusations in this… If it is a forgery, it is a good one. Is it an attempt to blackmail me? Which brother hired you?"

"No one hired us! His home is cursed and this letter is one of the few things that could explain it. You have no idea what trouble we went through to get here. Do you think we'd pick a party to show this to you unless we were desperate?"

"A party would provide an adequate escape route, if whatever plan you held went wrong," said Corvus, unswayed.

Crow took in a breath, composing his nerves, and then spoke, "But you are aware that there was an enchantress in the area a decade ago."

Corvus' eyes flitted to Crow.

Crow's head gave his own small twist, "Ah, I see you were. Then are you aware of what she did?"

Corvus momentarily looked as though to deny it, then revealed a slight, congratulatory smile, "Your shy friend is observant. I won't deny I had some suspicions. But it's not wise to speak of magic in these areas or times."

"Please, could you at least tell us which brother was associated with her and where she went?" said Crow.

Corvus' smile disappeared and he frowned, studying Crow and ignoring Roi.

"Who are you?"

"The only name I know is Crow," answered Crow, finally daring to meet the man's black eyes. "My friend and I are trying to track this enchantress to get her to remove the spell on my master's castle. My master is stuck in the body of a beast. You are our only clue and much has been sacrificed to get to you."

Corvus looked stuck between disbelief and concern, then settled with coldness.

"I don't know what you're playing at, talking of fairy tales. If you're seeking dark magic for its uses, go home, boy. If its blackmail, I guarantee I'll get the better of it. The woman you claim you're seeking disappeared shortly after she did show at court. I don't know where, nor do I care. I avoid such things. As for the wisher, if the rumors at the time are true, it would be this party's host. Now, for that information, I don't want to encounter either of you again. If I do, it won't end pretty for either of you. Am I clear?"

Roi did a deep bow. Crow stood still as Corvus strode away, too upset to speak. The associate Corvus had been with earlier, who'd settled to watching a short distance away, did a jog to rejoin him, giving the boys a brief, sardonic look before putting pleasantries back on his face.

"Let's get out of here," whispered Roi, pulling Crow out of his angered state. "I'm pretty certain Corvus considers everything he said a favor to us. I think that he's more than capable of having us stabbed here and now, and getting away with it."

Crow winced and followed Roi as they dismally wove their way through the crowd.

"Well," whispered Roi, trying to cheer Crow up. "At least he confirmed that an enchantress was here. She probably changed form and fled. Rumors say enchantresses are wise to when people start to know up on them. I wouldn't be surprised if Corvus chased her out... like he's doing to us."

"But a decade gone! There's no way we can pick a trail up from that. We're back at square one. At least he could have described her."

"Well, he did confirm our suspicions of which brother," said Roi, stopping.

"I searched his office when I first flew here. I found nothing."

"But maybe he knows the enchantress' location."

"Why would he tell us?"

"Because I'm starting to think that the curse must have affected him too," said Roi. "Think, any normal human no longer remembers the castle. Even Corvus. The Lord Heir may be a high noble, but he's just as human as us... well, me. He might have forgotten what he had her do, but he might still know her."

Crow carefully looked around for the heir but couldn't spot him.

"He left with some woman a short while ago," said Roi. "I've been keeping watch of him. His wife is handling it pretty well, too."

Roi discreetly pointed to a beautiful, tall brunette who was talking with a few other women by a gold statue of a goddess. Her dress was a combination of white and green, emphasizing her womanly figure while not being too revealing.

"She saw him leave and pretended nothing was amiss," said Roi. "If I was her, I'd be on him right away. I don't get noble women."

As they walked past the wife, she looked up and she and Crow made eye contact.

Crow swerved in mid-stride and stood absolutely still, staring intently at her. Roi took a few steps before realizing Crow had stopped and impatiently cleared his throat to get him moving again. Crow ignored him. The wife spoke a few more lines to the women she was with, looked up at Crow again, sharing a much longer eye connection, and then she turned and left through a double set door.

Crow immediately stalked after her.

"What's the matter?" hissed Roi angrily. "We need to get out of here before Corvus decides to change his mind."

"She's her," hissed Crow. His confidence grew with every step. "Initially I just thought she was cursed or magicked. I can tell in her eyes… But when we looked at each other longer, I could tell she was something more. She knew I was here meddling."

Crow exited through the doors into a dim hallway. Gold and green painted leaves decorated the panels and ceiling.

Roi struggled to keep pace.

"Are you absolutely sure? Crow, slow down. We've lost her."

"No," said Crow, gritting his teeth. His fear was rapidly diminishing into anger, giving him foolish bravery. "She's behind that door."

Roi slowly approached, looking around for signs of anyone else. He hesitantly reached for the handle, freezing as a maid servant opened the door from the other side. Her brows arched.

"You're right, milady," said the maid. "There is a gentleman visitor." She noticed Crow. "Two."

From inside the room, Crow heard a lovely voice say, "Please invite them in."

Roi straightened and tried to live up to the 'gentleman' address. The maid gave him a suspicious look, but barely gave Crow a second glance as they entered.

The room was scented sickly sweet. Too much perfume for Crow's sensitive nose. The lady sat in the room's largest, royal blue chair, her dress's hems draped to the side. She leaned, her arm resting expectantly on the side of the arm chair. She signaled her servant to prepare some tea, but her focus remained on Crow and Roi.

"I am Lady Valvern East," said Valvern. "My husband's party is grand so I'm afraid I don't know all of my guests. Pray tell, young sirs, what your names are and please have a seat."

Is she playing us? thought Crow, his eyes narrowing.

Something about the woman, aside from the scent and beauty, seemed siren-like to Crow. Roi, giddy and unnaturally wordless, took a seat on a long padded bench covered with luscious purple velvet and embroidered with forget-me-not flower designs. His eyes were stuck on Valvern. Crow hated to imagine what Roi would be like if he didn't favor men. Crow refused to be enchanted. His curse, his anger, kept him safe from the drawing powers.

Valvern gave Crow a pleasant smile, tilting her head to signal he should sit. No sign of hostility. No sign of recognition.

Confused, he met her eyes again and felt like he was looking ages back. He released a breath like he'd been holding it under water. Looking to the ground, he blinked several times. Carefully, he sat on the same bench as Roi.

"Your names?" she inquired politely again.

Without hesitation: "I'm Roi Duval. I keep books and records in the town of Beauclair. It is an honor to meet you, my lady."

Valvern smiled, then looked at Crow, "And you?"

Crow would have liked to have given her nothing, but forced out as neutrally as he could, "I don't know my birth name."

"What do others call you?" pursued the lady.

"Crow."

The maid shook her head in disapproval at Crow's bluntness. Roi remained oblivious.

Valvern giggled lightly, with a hand pressed against her lips, "How suiting, young crow."

"And what other names do you go by?" Crow asked coldly.

"Well now," said Valvern, looking secretive in a girly sort of way. Crow wondered her real age. "There's too many to discuss here. But I think we both know what drew us together. And this young man… Master Duval, I'm curious how he is involved."

"Do you know where I'm from?" asked Crow.

The woman's eyes grew distant as she thought deeply for a moment.

She recognizes me as someone she's affected by a curse, but not which curse, realized Crow. *How many curses has she strewn!*

"Aha," she concluded. "The southern East estate."

Crow nodded, then said, "His sister is our current hope at eradicating your spell."

The maid made a sound indicating "Oh please", as she poured them tea. Crow's was half filled. Then the enchantress had her sit down. Crow felt his hairs stand on end as a glaze started over the servant's eyes.

"Careful when you speak of magic, young crow," said Valvern. "It's not a prominent topic of conversations these days." Then she turned to Roi, who after hearing his sister mentioned, was struggling against the effects the room had. "Mr. Duval, what is your sister's name?"

Crow wanted to shout at him not to say, but he felt an unsettling force nudging him to stay quiet.

I hope it's just my instincts and not her doing!

"Hélène," answered Roi. "Then… you're the… enchantress?"

Valvern gave another beautiful, full smile.

"Why did you do it?" persisted Crow, struggling not to choke up. "What did we do to you? Master Goodwin, if he did something, I can understand just cursing him… but so many lives are…. because of this."

I've always been a loner at the castle, but there were a few servant children I had occasionally interacted with. They were some of the first to go, along with the very elderly. White is the only main elder still holding strong.

"Did you come seeking me out?" asked Valvern curiously.

"Not directly," answered Roi, still struggling under the sickly room's spell. "We were seeking Count Corvus, hoping he'd lead us to you."

"Corvus!" said the enchantress. For just a second, her face revealed a more realistic expression by the furrowing of her brow, then it was back to pleasantries. "I wasn't aware he knew who I'd changed to."

"He didn't," said Crow. *I need to protect him. Corvus treated us coldly, but he had tried to warn someone at the castle. That counts as something.* "We were leaving unsuccessfully when you and I caught each other's eye."

"And what lovely, rare dark eyes you have," said Valvern. She looked at her maid, "Emily, please fetch Count Corvus."

The maid obediently left, shutting the door after herself.

"It's not that I don't believe you," said Valvern. "But I must admit I'm curious as to why you think Corvus stood a chance of leading you to me. But that fact aside, why were you seeking me?"

"My sister," said Roi. "She's being held captive as they try to have her and Goodwin fall in love."

"That is one way to keep a lady around, but only unsullied love will break it. You cannot use magic on the girl to make her fall in love."

"Captive," spat Roi, frustrated that the room was keeping his full emotions at bay. Crow watched his lips thin as he mentally worked against the magic.

"It seems my room's spell isn't quite suited for your friend," said Valvern to Crow. "Most men are groveling by now."

Crow couldn't restrain a smirk.

"Please undo the East spell."

"I can't. Enchanting is particular. When the deal is complete, it cannot be destroyed. That's why I always put escape routes in, just in case. Goodwin should be grateful his is rather simple compared to some."

"Oh yes, falling in love with a creature is oh so simple," snapped Crow. "Especially when you can't even look at it without cringing."

A short knock sounded at the door. Emily poked her head in and then opened the door for the count. Corvus remained at the door, his expression unreadable as he took a swift look around the room before his gaze rested on Valvern.

"Count Corvus," said Valvern welcomingly, her arms sweeping dramatically. "Please come in. Emily, close the door and wait outside."

The maid looked reluctant but a glaze came over her eyes and she obeyed. Corvus didn't notice this. He hadn't allowed his eyes to leave Valvern, yet he appeared unaffected by the room's spell.

"Please sit," requested Valvern, with extra sweetness she had not needed for Roi or Crow.

Corvus entered the room, but seemed to sit because he preferred to, rather than at Valvern's request. He sat as far forward on his seat without looking awkward, and sat so straight and alert that Crow concluded he was resistant to magic.

"I believe you know my new acquaintances?" said Valvern, gesturing to Roi and Crow.

Corvus didn't look at them, just grimly nodded.

He's figuring out the situation before he says anything, realized Crow. He looked at Corvus' pocket where the letter had disappeared.

"So, I'm curious," said Valvern. "Of what they spoke to you about?"

Corvus took in a patient breath then said, "I only just met them. Frankly, they were eavesdropping and I sent them away. I wouldn't advise their company, milady."

"Oh, Bertok, that doesn't quite match their tale."

Corvus' mouth twitched.

"She's an enchantress," Roi forced out.

Corvus let out a couple dry chuckles. Then, when seeing their expressions remain serious, he became very still as his eyes narrowed.

"It's not wise to associate with magic."

"I associated with it long before you were ever born," said the enchantress amidst laughing. "I am more magic than human."

Corvus' grip on the chair tightened, "You're Giselle."

"I was in a more haggard form when playing cat and mouse with you, Bertok. And I must say, it seems you got closer to finding out my dealings with East than I thought. Such a rare breed."

"Why would you tell me this? Do you intend to silence me?"

"No, I just wanted to know what you know. Relax, it's evident you were not suspicious of my current form."

"And now I know the truth," said Corvus. His hand hovered by his sword's hilt.

"Oh, I abhor violence. I'm strictly a deal maker."

"Then make a deal with me," blurted Crow.

"You aren't able to pay any price I want," said the enchantress. "Heir East paid me with unknowingly marrying me and never having an heir. Besides, young crow, you are already involved in a deal."

"As collateral," said Roi between his teeth.

"Can't we break it some other way?" asked Crow. "We can't have her fall in love with him."

"Oh, sweet thing," cooed Valvern. "There's always ways to manipulate love and still have it true."

"We know we can't use magic on her to make her fall in love," said Crow.

"We won't even if we could," added Roi roughly.

"You need to leave this land," interrupted Corvus, not caring for their conversation. "But first tell me exactly what mishaps you've ruined on it."

"What makes you think it's all bad?" laughed Valvern. "Besides, what threats you're collecting in your mind are wasted energy. You won't remember anything when you leave the room."

Corvus and Crow rose to their feet simultaneously.

"Witch," Corvus snapped fiercely. "I should have taken more action back when I suspected something. What did you do?"

Crow was impressed the man was taking direct action. *He'd seemed more the dangerous behind the scenes sort.*

"You would have become a casualty then," said Valvern.

"Give me one reason not to rid the world of your tainted form right here and now."

Valvern stood up fluidly. Her hands lightly touched Crow's shoulders before he could jump back. From her touch, the sensation of cool water ran over his body. His muscles relaxed, his cares disappeared. Valvern moved him in front of her. He stared forward, past Corvus, his mind blank.

"I'll go through a boy if I have to," growled Corvus.

"Oh," said Valvern, delightedly. "You are a cold one! You'd harm your second son to get to me?"

"Crow, get out of the way!" said Roi.

Corvus' eyes narrowed, "I have only one child."

"On the contrary," said Valvern. "Let me enlighten you while you're in this room."

Crow saw the blurred movement of the enchantress's hands. Through his foggy mind, he struggled to focus. Corvus reached for his sword, but abruptly stopped and stumbled back into his chair. His hands grasped his head, horrified.

"May the gods have mercy," said Corvus miserably. He looked towards Crow with an expression he hadn't shown before. "Corbin."

"A lovely reunion," said Valvern. "And he was your favored son as well. Sending him off to befriend Lord East's favored son. Such an ill choice of time."

Corvus gave an uncharacteristic gasp, "He hasn't aged a day. What have you done to him?"

"She's dazed him into obedience!" snarled Roi, ripping from the remains of the spell. "He'll turn crow!"

"It was a risk he took coming out this far," said the enchantress. "Besides, you're still here to carry your message back to the castle residents."

"If you don't free him, I will make you regret it," threatened Roi. "I will hunt-"

"Don't underestimate me, book keeper! I do as I will." Valvern smirked. "Crow... Corbin, be a gentleman and bow down."

Crow turned, smoothly getting down on one knee.

"Milady," he said softly.

"See? I can control anyone at my will, but I don't, because I am not so wicked as you wish to see me."

"No," said Corvus, his shock wearing off, but a dark anger setting in. "You don't do this because you must pay a price each time. When you make deals, the dealmaker pays the price of their request for you. I'm sure you pick and choose, so you get the most out of it."

"Bitch," snarled Roi. "Let Crow go."

"Gentlemen, losing your manners. You won't get anywhere like this." Corvus reached for his sword. "Stand down, Bertok Corvus, or I'll make him do worse."

"Crow," said Roi miserably.

Crow struggled behind the shrouds. His fingers twitched as he fought it. Little by little he raised his head.

"Oh, what a noble little fighter you are," said Valvern. She pinched his cheek. Through it, he felt another rush of cool liquid. Valvern looked over at Corvus, "He has enough of his father's line in him after all. Corvus' were always hardy against magic. Now Corvus, I thank you for helping relieve my worry. As for you, Duval, my advice is to not return to the castle, but then, as you seem close to your sister and struck with this boy, I suspect you will, anyway. I will allow you to remember this conversation. I personally won't interfere with that castle, for good or ill. It will essentially be like your visit here never mattered." Valvern stared into Crow's glazed eyes. He could barely register her. "Corbin, I will give a helpful hint. Love's magic is not a one sided affair."

"For all the good giving a hint will do," said Roi. "He'll be lost to perdu the moment we're out of the room in this state."

"Oh, Duval," laughed Valvern. "Have you not picked out my favored pattern to spells? It is why people who are loved are protected from so many small curses. Corbin's daze can be cured by love. A true gesture, such as a kiss. He'll still have the East curse, but he won't become lost with my late colleague's magic still dissipating in his stomach. But the act of kissing won't do alone. It has to be with love reciprocated from both sides. Family is one effective stream of love often overlooked." She stroked Corbin's cheek while looking at Corvus, then said, "Let's demonstrate, young crow."

Crow felt the magic compel him to stand and bring his face close to hers. He kissed her powdered lips, holding for a few seconds. Her hand stroked his back. When he released, specks of powder remained on his lips.

"See, no broken spell," said Valvern. "Not a hint of love. Now, parental love-"

Before Valvern or Corvus could react, Roi grabbed Crow, roughly turning him around and pushing him into Valvern's empty chair. Holding both wrists down on the arm rests, Roi gently, compared to his other actions, pressed his lips against Crow's. His grip on Crow's wrists tightened and the kiss became stronger and more passionate as Crow didn't respond.

A light of pleasure erupted at the back of Crow's mind.

Roi is kissing me. I'm not sure why this is happening, my mind is too muddled, but this feels right. I want this. I want him.

Crow leaned into the kiss. He nearly pulled away when Roi's tongue moved in, but Roi pushed harder, preventing Crow from pulling back. Crow simply allowed the pleasure of Roi's kiss, closing his eyes and enjoying the new sensation.

When Roi pulled back, his hands still grasping Crow's wrist, he whispered, "You back?"

"Only to tell you to learn to kiss properly," said Crow slightly slurred, too embarrassed to admit how wonderful it had been.

He opened his eyes as he remembered the situation they were in. He licked his swollen lips nervously. His gaze slid past Roi to Valvern. She now stood by the door, looking surprised, but amused. Corvus just looked confused and empty, an expression that didn't belong on his face.

Crow gave a little struggle and Roi released his wrists apologetically. He gave Crow a helping hand up.

Valvern opened the door behind her back, "I suggest you boys leave these grounds immediately. I'll be having the guards searching for two young trespassers in five minutes. I, myself, shall be disappearing in a few nights. I've played this role far too long anyways. Best of luck on your quest. I truly hope you find a way as quick and strong as your own love."

Roi and Crow raced to follow her out the door, but as they stumbled into the hall, it was empty. The trace of perfume was gone.

"We need to get out of here now," said Roi, worried.

Crow looked back in the room at Corvus. His father.

"We don't have time," said Roi urgently. "We can barely make it out in five minutes!"

Roi grabbed Crow's hand and pulled him along the hall. Crow pulled out of his grip but followed. The image of Corvus was stuck in his mind. Left alone in the room, frowning in confusion at why there were tears on his face with the feeling of great loss- Corbin Corvus once again forgotten.

CHAPTER 12 – DISCREET SERVICES

Sneaking back to the castle proved easy enough. Crow believed White was still directing the servants to be away from the areas they needed to cross. The last of the enchantment from the mirror's glass had worn off shortly after leaving the heir's estate, having been consumed by the enchantresses' magic. Crow had ridden Roi's shoulder the way back, fighting the daze.

They said very little. Crow could see Roi holding back on several things, aware that Crow could not speak normally until they got back to the castle.

When they arrived at the passage's exit in Hélène's room, she was not there. The sky was getting dark, as they had stayed at their hotel until the next day to leave, for Roi needed a horse, so they concluded she was still at dinner. They crossed over to Roi's room, where Crow changed back to his human form and they both sat down at the table and wrote their own version of the estate visit, worried the enchantress may have messed further with their minds.

Crow wrote his bluntly and to the point, while Roi's appeared to be a novel. They didn't share the versions until they were done. Crow then bundled them up, binding them with string. He would deliver them to White tomorrow.

Exhausted, Roi fell asleep on top of the covers and Crow, in crow form, slept above him on the head board.

The next morning, Crow found White in the staff mess hall, where several members were eating. She placed on an excellent look of concern as she stated, "Crow, dear boy, you should not be out of bed."

"Like I'd told you last evening, Madam, I am feeling much better. I really must return to my duties. But I thought these poems you leant me would best be returned."

White accepted the papers, all the while lecturing him on taking better care of his health. Crow bowed from the room, seeking to check on Hélène on Roi's behalf. Roi figured he best stay ill a little longer, both for the welcomed privacy to plot uninterrupted and to avoid suspicion if both of them recovered at the same time.

His check of Hélène was brief, but he could see the relief in her eyes when he informed her they were recovering. To keep up appearance, Crow took a patrol, checked in with Fierté, who was more concerned about not hearing from Crow during his illness than about Crow's wellbeing, and then returned to Roi, where they discussed the outing.

Dinner was delivered at the door by Doe. Roi had quickly slipped under the covers before Crow opened the door and took the tray from her. When Crow reached for the usual napkins used by Roi on the cart, Doe insisted on him taking the older napkins. Crow immediately unfolded the napkins after the door was closed.

Inside the last napkin was a message written in White's cursive writing. *1 hour after dusk, meet me in my office. Tell Pont you're taking Roi for medication I've put together.*

Crow doubted Pont would accept the lie, but the cat merely yawned at Crow's brief explanation as he moved a towel-wrapped Roi from his room down to the basement. White's office door was open and she was sitting there waiting for them. The room was cozier and simpler than Fierté's or Boar's. Their written notes were spread along her desk.

Crow shut the door and Roi dropped his recovering illness pose.

"Bless your souls," White greeted them. "You got something."

"Did you figure out the hint the enchantress gave, as well?" asked Roi.

"What?" asked Crow, feeling left out. *Roi didn't tell me the enchantress' specific words.* "Forgive me, but some of us were muddled in a spell while she said it."

"She ranted a lot, but there were two lines she emphasized," said Roi. "The second didn't really sink in until my dinner."

"The enchantment words we wrote down those years ago are similar," said White. "But all we had was a mix of the majority's jumbled memories. If we'd remembered the specifics, perhaps we'd have solved this sooner. I suspect the words you wrote her saying, Monsieur Roi, are word for word, knowing your keenness for language."

"Or she had intentionally told you a more generalized clue at the time to mess with you," said Roi. "It's not beyond her character. Allow me to clarify what I've concluded. The first emphasized point was that both sides must fall in love."

"We are aware of that," said White. "It's not the master falling in love that's the concern."

"That's not his point," said Crow, catching on based on their discussions earlier. "Love is the key word. There is no mention that it has to be romantic love. Didn't she also mention something about parental love back at the estate? And why stop there? Love could go all the way to loving a hobby, a toy, a pet!"

"And there's no mention that this love can't be a fleeting moment; nor with external party tricks."

"But it must not be confused with lust," warned White. "And it still must be the genuine person they love."

"Don't worry, I have no intentions of tricking my sister, nor would she fall for any parlor ticks. What I was getting at was the specific wording the enchantress used, 'You cannot use magic on the girl to make her fall in love.' This is the second emphasis. There's nothing against using magic on the beast."

"Obviously not magic that would directly press upon Hélène as a result," said Crow. "But one that would affect the master in such a way that it would indirectly affect Hélène... in a non-magical conclusion... if that makes sense."

White's lips thinned as she looked at them severely, "So you are proposing we enchant the master. Play with fire. Even if that were acceptable, I wasn't aware you two were trained magic users. Magic of any sort is no longer common. Any magic workers are secluded far away or shy. And if you are implying something that is pre-enchanted, I have not heard of anything found in four decades."

"The mirror-"

"Does not nullify," said White. "It merely freezes the consumer's current state."

"This is all in theory," stated Roi. "But if there was a spell that would help, would you use it?"

White was silent as she gazed down at her hands.

"It couldn't hurt to try finding something," muttered Crow.

"I must reluctantly agree that your drastic measures may indeed be the only hope," said White. "But this does not mean we do not continue the search for non-magic alternatives."

"Is it at all possible," said Roi, "that the rules can be bent, and I can have access to that library?"

"With the master's good mood in the last few days, I might see about some exception. But it would have to be under my supervision, and with my schedule, it would mean at this hour."

"Night is fine," answered Roi. "Why is the beast in a good mood?"

"Hélène has been playing her role vigorously," said White. "I dare say in effort to keep everyone's thoughts on her rather than lingering over you."

Roi grinned proudly. Then he fiddled with his clothes, trying to maintain some humility in White's presence.

"Now, I think our meeting best be wrapped up," said White. "I intend to reread your experiences tomorrow in search of further clues."

She worked at gathering the sheets together.

"What's amusing?" asked Crow, noticing Roi's grin become a full-fledged smile as he fiddled with the cuff of his outfit.

"It's just occurred to me, I'm wearing your clothes. A little tight, but fits well enough. Shouldn't you start wearing your old things again? In fact, you shouldn't need to be a servant anymore! As a count's son, you're more than entitled to enjoy your remaining days at the castle in the library."

"It won't happen," sighed Crow, as White shook her head.

Roi's smile disappeared.

"There's no proof of Crow's nobility at the castle and we can't inform people how you have acquired this knowledge," said White. "It would not even be wise to fake documents to alleviate Crow of this position."

"Corbin," corrected Roi firmly. "And I'm sure now that we know what to look for we could find proof somewhere. He's been mistreated all these years."

"It's none of the servants' fault," muttered Crow. "We all forgot."

White took in a breath, "We must work discreetly, and this requires Crow, not Corbin. I must request you keep this knowledge to yourselves for now."

"I'll think about it," said Roi, giving an untrustworthy grin before opening the door and stepping out. He let out a yelp as he nearly stepped on Pont waiting outside. "When did you get here? I'm still too sick to deal with you. I swear, do anything unexpected and-"

Roi's voice drifted away as he headed back to his room, Pont following him.

"Do you understand?" asked White, when Pont was out of earshot.

"I wasn't expecting any changes," replied Crow. "It is nice to know, though, why this role never felt right."

"Well then, let us get a head start," said White, wrapping her evening shawl around her shoulders.

"A start of what?"

White directed him out and they passed a few servants in the hall.

"Hélène has lost a charm in the library today. I need to find it and I believe crows are good at picking out shiny things."

White opened the library door with a skeleton key. The ever-burning fire was used to light candles to read the spines of the books further back.

White had them turn books that addressed anything that involved magic or might help them upside down upon the shelves, this time not limiting their focus only on curse-breaking. The hope was to research now to increase the reading time tomorrow.

They stayed late sorting the books. White was a slow reader, and Crow simply didn't know if his choices were good or not. He suspected Roi would have better ideas.

It would help if I wasn't having difficulty focusing on task, thought Crow. *Remais. Bertok Corvus. I still have no old memories of him. I hate the conflicting feelings I'm having. It's a relief to know my name, but I'm feeling apathetic towards it all. I suspect I shouldn't be. Even Roi made a big deal of my identity. I wonder if there is anyone else with a significantly misplaced role at the castle.*

#

The following morning, Crow decided to postpone morning patrol. Nanny had given him a note telling him that Roi wanted to meet him in the ballroom for breakfast, rather than the bedroom.

Roi was already ten minutes late, much to Crow's irritation.

Crow sat in a spare chair in the corner of the ballroom. Tired, he rested his head on his arm that in turn rested on the handle. It had been tempting to stay in crow form, but he suspected Roi would want him human.

Fierté entered the room and stopped to talk to a couple servants prepping the table. Crow watched absently until Fierté turned and walked over to him. Crow nervously perked up, but was unable to brush off his weariness.

"Morning."

"Morning, sir," said Crow.

"Taking to sitting in public, in a room our guest will shortly be attending?" asked Fierté, emphasizing sitting.

Crow felt relieved it was just a reprimand. He put his hands down on the chair arms, using them to push up.

"Corbin!"

Crow's heart jumped, and his and Fierté's heads swiveled towards the doorway to the main hall. There was a brief pause, then Roi strode confidently into the room, looking back and forth, until he spotted Crow and Fierté.

"Corbin!" shouted Roi again, walking towards the cringing Crow, barely showing any heed to Fierté. "I thought I'd told you yesterday to meet me by my room door!"

"Corbin?" asked Fierté curiously.

"Ah, good morning, Fierté," said Roi absently, giving the head servant a nod.

"Why are you calling him Corbin?" pursued Fierté.

Crow inwardly groaned and lost his will to stand, flopping back into the chair. He saw Fierté's eye twitch, but Crow was too pissed at Roi to care.

"That's his name," Roi bluntly stated, staring Fierté straight in the face. Fierté blinked slowly.

Crow cleared his throat, desperate to amend things, but Roi continued, "We figured it out yesterday."

"Figured out how yesterday," said Fierté. "...Crow?"

"Corbin," correct Roi. "You see we were-"

"Bored in his final stage of recovery," said Crow, giving Roi the dirtiest look he could muster, glad that Fierté wasn't focused on him. When Fierté did turn to look at him, he continued with his face more innocent. "He decided to make it his mission to find what my original name was. He suffered me through lists of names until the Cs. Claims I reacted best to.... this 'Corbin' name he's been calling me since."

Behind Fierté's back, Roi narrowed his eyes while grinning impishly. Fierté gave a click with his tongue.

"Monsieur Roi," sighed Fierté, turning back around to Roi, who changed his face back. "I'm afraid there is little proof that that is in fact Crow's name. So please, respectfully call Crow by his proper name in public and before others."

Crow gave Fierté a bow, hinting a thank you in it. Fierté noticed Crow glare at Roi but misinterpreted and chuckled, thinking he'd helped Crow out. He had, to a degree. Crow did not want his original name being flung about here. They still didn't know enough.

Fierté excused himself and headed towards Pont, who had taken up post at the door, cleaning his paws. Crow knew he would double check with Pont what Crow and Roi had been up to yesterday. Pont's limited knowledge would put Fierté at ease.

Roi leaned onto Crow, like he was going to goof around further, but whispered seriously, "He knew that was your name."

"What?"

"I watched his response," added Roi quickly, before backing off, a grin back on his face and hands up in surrender. "Okay, okay, I'll stop bothering you. But you owe me another game of Rindles in my room after breakfast. Mr. Touchy."

Crow moved to stand back to the wall, his mind racing. *Roi must have come up with this test last night on his own, probably thinking of this as a side project, a presumed favor to me. Fierté gave some reaction Roi was looking for. But it doesn't make sense. Fierté has lost his memories too. Only his journals-* A bitter taste rose in

Crow's mouth. *I should have suspected this. With his vast collection of detailed accounts, Fierté could have relearned everything, known everyone's identity. It has always been odd that he demands his notes be private; severely claiming they were for memoir and archive's sake. Fierté knew I wasn't a servant all along, that I was a Corvus, and had simply played none the wiser. Perhaps that is why Fierté kept his hands off me all these years. But with everyone slowly going over the edge, so many lost, Fierté is losing his self-control.*

Crow realized he was glaring towards Fierté and quickly looked away, calming himself. There were more important things to focus on right then. It was better Fierté continued to think Crow was none the wiser.

Roi wolfed his meal down, then requested a servant take him to White. Crow was debating to follow or go on patrol first when Fierté gripped his arm. Crow resisted yanking himself free.

"Go with him," muttered Fierté softly. "I pray I'm wrong, but I suspect White's up to something. Has she said anything to you? Have you noticed anything out of ordinary?"

"No sir," said Crow. "He's just seeking her out for medicine."

"Alert me to anything."

Crow curtly nodded.

"And Crow," said Fierté, releasing him. "Don't forget your alignment."

Crow raced to catch up with Pont, deciding he would definitely not join in on the discussion. It would likely be behind a closed door and if Pont sent word to Fierté that Crow was privy to it, Crow would have to tell him something.

At White's office, Crow settled next to Pont, loudly complaining about not wanting to watch Roi strip for his medication so that Roi caught on and closed the door after himself.

#

During patrol, Crow found a group of desperate poachers in the forest. Crow followed them through the day to make sure they left without incident. The poachers eventually gathered their traps and left as the sun set. Crow gave one more sweep of the land before returning to the castle.

He encountered Roi on his way to the library.

Roi greeted him with a side hug, which Crow returned before Pont rounded the corner.

Crow nodded to Pont, then tried the library door, grateful that it opened with ease. He held it open for Roi to pass through, then closed it before Pont could even consider entering the room. The roaring fireplace would be a temptress to the cat who normally didn't enter the rooms after them.

The room was empty of any occupants. White was not yet there.

Crow eagerly hopped over to the fire place, where he hunched down and held his hands out near the flames. Roi crouched down behind and wrapped his arms around Crow. Crow released a sigh as warmth from Roi heated his back. He leaned his head back, letting Roi's neck warm his ear.

"With you and all these books, I could lose myself in here," said Roi.

Roi's voice sounded deep and vibrated against him. Crow liked it. He remained still as Roi nuzzled against Crow's cheek, tickling him with his hair.

"Did you want to start without White?" asked Crow, against his wishes to remain like this.

"I'm quite content to wait," murmured Roi. Crow chuckled as Roi struggled to finish his sentence when Crow dared to brush a caressing hand along his face. "I didn't get you to myself at all today. Affection is overdue."

"Fine by me."

Crow closed his eyes and leaned in closer, allowing Roi to better wrap his arms around him. Like this he felt happy and safe. He didn't have to keep his guard up. He could let his thoughts loose, drifting and dreaming.

A swift knock on the door tore Crow from his doze. He leapt to his feet, leaving Roi sprawled from the sudden departure.

White entered, the door closing behind her just as quickly. She spared Roi no second look. She immediately took charge.

"We'll divide roles. Crow, you will be half on door duty, half reading." White handed Crow the fattest book, which Roi eyed hungrily. "We will read broadly in hopes that something will come together. Monsieur Duval, I will have you reading through all the books mentioning magic."

White went over the shelves again, humming a lullaby as she hunted for any books they might have missed turning yesterday.

When the grandfather clock in the hall chimed midnight, Crow realized he'd been staring at the same page, on the East health history, for half an hour. He plunked the book down and raised his arms, feeling satisfied as little pops sounded at his stretch.

White had fallen asleep in an armchair by the fire, looking even older and worn.

Crow walked over and tossed a log onto the low flames. He leaned on the table where Roi had seated himself directly on the table. His legs were crossed as he leaned down to read the tenth book from the stack of twenty he'd picked from.

"Anything?" Crow's voice rasped into the quiet. With only the crackling of flames and the turning of pages heard for hours, his voice penetrated the room.

Roi blinked fiercely, drawing back from the written world. He looked owlishly at Crow and Crow gave a tired smile.

Taking in a deep breath and rubbing his face, Roi leaned his head back and groaned, "Nothing."

Crow looked at the page left open. In the right hand corner, an ink drawn scene depicted several plant leaves.

"Is this on alchemy?" asked Crow, flipping the book to see the cover.

"Ancient magic," groaned Roi. "Stuff witches and demon worshipers these days scoff at. Most of it is actually just using herbs for basic illnesses. Laughable, really. It's not magic."

"So magic didn't really exist back then," exclaimed Crow.

"Oh, it did," said Roi, righting himself up and grabbing a book from the been-read pile. "It's just that the really magical stuff no one attempted to record until much later. You were lucky to find a literate king in those days. Word of mouth passed it along, but by the time they got around to recording it, half of the magic was forgotten. The common stuff, the herbal stuff most medicine women in villages could manage, was all that was left. I actually suspect this enchantress, at least her magic, is ancient-based. There were some interesting pages towards the back of this one, I suspect copied from an older manuscript."

Roi flipped through the pages with scholarly intent.

"Wait, what's that?" asked Crow, flipping the pages back.

"Lycanthrope," said Roi. "It's a spell said to reveal their true nature, so they couldn't hide as humans. That was back several centuries when-"

As Roi stopped, his eyes started to dart back and forth on the page. His fingers twitched as if flipping the pages of an invisible book. He reached for the pile, tossing several books aside to get to a thicker volume.

Roi's mouth moved slightly as he flipped recklessly through the pages, stopping a quarter way into the book. He placed his finger as a marker and then continued to flip, stopping at a page that predicted planet alignments and moon cycles. Roi folded the page, then flipped back to the finger bookmarked page. The book was held up, revealing the lycanthrope page again.

Roi began to mutter words under his breath, "...pinus conis, taraxacum folia, tussilago farfara,..."

"Plant names?"

Roi nodded approvingly, "Fancy names for pine cones and dandelion leaves. Then there's mention of symbols drawn in mouse blood, a string of hair or drop of blood of the target... It's actually rather a disgusting concoction."

Crow moved over to White, taking her hand and gently shaking it until she woke.

When his listeners were ready, Roi laid the books out before them on the floor. He pulled an herb book from the pile for later reference.

"I've figured a way to use an ancient spell used to show the true form of beasts hiding as humans. I think this spell would have the same effect on a human hiding as a beast- intentionally or not. The list of ingredients are a ridiculous two pages long and appear to require two days to make." White picked up the book and started to read the list of ingredients. "Fortunately, most of the ingredients are easily attainable. This spell also requires certain positioning of the planets. First, the moon must be over half shining, but not full. Easy enough. And a planet must be blocking another in line for earth. There's one three days from now, and another next month. You won't get angry if I smuggle the herb book out? I'm going to look up their modern names tonight in my room. I can do further research on the spell portion tomorrow night. If we want to make use of this first alignment, we should gather the ingredients as soon as we can."

"I will be able to acquire most of these ingredients well enough," said White. "Crow, tomorrow I will need you to find pine cones from the top of a tree, preferably dry, birch bark, and water from a fresh stream." White pursed her lips. "You will also need to catch ten mice. I believe I won't need to remind you to make sure they aren't staff members."

"Mice?" said Crow. "I've never caught a mouse before. I've never tried."

"Perhaps this will be an opportunity to test out your crow instincts," said Roi.

"My crow-self is a scavenger," said Crow. "Can we use already dead mice?"

"We will have to bring in a third party," said White, placing the book down. Roi and Crow exchanged reluctant looks. "I know what you two are thinking, but we are too short in time to be picky and it is the blood of the mice that we require. We need a cat. One that won't eat the fresh prey it catches."

"Pont," said Crow. "You can't be serious. I can give you a very long list of why we can't trust him."

"And I can give you a list of why we should," replied White, puffing up her chest. "He has a grand resume for rodent catching. Pont is well known to be bribed and he has held his tongue for me once in the past. He is a man of his word, though you need to listen to how he phrases his words carefully. And if we phrase things carefully to him, he will be none-the-wiser to our full plan."

Roi looked towards Crow with a slight furrow to his brow, then shrugged apologetically, "We don't have the time for you to learn how to hunt."

"Fine," snapped Crow. He crossed his arms and looked away.

White licked her lips nervously, "Crow… I would like to task you with bribing Pont. If I approach him, it would appear too suspicious."

Roi noticed Crow stiffen.

"I can do it," offered Roi.

"No," said Crow. "You still don't know him well enough. Merde. I'll do it. But if hell rains down from this, I'm not taking the blame."

Crow stared directly at White. White subconsciously touched her neck.

"On my head, then," said White. "Only reveal what's necessary to get Pont to hunt the mice. Promise him anything within my range to bribe with."

Pont, per usual, was outside Roi's door the next morning.

Catching Pont's attention, Crow opened a door a few rooms down and indicated the cat enter with him. Intrigued, Pont surprisingly gave up his post. He transformed into his human form, faking a disinterested expression. He closed the door, sensing Crow's anxiousness.

"I've been sent to offer you a task that requires discreet services," said Crow. "And of course, you will be nicely rewarded."

"I imagine this is for Madam White?" said Pont. "Strange that she enlists for something requiring secrecy. Suspicious."

Crow didn't bother denying White's involvement.

"Ten mice," said Crow. "A few more would be good, though, as extras."

"Mice," said Pont dully. "Is there a rodent infestation in the women's ward?"

"It doesn't matter where you acquire them," said Crow. "If dead mice are more convenient, make sure it's not dried bodies you bring. You need to catch them today."

"Fresh sheets, pillow, and a quilt," said Pont. "That will cover the mice. As for my secrecy, which I assume she does not wish the remaining triumvirate to know, a future favor owed."

"Done."

"So this all has to do with you meeting behind closed doors with White," said Pont. "First the office, then the library, and now, it seems... I don't really know what to make of it. Magic, I presume, since your enchantress discussion."

"You heard us that night at the door?" asked Crow darkly. His fingers furled into fists.

Pont looked at his hands, a villainous smile forming. He leaned against a table and looked back, as if surprised at its existence. He seemed tempted to lie on it.

"I heard bits and pieces."

"So you knew- know what we are doing? You seem well versed in blackmail."

"You have no idea the number of scandals I'm privy too," smirked Pont. "But I don't blackmail unless it's necessary. Too much work, you see.

And, you say it like you're up to something bad. I did not inform Fierté of anything aside that you and Roi went into White's office for a period of time longer than it should take to administer medicine, with the door shut. Fierté didn't even questioned whether I held anything back. Of which, you should be wary of appearing with White so often. You know how the triumvirate don't like us associating with the other heads too much. And you must remember that, even throughout this apparently noble pursuit that rises above regular rules, we are Fierté's. I won't take any action until you can ensure that my part in this is unmentioned. Should any of this get out-"

"Done easily enough," said Crow. "Acquire the body count and we won't ever credit you for it."

"Make sure the new sheets brought to my quarters are fresh," said Pont, changing back to his cat form as he headed out. "And keep the rebellious one in his room, so my missing presence for the next couple hours is not heeded. I will be at the barn."

Crow pondered whether to tell White all this, but other than Pont's price, he settled to let it be. Pont catching mice was all that mattered. He wrote Pont's requirements down and folded the paper up, giving it to a maid he knew couldn't read, to give to White. With his first task completed, Crow flew out the open window, pursuing the next ingredient. Dried pine cones from the highest branches. They weren't dry yet, but he suspected White would know a few tricks when he brought them in.

When Crow had acquired all ingredients, he returned to White's office. He placed his them on the table, including a flask filled with the stream water. That had been the toughest acquiring. He'd stolen the flask from a townsman and then had to find an unfrozen stream.

"I've come up with a plan to administer the brew, if we succeed," said White. "I cannot think of anything more entertaining and positive than a ball. Master Goodwin will look his finest and they can enjoy physical interaction together. But of course, no preparation for this will begin until we are certain of the brew and have all the ingredients."

"I've acquired all mine," said Crow.

"And Pont has left a bagged present at my door," nodded White. "I checked with Boar and he has two of the three flowers. We're still missing tussilago farfara, and Roi's research in the herb book indicates it is not locally grown, not that this would help much, being winter."

"I can check the towns," said Crow. "But I have no idea what it looks-"

Crow's eyes went distant. White lightly grabbed his shoulders, ready to shake him.

"Are you alright?"

"I'm fine," said Crow, stepping from her reach. "I just remembered, Fierté has herbs in his office. They're practically ingrained in my mind from spending… He has it. I can't believe it didn't occur to me right away. He has a flower of tussilago farfara… but only one."

"That would be his personal collection," said White, closing the box. "He keeps them nearly as close as his journals."

"Do you want me to ask for it?" asked Crow. *I doubt Fierté will part from it without a good explanation.*

"No," said White, thinking along the same lines. "He would figure this out if we do anything direct. And without any certainty yet, I would not risk even hinting to him."

"Steal it?"

"I'd rather not," sighed White. "I hate to think we need to lower ourselves any further. This secrecy is not healthy for my old heart. And his room is locked when he's not in it. Perhaps if I suggested I wanted to brew a special tea for Hélène, Roi told me it is edible… no, it is not a strong enough idea for him to part with it."

Crow flicked one of the pine cones along White's desk and watched it role a couple times before rocking to a stop.

"Marvelous," said White. "Absolutely brilliant! I can win it from him. We haven't for several months now, but Fierté, Boar and I used to get together to play black gammon as we discussed whatever struck our minds. Betting was more Boar's pastime, but Fierté and I would appease him, especially with nice glass of wine."

"Do you want Roi to discuss this with?" asked Crow. "I reckon he holds experience in cheating."

"Cheating!" said White, alarmed.

"You'll want a way to get Fierté to bet his flower, but you'll also need a plan to make sure you win. This all won't matter if you don't win."

"I abhor the thought, but you are right," said White. "I'll go see Roi during tea, after I've arranged the game for tonight." Her frown deepened. "I must limit my interactions with him. Gustav has been popping up a little too often and I suspect it is Fierté's doing."

CHAPTER 13 – DRUGGING THE BUTLER

Waiting made Crow restless. He paced Roi's room while Roi lounged on the bed, reading pages for any herbs that might substitute in use for tussilago farfara. Crow suspected Roi had become enthralled by the book and was reading it entirely page for page.

"Relax. I taught her everything I know, including how to load dice."

"I doubt she'll use half of them," said Crow. "The expression she wore on the way to Boar's office for the game was one of someone who believes the right thing will happen because it should. She should know better."

"Lay down next to me before you make a rut in the floor," said Roi. He patted the extra pillow, though his eyes remained on the pages.

Crow looked anxiously at the door one more time before striding over to the bed and flumping down next to Roi.

Roi gave him a quick kiss on the cheek, muttering, "Good crow," before returning to his book. "I can read out loud, if you'd like. There's three natural herbs that grow in this province, each designed to send the consumer to sleep. Some react faster than others and some…"

Crow tried to force himself to relax. He stared at the pages, but found his gaze sidling away to Roi's face. Giving up, he studied the man, memorizing the short eyelashes, slightly darker than his hair, the thick eyebrows, the fading freckles-

"It's no use," grumbled Crow. "I'm going to watch the halls."

He got up from the bed, hesitated, then leaned down and kissed Roi. It still amazed Crow how soft Roi's lips were and he pressed a little harder, seeing how far he could push himself.

Roi's chuckling had him pull away, reddening in the face.

"You really want attention, don't you?" said Roi, his gaze finally fully focused on Crow.

"That's your goodnight kiss," said Crow. "I might not come back if I encounter White. She'll want to start the final brew tonight."

"Then who's going to inform me if you got it?"

"I don't think it will be a problem for you to wait till morning," said Crow, grinning mischievously. "The world ceases to exist for you, when you're reading."

Crow left to the hall, transforming and heading down to the servant quarters. He heard a clock chime ten distantly. Boar's hallway was empty of all normal servants and those on night duties wisely steered clear.

His slim bird form fitted with ease behind a mantle of a knight's armor at the end of the hall, hidden in the shadows. When the triumvirate exited from the room, Crow waited for White and Fierté to pass before pursuing after White as she headed towards the female servant quarters.

He transformed midflight, matching step with White.

"It failed," said White, trying to hide the quiver in her lip as she continued her pace. "At this rate, with the time the ingredients need to simmer together, we will be too late even if you fly out tomorrow and miraculously find some. Please inform Monsieur Roi for me and get some sleep."

Crow wordlessly stopped. His eyes narrowed as White continue without looking back. A scowl formed along his lips.

"No," he muttered under his breath.

We were so close. White, you're too incompetent at this sort of thing. It should have been left to me or Roi. We should have just stolen it. We could have even used some of those sleeping herbs Roi was reading about.

With a final glare at White, Crow quietly rushed to Boar's storage where he kept his special kitchen stock and medicinal herbs. He carefully tiptoed over the skunk and duck until he reached the back counter. At the very back, dustier than the rest, a series of shady, enclosed jars were labelled from diuretics through death. He lightly ran his fingers over the dusty labels.

Boar will skin me if he finds out I'm poking through his collection, but it's his fault for getting drunk last winter and bragging about it. Which one will work for me? The ones furthest to the left are fast-acting. Well, well, this one in the middle is labelled "sleep." Perfect, if the instructions on how to administer, dosage, and side effects hadn't been smudged at some point. No time to sleuth this out, though.

Crow delicately picked up the sleep bottle and worked at getting the tight lid to loosen. His hand slipped from the effort and his elbow hit down against the corner of the counter. Crow squeezed his eyes shut as he bit his lip to restrain from adding to the noise. He bent down, enduring the pain shooting up his elbow. He opened one teary eye, and slowly relaxed as he saw the animals were still asleep.

Shaking his arm as the pain diminished into tingles, he stood back up, more carefully working at the lid until at last it gave way with a slight pop. Crow reached in. The contents inside felt like dried peas. Pulling one out, the ingredients appeared to be rolled in a small ball of hardened bread. He checked his pocket to make sure there were no holes, and then tucked the small ball in.

Crow transformed and took flight, flying faster than ever through the halls, taking the shortcut up to the third level. As he entered the hall, he saw Fierté holding a lit candle in one hand while pulling out the keys from his deep pockets to his office's door.

Transforming swiftly, Crow strode towards him.

Tired from the evening, Fierté didn't notice Crow. He placed the key in his door's lock, turning it with the dazed expression of one used to performing the mundane routine.

"Fierté," Crow called out, picking up speed.

Fierté's head jerked to look at Crow.

"The hour is late," said Fierté, opening the door. "Report-"

"This isn't a patrol report."

Fierté stood still for a second. His facial expressions showed a battle between fatigue and curiosity. There was also the hint of irritation at having been interrupted. Then he stepped into his office, distractedly signaling Crow to follow. Crow entered and closed the door behind him. Fierté seated himself wearily behind his desk, watching Crow carefully.

"I think you're right, that White is up to something," said Crow.

Fierté perked up. He leaned forward onto his desk. His hands grabbed the nearest quill and began to eagerly fiddle with feathering.

"You've found proof?"

Crow shook his head, "Nothing distinct, but she is always speaking privately with Hélène. I don't know about Roi. I'm with him most of the time, so-" Crow shrugged and sat down uninvited on a chair. "I happened to overhear something earlier, though."

Fierté's jaw started to work back and forth, nearly imperceptibly.

Alright, I have his full attention. My heart's pounding so fiercely, I wonder if he can hear. Crow's eyes darted to Fierté's cabinet, the flower hanging right where he remembered it. *I'll have you before the night is out.*

Crow's eyes lowered down to the counter beside the cabinet; holding a tray with a few of Fierté's favorite bottled drinks. He energetically jumped to his feet and grabbed a chalice, placing it before Fierté. He then selected the darkest wine and set about opening it. Fierté remained patiently silent.

He must think I'm trying to be dramatic.

"You're going to need a drink," said Crow. As he poured the wine he looked towards the window. Moonlight shone in, helping the lone candle on Fierté's desk light the room. "Lovely moon tonight."

Fierté looked back at the moon for a moment, which was all Crow needed to drop the drug into the drink. The bread cover was so dry it dissolved in a second.

"What do you need to tell me about White?" demanded Fierté, picking up the wine and leaning back in his seat as he took a sip.

Crow returned the bottle to the side, retaking his seat.

"As you know, Roi has access to the library now, under White's watch, every night," said Crow.

I hope I can keep everything straight as I make this up. How can I have this lasting long enough for the drug to take effect, without Fierté catching on. Of course it's the slyest of the three I have to steal from!

Fierté drained the cup with two swigs as Crow continued, "At first I thought it was her taking pity on Roi. Maybe she thought he was getting a little too rambunctious again and needed a distraction. The books make him ridiculously docile and unresponsive. It was then that I noticed that White wasn't merely sitting in the room watching. She'd walk the shelves, checking various books and putting them back. I thought little of it. I was just content to be by the fire."

Crow stopped as Fierté stood up. He swayed slightly as he rounded the desk and sat opposite of Crow. He leaned his elbows on his knees as his focus didn't waver from Crow.

"Keep going."

"Well, it might be nothing… but it weighed on me all today. She mentioned something about journals under her breath. I know there are journals kept in there, but I couldn't understand why she might want to read them. She's agonizingly slow at reading. And then I wondered if it might reference to your journals. I know we're not supposed to mention them, but-"

Fierté whispered something so fiercely under his breath, that Crow feared Fierté was angry at him.

"Sir?"

"White tried to initialize a strange method of betting at our meet tonight," said Fierté distractedly. "Boar and I overrode it with the usual betting rounds… but-"

Fierté grabbed Crow.

"Are you sure you heard her mention journals? Did she mention my name? Anyone's name?"

"No sir," said Crow, his eyes widening.

Fierté was acting off, but sleep did not seem to be taking effect as quickly as Crow had hoped. That was when Crow noticed Fierté's pupils. They were large.

"Shit," swore Crow under his breath.

"Such dark eyes," said Fierté, his mind trailing. His face drew close to Crow's, "What a waste of good looks."

"Sir?" repeated Crow, swallowing nervously.

Fierté let go of Crow, leaning away. He raised his hand and ran it over his face, struggling to restrain himself.

"If that's all you have to report, you'd best go."

Crow slowly stood up from his chair, struggling over what to say next.

"But you know, Crow," said Fierté slowly. "I think there's still things you're not telling me. Not significant things... just small things, that I don't mind overlooking... even if they do irritate me."

The drug is speaking now.

"Sorry sir?" said Crow.

"Corbin. It is not a name someone might think to list. But you couldn't have remembered... so, did you find something in the guest room?"

Fierté stepped closer to Crow, causing him to back away so he wouldn't trip into the chair. Fierté backed him towards the wall.

"It was carved into some wood."

"Ah," said Fierté, accepting it easily in his drugged state.

"Are you feeling well?" asked Crow. "Perhaps you need to rest?"

Fierté narrowed his eyes as an eerie smile crept on his face.

"I thought it was weariness and love-loss, but Crow, you crafty boy, you've drugged me. Has White gotten her hands on you?"

It would have been better to have denied it, but Crow guiltily remained silent. The plan was changing, but he could still work with this. He felt determined to prove himself more resourceful than White.

Fierté stumbled forward and grabbed the front of Crow's shirt, "Why?"

Crow opened his mouth, but froze, his voice catching in his throat.

If I was Fierté and Roi was me, he'd flirt to get what he wants. Crow clenched his jaws. *Fine. The pigs can fly while I flirt with Fierté.*

Crow let Fierté keep a hold of him as he ran his hand through his own hair. Fierté avidly watch. Crow prayed Fierté wouldn't remember any of this the next day.

"I just... wanted to..." said Crow. Forcing the words, Crow winced at the painful stop starting. He swallowed deeply, realizing this actually made his speech sound authentic.

His insides squirmed in a knot as he stepped up against Fierté. Not too close, but enough that the fabric touched. Crow reached to play with one of the gold buttons reflecting the candlelight on Fierté's outfit.

"I was always envious of you and Elliot," Crow managed to usher out. "I've always liked men too... but couldn't exactly go tromping about-"

Fierté ran the back of his free hand along Crow's hair. He bent to smell it. Crow winced.

"Young fool," slurred Fierté. "I'd have fucked you in a heartbeat if you'd ever came to me."

177

Crow looked up at Fierté. Fierté's eyes were hooded, but still sharp. Crow was the only thing in his sights, on his mind.

Why isn't he passing out? thought Crow desperately. *Foreplay. What do people do as foreplay?*

Crow wrapped an arm around Fierté, grabbing hold of some decoration on the back of his uniform. Crow rose on his tiptoes and aimed his lips for Fierté's.

This isn't a kiss, not like what Roi and I do. That's special. This is different. It has to be different.

Fierté leaned down, greedily returning with his own passionate kiss. Crow pushed forward, stepping Fierté back until he hit the chair. Crow closed his eyes, imagining Fierté was Roi. As Fierté sat into it, he wrapped his arm around Crow's neck, pulling him down with him. Crow released a groan, which he abruptly cut off, remembering who he was with.

Crow struggled to stay standing while bent. Pulling Crow closer, Fierté lightly nipped his ear, then whispered, "Did you ever fuck around with Duval?"

"What?" hissed Crow.

He looked, alarmed, up into Fierté's eyes.

Fierté gave a low chuckle.

"No? He's like us, you know. Well, allow me to help relieve you."

Fierté's hand slid under the shirt collar and trailed like a snake down Crow's back. His fingertips scratched lightly against Crow's skin, causing Crow's hairs to stand on end. A growing warmth started inside Crow, his skin tingling wherever Fierté's experienced fingers touched.

No. I'm not supposed to react like this. I'm just... I'm supposed to fake my way.

Crow made to pull back, but couldn't pull fully away without causing suspicion or a ruckus. Fierté's arm remained slung over Crow, but the scratching stopped. Crow jerked, realizing his eyes had settled on the bulge in Fierté's pants. Crow felt a blush race across his face as he looked up at Fierté's smug expression.

Fierté chuckled, releasing Crow and leaning ruggedly back in the arm chair. Slouched and at ease, he wasn't as imposing... but still awake and capable.

"Have you ever gone past this point?" patronized Fierté.

Of course not, thought Crow. *I only have an idea. Why can't you just fall asleep?*

Fierté laced his fingers through Crow's and brought them up to his lips, briefly biting each fingertip. Then Fierté leaned forward, his one hand running through Crow's hair. Crow opened his mouth to object, but Fierté's fingers curled and pulled, drawing him forward. His long, bony fingers held a strong grip. Gone was the veneer of sophistication and class, revealing a more direct, brutal, selfish individual.

Crow swore under his breath, his eyes tearing up from Fierté's hold. Closing his eyes, Crow distanced himself by focusing on his goal. And suddenly, the fingers loosened, slipping out and falling heavily at Fierté's side. Fierté slouched to the side, asleep.

Shivering, Crow straightened up. He stumbled, his muscles weak and his thoughts groggy. Crow's hand brushed against his own slightly aroused bump. He dug his nails into his palms, determined to use pain to repress the shameful reaction.

In dream-like fashion, he made his way over to Fierté's desk, retrieved the key, and unlocked the cabinet, recovering the flower. He then, with extra detail, put everything back. Crow downed half of the dark wine.

Fierté owes me at least that much.

Crow snuck from the room. Carefully checking the empty halls, he returned to the women servant hall. He spotted Sparrow and had her fetch White. Crow leaned against the wall, disheveled, wishing he'd drunk more of Fierté's wine.

"What's wrong?" asked White.

Crow took out his ill-gotten prize, passing it to her, "The flower."

White took the flower, inspecting it in the dim candle light. "How did you get this?"

"I had drinks with Fierté," said Crow.

White sniffed the air and her nose wrinkled slightly.

Crow gave a weak smile. "Will it do?"

"It should," said White, eyeing him closely. "Is he awake?"

Crow shook his head no.

She suspects I told Fierté our plan... perhaps even thinks I'm a spy for Fierté. The old croon. Though, truthfully, I don't want her exactly knowing the truth either. No one should learn about that. Ever.

"Does he know?" persisted White.

"He might notice it missing, though not right away," said Crow.

White released a long breath, raising the flower before her eyes for closer inspection.

"Wash up," said White. "You reek of drink. I'll start the brewing."

Crow remained wordless as White turned to leave.

I'd drink three more bottles if they were around.

CHAPTER 14 – THE BREW

Crow gazed absently out of the window in his attic. He had not slept. His senses were dull and slow. He knew he wouldn't be able sleep for some time. Even if he could, he wouldn't allow himself. He didn't deserve it. He needed to see the plan through.

There were whispers that morning amongst the male staff that something was going on with the female staff. And rumors that White had met with the master earlier that morning quickly allowed Crow to conclude the brew had been successful. He wasn't sure how much White had told Goodwin, or how much she wanted the various staff to be informed, so he kept to himself.

It was to his surprise that on his way to Roi's room, he spotted Roi already down the hall. Roi beamed at him, clearly having been informed of the brew's success. For the briefest time, Crow's worries ceased to exist.

"Pont's running errands," said Roi, signaling Crow down an unused hallway.

"Freedom at last," said Crow. "Are you ready for today? It's going to be… unusual."

"Tonight will be the telltale," said Roi, skimming his finger along Crow's jaw line. Crow closed his eyes and enjoyed the stroking. He wondered if there was some cat in him. "The potion is brewed. The symbols are in place. The beast is informed of the basics. We can only wait."

"The extent of our involvement and how much we snuck around still needs to be kept secret," warned Crow. He envisioned Fierté and shivered. He would avoid the man entirely today, even though the drugs should have done the job in making Fierté think it a dream if anything at all was remembered.

Roi nodded in agreement.

"And White told me this morning that Fierté and Boar will be informed around noon that this is far more than just a dance. Most of

White's ladies already know various portions of the plan. I'm supposed to be informing Hélène, but I wanted to see you first. I'll likely be with her all morning and I suspect White will keep you tasked."

Roi's hand wound around Crow's waist. He smelled slightly of smoke and cinnamon. Crow breathed in, relishing the scent. It would have been perfect, were he not feeling disgusted with himself.

Roi moved to kiss him and Crow hesitated before meeting his lips. Roi's hands rubbed lightly against Crow's back, causing Crow to stiffen and when Roi stepped forward to move Crow against the wall, Crow broke.

"I can't do this," said Crow, ripping from Roi's hold. He could see the confusion in Roi's eyes, so he quickly made an excuse. "We don't have time for this."

"This isn't about time," said Roi. "You're off today. What's wrong?"

Roi reached for Crow, but Crow slapped his hand aside, wincing at the sound. He hardened his gaze.

"You," answered Crow firmly. "We've only a day to prepare for the event that could end the curse and you're focused on triviality."

Roi looked taken aback. Crow kept his face cold.

"This thing we have is not beneficial," snapped Crow. "Especially now. And it's not like we were going anywhere."

"It's beneficial for both of us," said Roi, his voice getting tight as his temper rose. "And I wasn't developing our relationship further because of you! You still freeze up at anything new."

"And it didn't occur to you," said Crow haughtily, reminding himself of Corvus, "That perhaps those were hints it wasn't to be?"

"No!" said Roi angrily. "We're fated! I know it. The kiss in Remais that broke the spell proved it. You love me."

"Such a romantic. When have I ever said I loved you?"

Crow felt like he'd hit himself in the stomach, regretting the line as soon as it had left his lips, and his guilt multiplying from how smoothly he'd executed it. He stoically watched, internally screaming, as Roi paled, his body deflating and jaw clenched, as he wordlessly turned, heading to Hélène's room without a second look back.

Crow resisted running after him. Even before the incident with Fierté, he'd never forthright told Roi he loved him. Roi didn't deserve a cold-hearted coward like him. Roi would find someone better after all this. It was for both their own good. And yet, Crow's eyes threatened to flood as he turned and marched away opposite.

Crow's sulk was short lived. White spotted him and had him living up to his messenger role by flying around the castle to inform staff of what to prepare. He was grateful for the distraction, while avoiding Roi and Fierté like the plague

After having delivered a request to the seamstress to bring her finest clothes to Hélène's room, Crow found White heading up the stairs in the main hall. He transformed and walked up alongside her.

"Everything is in order."

"Excellent," said White. "Stay with me, I was on my way to speak with Roi on how Hélène is doing."

Crow stopped just before the top step.

"There's, um, some things I need to head off to-"

A loud click echoed the hall as Hélène's door opened. Roi exited, his face unnaturally cheerful, chuckling.

"I promise I'll ask," he said. "Wait there, and I'll find out."

White cleared her throat impatiently at Crow. Crow moved from his rooted spot, but was careful to have White between him and Roi. He tilted his head warily, not wanting to ruin the good mood.

"Madam White, you will not believe what my sister has requested," said Roi, his eyes alight when he spotted her. "She wants any staff that can hold human form to also attend the ball. She claims, and I admit I agree, that dances are not fun when only two people are dancing the entire time."

White's smile reached her eyes.

"The idea is precious. But without human forms to manage their duties, the dance will not be possible."

"Could they alternate between dancing and responsibilities? During the actual dancing, we only need the musicians to maintain their jobs."

"Perhaps." White lowered her tone and signaled Roi and Crow to walk with her, "But we must make sure Hélène's eyes are only drawn to the master."

"She has no interest in Fierté, Pont, or Crow, and I'm pretty certain of all the human-form staff I've seen, that they're your prized ponies. I saw the dusted portrait in the hall near the library. That's Goodwin East, isn't it? He's got an old-fashioned handsome look. If his manners can finally match those looks, there might be hope."

"He did enjoy balls once," sighed White nostalgically. "I've just finished informing Fierté and Boar that I'd found some old magic that will present the master in human form for a moonlit evening. Fierté is lecturing the master at this very moment, although he's been oddly standoffish of late. Boar has isolated himself to the kitchens."

"Making every which dish possible?" asked Roi, grinning.

"There will be a banquet on the side, but I think its best that no one further mentions the spell to Boar. I suspect 'witch' was on the tip of his tongue by the way he looked at me."

"He does know that old magic has to do with alchemy and the heavens," said Roi. "No demonic dealings, sacrifices, or dark rituals."

"Boar is narrow-minded," reminded Crow.

Roi's eyes flitted briefly to Crow, before focusing back on White. Crow lowered his head and moved to be a step behind them.

"Magic is a blade," said White, stopping them at a servant backstairs. "I've never liked weapons, but I can understand their need to be used in desperation. There is a reason magic is shunned by the kingdom."

"I guess I've read too many old tales of magic," said Roi. "Inspiring in theory and story, but terrifying in reality. So, what am I to tell Hélène of the dancers?"

"I will gather five women and four men to attend- Crow, you will be one of them."

"Why four men?" asked Roi, at the same time Crow objected, "Why me?"

"Monsieur Roi," said White, "You would make the fifth member of the men. We don't know how long the ball will last, though I suspect between two and four hours, so we need those who can last the entirety of its length. Don't you both still have your outfits from your previous outing?"

"I- I can't dance," stated Crow.

"I highly doubt that, Master Corvus," said White, a humor shining in her eyes. "I've never come across a noble who doesn't know a few moves."

Crow stood in front of White, his hands up, "Then I'm the first."

"Perhaps Monsieur Roi might re-familiarize you with dancing," suggested White, her eyebrow arcing.

Crow met her gaze. She knew. She definitely knew Crow had a relationship with Roi. Little did she know of their argument though, which was more of a concern for Crow right then than the fact that White knew they were more than allies and friends.

"Before noon, speak to Pan and have him find the frosted masks we used to use for winter balls. Covering the servant faces with them will maintain an eloquence, but keep Hélène's eyes from wandering astray from the master."

White moved around him. Crow struggled to come up with a better excuse.

"Meet me in the guest room," ordered Roi, drawing Crow's attention back. "I can show you some humble town dances. I'll be but a moment with Hélène."

"I don't want to take away from your time with your sister," Crow politely objected.

"Not to worry," said Roi. "The lessons will be fast. I know when you're lying."

Crow knew some dance moves, though he couldn't recall their names. The nearest memory he could draw on was years ago, when hope was still young that the spell would be broken, when the younger staff had decided to have a humble dance in the basement. There was more of them then and many could still transform. The servants had dressed in their best. He'd danced with a redhead. He couldn't remember her name. She wasn't around anymore. He remembered the fun, the smiles. Even he had fun, though he remembered thinking of the dance as common; residue of an elitist's mentality.

"You are still my servant here, aren't you?" asked Roi. "White calling you by title isn't getting to your head?"

"As you wish, sir," grumbled Crow, waving his hand while giving an extra low bow.

Roi returned to Hélène's room.

"Roi recuperates always so quick," muttered Crow, entering Roi's room. "If he still holds any anger from earlier, he's doing an excellent job of hiding it. He must have told Hélène and she calmed him down. Hélène has a talent with that. He must want to get me on my own to either fix this or make everything to go back to before-"

Crow thought he heard a rustle coming from behind the tapestry and he froze. He held his breath, listening intently. When nothing further sounded, he released a shaky breath.

No more talking out loud. Roi must want to get me on my own to either fix this or make everything go back to before- How I want this to be fixed. Crow felt his heart pang against his chest. He kicked the bed, trying to shove the hope back down. *No. I can't accept this feeling. I'm cowardly and low levelled; tainted. Roi deserves better... Dammit, I still want him.*

Agitated, Crow grabbed the outfits from the wardrobe and spread them out on the bed. He piled the pieces that needed ironing.

"I'd forgotten displaying public affection is frowned on by the staff here," said Roi. Crow jumped around and Roi closed the door as silently as he'd opened it. "In the hallway… if we were seen, it would have at least affected your reputation. Please don't withdraw further. I want us… I'd like to continue the trust we had. I swear, I'll be more careful. And I know there is a lot I still don't know about you, but I'd like to find out all."

Being caught by other servants hadn't even been in Crow's mind. He was certain Roi's conclusion had been shaped with Hélène's help. Roi didn't care as much for people judging him, and it wouldn't have occurred to him easily that others would.

"Forgive me?" asked Roi sincerely. "We can start over? I'll do whatever it takes!"

The sincerity in Roi's eyes made Crow's heart tremble. He stilled his trembling fingers as he ran his hands through his hair. Slowly his frown relaxed into a slight smile. He felt like a good chunk of burden had been removed from his shoulders. The incident with Fierté would always be there, but he could redeem himself. He could make himself actually worthy for Roi- because as damned as he was, the man had become the center of his world.

"We both were hotheaded."

Crow held his hand out, his smile growing as Roi accepted and they shook. Before releasing, Roi's thumb drew across the of Crow's hand. Crow's smile wavered as he felt a conflict of pleasure and worry. After Roi released, his fingers lingered over where Roi had touched.

Sparrow flew into the room, landing on Crow's shoulder, "I need your help placing some strange ingredients in the corners of the ballroom, up high on the ceiling ledges. White won't explain what are in the bags, but they're too heavy for me."

#

The castle came to life. The drapery covering the massive windows to the ballroom was entirely removed. The dining table was moved to the edge and replaced with smaller serving tables boasting many delicious looking treats. Flowers were arranged on stacks and stands throughout the room. A small stage was set up in the far end, rimmed with lacing and silk for the musicians. They had three on staff who could play decently together, and they practiced all afternoon. The chandeliers were fully lit, and as the sun set, the room took on a golden hue.

At this time the servants took their place. Several were in full gowns and suits, their faces covered by masks. Crow was sent off to change. Roi was not in the room, but his outfit was missing. Through Hélène's open door, Crow heard the siblings laugh as Hélène got dolled up by Nanny.

Not wanting to disturb their fun, Crow returned to the guest room and got changed. He felt more comfortable in the tailored clothing. He looked at the rest of the clothing in the wardrobe, curious if it was all tailored like this. None of it looked familiar to him, though he knew it was his.

"Crow?" asked Pont, poking his head into the room. "Ah, you're ready. Good. You need to come to the ballroom. Everyone needs to be there, ready for Hélène's entrance. White will be to the master's left, with the line of five women. Fierté will be to right with you leading the line of four men."

"Fierté?" asked Crow.

"You've heard," said Pont, nodding grimly. "If I hadn't been with White's minions under her supervision the whole day, I guarantee she'd have blamed me."

Crow stopped, confused.

"What are you talking about?"

"Fierté spoke with White a short while ago," said Pont. "Apparently, he knows all the juicy details she'd held back from telling. Fierté and White have given each other the cold shoulder since, angry that the other doesn't trust them. At least they're cooperating for this evening. Tomorrow will be hell. For now, White has charged me to hunt out who the spy is."

"What does he know?" demanded Crow, holding his breath.

"That I helped," said Pont, for once revealing a slight snarl, but quickly he hid it in his usual lazy demeanor. "That this all originated from Roi. That you left the castle with him. I won't go down the list."

"But only five of us knew about the trip to Remais..."

"Apparently White told several of her girls bits and pieces this morning," said Pont. "And someone put it together and told Fierté. I don't think any of Boar or Fierté's men would have acquired all the information as easily."

Crow swallowed nervously.

"You're not at the top of my culprit list," chuckled Pont as they approached the ballroom. "You invested too much into this. Though truthfully, you're not at the top of my most trustworthy list either."

Crow chuckled under his breath.

"I don't trust myself either. Are you being this chatty because your stressed? I find it hard to believe you experiencing such a symptom, but you've never talked this much to me nor given so much information for free."

Pont didn't answer. They'd arrived at the ball room's entrance. The cat slipped away from Crow's side.

Crow looked across the floor and saw everyone was in place. The moon was low, sprawling its line through the windows and across most of the room. In the center of the light a tall man, thickly muscled, clean shaved, and wearing an assortment of red, gold and blue clothes.

"Goodwin," Crow said in awe under his breath.

He walked across the room, intentionally avoiding any eye contact with the men's side. When he arrived before Goodwin, he took a low bow, tucking his left foot behind his right. He could see the pride and happiness in Goodwin's eyes. And yet, there was also fear.

"Master East," said Crow as he finished his bow.

Goodwin stepped forward, holding out a hand and the room went dead silent.

"I believe you are one of two to thank for this evening," said Goodwin. His voice did not match his appearance, nor was it his usual growl, soft and fluid instead. Yet, it possessed the power to silence the room with a single word. "I've been informed of everything."

Crow curiously shook the gloved hand. Goodwin squeezed hard. Then even softer, so no one else could hear, "To your spot, Monsieur Corvus."

Swiftly Crow took his place, thanking the servant who passed him a mask. With the mask overtop, he felt slightly more anonymous and relaxed.

"Mademoiselle Hélène Duval, accompanied by Monsieur Roi Duval," announced a duck at the room's entrance.

Crow lightly shook in amusement at the absurdity of a duck announcing. Then he grew solemn, realizing the duck must no longer be able to turn human, even for a brief announcement.

Under the chandelier's light, the beads sewn throughout Hélène's dress reflected like small jewels, drawing Crow's gaze. His mouth opened. Hélène was beautiful. Her hair was strung in loose ringlets. The makeup enhanced her eyes, giving an even more doe-like appearance. Her dress was the most beautiful one Crow had ever seen; a mix of light and dark green silks.

Escorted by Roi, Hélène steadily walked to the center of the room before curtsying. Her eyes widened at the sight of Goodwin and she blinked several times when Goodwin stepped forward, bowing in turn.

"May I have the first dance?" he asked softly. Crow barely heard him.

"You may."

Hélène placed her hand onto Goodwin's offered arm. They moved closer to the musicians and the servants cleared out of the way. The first dance was only for them.

Roi moved next to Crow.

"Goodwin says thanks for everything," said Crow quietly, unable to take his eyes off the dancing.

"Hélène says the beast doesn't look half bad."

Crow jabbed Roi with his elbow.

"She didn't say that! She hasn't said a word since entering the room."

"She was thinking it. I could see it in her expression."

"And what is my expression saying?"

"Take your mask off and I'll tell you. Though I might have to inspect you a lot more closely... so close our lips might touch."

"No joking around. Focus. This dance is about your sister."

Roi released a mourning sigh.

"I assure you, I'm more than aware of that. I need to distract myself though. You have no idea how difficult-"

"Quickly now, prepare for the next dance," whispered White, separating Crow and Roi and pairing them with two of the servant women.

Crow hesitantly escorted his partner to the dance floor, just as the first song ended.

"Do you know how to dance?" he asked his partner. He couldn't recognize who it was under the mask, makeup and jewelry, but based on the wrinkles around the neck, he guessed she was one of the more mature staff members.

"Decently," replied the woman stiffly. "Though I haven't had practice like you, when you visited to Remais."

Crow groaned.

"I didn't dance- That doesn't matter. Does everyone know about Remais now?"

"Never mind that," said the servant. "What did the master say to you?"

"When?"

"When you shook hands and he whispered something. I don't think I heard right."

To Crow's relief, the music for the second dance began. He placed his hands in position and managed to maintain a decent composure, intently watching others for the dance's steps. By the third song, this moves came naturally and Crow's stiff posture started to relax. Able to enjoy more of the environment, he found his eyes kept drawing towards Roi and his partner.

The woman wore a faded pink gown and her long, auburn hair had been braided back. Unlike the rest of the women, scars showed on the small amount of revealed skin, giving Crow suspicion Roi was dancing with Fox. Fox and Roi moved fluently together, making them lovely to watch. Roi whispered continuously to her, and a smile built on the shy woman's face. Crow grinned, imagining what ridiculous things Roi was saying to lighten the mood.

Crow slipped from the dance floor during a break between the sixth and seventh song when partners amongst staff were traded. Crow was relieved to see only four women left, so his absence would not cause discord.

Goodwin and Hélène chatted while dancing, with everyone eagerly watching. Goodwin grinned with happiness and Hélène with curiosity. Not the desired result yet, but Crow was certain Goodwin was definitely in love right then.

He found the drinks and consumed a couple glasses before two animal servants of White's joined him, asking him what he thought of dance, the outfits, if this would work for Hélène. Crow, unused to his opinion ever mattering before, less so even being sought out, answered awkwardly before managing to sneak away as the second hour approached

Crow hid behind the stacks of false floral, within the shadows. Here, even the chandeliers did not reach well with their light. He sat on the collection of cloth bags the flowers had been kept in and watched the dance between the decoration's cracks.

As Crow removed his mask to wipe the sweat off his face, Roi sidled in next to him. Roi sat so close their shoulder's met. A slight throbbing started in Crow. The effects of the alcohol made him bold.

"I'm glad for your fetching company, but how did you find me so quickly? I thought my hideout foolproof."

"You couldn't possibly be more handsome tonight," said Roi. "I couldn't keep my eyes off of you."

"What's with the flattery?" said Crow, turning his head and receiving a surprise kiss.

"I've concluded the full truth, Corbin," whispered Roi, near Crow's ear. "I was too fast. I will slow down. For now, only kisses."

"Even after I was such a jerk? You won't stop?"

"Never," whispered Roi. "I love you. I've never felt so strongly for someone before. I- It's to the point where I could see us being together for the rest of our lives."

"You're a happy drunk, aren't you?"

Roi's breath indicated he'd also consumed a good portion of alcohol. Crow imagined the main reason would be his concern for his sister. He was handling everything remarkably well, but Crow could see the lines of tension around Roi's eyes. He needed a good distraction.

Crow firmly pressed his lips against Roi's and wrapped an arm around him, bringing them closer. He could feel his heartbeat against his chest. Crow maneuvered his leg to straddle over the man's body and fell down with him as Roi's muscles relaxed with surprise and welcome.

Crow released the kiss, opening his eyes inches from Roi's face.

He felt Roi's hand snake delicately through his hair, then gently pull their faces down together again. Crow's stomach flip flopped at the care the man was giving.

"Swear to be mine forever," whispered Roi.

"I'm yours."

Roi smiled as Crow pecked him with decisive kisses several times around the face.

Approaching steps had Crow quickly return to a seated position, pulling his mask clumsily back over his face. Roi remained laying down. Crow nudged him.

"Tell them I'm too drunk," said Roi between chuckles.

"You are."

Crow lightly touched Roi's hand as he got up. He went back to his duties, feeling much more lighthearted.

With the light on the ballroom floor shortening as the moon moved past the windows, the ball was ended sooner than desired. But they wanted to leave a good impression for Hélène with Goodwin's human form being the last thing she saw. Hélène was escorted back the room and the servants, with the exception of Boar's, were excused for the night to recover.

While placing his mask on the table, Crow spotted Fierté, White and Boar talking with Goodwin in the center of the room. A divider was being put up around him, so that he could change out of his wealthy clothing before the regression occurred and stretched the fabric.

Crow sought out Roi, finding him where he'd left him, albeit now sitting. Roi was watching Goodwin, a thoughtful look on his face.

"Do you think it worked?" asked Crow, helping Roi up. "The curse is still in effect but if this has helped, even just a little…"

"Honestly, I'm not sure. Hélène definitely had fun and the beast was charming-" Roi grunted as Crow elbowed him in the side. "Master East was charming. Who would have thought it possible! We'll have to find out tomorrow when she has breakfast with us."

They walked out from the shadows. Roi leaned lightly on Crow. He wrapped an arm around Crow when he nearly tripped. They headed across the floor, for the main exit.

"I'm definitely feeling the magic tonight."

"No more drinks for you," stated Crow.

Roi groaned, but it quickly changed into laughter as he started to play with Crow's outfit.

"Will you still give me a bedtime kiss?"

Crow held his breath when he caught Goodwin watching them. Their actions would be perceived as drunk play, Crow thought. He could have sworn there was an amused look on Goodwin's face. Crow started grinning, then noticed Fierté next to East. His expression was not amused. Crow sobered.

He yanked himself free, swiftly transforming and flying up to the chandelier.

"You know, when the curse is broken, you won't be able to fly away!" shouted Roi. He sounded drunker than Crow had thought. Perhaps Roi was acting again.

Roi stumbled his way out of the room. Crow hopped from one high point to the next, watching until Pont took over supervision, catching Roi as he nearly fell over outside the room. In his lengthy human form, Pont had no trouble in keeping Roi upright, though Crow suspected Roi was attempting to see how far he could push Pont.

A couple animals passed by where Crow perched and he caught, "-Improper behavior."

"You can't blame him really. To watch his sister-"

The servants went quiet.

Then, as they headed out of ear shot, "I would not want Pont or Crow's position."

Crow flew to the attic where his welcoming nest awaited him. He'd wake up to do his patrol before dawn, he decided. That way, he could report and then meet with Roi early. They could spend some time together before checking with Hélène.

His heart fluttered at the thought. And he fell asleep dreaming sweet dreams.

CHAPTER 15 - THREATS

Crow slept past dawn. He'd had so little sleep the past few days that even his bird instincts had not helped at the rising of the sun.

Cursing himself, Crow headed out into the cold sky. The clouds that had rolled in had dropped a foot of snow.

The usual locations of human travelers were clear, except one. Crow landed down near the camp, but quickly concluded they were harmless; a group of pilgrims heading for the monastery. Crow as about to take off as the pilgrims packed to move on, when he froze.

"Where is this castle the mercenaries said they were heading to?" asked the woman.

"Further in the woods, I suspect," commented the man. "Let's not speak of it here. Cursed places have a way of knowing you're speaking about it... especially so close."

"But if it is so isolated, then how did those men learn of it?"

"I heard their sponsor-"

"The mustached treasurer speaking at the inn? Wasn't he Lord East heir's new treasurer?"

"Yes, that one," said the man. "At the inn he claimed two of the castle residents came to Remais in search of more dark magic. They intend to spell the kingdom. Apparently even the heir claimed he'd heard rumors of a castle where beasts spoke and served the devil, hiding some rare, enchanted object. But, he's claimed many strange things since his wife disappeared."

The woman shivered. The second man, glared at the other two for talking about it.

"Let's hope they succeed, then," said the woman, looking around as if to spot demons in the trees. "Perhaps we should have travelled through the woods with them. Would be safer."

"Vignon was their last stop," said the first man. "Their goal is to reach the castle tomorrow midday. They're speaking of attempting to reason with the residents, but the residents are mad. It will be a battle. No beast left by the end. Only then will the woods be safe."

Crow waited until they'd left camp, then flew towards Vignon. He arrived to see that the human population had increased but not the horses. They would be on foot. Even if they left today, they'd arrive at the castle too late at night for an attack. They would likely travel into the woods today, camp, and then strike the castle the time the pilgrims had stated.

Crow took off to return to the castle.   Fierté's window was open, so Crow took the shortcut and landed on the office floor. If Fierté had been startled by his sudden intrusion, he hid it as he eloquently stood up from his chair.

Crow transformed, trying to catch his breath.

"Somehow the castle's inhabitation has reached external ears. Villagers and local mercenaries have gathered in Vignon. They plan to confront us."

Fierté stood straighter.

"Calm yourself and tell me in detail," said Fierté sharply.

Crow took a breath and relayed what the pilgrims' said word for word. Then he gave a brief description of Vignon.

Fierté paced the room, flexing his fingers. His movement grew agitated, while his face remained calm.

"We've faced violent intruders before, though never of large scale," muttered Fierté. "This couldn't be more ill-timed. Fortification needs to begin before nightfall.."

Fierté picked up a pen and began writing fiercely on paper.

"I'll go inform White and Boar," said Crow.

"You will not!" snapped Fierté.

Crow stopped, startled. Fierté threw the pen on the desk. He moved between Crow and the door. His expression softened as he saw Crow's alarm.

"It's my duty to discuss this with the others," said Fierté. "And then we will inform Master East. Depending on the circumstances, I may bring you along then."

Crow nodded, not wanting to say anything that would set Fierté off again. It was clear Fierté was feeling troubled long before the news. He was off.

"May I take my leave?" asked Crow quietly.

"There is something else I wished to discuss with you. You missed your reports yesterday."

Fierté drew closer, massaging his writing hand. Crow stiffened.

"You seem to have not heeded your pre-lesson well," continued Fierté, as if chiding a child. "I lecture and you half listen. I warn and you ignore. Your misbehavior is taxing. I've restrained giving you a proper lesson, but it's become necessary in light of recent events."

Fierté started listing about loyalty and obedience.

Crow's mind impatiently turned to thinking of the attackers. The leader description matched the man he'd seen talking to Corvus at Remais. It was possible the man had waited close enough to overhear them through the chatter. Crow grimly started to wonder if they'd been followed.

"You're not listening," grumbled Fierté, inches from Crow's face.

Crow jerked back to reality. He released a hiss, stepping back and tripping into Fierté's armchair.

"I don't need one of your lessons!"

"Talking back, consorting with a different head servant and conspiring. Shameful. Oh, and my favorite, drugging and stealing from me! Crow, your lesson is overdue- and I will make sure you learn well."

Crow's breathing quickened. He wasn't sure how much of the night Fierté remembered, but saying Fierté felt deceived was an understatement. Crow raised his right arm protectively as he attempted to stand up.

Fierté's grabbed Crow's arm with his long fingers. Sliding his grip to the wrist, he restrained it down at the top of the armchair. Crow took in a sharp gasp when the angle Fierté held it at hurt. Crow slid backwards to escape the pain. His back pressed against the armrest.

Crow swiped at Fierté with his free hand, but Fierté caught it.

"The first rule of the lesson," said Fierté. "Every foul word you speak owes me a kiss."

"Not-" Crow started, only to be stopped as Fierté pressed his lips zealously against Crow's, lightly biting Crow's bottom lip with his teeth at the end.

Crow whimpered as Fierté pressed down harder on his pinned wrist, causing the wood to indent into his skin. He clamped his mouth shut as he struggled to shove his freer hand up against Fierté's chest, but Fierté's grip of that hand too became a vice. Fierté curled his fingers so that his neatly trimmed nails started to press down, through the fabric, into Crow's wrist. Fierté loosened and tightened teasingly.

"Be good," warned Fierté.

"You bastard!"

Fierté moved in again, fervently kissing Crow; wetting lips and surrounding skin.

Crow leaned away, but released a cry as Fierté's fingers dug to the point that the skin broke. He pressed his back so painfully into the armrest that it creaked. He brought his leg up to push against opposite armrest in weak endurance.

Fierté smiled condescendingly. His fingers, one at a time, released their grip of Crow's injured wrist. The cool air stung at the small cuts. Crow brought the free hand down to the armrest, digging his fingers into the wood in frustration, feebly attempting to build his resolve to strike and run.

"No more fighting, Crow," said Fierté. "Accept this lesson or I will punish Roi, too, for this to sink through your headstrong defiance."

Crow stopped sidling back. His mouth partially opened as he met Fierté's lofty gaze. Fierté meant what he said. He squeezed his eyes shut, then opened them to look past Fierté, out the window that showed endless gray crowds.

Fierté hummed victorious at Crow's surrender and he rested a knee on the couch, between Crow's legs. He loosened his grip, just slightly, on Crow's still pinned hand against the back of the seat. Then he leaned in, kissing Crow's neck and working his way slowly along to the collar bone. His free hand moved along Crow's thigh, causing Crow's muscles to twitch. Crow closed his eyes.

The door opened.

"Fierté, I have-"

Crow's eyes flew open at the unsuspecting arrival.

Roi froze mid-step, blushing furiously. White, behind him, went pale and immediately turned around. Three long, frozen seconds passed.

"Sorry to disturb you," Roi retreated.

Fierté irately stood up. Free, Crow grabbed the edge of the chair, sliding over the arm rest. He fumbled to do his pants up as he desperately raced across the room.

"Roi, wait! I can explain."

"Discreetly, Crow," warned Fierté, but any further words were ignored.

Racing out the door, Crow passed White, who stood just outside with her face hidden in the shadows. Crow ignored her.

"Roi!"

Roi raced down the servant stairs. Faster than Crow could pursue, reminding Crow of how fast Roi had been in the woods.

"Please wait," pleaded Crow, but as he exited the stairwell, he pulled back. Hélène was in the hall with Nanny and another servant. Roi rushed passed them, with little attention. Quickly Crow did up his belt, arranging in his shirt and vest with shaking fingers. His hair still disheveled, he entered the hall in time to hear Roi's door close.

Crow passed Hélène with a nod, hoping he didn't appear too disordered. Quietly at Roi's door, he tapped before turning the handle. Something blocked the door.

"Are you sitting against the door?" hissed Crow.

"Sorry to have disturbed you and Fierté," said Roi sharply. "Pray, give me some time to erase that scene from my mind."

"Dammit, Roi," started Crow, but stopped when he saw the others looking. Crow clenched his hands, wanting to hide, but he didn't want to leave Roi with this misconception. At the same time, he didn't want to admit what had happened. He lowered his voice. "We need to talk. It's not-"

White rapidly approached with clipped steps and pinched his ear, pulling him away from the door. She pulled him two rooms down, to an old music room, where she shut the door after Pont entered after them.

"What's going on?" asked Pont curiously, transforming to human and lightly brushing against the fabric covered furniture and instruments.

"I'd sooner expect Pont to be kissing Fierté's hand than you," said White disgustedly. "But I had wondered if Fierté still secretly had you in his pocket. I guess my suspicions were correct."

White stared daggers at Crow.

Crow scoffed at her accusations. Trembling, he gave into a bitter, hysterical laugh. Frustrated tears ran down his cheeks as his clutched head, striding towards the window.

"I'm not putting up with this," snapped Crow.

"Pont, stop him."

Crow pulled the curtains aside and struggled at unlocking the window latch with trembling fingers. Pont's hand moved in and blocked the latch. Crow yanked away when their fingers accidently touched. He crossed his arms and leaned against the cold panes, staring at the floor through blurry eyes.

"What's going on?" Pont asked directly at Crow. "Shit, why are you crying?"

"While I'm not proud of witnessing it, those would be tears of guilt at being caught in the act," said White stiffly.

"Act?" asked Pont.

"He has a much closer relationship with Fierté than anyone would have suspected. Is this how Fierté got the information, Crow? You were working with him all along? My God, he had you moled in well."

"I didn't tell him anything on this," snarled Crow. "After everything I've done, you don't trust me! I don't work for him. I'm not a servant!"

"Of course, young Corvus," said White smoothly, but there was a venomous sting to her words.

"He's not the spy," said Pont pointedly. "I've traced an eavesdropper. If anything, Fierté must hold a grudge against Crow... or is that not your name anymore?"

"Fierté must have more than one spy," said White. "You did not witness the relations they were having not minutes ago."

The room went silent. Crow trembled and seethed. Then through the quiet, he released a sob and sank to the ground. He brought up his hands to hide his face. His revealed wrists sent another throb of pain and his cuts seemed to sting even more.

Pont released a cat-like hiss. His voice came out in an angry growl, "He was giving a specialized discipline lesson, wasn't he?"

White's eyes widened and her hands went to her heart. She crouched in front of him, grabbing his bruised wrists and lowering his hands to see his face. Crow didn't fight. He swallowed as he looked up at her.

"Dear, precious boy, has he harmed you before?"

Crow could bring himself of answer.

"I will speak to the master," said White harshly. "This is unacceptable."

"No. Just… forget it all. I'll steer clear of Fierté until this is all done."

"We both know it will be too difficult. And if Fierté has stooped this low, it may place others in danger too."

"I agree with Crow on different reasons," said Pont coldly. "We currently can't afford internal strife. We are so close to breaking the spell. We need unification. Though I will spread rumors to make others on guard."

White closed her eyes so tightly her wrinkles triple-folded.

"Pont, would you at least inform Fierté that Crow is now under my protection. Hopefully that will have him putting his lust on hold."

Pont nodded and left.

"My dear," said White tenderly. "Are you injured anywhere else?"

Crow's throat felt to swollen to say anything further. He gave a half-hearted shrug.

White's scrutinized him again. Her fingers twitched, wanting to inspect him more closely, but reluctant to touch him. She finally clutched his hand one final time, squeezing it tightly.

"Stay here as long as you need. I need to go tend to some things, but if you need to speak to someone, I'll always make time."

Crow grunted in response.

With White's retreat from the music room, and in the absence of any further company, Crow brooded and simmered in misery. He inched over to the back corner, half-hidden behind an old curtain. He coughed as this stirred up dust from the fabric.

His mind wrangled with the desire to rush to Roi's room. He feared that even if Roi learned the truth, he'd see Crow as truly tarnished and weak. Worse, Fierté may be harsher with Roi, since Crow hadn't completed the lesson. At least Pont and White knowing could help Roi avoid any repercussions.

Gathering what little composure he could, Crow slowly got to his feet, his muscles objecting. He knew Roi needed to hear the truth, despite what may result. He made it half way across the room, when he froze in spot as the door handle turned.

Nanny's voice whispered into the room, "Crow?"

Her slim figure entered in through the small opening. Her eyes widened as she saw Crow standing like a deer caught in the headlights. She held up a cup, her hands slightly shaking. Then she reached into her apron pocket and brought out a napkin, unwrapping it carefully so Crow could see a freshly sliced piece of bread. She placed the food on a near piano seat.

Nanny brought her hands together, holding them nervously to her chest.

"White asked me to bring you something to eat and drink. She would have brought it herself, but everyone is busy preparing, since word of an attack has spread through the castle."

Crow didn't respond.

Nanny silently set the cup beside the bread and left.

Crow's stomach growled at the food, but he couldn't move his feet closer to the door. His self-loathing had become too strong again. Preferring to starve, Crow stumbled back to the corner. He grabbed the edges of the curtains, wrapping them around him, pretending they were Roi's arms embracing him. But this only seemed to increase his guilt. Bringing his legs up against his chest, he leaned his head on his knees, the morning replaying in his mind and Roi's expression looking increasingly worse, each time, at seeing Crow and Fierté. Frozen in this dreary state, Crow remained in this position, unaware of the passing time.

The sound of the door opening again had Crow look up, alarmed at being woken from his dark thoughts. White opened the door wide, but did not enter the room or even look for Crow. She signaled someone else to enter.

"Healing is hard. Often, it's best to hear the other's side of the story before making judgment," said White wisely, closing the door behind her as she left a bewildered Roi inside.

Roi stood facing the door, speechless and confused. Finally he turned to the room, running his hand over the cloth covered piano. He stopped when he noticed the water and bread. It was then he spotted Crow sitting, half hidden in the drapery. He took a step back.

Crow could read the anguish in Roi's eyes. His heart hammered painfully in his chest. The misunderstanding needed to be cleared up. And yet, he couldn't find the words. And Roi, probably having thought up several crazy conclusions, was not going to approach him.

Slowly he unclenched his jaw, but his mouth refused to work. He used a music stand to help himself up. His legs visibly shook.

"We're not lovers," Crow finally rasped.

"What?" Roi mouthed, listening out of respect but clearly wanting to leave.

"Fierté and I… A lesson. A punishment. We… I don't love him, Roi. I love you."

Roi said nothing, his eyes furrowing in desperation to believe Crow, but the images of the scene were clearly in his mind.

Crow shakily made his way around the piano. Roi held his ground, but didn't reach for him. This caused Crow to flinch, cursing himself for even hoping for the slightest sign of caring.

"I would never-," a sob interrupted Crow's speech. He looked away, trying to gather himself. "You probably don't realize this, but you rescued me by entering that room. I was fucking stupid and weak. If you hadn't arrived, I would have been-."

Crow couldn't finish the sentence.

Roi's mouth parted. His hands were flexing and Crow could tell Roi was processing every word carefully. Crow feared a punch would be coming his way soon. His monologue sounded dull and pathetic to his own ears.

"You must be disgusted with me now," said Crow wretchedly. He laughed bitterly. "It's so strange; me not shutting up and you listening. It's like we've traded spots. Not- Not that I'm saying you're like me. No one should be like me. Damn. Here come the stupid tears again."

Crow started to turn away.

Roi's boots thudded intently as he crossed the space between them and engulfed Crow in his arms. Crow stiffened, waiting for shaking, shouting, something to finalize the death of their relationship. When he nuzzled his face against the side of Crow's head, Crow felt as though he would melt.

"I understand," he whispered.

Crow rested his head onto Roi's shoulder, shivering. Slowly Roi got them seated on the floor, his legs stretched out on each side of Crow. Crow remained curled against him, crying silent tears as Roi's hands started to rub his back.

"I'm so sorry."

"Don't say that," said Roi. Then he growled, "I'd like to feed Fierté to Wolf, but you have nothing to apologize for. No more. I'll protect you."

Roi nestled his head against Crow. They rested against each other until a knock sounded. White entered, her pinched expression relaxing at the sight of them.

"I'm sorry to interrupt. Monsieur Corvus has been requested by Master East to his study. We would like to hear of these encroachers in your own words." She hesitated. "Fierté is busy elsewhere."

Crow unwound himself from Roi. They helped each other up. Crow's limbs felt stiff, but the heaviness he'd felt earlier was gone.

"May I come?" asked Roi, surprisingly polite.

"That may be acceptable," said White, opening the door wider for them. "The master sees you in good eyes these days."

White ushered them at a brisk pace down the hall, eventually slowing before Goodwin's closed bedroom door. Crow thought he could barely make out the gruff voice of Boar speaking on the other side.

"Enter when you're ready," said White, giving them both a fond smile. "I'll let the master know you're here."

White gave a warning knock before slipping and closing the door after herself. Crow worked at clearing his throat and rubbed his face, trying to hide any evidence of his tears.

Roi quickly leaned over and gave Crow a kiss on the cheek, then whispered in his ear, "We will manage all this together." He took hold of Crow's hand, entwining their fingers. Crow squeezed tightly, not wanting to ever let go.

Upon entering the dark room, Crow's eyes quickly adjusted. His eyes rapidly scanned for any sign of Fierté, and he softly gave a relieved sigh at his evident absence. White stood quietly by the lit fireplace, her hands held loosely in front of her, while Boar was seated on a stool next to her. Opposite of them sat Goodwin, stooped in his armchair.

Crow's eyes lingered momentarily on Boar. He hadn't had to deal with the hot-tempered man for a while now. His earlier beatings had paled with time and Boar no longer appeared as threatening. Then again, knowing his real identity and having Roi steadfast beside him, might have been giving him some added confidence. Crow bit his bottom lip, hoping that time would also help heal his experiences with Fierté.

"Tell me exactly what you overheard in the forest," ordered Goodwin, his eyes settling directly on Crow's face.

Roi inched closer to Crow so their shoulders were touching. Crow saw Boar's eyes trail down to their hands. Crow couldn't resist a slight smirk. Boar's eyes darted up in time to catch the fleeting expression and Crow wondered the whether the Boar's face had been quite so deep red before.

Goodwin cleared his throat, drawing Crow's attention back onto him. Crow recited everything he could about his morning flight, limiting the end with a stiff line of, "And so I flew back and told Fierté." Goodwin asked a number of questions, his temper remarkably restrained, to which Crow did not have answers for; what weapons they had or a specific number count. Crow could only offer speculations.

"Thank you for your report, Monsieur Corvus," said Goodwin. Crow blinked several times in surprise. "I appreciate all the sleuthing you have done. But I must request more of you. I need you to fly out and find answers to these unsolved questions."

"Tonight?" said White surprised.

"Why not tonight?" demanded Goodwin.

White's eyes shot over to Crow. Crow forced a simmer of a smile, trying to silently convince her his mentality was healed enough. Roi rubbed his thumb against the back of Crow's hand.

"The sun has gone down and the clouds are too thick for any moonlight to shine through," said Roi.

"I also suspect there will be a snowstorm all night," added Boar. "He should leave at dawn, when it is cleared up."

Crow looked over at Boar, wondering what the man might know. His face remained stoic, until he caught Crow looking at him and an expression of loathing formed along his lips. Crow grinned. Still the same Boar; ignorant of all and any drama.

"Well then, Corvus, do you accept the undertaking of this task at dawn?" asked Goodwin.

Crow released Roi's hand and gave his best gentleman bow he'd seen at the party, "Of course. Am I excused now, sir?"

Goodwin's lips twitched. Crow was uncertain whether in irritation or amusement at his pertinence. But Goodwin gave a dismissive snort as he waved his hand towards the door. Roi was quickest to the leave, opening the door wide for their escape of the dark room. Crow grabbed the handle, slowly closing the door after them.

When the door was barely a crack, White spoke, "Fierté should soon be done placing the extra watch on the castle grounds. We should determine a few more things until Crow's report tomorrow."

"Forgive me, but Master, why were you calling him Corvus?" interrupted Boar, trying his best to sound polite in his gruff manner.

The door clicked shut. Crow turned from the door with a smile brimming on his face, amusement and relief from everything making him giddy. He nearly jumped into Roi's hands when he saw Pont's eyes watching them from the dark shadows of the hall.

"Pont!" snapped Crow. "Are you trying to scare the shi-"

"Roi," Pont asked, unperturbed, stepping into the dimly lighted section. "Are you familiar with siege tactics?"

"I've read on them."

"Then I need you in the library. I've experience fighting, but not planning battles. We need to have a plan of defense. And as you can imagine, our soldiers are going to be quite unique."

Roi's eyes gleamed as ideas already cropped up in his mind.

"It's almost advantageous having animals. Even those who aren't used to fighting have claws, horns, and teeth. Speed, size, agility. All with human intelligence."

"Don't forget the crazy ones in the dungeon," muttered Crow.

CHAPTER 16 - SIEGE

Crow's talons flexed into the bark of the branch he perched on. He watched the mob of forty-seven men march by. The leader was at the center, continuing to keep the group rallied. It was the same man Crow had seen at Remais watching him speak to Corvus.

The man signaled his mercenary leaders to the side with a nod of his head. He rubbed his fingers together.

"Remember, you all get to keep what you can find and carry, but no looting until after the castle occupants are cleared. The castle will be mine after this, so avoid wrecking anything. I want my money's worth out of this place after all this effort."

Greed, thought Crow. *That's what I'll name him.*

"But isn't this place rumored to be a long lost castle belonging to the Easts?" asked the mercenary captain.

"I looked up the records," said Greed. "The place is lost from history, so it is open for me to take. I'll show Count Corvus that having some backbone and ambition will make me far more successful than even him."

"I heard managing the treasury is a front for Count Corvus," muttered the captain. He shivered. "I encountered his servants in an alleyway once. He's not one to cross."

"I'm not stepping in his way for this! I respect the Corvus family immensely. Proactively obtaining financial assets will be my mark in this world. Focus on our task. Think of the great treasure these creatures must have massed over the years."

Clacking his beak in irritation, Crow took off back to the castle. He'd reported back and forth three times now, keeping the defenders updated; only the mercenaries had muskets, the townsfolk had pitchforks, knives and clubs, they were taking the path that would bring them to the castle front.

The library had become the assigned headquarters.

Crow stopped outside the library door in human form. He could hear Pont and Roi talking about hidden passages inside; White and Boar adding in pieces of information. Crow peered in. Goodwin was glowering in a chair, leaving most of the planning to the others.

Goodwin's eyes flickered towards Crow and Crow felt his stomach roll nervously.

Crow swiftly trained his eyes towards Roi, who leaned over the long table, moving a couple markers on the castle's blueprints. His long fingers were covered in ink and lines furrowed his brow.

"I'm not saying using the passages for floor changes isn't a good plan," said Roi, using his free hand to rub the dark lines under his eyes. "What I'm concerned about is the speed of everything. If we completely rely on all this trickery, they're going to start noticing the patterns and the tricks will run out quickly. If the mercenaries are as efficient as Crow reported, they'll cross all the traps within the first twenty minutes."

"Timing doesn't matter if the traps work," replied Pont.

Roi turned away from the table, waving his hands in frustration. "How many times do I need to repeat this? Fighting shifters will initially shock them, but they'll get over it. They'll adjust to our guerilla tactics. And we are barely acknowledging the fact that with each trick we use, we will be with less people. Especially with the- Crow you're back."

Roi's furrowed brow smoothed out and a genuine smile spread along his smooth lips.

Crow returned it with a slight grin, but it didn't reach his eyes and shortly fell from his face.

"The mob is a little over half an hour away."

"Then it's time for the Duvals to leave," said White, nervously fiddling with her apron strings. "Henry is ready at the back."

Roi looked over at Pont.

"I can stay and help."

"No," growled Goodwin. "You must protect Hélène."

Roi opened his mouth, but swiftly shut it when Crow shook his head.

White looked at Crow, "Would you send them off? Then keep watch outside."

Crow nodded, a lump in his throat. He stepped back out into the hall. Roi wordlessly followed him out, in a pout. They looked down at a small group of rodents working at getting a line of string strung out under the carpet. Crow bent down and tucked a piece under.

"Hélène should already be packed," said Roi, pulling his eyes away from the rodents. He helped Crow back up and placed an arm around Crow's shoulder as they walked down the wing towards the main hall. Roi ran his fingers along the bannister, slowing their pace even further. They stopped outside Hélène's door, enjoying the last few minutes of each other's company.

Roi caught Crow's hand, as Crow raised it to knock. His fingers wove around and through Crow's until they were interlocked. Roi knocked once, and opened the door only large enough that his head fit through.

"Hélène," said Roi. "We're leaving in five minutes."

Roi swiftly pulled his head out, closing the door to cut off the exaggerated, bleak sigh made by Hélène.

"Why, she sounds just as pleased as you," said Crow sarcastically.

"I might have to tie her to the horse to leave, and then you'll have to tie me."

"After being trapped here for so long, you should be happy for the freedom."

"Hélène definitely needs to leave," muttered Roi. "I'm just not happy that I'm being sent off like a damsel as well."

"Goodwin already said your job is to protect Hélène."

"She's a better rider than me, and she's surprisingly handy with a sling."

"You know that's not-"

Roi leaned over and gave Crow a kiss.

"If I have to leave, you should come with me," whispered Roi. "Don't give me that look. I know you won't and I know your reasons are justifiable. I just wish- Ugh. Just let me enjoy these last few minutes together."

It felt so right, whenever they pressed against each other. And inside, Crow felt his heart quiver that this might be the last time he'd ever kiss Roi. He felt a surge of possessiveness and flushed with guilt.

Roi will leave and return to his life. He will go to old partners or find new ones. But I can't have him stay with me. He needs to be safe.

"If there was no curse, if this raid wasn't happening, you know I'd go with you," said Crow, breaking the kiss. He brought his hands up to Roi's chest, fiddling with loose stitching sticking out from the seams. He stared up, but focused on Roi's bangs, unable to meet Roi's eyes. "Four minutes left, what to do?"

Roi wrapped an arm over Crow's shoulder, his hand gently pressed against the back of Crow's neck as they went for a more passionate kiss.

Crow's need for this connection felt like it would burst, their kiss only breaking when they needed to breath. Roi slowly backed until his should hit against the male guest room door. Crow kept pressed against him, desperately wanting to make this moment memorable.

Roi opened his mouth, sucking along Crow's bottom lip, then began to tentatively press his tongue against Crow's lips. Crow slowly opened, allowing Roi's tongue to snake between them. Crow slipped his arms around Roi, his hands massaging against Roi's shoulder blades, clutching their chests against each other.

Roi gave a pleased moan at Crow's sudden aggression, as they passionately stroked their tongues against one another. His hand released Crow, fumbling behind him to blindly turn the door handle. At the click of the door, Roi drew back from Crow.

Crow opened his mouth to object, but Roi grabbed the front of his vest, dragging him into the room and slamming the door shut behind him. Roi didn't bother locking the door. He shoved the nearest furniture, a footstool, in front and left it at that. He was immediately back on Crow, lining kisses along Crow's jawline.

Running his fingers to the top of Roi's shirt, Crow undid the draw string, his fingers poking thought the shirt opening and running teasingly against Roi's chest.

A purring sound escaped Roi. He broke from their kiss to grab the bottom of Crow's vest and began to slide it up. Crow scrambled at the vest's buckling, and it fell to the floor as it slipped off half undone.

Roi ran his hands over Crow's chest, against his stomach, up his sides again. Crow moaned his pleasure at the touch. It came out slightly jagged, uncertain and naïve, but as Roi's hands massaged his body, teasingly avoiding Crow's crotch, Crow felt he couldn't take much more.

"My legs aren't going to be able to hold," slurred Crow, finally looking up into Roi's smoky eyes.

Roi passionately leaned forward against Crow as they kissed again. Crow nearly melted. Roi released a couple huffs of laughter, his arm supporting Crow's lower back tightened and Roi stepped towards the nearest furniture.

"No, not the armchair," objected Crow. Roi placed a hand against Crow's cheek, his own lips red and swollen.

"Where ever you wish," he whispered, moving his hands to Crow's shoulders. He lightly skimmed down the loose shirt. Crow shivered at the tingles the touch alone sent through him.

With Roi in pursuit, Crow stepped back until his back pressed against the tapestry, the long, blanket-like fabric slightly enfolding around them.

Roi ran his fingers around Crow's waste, stopping at the back and slowly wedging themselves under the belt, past the tucked shirt and arriving against Crow's flesh. Crow's breathing hitched as the fingers lightly kneaded against his butt. Roi pressed against Crow lightly, delicately. But the pressure in both of their cocks could be felt through their clothes by the other.

If our clothes weren't in the way… thought Crow, shivering as his imagination swept him away. He shifted, grinding himself slightly against Roi and jerked at the unexpected pleasure the instinct had given him.

Roi leaned his forehead down on Crow's shoulder. He slowly turned his head, briefly looking lovingly at Crow's hazy eyes before focusing on

Crow's neck. He started to nibble, then suck, running his tongue over the patch of skin.

"A hickey," muttered Crow, the word popping up from the back of his mind. He felt Roi's chest vibrate as he chuckled lightly again. Roi finished his artwork by biting around the suctioned skin. His teeth didn't break skin, but Crow could feel them indenting. The light pain that came with it caused Crow's cock to thrum even harder.

Warmth and arousal flooded the remaining thoughts Crow had. He didn't want it to end. He reached down and encompassed his hand around Roi's crotch. Roi released a breath, both surprised and pleased. Crow felt a wave of sexual euphoria from being successful in his daring.

Roi's fingers flexed from where they'd been kneading against Crow's butt. Roi leaned harder against Crow, grinding against Crow's hand and thigh.

"Are you sure you want to go further?' whispered Roi, his voice hot and wispy against Crow's ear.

Crow could feel his heartbeat matching Roi's. He closed his eyes as he ran his tongue along Roi's swollen lips, savoring the salty taste. Roi's soft flesh was addicting.

Roi shuddered in arousal. His warm hands slid up, pulling away from Crow's skin. His waist leaned away from Crow's body. The sudden cool air in place of Roi caused Crow's brows to draw together. He opened his eyes to slits, fearing Roi was stopping. But he heard the ruffle, then felt Roi's hands, as Roi worked to free his tenting cock.

"Let me," muttered Crow, sliding his hands against Roi.

He undid the remaining strings, closing his eyes as Roi leaned forward and joined their lips once more. Crow's fingers curiously brushed against Roi's member. Soft, yet hard; like a smooth, warm metal bar. Crow slowly wrapped his fingers around the cock, playing inquisitively with the skin. Roi whimpered happily, his shoulders leaning forward and pinning Crow back. Crow blindly started a pattern motion of up and down. He could smell the precum. Not all of it was Roi's.

A heavy knock on the door had them freeze.

"Roi?" Hélène's voice barely sounded through the thick wood, but they jumped apart like she was in the room.

Roi stumbled towards the door, doing up his pants clumsily with his fingers. He stubbed his foot on the footstool as he tried to kick it aside and slipped out a curse as he gave it a second kick that sent it across the room.

He opened the door, but only a crack.

"Give me a few minutes," said Roi.

"Are you alright?" asked Hélène.

"Yeah," said Roi wistfully, before shaking his head and clearing his throat. "Er, yes. I'll meet you at the stairs in a few minutes."

"I've already packed your bag," said Hélène. "It should just be Corbin's stuff that's left in there. What else do you need? Roi, open the door properly."

Hélène pushed against the door, but Roi placed his boot down firmly in its way, wincing as it pressed against his already sore foot.

"I'm just saying a special goodbye to Corbin," hissed Roi through his teeth.

"He's- oh…" said Hélène. "Ohoho!"

"Oh, for fucks sake," groaned Crow, thumping his forehead against the tapestry's wall.

Boar's loud steps were easily heard as he stomped by, and his gruff voice sounded past Roi and Hélène, into the room.

"Get out of the castle now, Duval! You're holding up our eyes in the sky."

Crow sunk down to his haunches, seething in embarrassment.

Roi shut the door with a sigh. He scooped up Crow's vest on his way back and held it out.

Crow slowly eased himself up.

"And I almost had you," said Roi, hiding the disappointment in his eyes with false mirth.

Crow slipped the vest over his head and did up the buckle.

"The way Hélène interpreted it, you did have me," said Crow. "Why don't you tell the whole castle next time."

Crow clamped up, remembering there wasn't likely to be a next time.

Roi kissed Crow on the temple in an attempt to pacify him as they opened the door. Roi let out a sudden chuckle. "You're not the one that's going to have to sit on a horse with his sister, while trying to get down his boner."

"I didn't need to hear that," hissed Crow, lightly hitting Roi on the head as he spotted Hélène waiting at the top of the stairs. He hoped his own half hard cock wasn't showing too prominently against his pants. He was too embarrassed to check.

The small amount of humor Crow and Roi tried to maintain quickly dwindled when Hélène gave Roi his coat. Though she had smiled at the sight of them, her gloomy mood showed in how she moved sluggishly and sniffed every other second. They hurried out to the back courtyard where Henry waited.

The horse nuzzled Roi, recognizing him.

Hélène released a long, dramatic breath into the air. She dropped her bag into the snow and crossed her arms, turning to face Crow. Despite the firm line on her lips, her eyes were watery.

"Perhaps we can bring help? There has to be something more we can do. We could stay in-"

Crow picked up Hélène's bag, carefully brushed the snow off the bottom, and strapped it to the side of Henry's saddle. He wiped the melting snow off his hands on his pants, and then faced Hélène, holding his hand out to help her up on the horse. His fingers were turning pink from the cold's bite.

"You've given hope to a beast, you've done more than we ever deserved," said Crow. "Goodwin cares for you. He wants you safe and happy."

Hélène scrunched her forehead, but accepted Crow's hand up.

"If either of us should stay, it should be me," said Roi. "There's only a few people here who understand strategy. One more can make a difference. You said some of the men approaching were from Beauclair, perhaps I can talk some sense into them."

"They'd think you were one of us, since you were seen with me at the party," said Crow. He forced on a grin. "Besides, we can handle a fight. Goodwin East is stronger and taller than any man. Wolf will take out half of them before they even touch the castle."

"And you?" asked Roi, placing a light hand on Crow's shoulder.

"I'm good at surviving. In fights, they never look up."

Roi raised an eyebrow, unconvinced. He took in a deep breath to give off another rant. But looking at Crow, his words caught in his throat.

Crow tried to force a smile. It wobbled away on his face.

"Be safe," Crow added softly.

I love you.

Roi reached out and pulled Crow into a hug. He breathed heavily, his hands grasping the back of Crow's vest. Crow hugged Roi back just as fiercely.

"When Hélène's safe, I'll come back for you," Roi whispered.

Crow said nothing as Roi got on the saddle behind Hélène. His mouth was firmly shut, fearing his voice would waver. He watched them take off into the woods and stood as still as a sentinel statue until the last signs of them disappeared. He looked down at the tracks in the snow. The castle would have to make sure they won, or the raider victors might follow the trail and track the siblings down.

Crow transformed and took post on the roof. This gave him time to attempt burying his feelings and take on the coldness needed for battle. No matter how much he tried, though, it was impossible to rid the unsettling, empty space growing inside him since Roi's departure. He shivered when he realized he could closest compare the feeling to perdu.

When the mob was sighted five minutes from the castle, Crow gave the warning call through a series of caws. He held at his spot, flinching as the mob cheered upon spotting the old structure. A red anger started to boil inside him as the group maliciously vandalized the gate open and stormed into the front courtyard.

The men's bravery dwindled as the silence of the place soaked in. They stopped before the entrance steps. The foreboding doors loomed down at them, daring anyone to try opening them.

Greed worked his way to the front, making sure his largest mercenaries were by his side. He walked in a small circle, his eye's devouring everything within sight. Crow stood still, hoping to pass as a gargoyle when Greed's eyes scanned the roof.

At last Greed stood proudly facing the doors, raising his chin challengingly.

"Hail," he called to the silent grounds. "I know you are watching! I am not an uncompromising man. Prove yourself respectable, monsters, and send out a representative to speak on your behalf."

Crow took off, quickly entering the castle through a back window. Half of the servants were watching at the windows, their animal ears attentively twitching. Goodwin paced the main hall, a large, burgundy war cape draped across most of his body, fluttering about with his agitated movements. The triumvirate stood nearby in animal forms.

They're more formidable and dangerous with antlers, tusks, and canines.

Pont stood at the bottom of the stairs in human form, his arms crossed. He spotted Crow and nodded. The traps were set, the strategies in place.

"Should we send someone out?" asked Boar.

"I will go," growled Goodwin. "Maybe they will be satisfied with me. This could protect the rest of you if you hide and let them loot."

"Not a chance," said Fierté. "Sir, we are a family of one here. We will stick together against those barbarians."

"Then will you go out?" Boar asked Fierté. "I know I will not. We should just let loose the perdu and start this."

"They must initialize it," growled Goodwin.

"I'll speak to them," said Crow, flinching as his voice echoed in the hall. No one objected, though White gave a whine. He finished in a whisper, "Though it will likely be in vain."

"Open the main door," said Goodwin.

Crow flew down before the door, transforming as he reached the marble floor. He started to bite his lip, but caught himself. He wiped his hair back and straightened his posture. Pan and Steven unlocked the door. It was opened wide enough to only reveal to the trespassers Crow from the dark room. He tried to pretend he was back in Remais, facing harmless party guests.

Crow stepped forward and the door groaned closed behind him.

"Good evening, gentlemen," said Crow, dramatically bowing as he saw the guns train on him. His breathing quickened as he fought his instincts to flee.

"It's a human," declared a farmer.

"Don't be fooled!" said Greed, taking a few steps towards Crow. His eyes narrowed as they seemed to strip away Crow's form. Crow took a large step back, determined to remain out of reach. "This was one of the spies at Remais. He works for them."

Crow swallowed and continued to speak like they'd said nothing, "I speak on behalf of this castle's master. He sends an offer of peace. We've done you no harm, nor you to us." *Yet.* "You are requested to leave immediately, so no bloodshed will be necessary."

"One of your monsters captured one of our girls!" shouted a man from Beauclair.

Crow fidgeted with his fingers behind his back.

So, Hélène's father finally told the story? He must have done so when Greed visited the town and promised to take us down.

"Hélène Duval is returning to Beauclair as we speak," said Crow calmly.

"Lies!"

"Death to the creatures!"

"Death to magic!"

Crow sighed, raising his hands in exasperation. The abrupt silence surprised Crow, giving him a strange sense of being like a conductor. But the experience was fleeting as his focus trained on Greed, spreading a coldness through him. His eyes darted from one man to the next. The looks of animosity and fear made it clear the time to speak was near an end.

"Remember, you bring this upon yourselves."

The click of a gun cocking startled Crow to transform mid-step. The men shouted as he flew past, and he would have found it funny in a less dire situation. A shot was fired before they had aimed properly and luckily missed. He quickly rounded behind the castle, landing on a weather vane. In bird-form, his heart pumped even crazier and he couldn't keep back the shivering.

He closed his eyes tightly as he heard the doors open and the perdu animals set free. He didn't want to see the first wave of attack. Yowls, growling, screeching, and barking sounded, joined shortly by human screams and yells.

Crow entered the castle only when the attackers started finding ways in. He stuck up high, overseeing.

"Two enemies hiding in the drawing room… Don't go down that hall, Boar's special concoction is there. Squirrel needs assistance in the rafters. Use the third passage and double back."

In the servant quarter's hall, Crow came across Pont holding out on his own, armed with his fencing rapier. Sweat dripped down Pont's temples and his knuckles were lined with scratches and bloodied. The remaining mercenary in the hall ran back towards the ballroom as Pont swiftly took out his friend.

"Quite the body count," said Crow, landing beside a three-man body pile and avoiding the grisly temptation to view their faces. If he did, they'd always haunt him.

Pont grimaced, leaning back against the wall as he cleaned his sword on a blood-splotched rag he familiarly drew from his pocket.

"Steven gets half of the credit and the two bodies around the corner are only unconscious. I'm trying to dispatch the townsfolk mercifully, but the mercenary bastards are asking for my blade."

"Aren't you supposed to be positioned by the library for the west wing tricks?" asked Crow.

"No point. They were all used up in the first few minutes. Roi was right. Though there's little we could have done to get any better results. It's chaos. Every man and woman for themselves. The servants aren't tactical soldiers and neither are most of the villagers. I just hope everyone stays in their assigned zones, to disperse the fighting and keep us on par with the mercenaries. Do you know if the master and the triumvirate are still holding their position in the main hall?"

"When I flew by, they were at a standoff. The attackers there have no guns and no one really wants to go up against the other side."

"I'm certain it won't take much to set either side off though," muttered Pont. He wiped his face with his sleeve and noticed with distaste the speckles of blood on his clothing. A shout rang out from around the corner in the dungeon stairwell. Pont set off running towards it, his sword raised for another bout. "I'll manage the main floor. Go help second and third."

Crow reluctantly took off, using a servant stairwell to get swiftly up to the second level west wing. He winced as he flew over two still duck bodies near Goodwin's bedroom. He let his gaze linger, recalling memories of them.

Ahead, around a corner, he heard the yelp of one of the servant dogs.

"Cursed beast, trying to take my stave from me," snapped a voice.

The sound of repetitive beatings made Crow tremble in anger. He picked up speed, turning the corner, ready to wreak havoc. He released a surprised screech when he flew into the back of a human. He landed on the floor and hopped swiftly to the side before he might be kicked.

The human ignored him. Instead, they held a fire poker in their hands like a bat and swung it at the back of a second human. The second human, a balding man with a slight hunched back, cried out as he stumbled from the hit. The first figure raised their boot and pressed it against the balding man's back. The man hit against the wall and went down, clutching his head.

The dog whimpered as it picked up the balding man's stave, its jaw amuck with blood and cuts. It brought the blunt end down against the man's temple. The man went still.

The first human bent down and felt the man's pulse, releasing a relieved breath, "Only unconscious".

The dog gave a few weak wags of his tail, before turning and limping down the hall.

"Wait, where's Goodwin?" called out the human. They pulled down their shawl.

Crow transformed and grabbed Hélène's arm, raising her up to stand and turning her around. Hélène's stiffened form, braced for attack, immediately loosened at the sight of Crow. Her lips held a firm, resolute line, and her eyes stared at him unwaveringly.

"Hélène, what are you doing here?" demanded Crow.

He moved her away from the body, looking for an open room he could hide her safely in. Hélène yanked her arm from his grip. Her boots planted firmly on the floor and she folded her arms.

"Where's Goodwin?" she demanded. "I heard the cries all the way in the woods and I knew I had to come back. I need to stop further bloodshed. I need to try talking to the people from Beauclair and convince them to put down their arms. If I can speak with Goodwin first-"

"You need to get out of here!" said Crow, looking back and forth to make sure no enemies were coming their way.

"Tell me now!"

"This is no place for a girl!"

"Crow!" yelled Hélène angrily. She pointed at the fallen figure. "I can handle myself well enough."

"I hope you're ready to do that again, because no one is in a negotiating mood. Do you realize both sides have now killed in mass? Revenge has become the new motivator."

"Where is Goodwin?"

Crow ran his hand through his hair agitatedly, biting his lip. He released an angry hiss.

"Grand hall."

Hélène raced past him, Crow's hand skimming the edge of her cloak, but too slow to catch her.

They came back to help us! Foolish, really. But where is Roi? I doubt he would have left Hélène on her own. He's must have gotten caught up along the way.

Crow took off opposite. He transformed and flew out the nearest window into the yard, scanning the grounds for Roi.

Only a few lifeless perdu bodies and several injured villagers lay there. He caught sight of Wolf lying injured in the snow near the back of the property. A mercenary, just as mangled, pulled himself over to Wolf, raising a knife to strike Wolf's neck.

Crow swooped down, his talon's scratching the man's scalp. The man fell backwards, cursing Wolf and Crow, but too weak to get up. Crow landed and transformed. He kicked the knife out of the man's hand and out of reach. Then he leaned over to inspect Wolf. There were so many injuries, it was hard to tell which was worse. Crow reached out to pull a shard of wood from Wolf's leg.

Wolf gave a whine as he flinched. Crow jumped, unaccustomed to anything but snarls and growls from him. Wolf stared at him, his eyes surprisingly lucid. His mouth opened and closed, trying to form words.

"-human," gasped Wolf, coughing painfully. He shuddered, and then transformed. A shaggy man in a soldier uniform lay sprawled out. His eyes held mostly bitterness, but also pride.
Crow felt a lump in his throat as he watched the life disappear in the man's eyes.

"You did well," Crow whispered quietly. While he had never really thought of Wolf as a good person, he had not wanted the man dead either.

A panic bubbled up in Crow. Wolf was a better fighter than Roi and had fallen. Roi didn't stand a chance!

Crow transformed, flying back to the castle. He entered in through the guest room, looking wildly around. Finding it empty, he headed directly to the main hall. He landed on the bannister, overwhelmed by the scene and reaching a loss.

The mob's remnants and the castle occupants had mostly grouped here. Goodwin was cornered in the far end of the room. Blood, his own and others', matted his fur. White lay at the top of the grand stairs, struggling with an injured leg. Boar could be heard squealing down a side hall. Fierté was at the bottom of the stairs, motionless, but it was unclear whether he was unconscious or dead. Two humans lay under him with slashes across their arms and faces.

Hélène's screams drew Crow's attention. Two men had her by the arms, dragging her towards the open main doors.

"No, no, the animals are good!" Hélène squirmed enough to free one arm, and gave a good hook to the nearest man before he reacquired his hold.

"You're lucky you're Duval's little brat," said the man angrily. "Foolish girl, thinking these creatures can be negotiated with."

"No. They can. They're good. Let me go! Goodwin. Goodwin!"

Goodwin looked up, wrinkling his gash covered snout, and released a roar as he charged through his foes, ignoring the injuries created on his shoulder from a pitchfork stabbed forward. He crossed the bloody, marble floor in a few paces, grabbing and throwing the nearest man away from Hélène. He sheltered her in his arms as the second man leapt out of the way, yelling, "Traitor!"

Through the noise, Roi's voice rose, "You can't believe this is right."

Crow whipped his head to look down at the entrance leading to the dining hall.

Roi was leaning against the door. There was some blood on his outfit, but he appeared otherwise unharmed. His furious gaze kept shifting from someone just out of view, to Hélène. A hidden figure seemed to compel Roi to refrain from running to his sister.

Crow's talons tightened on the bannister, straining his eyes to see through the dining room's dark entrance.

Greed cockily stepped into view, brandishing his silver gun and unwaveringly he aimed at Roi.

Roi stumbled back, raising his hands up. Greed cocked his gun, "I can't expect a monster's pet spy to understand."

A numbing darkness swept over Crow's mind; everything flickered from existence, leaving only the three of them. Crow took flight. Murder building with the rush of air under his wings. He swooped over Roi's head, his tail feathers barely tussled Roi's hair. Now between Roi and Greed, his talons raised up, intent on ravaging Greed's face and blinding the man.

Roi yelled.

The trigger pulled.

The sudden weight and agony that exploded in Crow's arm had his vision go red. High pitched ringing superimposed the rest of the room's noise. He thudded to the ground, grunting. Blinking his eyes clear of the reddish haze, the sounds of the room slowly returned through the ringing.

The warmth from his blood trickle down his arm.

Warm, like Roi. He's safe. He didn't get hit.

Crow gritted his teeth, realizing he was in human form. He managed up to his knees, confused.

He wavered.

I didn't choose to transform…

"An abomination that eager for death?" muttered Greed, swiftly reloading the gun. "How rare."

"No!" screamed Roi. He made to step forward, but slipped on the blood on the floor.

Please, Roi, get Hélène and run, thought Crow.

Clutching his injured arm, Crow's eyes steadily watched the weapon. His executioner stepped forward, placing the metal end against Crow's head, then moved slowly down until it held steady at his chest, lined with his heart.

"One less abomination," said Greed.

The gun cocked.

"Corbin!" wailed Roi. Crow could hear him struggling to his feet.

Crow swallowed, refusing to close his eyes. A tear ran down his cheek. *Goodbye, Roi.*

A sudden flush crept up along Greed's neck, running all the way to his ears. His eyes widened, the malice replaced by horror. The gun dropped from his hand.

"My god, Corbin Corvus!" he stuttered. Several shouts sounded across the room. Greed's gaze shifted towards the cause. "Goodwin East," he moaned. "What have I done?"

"Attacked a castle in fear and greed," seethed Roi vehemently, dashing forward and grabbing the gun. He positioned himself between Crow and the man, shoving the shocked man to his knees. Then he too noticed where everyone was looking.

Goodwin and Hélène clutched each other closely. Blood on and around them, they ignored everything but each other's eyes. Surrounded by townsfolk, now lowering their weapons, they believed all was over, after having so valiantly trying to defend each other. Goodwin was human.

They'd felt love.

The spell was broken.

For everyone.

CHAPTER 17 – CORBIN OR CROW

Their memories were frazzled bits and pieces, but there was a confidence it would return in time, especially with familiarity. Goodwin was the only one whose full memories returned nearly immediately. Unfortunately for those who had fully entered perdu, they remained animals.

Greed had called off the attack, not that there were many remaining who hadn't run away by the end. He apologized profusely to Goodwin, who vindictively assured him the attack would be heard of by his father, but he wouldn't be killed- yet. Greed had turned to also speak with Corbin, but was met with an infamous Corvus glare that had him shuffle sullenly away to where they were holding him.

And my father will hear about this too, thought Corbin darkly. *I remember I went to school with you. I never would have thought greed would change you so badly.*

Evening was approaching.

Corbin sat on the bottom steps of the grand hall stairwell. A strip of cloth was tied around his wounded arm, waiting for proper medical attention, but he knew his injuries paled in light of others in the room. Cots, bedding, couches, as many transferable objects of comfort had been set up in the vast room. Trespasser and staff alike were being treated, though there were far too few who knew enough to play doctor or nurse. This made the wait long.

Fierté lay on a makeshift cot, two cots away from the stairs. Awake, he was too injured to move, but this didn't stop him from giving orders. Gustav, with a nasty bruise over one eye, eagerly listened to his instructions and then ran off to pass them along. Corbin half-heartedly watched, his mind still replaying what happened, counting losses, and wondering towards what would happen next.

"Where are your injuries?" asked Nanny, as she walked down the steps, carrying a load of freshly stripped sheets. "I'll need you to move if you aren't in need."

Corbin looked up at her, too tired and weary to fully turn around. Nanny's eyes widened as memories of Corbin's original identity and status returned to her. His head started to buzz with a petty headache as he remembered her from before the curse. Memories aside, her personality had remained the same throughout it all.

"Am I in the way?" asked Corbin. He looked at her apologetically, then indicated his arm. "I didn't want to take up the bedding spaces when it's not necessary for me to lay down."

Nanny got to the bottom and dumped the sheets at Corbin's feet, one of the few places in the room that was blood free. She raised a thumb and began to bite her nail as her eyes quickly scanned him.

"Sorry if I sounded abrupt," said Nanny, blushing a deep red. "White's broken her leg, so she can only tend to so many people, and there's so few of us who've been taught the basics. With only so many spots for the wounded to lay and sit-"

Corbin laughed softly, trying to calm her, "I was shot in the arm, but the bullet went clean through. Doesn't mean it's not hurting though."

"Where are Hélène and Roi?" asked Nanny, sitting hesitantly next to Corbin. She helped untie the knotted cloth wrapped around the wound and then rolled up his blood-soaked sleeve to get a clear view of the whole arm. Just above his biceps, the wound started streaming once more.

Corbin bit his tongue to keep from moaning. He watched the lines of red slowly make their way down along his arm. His thoughts slowly dwindled into nothing, his vision fascinated by the color.

"Do you not know?" asked Nanny.

Corbin blinked a few times and looked at her, "Sorry, what were you asking?"

Nanny shook her head.

"Never mind, you're anemic," she muttered.

She rushed over to the collection of washbasins and bowls that had been collected in the corner near the dining room door. Corbin looked away from the location, unable to rid his mind's association of pain and weaponry there.

Nanny set the bowl down on the steps and wiped her brow.

"Please hold your arm out with your hand on your knee. Thank you." Nanny dipped a cloth in the water and began to clean from his wrist up to his shoulder. She held a second rag around his injury when it kept sending down fresh streams of blood.

An alcohol concoction was poured over the gash before Corbin's arm was quickly bandaged and placed in a makeshift sling. Corbin wished for something to dull the pain, but he didn't want to take up more of Nanny's time. He knew where those remedies were kept and could fetch them himself.

It was as Nanny did a final knot of the sling behind his neck that he realized she'd been quietly talking to him still.

"Either way, you really should lie down. I need to go elsewhere, so promise you'll find Roi and have him help you."

Corbin's eyes skittered up to Nanny's face, her lips tightened as her hands lay gently on his shoulder.

She's nearly overwhelmed. But she's remaining strong.

Corbin nodded.

Nanny gave him a shy smile and headed off to help others.

Hearing another person make their way down the steps, Corbin gritted his teeth as he placed his good arm on the cool marble to help slowly ease to the side, out of the way. His injury sent a trill of sharp pain through his nerves, causing him to swiftly give up.

Arriving from behind, Roi sat down next to Corbin, wiping his hands on his pants.

"I finished settling Hélène in her room," said Roi. "She'd be out here helping, but Goodwin, even half dead, insisted she rest. Her hands were shaking so badly. What's happened today will be hard for her… and me." Roi took in a deep breath, rubbing one of his hard won bruises Crow had failed to notice earlier in the fight. "But the Duval's are hardy. We'll both be okay… Are you-"

"I've been shot in the arm, watched allies die, surrounded by blood, and yet, I'm the happiest I've been in ten years," said Corbin.

"Such optimism," said Roi. "I like it. I'm just glad no one's asked me to take care of the bodies or mop up the blood."

"You're a guest and your sister just saved us all from the curse; I assure you, you're safe from those duties."

"And no one's asked you to help?"

Corbin held up his wrapped arm, winced, and then settled just for wiggling his fingers.

"Injuries aside, anyone who didn't remember my status, remembers now, after Greed's little begging for forgiveness performance."

Roi looked down at his clothes. A grin dawned on his face.

"Leave it to you to find humor in all this," said Corbin, watching curiously.

"I owe you new clothing," said Roi. "I wore these from the wardrobe this morning. That room is yours again."

The clearing of a throat caused Corbin to startle. His eyes drew to Fierté, who'd been quietly watching them.

"If I may interrupt," rasped Fierté hesitantly.

Corbin's mouth formed a grim line.

"You already have," said Roi, his eyes narrowing in anger while the rest of his face took on a snarl.

"Easy," whispered Corbin, under his breath, so only Roi heard. "He's no threat anymore. He helped us win."

"He still attacked you," growled Roi.

"And he and I will deal with that when he's not so out of commission, I assure you," said Corbin darkly, this time loud enough to be heard.

Fierté flinched. "I can have the eastern corner room set up for Monsieur Duval for the remainder of his stay, if you would like, Master Corvus."

Corbin smirked, "No, Roi and I will share my room."

Roi's scowl disappeared.

"Really? Well now, I'm feeling weary. Are you feeling tired, Corbin? I think we should retire early."

"Let me find some herbs first," said Corbin, letting out a laugh. It felt good. "I'll meet you in my room."

Corbin grabbed the stair rail and staggered to his feet. He wobbled. Roi reached out to help. "I'm okay. Just a little low on blood."

"Let me help you up the stairs," insisted Roi. "We'll get you to the room and then I'll grab the herbs for you."

Corbin slipped his good arm over Roi's shoulders as they carefully walked up the steps.

"Thank goodness the fighting avoided the guest rooms," said Roi, as they entered Corbin's room. They hobbled to the armchair, where Corbin eased down with a relieved groan. "Wait here."

Roi was half way to the door when Corbin started laughing.

"Do you even know what type of herbs to select or where they are?"

"I've read books on different types," said Roi. Then grinned, "But I could use a hint of where they're stored here."

Corbin gave directions and his smile remained on his face until Roi disappeared.

As soon as Roi was gone, Corbin got up, gripping the chair and then the fireplace mantle, as he made his way across the room. He released a relieved breath when he saw the filled water basin. He leaned against the counter, pulling off his vest and shirt. He paused to catch his balance.

He'd expected some memories to return from the room's familiarity, but the sudden headache that had come with it had been a surprise. None of the servants had expressed any pain as their memories had crept back to them. Instead, they had shown joy and celebration, even towards dull, benign recollections.

Corbin winced as the headache thrummed more intensely when he tried focusing on his old personality and thoughts. Panting, he stopped dwelling so deep and concentrated on more basic memories; like how he loved open windows letting in a fresh breeze or the compulsion to check every door, including the wardrobe, before going to sleep.

The headache persisted, but trickled down to a light throb.

When the room stopped spinning, he picked up the wash towel, wetted the end, and began to clean the blood around the area Nanny had carefully cleaned and bandaged. There wasn't much, but blood had soaked through the bandaging already.

Corbin held the counter with his good arm as he looked down in the basin. A blurred reflection of himself reflected on the surface. He dunked his face under, letting the water clean his sweat and grime. With his ears submerged, the watery isolation gave Corbin a sense of relief and a stronger sense of focus.

I liked being alone, Corbin realized. *I thought more clearly on my own. People my age always seemed to hold me back. I viewed nearly everyone with suspicion, though father taught me how to hide it. I knew how to manipulate them. Know how to manipulate them!*

The pain in his head started to pound with returned vigor. Corbin gritted his teeth.

I understand. The headaches are my own doing. I'm afraid. I'm afraid of who I was. I'm afraid how different I might be if I remember my old self too much. I don't know if I will be the same person or- I don't want to become someone Roi will hate! Or worse, what if I stop loving Roi?

Someone lightly tapped his back, a warm finger on his cool skin. Corbin pulled his head out. He blinked his eyes open and saw Roi.

"Are you sure you're okay?" asked Roi

"No, not really," said Corbin.

He grabbed for another towel to dry off, but stumbled. Roi caught him and assisted him to the bed. Corbin sat on the edge. He felt tears surge in his eyes.

Seriously, I'm going to cry? Shit. Stop looking right at me, with those gorgeous eyes... and now they're narrowing.

Corbin angled his head to look at his initials, *CC,* on the counter. He remembered carving them. It had been back when the curse had first started. He'd been afraid of losing his identity.

Smooth, soft lips lightly pressed against Corbin's temple. Then once again, followed by another, moving along the right side.

"Let's forget all our hardships," Roi whispered into Corbin's ear. "Even for just an hour. If you want to cry, let the tears run. Let them leave you. I promise I'll make you happy."

Roi's hands feathered through Corbin's hair as he shivered. They skimmed down to the back of Corbin's neck, right at the hairline. Roi began to draw loose circles. Corbin felt like his skin would burn in his yearning for more of Roi's touch.

Corbin blinked back the tears and turned to look properly at Roi. They studied each other's face, as if reaching beyond flesh and bone, into their thoughts. Roi's face drew closer, until at last their mouths met. Corbin whole body ignited. The thrill of desire sparked through him as their mouths opened and Roi's tongue started sliding against his.

Roi's hands blindly massaged Corbin's back muscles, progressing downwards, until they got to the bottom, where they teased their way to the front of Corbin's pants.

Corbin broke from the kiss and began to undo Roi's shirt. He bit his lip in frustration as he struggled to do so one-handed. His headache did not help his impatience. Roi captured Corbin's trembling fingers and brought them up to his lips, kissing them like Corbin had seen in images of knights and princesses. His cock jerked.

Roi undid the top of his own shirt and pulled it off with ease. His eyes never left Corbin's body. Roi tossed the shirt to the floor, straddled over top of Corbin's thighs, and lightly pressed down against Corbin's chest. Corbin grinned, allowing himself to be guided back so he was laying on the bed. He flipped his head to the side, to get his wet hair out of his face. He slipped his injured arm from the sling and spread his arms out; inviting.

Corbin's gaze kept lingering towards Roi's erect cock, pressing against his pants. He felt his flush deepen. He tried to focus only on Roi's face.

Roi grinned, shifting so his cock lightly pressed against Corbin and loosened his pants, taking on a revealing pose.

"You can look at me anywhere you like, my lord."

"I'm not a lord," Crow managed through numb lips. He bit his bottom lip as he gave up being proper and allowed his gaze to linger on Roi's full body.

"You're a lord to me," said Roi, gracefully stretching and rippling his muscles. "You're my lord."

Roi leaned down, resting his elbows just above Corbin's shoulders. His head drew closer, and Corbin greedily prepared for another kiss. He closed his eyes, anticipating. But instead, he felt Roi's cheek slide against his own. Roi lowered himself further. Corbin could feel Roi's arousal even stronger and this caused a jump in his own.

"So perfect," Roi murmured against Corbin's ear.

Corbin felt his throat swell and a guilt sweep over him. Though still feeling flushed and aroused, his desire started to dwindle.

"Perfect?" he whispered back, desperately trying to hammer back the despairing thoughts.

Roi felt the sudden slack in Corbin's body.

"Did I hurt you?" asked Roi, going back up on his elbows. His lust filled eyes started to shift back to the caring, discerning Roi Corbin knew. He looked at Corbin's injured arm.

"No," said Corbin. A severe throb from his headache made him flinch. "It's this damn headache."

"Right! The herbs! Your arm must be in pain too."

Roi leapt off of Corbin and rushed over to the counter where he'd left the herbs behind. He grabbed a cup forgotten on the table and filled it with some water before breaking the herbs into small pieces over it.

"It should be in hot water, but this should do."

"Roi," said Corbin hesitantly. He hadn't moved since Roi had left and felt like he was missing something without Roi's touch. "I... my memories are starting to return... a lot of them."

Roi looked over happily, not sharing Corbin's concern.

"Excellent! You're recovering quickly because your family naturally resists curses, right?" He brought the cup over to the bed and held it out, but Crow remained lying, covering his face with an arm. "Are your memories giving you the headaches? Did you remember something bad?"

"I want to be with you more than anything. But my personality and experiences... it wants to come charging back in and I'm terrified. Should I just let them come? Let them change me?"

"You will be you," said Roi softly.

Corbin peeked over his arm. Roi's gaze at him was soft.

"We don't know that."

"Look at the others. Fierté's still a controlling, slick bastard, albeit he's subservient to you now. Nanny's a little braver, but still the shy, kind, caring maid we know. And Goodwin's still a self-entitled, gentleman brat, who'd risk his life without hesitation for my sister again. So there's a good chance you're still that loyal, clever black bird of mine."

Corbin lowered his arm, but remained doubtful.

"I don't want you to suffer," said Roi. "I can see your anguish holding them back. I won't leave you. Let them return. And if you have any changed feelings after this, well then, we'll deal with it then. But right now, we both want each other. We've won against the curse. Let us celebrate. We've earned it. We can sort everything out, any changes, good or bad, tomorrow."

Corbin looked fearfully into Roi's calm eyes then nodded. He took in a deep breath, then let go of his worries, accepting what would come. Nothing struck him right away, nor did any memories pop out, but the headache disappeared, like a puddle drying under a hot sun.

Corbin's eyes widened as Roi took a swig of the cup and placed it on the counter. Roi moved back on the bed, crawling over Corbin and bending down, he placed his lips over his mouth. Corbin closed his eyes and opened his mouth. The herb water entered his mouth little at a time.

Corbin swallowed the last of it and held back a moan. He opened his eyes in slits, to watch Roi's expression. The man's own eyes flew open as Corbin's hand flitted against his thigh, moving in circular patterns up along Roi's butt, his finger slipping along the fold line and running down. Roi drew in a sharp intake. His body lifted up, as if inviting more. Corbin grinned, his hand instead slipping around Roi's thigh and under the opening his body gave. Between Roi's legs, he ran his hand from furthest back, through his hair and made his way to Roi's balls.

The sharp, pleased sounds Roi made encouraged Corbin. He began to massage him, teasing, but never quite touching his lover's cock.

Roi finally groaned and rolled over, unable to support himself over Corbin.

"You're not a virgin, are you?" whispered Roi delightedly as Corbin's hand trailed in pursuit.

Corbin raised and lightly skimmed his fingers over Roi's tip. He hadn't even thought about it, but these moves had come from half-remembered experiences.

He gave a half wicked, half worried laugh, as Roi's breathing became staccato.

"I guess I'm not so innocent as Crow. Are... are you alright with that?"

"As long as you're mine," whispered Roi.

Corbin leaned on his injured arm, ignoring the herb dampened pain. He bent over and covered Roi's mouth in another soul-stealing kiss.

#

The following day, Goodwin made arrangements to go to Remais, to refresh his presence and detain his devious brother. He sent out servants early morning to buy horses for the journey and they returned within the day.

Corbin and Roi sat in the garden, watching the horses get harnessed and saddled. Roi scratched at his hickey on his neck.

"Do you really have to go with Goodwin?" asked Roi.

"Are you going to miss me?" asked Corbin, nudging Roi. "I'll be in Remais' grand court, surrounded by dozens of gorgeous nobles."

"You joke, but I'm serious."

"You, serious," laughed Corbin. He sobered up as he wrapped his good arm around Roi. "It will only be for a week, to sort everything out and play witness against Goodwin's brother. Apparently my voice has more weight than Pont's or White's."

"I'm pretty certain Goodwin's accusations alone will do the trick," grumbled Roi.

"You know I'll find you afterwards."

"We don't know that for sure. Your memories are still returning. What if you have a love waiting for you? And your family... they'll want you to stay."

"Bertok will be happy I'm alive, but, well you've met him, we aren't exactly a hugs and kisses sort of family. He's got my older brother as his heir and will likely feel some responsibility in me getting caught up in all this," *though he'll probably tell me I was stupid not to leave when I got his warning letter,* "so I'm pretty certain I'll be free to do as I please without hindrance. Come on, Roi, you're worse than Goodwin fluttering over Hélène at breakfast. Even if all my memories return, I know you're the one. Nothing will keep me back from returning to you."

Roi shook his head.

"My sister was pretty strict in her instructions to Goodwin. I almost pity him."

"Really? Having to come to Beauclair after everything is sorted in Remais and re-woo her sounds fair. Perhaps their courting as humans will not be the result of a kidnapping this time. She's going to live with you, instead of returning to your father, right?"

Roi mutely nodded.

Goodwin strode around the corner, followed by Pont and White. White's leg was heavily wrapped, but she was the only triumvirate in riding condition. She'd determinedly declared she would see this through to the end. Corbin intended to help care for her during the ride.

"I'll be waiting," said Roi, slipping an arm around Corbin and giving him a kiss.

"I'll be there."

64486528R00125

Made in the USA
Lexington, KY
09 June 2017